PRAISE FOR THE
NOVELS OF J. BARRETT

International Impact Award Gold Medal Winner for *Orabelle*
Red Ribbon Award Winner for *Blaise*

"Fans of fantasy novels featuring action and fascinating people will inhale this story. Readers will find a gritty adventure full of heart, loyalty, intrigue, deception, and a host of bitter-sweet emotions. This fantasy has the depth to cross genre boundaries and provide a provocative, captivating read. I heartily recommend this read." - *Reader Views 5 Star Review (Orabelle)*

"A crackerjack yarn featuring a strong heroine, plenty of action, and genuinely surprising twists and turns. Get it." – *Kirkus Reviews (Orabelle)*

"Barrett's storytelling prowess shines, offering readers a riveting journey into a world where shadows of the past converge with the uncertainty of the future. A must-read for fantasy enthusiasts craving a tale of complexity, heart, and unrelenting suspense." – *Reader's Favorite 5 Star Review (Maialen)*

"An epic narrative unravels through intricate plots and surprising turns. Characters and events come to life, offering readers a cinematic journey. The author's words skillfully paint each scene, making it enthralling to imagine. For enthusiasts of fantastical tales, this story is sure to enchant." – *Author's Reading (Blaise)*

"An exciting new world filled with elemental magic and political intrigue. This is an excellent start to an epic new fantasy series." – *Reedsy Discovery (Orabelle)*

"There was never a dull moment, and I immersed myself in the depiction of another world...Fantasy, family drama, and more await. I recommend Orabelle to readers who enjoy action filled fantasy stories" - *Reader's Favorite 5 Star Review (Orabelle)*

"Orabelle was a unique fantasy incorporating fresh takes on elemental magic and political intrigue. My favorite parts of this novel were the ways it defied my expectations." - *Judge, 10th Annual Writer's Digest Self Published E-Book Awards.*

"A taut fantasy tale of bloodshed and politics with a complex hero battling her own personal demons. Barrett once again weaves together heart-pounding action and complex characters to create an epic tale that tackles themes of grief, forgiveness, and self-determination... Our verdict – GET IT." *– Kirkus Reviews (Maialen)*

"An enthralling journey infused with raw emotions, unwavering loyalty, and intricate webs of intrigue and deception; un-put-downable. Readers hungry for stories of adventure, betrayal, and the unwavering strength of the human spirit won't want to miss this one." *– The Prairies Book Review (The Keepers of Imbria full series review)*

"Author J. Barrett has crafted an exhilarating novel that kept me on the edge of my seat from start to finish...Eolande delivers a satisfying conclusion that will linger in the minds of readers long after the last page is turned, and I would highly recommend it and the series in general to fantasy fans everywhere." *– K.C. Finn, Reader's Favorite (Eolande)*

BOOKS BY J. BARRETT

The Keepers of Imbria

Orabelle

Maialen

Blaise

Eolande

BLAISE

The Keepers of Imbria Book 3

J. Barrett

ANTHEM IN ART

Blaise

The Keepers of Imbria Book 3

Copyright © 2023 by J. Barrett

All rights reserved.

This is a work of fiction. Names, characters, places, and incidents in this book are either the product of the author's imagination or used in a fictitious manner. Any resemblance to actual persons, living or dead, or actual events is purely coincidental.

This first edition published by Anthem in Art

IMBRIA

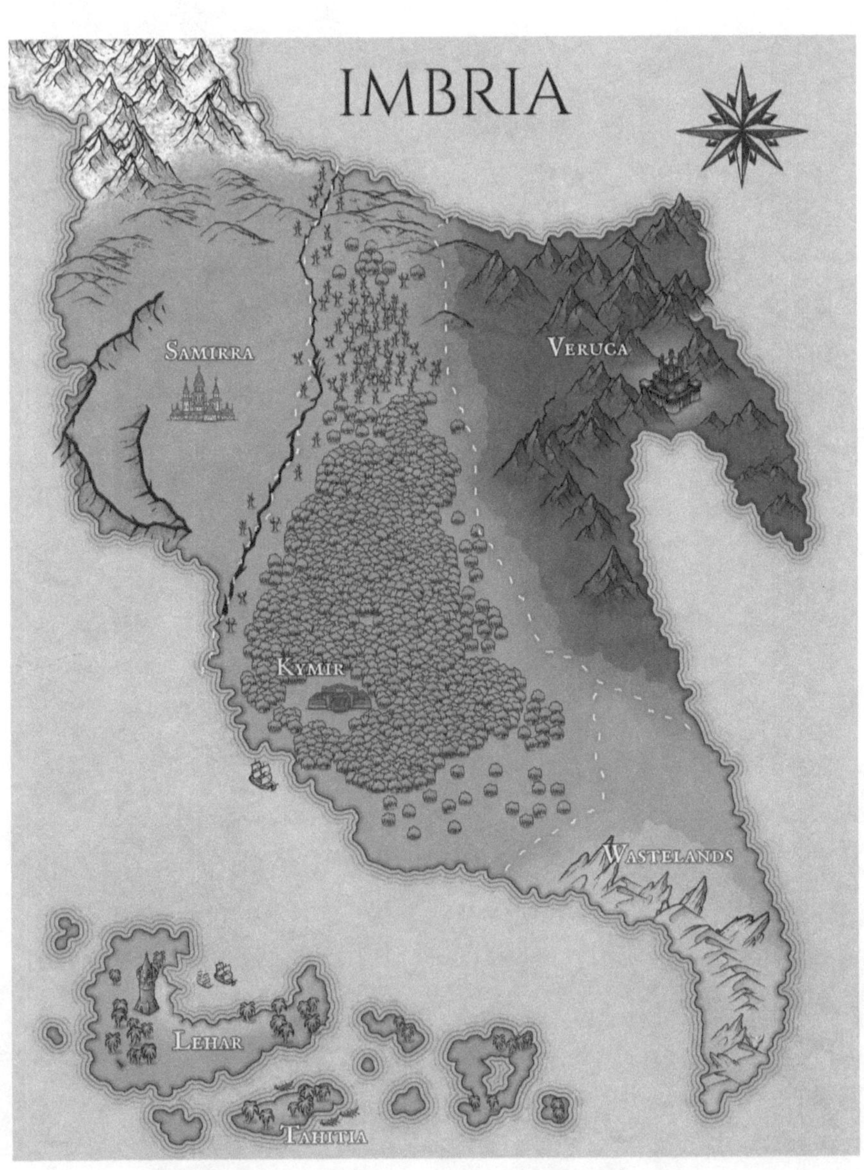

1

I was surrounded by the dead, stalking my prey through a world of shadows. With every step, soft plumes of dust and ash rose up to cloud the grey winter air. The blackened skeletons of burnt trees stood like sentinels all around, a ghostly army left behind to protect the remnants of the once great forest. I prowled around the lifeless remains, my senses trained on the thing I hunted. I sniffed the air where the metallic odor of blood lingered and my amber eyes searched the cold mist that encircled me. A shallow, almost imperceptible pulse of breath reached my ears. My prey was near.

My fingers flexed in the leather gloves that encased them and I gripped the hilt of the broadsword I carried, the weight of it causing the muscles in my arms to strain against my leather armor. Another step and another haze of ash floated into the frosted air. I could hear my prey's breath, louder now, and I searched for the telltale clouds of moisture that would float from its evil mouth. Within a tangle of charred branches, I saw the wispy tendrils of warm air rising in a steady rhythm. There was a subtle edge of movement, and a low growl rumbled through the wasting silence. I braced my feet, the heel of my boot grinding into the dead earth. I was anticipating an attack, for the thing I hunted also hunted me.

The blooddrinker leapt from the icy shadows with a furious roar, clawed hands tearing at the space between us. I stood still, sword held steady and muscles taut, my eyes following the bestial movements. A bead of sweat slid down the side of my face from beneath the blood-red hair that curled over my forehead. The creature's face was a deformed mask of rage as it snarled, putrid saliva dripping from blackened fangs. It lifted one of its hands, the razor-sharp talons aimed at my throat as I looked into glowing yellow eyes, seeing my death reflected in the sparkling madness of their depths. My hands swung in an arc, sword flashing against the dull winter landscape, and the right arm of the beast dropped heavily to the ground with a spray of black blood that curved through the air and spattered hotly across me. It screamed and the unnatural sound shattered the stillness of the forest. Before it could recover the boy was there, running silently from the shadows where he had waited, his own short sword curved in front of him. The yellow eyes of the beast widened in shock just before its head toppled from its neck and it collapsed in a pile at my feet, dusted with the ashes of the dead.

"Well done," I said to the boy, sheathing my sword and wiping at the foul black ooze that splattered the planes of my face.

Kaeleb scowled, nudging the shoulder of the Fomori beast with the toe of his boot. "What do you think it was doing out here alone?"

"Looking for us, I would imagine," I replied with bitterness. I was growing weary of being chased.

The boy turned his grey eyes up to me with a look of such solemn trust that it made my chest ache with guilt. Kaeleb was ten or eleven years old, and like most Leharans he was tall for his age with golden skin and narrow angular eyes. He was an orphan who had been used as a pawn since the day he was born. He was a decoy, a ruse to help hide the actual child of the late Water Keeper, Orabelle. The woman who was to have been my wife before her untimely death in battle changed the world forever. Her Guardian, Damian, gave the orphaned boy to two of the Queen's companions after her demise, claiming that Kaeleb was her child, the fabled Solvrei, the legend born of divine blood who would save Imbria. He lied to them, but they did not know this, and so they raised the boy accordingly, forcing him to endure trials and tests of strength that even grown men were likely to fail at. They relentlessly groomed him to be the thing they wanted him to be, a legendary warrior and a savior to the world, and in doing so they had shaped him into a strange blend of merciless killer, honorable warrior, and childish innocence. Then they brought Kaeleb to Maialen.

A shadow fell over me at the thought of the Earth Queen. Maialen was Orabelle's younger sister, and the Keeper of Earth and ruler of Kymir, the forested realm of central Imbria. A realm I had inadvertently destroyed a good portion of the last time I had seen her, when she was trying to kill Kaeleb and use his divine blood to defeat the Fomori. It has been a wasted effort on her part since Kaeleb was not the Solvrei and his blood was as ordinary as the rest of ours. I had stopped Maialen from killing him, but I would never be able to look at her the same way again. Any affection that I had felt for her, whatever had been between us, it died that day. I told myself it was for the best since Maialen had always wanted something from me that I could not give, and that was to have never loved her sister.

My mind drifted back to the day we had stood on the field that stretched between Kymir and Samirra, the day I saved Kaeleb from Maialen and took him away from her. He had clung to my back, hurt, his arm bleeding heavily from the wound she had inflicted on him. His blood was warm as it ran down my neck where he held onto me. It was then that I unleashed a torrent of fire, scorching everything in its path. The Fomori frantically retreated from the flames, their halfbreed leader cursing me as she vaulted onto her eagle to escape the lava that poured out of the rift Maialen had torn open in the land. I carried the boy away, ignoring Maialen and her desperate screams and curses, taking one of the eagles, not knowing where I would go. I was just as much an orphan as Kaeleb, and just as lost. My home had been stolen from me, and Maialen was my one ally on Imbria, but it was an alliance that I could bear no longer, not after what she had done. In my mind, she was too entangled with the memory of my mother, Maritka, a woman who was willing to kill a child, who had killed my little brother because he was a burden to her. After what she had done to Kaeleb, I could not see a way for Maialen to unravel the knot from the past she had tied herself to, and I could no longer look at her without also seeing my mother.

I had not known as I walked away from her that fateful day that the massive chasm she had opened in the ground reached further north than either of us could have imagined. When I had shoved all my power and rage into it, calling forth a deadly inferno to stop the Fomori onslaught, those flames had spread, filling the entire divide. The northern forest had burned, and none of us realized it until it was too late. In a fit of anger and grief, Maialen had vowed never to forgive me, and she had taken back her promise of helping me to reclaim my stolen kingdom.

"Where will we go now?" Kaeleb asked, interrupting my thoughts.

I brought myself back into the present, feeling the cold winter air biting across my skin. I waited a moment before answering him, considering our options. For the past few months we had been quietly threading our way through the outer towns and villages of my former kingdom of Veruca, stirring rebellion and gathering the support of those who were loyal to me or unhappy with the rule of my duplicitous cousin,

Logaire, who had stolen my throne while I was off battling the Fomori in the north. Logaire had gotten word of what I was up to, that I was fomenting insurgence throughout the realm, and she had sent soldiers after us, driving me back into the desolate forests of northern Kymir.

"We do not have the numbers to march on Veruca yet. Not without the help of the other realms," I pointed out needlessly. The boy knew where we stood.

"This is the Earth Queen's fault," Kaeleb muttered, kicking at the snow with the toe of his boot and covering the dark drops of Fomori blood with a dusting of pristine white powder. "The least she could have done was to help you take back your kingdom after you saved hers."

I felt a smile pull at the corners of my lips in response to the child's indignation on my behalf. "The Earth Queen does not see it that way. In her mind, I betrayed her and destroyed her land. Besides, she has her hands full dealing with the constant war the Fomori are raging against her. Chaote is determined that Maialen will be the next Keeper to fall."

"All the more reason to help us. We could fight alongside her if we had your army!" Kaeleb pointed out, shaking his head in disgust. "Kymirrans really are inferior in their ability to observe a situation."

"Just as we Verucans are not to be trusted?" I teased him.

He flashed me a sharp glare, his eyes like grey steel. "Look at your Verucan cousin, proof that Verucans are not to be trusted."

I gave a slight shrug to show that I would not argue with his logic. I myself had not been the most trustworthy of Verucans over the years. I had lied, threatened, manipulated, bribed and coerced to get what I wanted, but that was the price that came with power. No one held a kingdom without staining their soul with some sort of blight. Not even Maialen had escaped unscathed, and she had once been the most guileless of us all.

Where would we go now? It appeared that the hefty bounty Logaire had placed on my head was quite effective at running us out of the larger towns and villages of Veruca, for once I was recognized someone would inform the castle. If I was to lead a revolt and take back what was mine, I needed to stop running. I needed time to plan and organize. There was only one place I could think of going to where she would not look for me.

"We will take you home," I told the boy.

"To Lehar?" Kaeleb asked, raising a pale brow to express his doubt. It was so much like one of my own expressions that I was caught off guard for a moment. "Don't they hate you?"

"That is why Logaire will not think to look for us there."

"Why would they help us?"

"Lehar is in turmoil, their factions divided. Half of them are loyal to Thyrr because he is Orabelle's brother, and the other half wish to follow Colwyn because they want the reassurance of having a Keeper to protect them and Maialen has given the Captain her support. Lucky for us, both men owe me. We will be safe on Lehar, at least for the time being."

Kaeleb considered this, scowling into the approaching night that hung like a heavy curtain over the charred forest. "They do not have any decent food on the islands. Just salted fish and sour fruit."

I chuckled. "Then we had better find a way to take back my kingdom as soon as possible, so you can have all the pastries and treats you can steal from my cooks."

The boy nodded, his face set in determined lines. We trudged back through the ash and snow to where our horses were tethered and climbed on them. I was tired, and I knew the boy was too, but I wanted to put more distance between us and the Fomori. A lone beast was likely a scout, which meant a hunting party could be nearby and we needed to be careful. We rode in wary silence for the next few hours before reaching the edge of the fire line where the blackened skeletons of burnt trees gave way to soaring evergreens. The ash that had coated the world in a grey haze retreated from the icy forest floor in frothy black clumps beneath our horses' hooves.

I allowed us to stop and make camp there, just inside the shelter of the living trees, where the forest could provide cover. As Kaeleb brushed the snow away to make a clearing, I used my power to light a small fire, noting the shiver of his thin limbs. He looked up in surprise, for I had not used my power since that day at the Kymirran border.

"Are you sure you want to?" he asked me.

I shrugged, feeling the knots that strained the muscles of my back and neck. "I will have to use it eventually. I may as well be useful and keep us warm."

I had told Kaeleb about the power I wielded, about what it was like to be the Keeper of Fire. The constant ache within me to burn something to ash, the pull of the Element that clawed its way into my brain until I thought I would die if I did not release it. After what happened at the border it had been quiet, everything that was inside of me used up, incinerated in the inferno I called forth against the Fomori. It had taken more strength than I thought I possessed to fight back against the Warding Stones that Chaote wielded, stones which dampened the power of the amulets, swallowing the Elements in a void of emptiness. Since that day I had refrained from using my power, enjoying the brief respite from its insistent presence, not wanting to feel the awful pull of it again, the rage that threatened to overwhelm me. Not wanting to admit I was afraid of it.

"When I thought I was the Solvrei, the Harbonah told me the amulets were poisoning the Keepers. He said that was why I must take them and be rid of them," Kaeleb said in a soft voice tinged with worry, a frown pulling at his mouth. His pale hair gleamed against the darkness like the moon.

"I will be fine," I assured him with a careless grin meant to put him at ease. "The Harbonah are extremists, they exaggerate their claims to further their agendas. Whoever this old man was, he was probably clamoring for power in Samirra and thought saying such things against the Keepers would help his cause."

"But what if he was right? Could you not take the amulet to the Solvrei and be done with it?"

"And what if that little girl is just a little girl? What if there is no Solvrei? What if the only thing that can stop Chaote and her Fomori are the amulets?" I countered his questions with my own, questions I had already asked myself a dozen times. He sat, arms folded, staring at the fire, his face scrunched in thought and his shock of pale hair falling over his forehead. Around us, the fringe of pine trees shivered in the moonlight like splintered needles. The entire world seemed cold and harsh and brittle, the only warmth coming from the meager fire between us. I wondered once again if I had done the right thing in taking Kaeleb with me, or if I was condemning him to a fate he did not deserve, forcing him to fight my battles alongside me without having given him any choice in the matter. Though I could not see what other choice he had. The truth was, he had no one else to turn to, and neither did I. Like it or not, Kaeleb and I were in this fight together. I would just have to make sure I did not lose. That was the only way I could protect him.

I barely slept that night, listening to the steady rhythm of Kaeleb's innocent breathing as my mind ran through the myriad possibilities of what was to come. I watched the meager fire, the flickering waves of flame that twisted into wispy tendrils of smoke, and I tried to ignore the small ember that had been lit within me, the faint pull of my power already begging me to use it again. I flexed my fingers, feeling the muscles of my forearms pull against the black leather. I was strong, I could withstand it for now, but how long did I have until it was too much? How long until I needed to destroy something, until I lashed out against the ones closest to me because I was tormented by the power, by the way I both loved and hated it? It was the same paradox of emotions I had felt about Orabelle all those years ago, and in the end I had lost her.

I could still see her, as perfectly as if she were standing before me, and I wondered if her memory would ever stop haunting me. I closed my eyes and she was there, her white hair cascading down her back, her chin lifted in haughty arrogance and her blue eyes flashing. She was at the Council table, waiting for her father to enter so the meeting could officially convene. I had rested my booted feet on the hallowed table defiantly, wanting to impress her with my flagrant disregard of the rigid Council rules.

"You can support my claim to take her," Orabelle was saying to me.

I knew I was handsome, that women appreciated my looks, and in my arrogant youth I had assumed that this would apply to all women, including the Water Keeper. I was tanned, my skin swarthy with a healthy glow from being outdoors, and I had deep red hair that curled above the collar of my jacket. My muscles were firm and strong, trained from years of fighting in the former king's army. It never occurred to me that Orabelle would not feel the same way about me as I did about her, and I watched her with amusement, enjoying the fact that she needed my help and was swallowing her pride to ask for it.

"And what would I get in return?" I countered, dropping my feet so I could lean in closer to her. She smelled of the sea, fathomless and eternal.

She frowned at me, her eyes narrowing, flashing pale blue. "Name your price and I will give it."

I stared at her for a long moment. I could have helped her, I could have supported her claim to take her dying mother from Chronus and possibly saved Ursula's life, but I had not cared whether the former queen lived or died. Ursula meant nothing to me. All I had cared about was getting what I wanted and even though it was Orabelle herself that I wanted, it was not in her power to give herself to me. Her father was the one who would decide who she married and if I defied him now, he would make sure that I would never have her.

"Apologies, dearest, but I'm afraid you cannot give me what I want."

"Blaise, you cannot trust my father. Whatever he has promised you will cost you far more than you are willing to pay," Orabelle assured me, lowering her voice and leaning even closer. My pulse had quickened at her proximity, at the soft brush of her hair against my arm and the nearness of her radiant golden skin.

"I will take my chances," I had told her with a callous shrug.

"But-" she started to protest, slamming her palms on the polished table, her magnificent temper flaring to life. She was interrupted by the booming voice of her father as he descended into the chamber and I grinned at her, lounging casually, never taking my amber gaze from her. I wanted her to know I was superior to her, that I held more power than she did. I had been too young and stupid then to realize what I had really wanted was for her to respect me, but in my foolish youth I had believed that fear and respect were the same thing. I had not known enough of the world to realize she would always hate me for that moment, the moment I could have been her champion, but instead I chose to be her enemy.

I sighed into the frosty night and tried to let the memory fade, lacing my fingers behind my head and pulling my gaze from the fire to stare up through the trees at the relentless black sky. Perhaps Kaeleb was right and I should just give the amulet to the girl. Perhaps Maialen was right in her desire to be rid of it all, to go somewhere far away from it as Gideon had, to leave it all behind. But no. In the end, Gideon had not escaped us or his fate, and there was nowhere that would be safe on Imbria if Chaote and the Fomori had their way. I was not born to give up. I was born to fight and I would not quit now. I would take back what was mine, then I would crush the halfbreed and her army of demons. That was who I was.

It felt like mere moments after I closed my eyes that I was jerked awake, startled by a sharp nudge against my abdomen. Kaeleb was crouching beside me, making a gesture for silence, his short sword held in his hands. Dawn was rising behind the forest, the frosty ground glistening with cold droplets of dew, and I could hear the agitated huffs of breath from the horses as the first golden rays of light stretched their long arms around the trunks of the trees.

"Someone is near," Kaeleb whispered.

I rose to a crouch beside him, noting that he had already damped out the fire. We waited in silence, listening, and I felt the familiar pull of my Element, like pins and needles pricking along my skin as I drew the power to me.

There was rustling in the foliage nearby and I held my breath, rubbing my thumb over the flint that I carried in my pocket. All I needed was a spark. Kaeleb was silent, nearly breathless, his self-control far beyond his young years. I saw the white knuckles that gripped the sword, the slight wrinkle between his brows as he concentrated. The sound retreated, fading into the distance, and I narrowed my eyes, not trusting that the danger had passed.

"What do you think it was? An animal?" Kaeleb finally asked. He slid his sword back into its homemade sheath beneath his leather overcoat.

I stood and surveyed the forest that stretched out around us. "Possibly, but we should get moving just in case. If it was another Fomori scout, then they could be on their way back to us with reinforcements."

We quickly packed up the camp and began making our way in a southeastern direction. I wanted to avoid the southern Wastelands and the utter desolation of the harsh desert, but I also had no desire to attract Maialen's attention by traipsing through her kingdom. We would go somewhere between, skirting the edges of Kymir until we reached the ocean. I did not know how we would get across the sea to Lehar, but we could worry about that later. At the moment, our priority was not getting murdered by a pack of hungry blooddrinkers or captured by overzealous Verucan soldiers.

As we rode, Kaeleb kept twisting in his saddle, staring behind us with a distrustful gaze. Finally, after about the hundredth time, I slowed my mount to a stop, turning and looking into the distance with him. We had left the dense forests behind us and were now rounding the edge of the plains that stretched between Veruca and Kymir.

"What is it?" I asked him.

"I think we are being followed. There." He pointed and a shimmer of dusty earth could be seen far back on the plains, visible against the towering black spires of the snowcapped Verucan mountains that rose beyond.

I sighed. I had hoped to escape the area undetected, but it seemed I was not so lucky. "The Fomori?"

Kaeleb scrunched his face. "Not likely. Whoever this is, they are on a horse. And it is not your cousin or the Verucans. Those dimwits you call soldiers would have come barreling through here like a herd of stampeding cows."

"Do we wait for them? Or keep going?" I asked. I knew what I wanted to do, but I was curious what course of action the boy would choose. He was a constant source of surprise, his wit sharper than most grown men I had met. He was far more intelligent than Akrin, my adopted son, despite the other having at least a ten-year head start. I felt a twist of anger in my gut at the thought of the sullen young man I had taken in so many years ago. Alita's younger brother. She had also been the one to raise Kaeleb, and I wondered how the two had ended up so completely different. Akrin had joined Logaire in usurping my kingdom, bringing my entire army to her side and betraying me in a way that I never thought he would. Whatever she had promised him, I hoped it was worth it because one day soon he was going to pay for that betrayal.

"We wait." Kaeleb was resolute.

"Very well," I said with a slight incline of my head. I folded my arms over the pommel of my saddle and we waited, watching the cloud of dust in the distance as it drew nearer.

"They are taking forever," Kaeleb muttered impatiently a few moments later. He squinted up at the sun, judging how much time had passed.

"They are probably doing their best to be stealthy in their pursuit," I pointed out.

He snorted. "Well, they have failed terribly in that endeavor. A blind toad could see them coming."

I laughed again, thinking once more that I was glad I had kept the boy around. I drummed my fingers on the edge of the saddle, nearly as impatient as the child. It seemed an eternity passed before the lone figure was silhouetted against the sky. Their horse slowed to a steady walk as they approached.

"You!" I growled through clenched teeth, anger burning across my skin in a wave of hatred. I had not seen the man for more than ten years, but I would know him even if a hundred years had passed.

"I am not here to fight you," Damian called, lifting his hands in a gesture of peace. "I seek your help."

I stared at the big Tahitian as he towered over us, his shadow slanting across the ground, and I felt as if my insides were being torn apart. In my mind I went back to that day in Veruca, to the battle of Queen's End. The day Orabelle died. The battle, the bite on her neck, her blood staining my hands, her eyes glittering with hate as she stabbed me. It all came crashing back to me at the sight of him. Damian had been there, taking her from me, shoving me away as he held her hands while the light left her eyes. He had not let me explain to her that it was not me who had killed her first Guardian. He had not let me say goodbye. Orabelle died hating me, and Damian was as much to blame as Astraeus had been. It was the responsibility of her Guardian to protect her, and if he was incapable of fulfilling that duty, he should have entrusted her to me. I would have kept her safe. She would still be alive if not for him.

"Blaise," he began, and I felt a roar tear from my throat.

"Get down and fight me!" I shouted at him, leaping from my horse. Kaeleb's wide-eyed stare made me briefly wonder whether he understood the significance of the man standing before us, but I had no time for explanations.

"I am not here to fight. I need your help," Damian repeated, his deep baritone trying to maintain calm as he slid slowly from his mount, his movements steady and measured.

"I will never help you," I snarled. I began to call my power, feeling the burning, insistent rage of it filling me up, like liquid fire being poured out of my soul and coursing through my veins. I wanted to kill him then, more than I had ever wanted anything in my life. "It is your fault she is dead! You could not protect her! You should have left her with me, where she would have been safe!"

"You are right."

The pain in his words was like an arrow piercing through my anger. I stopped, the flint in my hand, my chest heaving, my power crawling across my skin like a thousand sparks.

"You are right," he said again, and his head fell forward, his long dreadlocks sweeping his ebony shoulders above the dark cloak that was shrouded around him. "I failed Orabelle and because of that she is dead. But it is her child that now needs your help."

"The Solvrei?" Kaeleb asked sharply. "Has something happened to her?"

"The child needs your help," Damian insisted, ignoring the boy.

I scoffed and felt the intense pull of my power ease as I relaxed slightly, my curiosity peaked. "What have you done this time?"

Damian's stern features were set and though his face remained impassive, there was a flash of something uneasy in the round, black eyes. "We have tried to give her the Pearl."

I arched a brow, my face splitting into a mirthless grin. "So, you had it all this time?"

"The Sirens held it."

I kept smiling though my mind spinning with his admission. The Sirens had kept the Pearl of Water. The Sirens that should not exist any longer without Orabelle to keep them alive. His short, cryptic answers were typical of the Tahitians, and I wondered what else he was deliberately not telling me.

"She is too young," I pointed out. "Why would you think she could control an Element at her age?"

Damian sighed, looking out past me into his own thoughts. "What choice do we have? This is the only way we can keep her safe. She must be able to protect herself from Chaote."

"You mean the deranged Tahitian woman that was trapped in a cave for centuries and wants to destroy all of Imbria? Seems like this is the Tahitians' mess to clean up, Guardian, not mine. Chaote is one of you, after all."

"You are the one who let her out. And do not pretend that you don't care what happens to the child. Seff told me about Gideon."

I stiffened at the mention of the woodsman, seeing Maialen's tortured face in my mind after she had killed her former Guardian. "Gideon's death was an accident."

"I know that. And after he died you tried to protect the girl. She means something to you because she is Orabelle's child. Do this for her mother. You owe her this much."

My fingers twitched as I took a step closer. He did not flinch, refusing to back away, his black eyes meeting mine. He towered over me but we both knew I could kill him, burn the flesh from his bones in seconds. It would only take a moment, a flick of my wrist. He had come here willing to die, knowing it was a possibility.

Kaeleb landed lightly on the ground, walking over to stand beside me, his shock of pale hair glinting in the sun. He glared at Damian. "You are the one who gave me to Sister Alita and Brother Kaden."

"I am."

Kaeleb considered this for a long time. He kicked at the dirt road with the toe of his boot, a gesture so childlike that it melted my fury. He said to me, "My entire purpose in life was to be the Solvrei. Now that I know it is not who I am, the only purpose I can think of is to serve the Solvrei. If she needs us, then we must help her."

I continued to keep my eyes trained on Damian, taking in the boy's words, envious of the childish simplicity of his thoughts. The world was not so straightforward. "How do I know you are not luring me to your island to steal the Opal from me and give it to the girl?"

Damian seemed annoyed at having to prove his intentions. "She cannot control one Element, let alone two. And if she truly is the Solvrei then once she learns how to call the power, she will not need your amulet and no one will try to take it from you."

I knew the islanders' code of honor, the ridiculous importance they placed on their word. "If I help you, then the Tahitians and the girl will fight for me to reclaim Veruca."

The stern jaw clenched and Damian gave a slight shake of his head. "We have bigger problems than your family squabbles-"

"You do this or I kill you now and walk away."

He was clearly displeased but he knew he had no choice but to agree if he wanted my help. "It is agreed. We will help you reclaim your kingdom, but not until the threat from Chaote has been dealt with."

I laughed. "You underestimate my cousin, Tahitian. If Logaire can find a way, she will align herself with this woman against us. Trust me, returning Veruca to me as soon as possible is in all of our best interests."

"When the time is right, you will have our help."

"Wise choice of words. I will accept your offer. Now, tell me about the girl," I said brusquely.

Damian told us how Seff had brought the little girl to Tahitia. Cossiana, Damian's mother and the island Elder, had convinced Maialen and anyone else who would listen that the Tahitians wanted the child dead, a clever lie told so no one would suspect them to be harboring the Solvrei. After Chaote took Samirra and began her assault on Kymir, the Tahitians knew they could not wait. If Eolande was truly the Solvrei, then now was the time to begin her training, for the war they had always feared had already begun. Damian brought the girl to the Sirens, and they gave the child the Pearl. It had not gone as they had hoped.

The girl had gripped the amulet in her small fist, her blue eyes bright with terror before she turned and flung it out into the sea, cursing it. Cossiana's mouth had fallen open in surprise and she had tried to calm the child, but the little girl had shoved her away, screaming at the Elder to leave her alone. The Sirens retrieved the Pearl from the sea, once again bringing it back to the girl, but this time she refused to take it, burying her face in her hands and screaming over and over till her throat was raw and she was exhausted. She had laid herself down on the warm golden sand, staring up at the sky, tears running out of her eyes, shrieking wildly anytime someone came near her. The twin brothers' ugly dog was the only creature she would allow near her. It trotted over, lying by her side, and she finally quieted, falling asleep with her arms curled around the beast. The Tahitians had left her alone for the rest of the night, and the next day they found her sitting at the edge of the sea, a fishing knife in her hand and her hair scattered around her in tufts of white where she had cut it short, her head scratched and scraped from the clumsy effort. They had tried again to give her the amulet, but it was the same. She refused to take the Pearl and when the Sirens tried to press it into her hands, she screamed and flung it away, becoming inconsolable.

"Is she mad?" I asked him, wondering if Gideon's death had been more than the girl could have endured. He was all she had known, the only parent she ever had.

Damian shook his head. "She was perfectly fine until we tried to give her the Pearl."

"Perhaps she realizes she will be better off without it," I suggested. "Your prophecies and destinies have cursed many lives, Tahitian. Maybe the girl wants nothing to do with the path you have set her upon."

I glanced at Kaeleb, saw the flicker of emotion cross his face, the toe of his boot still scraping lines in the dirt as he listened to our words.

"We need you to help her, to convince her to at least try. None of us know what it is like to be a Keeper, and, though I never thought I would say these words, you are the only one I can trust to do this."

I felt my grin widen. "Well, well, Tahitian, that is quite the admission. You must indeed be desperate. Perhaps I should have asked for more in return."

Damian glowered at me. "I have agreed to save your kingdom. I think that is fair compensation for a few hours of tutelage."

"There is something that I want," Kaeleb interrupted us. He lifted his head, squinting up at the heavily muscled frame of the dark Tahitian. "If we are to help you, then I want to know who I am. You were the one who took me when I was a baby, so you must know."

Damian had the decency to look guilty and I rocked back on my heels, waiting for his answer. The boy was right. He deserved that much, at least.

"You were nobody. Your parents were of no consequence and they did not want you. I do not know why. They abandoned you to the midwife and it was she who gave you to me."

Kaeleb's bottom lip quivered slightly, the movement almost imperceptible and yet so vulnerable that I felt my chest tighten. I wanted to punch Damian in the face for the callous delivery of his words, but he had already turned back to his horse, and there were bigger things at stake here than the boy's feelings. I needed an army to take back Veruca, and the Tahitians had just provided me with one. I gripped Kaeleb's shoulder and stood in front of him.

"It does not matter who you were. I came from nothing just like you, but where we come from does not define us. We were meant for great things, you and I, never forget that," I told him. He nodded and squared his thin shoulders, running to his horse and flinging himself into the saddle. I grinned after him, striding back to my own mount and wondering just how long it would be before Damian and I tried to kill each other.

2

The islands were different than I remembered. Or perhaps it was me that was different, and the islands had remained unchanged. Either way, it was a strange sensation setting foot on the shifting sands of the Tahitian shoreline. The world felt loose, dislodged from the solid black rock that I was so accustomed to. I squinted my amber eyes against the glare of the sun and regarded the gathered crowd warily. The Tahitians maintained a respectful distance, but their distrust of me was evident in the dark glances and whispered conversations that trailed after us as we passed by. We were following Damian up the beach from the pier where the small ship had docked. I had to admit, I was grateful he had effectively solved our problem of getting to the islands from the mainland, though I did not tell him that the islands had already been our destination. Let the Tahitians think they had taken us off course. It would make my sacrifice seem even greater in their eyes.

Damian had been mostly silent for the journey, staring out over the ocean in stoic solitude and giving veiled answers to any questions that Kaeleb or I asked. It was clear that he was not pleased with bringing us to his homeland, and it was a prudent way of thinking, because I was still toying with the idea of killing him anyway, despite our agreement. His very presence grated on my nerves, reminding me constantly of the past and of things I would rather forget.

"I have avoided the sea since her death," I said to him as we looked out over the waves, the ship dipping up and down in the frothy swells as we glided through the water. There was no point in pretending we both were not thinking of her.

"Hiding from what happened does not make it easier to live with," was his clipped response.

"I am surprised that Orabelle enjoyed your company so much. She did not seem the kind to tolerate self-righteous philosophizing," I tossed back at him. I thought I saw the corner of his mouth twitch with mirth, but he continued to stare out over the vast sea.

"She was full of surprises," he finally said in his deep, quiet way.

I chuckled, seeing her again in my mind's eye; the vibrance of her being, the keen intellect in her eyes, and the fearless and stubborn tilt of her chin. "That she was."

He had turned away from me then, moving across the deck to face the wind. I watched him for a while, wondering once again just how long it would be before the two of us could stand each other no longer.

On the Tahitian beach, we found Cossiana waiting for us. I inclined my head politely in greeting. The last time I had seen the old woman was when she had slapped me soundly in the Council chamber, and from the amused glint in her eye it seemed very likely that she was also reliving that particular memory. Kaeleb came to a stop beside me, casting a scowl in her direction. Cossiana gracefully bowed before him, her cascading braids and the trailing edges of the blue cloth she was adorned in gently touching the sandy ground.

"I owe you an apology," she said to the boy, the lines of her weathered face folding into a maternal smile. "I was unkind to you before, but I hope you understand it was to protect those I care about."

He shrugged, looking uncomfortable and twisting the toe of his boot into the sand.

"No apology for me?" I asked Cossiana with a wink, drawing her attention away from him. "I seem to remember your behavior towards me was quite unkind as well."

Her grey brows drew together as she glared at me. "You deserved it. The boy did not. And do not try your charms on me, Fire Keeper. I am too old to be swayed by a handsome face."

"Oh, so you find me handsome?" I teased her with a suggestive grin.

"Just because I am old does not mean I am blind," she retorted, making me chuckle. I was surprised at her candid humor, and I wondered if in another life the old woman and I could have been friends.

"Is it always this hot?" I asked, changing the subject and wiping sweat from beneath the thick red curls of hair that clung to my neck.

"You are dressed for the winter of the mainland, not the islands. Come, we will see that you are made comfortable," she said, motioning for me to follow her. "We have a place prepared for you in the village and the boy will be staying with-"

"The boy will be staying with me," I interrupted her, my tone making it clear that it was not up for debate. "You can understand, Cossiana, that my trust only extends so far and I have promised to protect him."

"Very well. He stays with you."

"Where is the girl?"

"All in good time, Keeper. She is safe for now. The Sirens are with her," Cossiana said. I could see there was a shadow in her eyes, and she was more concerned than Damian had let on. Whatever was happening with that child, the Tahitians were quite upset about it.

I followed the old woman up the beach, Kaeleb trailing behind me with his hand on his sword, shooting angry glances at anyone who looked his way. We entered the walled village and passed through a circle of huts, making our way over the packed earth of the central clearing to the far end. A small house made of thatched grass was shaded by heavy palms, the tree trunks bent by the wind so they sheltered the structure from both sides, like hands protectively cupped around a cowering animal. The house itself was cool and airy, and simple in design. There were two rooms with woven grass walls to separate them and what appeared to be a random scattering of carved teak furniture, brightly colored fabrics and decorative objects. Beaded curtains hung from the doorways and draped across the windows, which seemed to have been perfectly placed to catch the island breeze.

I pulled at the laces of the thick leather vest I was still wearing, grateful for the wash of cool air even if the rooms were a bit too cluttered for my tastes. A man followed Cossiana in and dumped a pile of clothes unceremoniously onto a chair, then turned and stomped out.

"I suppose not everyone here is happy to see me," I noted.

The old woman lifted her hands as if to say it was beyond her control. "You have made your own bed, Fire Keeper."

I felt a flush of irritation. "That is amusing coming from you, Tahitian, since it is one of your kind that threatens Imbria, not me."

"We will bring the boy what he needs. Please, change your clothing and then I will return to take you to Eolande," Cossiana said, ignoring my comment. She knew I was right. The Tahitians could pretend to be as sanctimonious as they wanted to, but the truth of the matter was that this was their mess to clean up, and they knew it.

After she had gone, I dug through the pile of clothing, holding up the long swathes of cloth that the fishermen folded in elaborate drapes to cover themselves. I had no clue how to wrap the dyed cloths, so I flung them aside in irritation, thankful to finally find a simple linen tunic and pants that tied around the waist. I pulled off my heavy leather shirt and vest and tossed them aside, my eyes straying to the jagged white scar that skittered across my ribs like a lightning bolt. The wound Orabelle had given me at the battle of Queen's End, just before she died.

I thought again how strange it was to be on the islands, to be in her realm. I had never wondered what her home was like for her, never bothered to learn why she loved it so much. Lehar and the other islands had always been an unreachable place in my mind, something far away and exotic, like the Queen herself. I felt her presence here more than I cared to, and I also felt the uncomfortable sensation of regret creeping through my body.

There was a light tap on the door and Damian was there, his massive frame filling the entryway. He had a bundle of clothing for Kaeleb, which he handed to him kindly. The boy took the offered goods and went into the other room, leaving me to face the heavily built Tahitian man in awkward silence. He was bigger than I remembered, all muscle and sinew, his dark ebony skin gleaming. There were silver hooks that pierced his ears, and his long dreadlocks hung down his back, tied back from his face with a blue cloth. I noticed his black eyes linger a moment on the curved edge of the Fire Opal that hung beneath the loose linen shirt I had donned.

"You afraid I will burn your little village to the ground?" I asked him with a grin.

"I am not afraid of you and never have been," he replied flatly.

"You should be," I warned, my tone laced with malice. It would be easy to kill him now. It would have been easy to kill him at any point since he had caught up to us and asked us for help. I wondered if he even realized how vulnerable he was.

"My lack of fear is not because I underestimate you," Damian said, as if reading my thoughts. "I know that you could have killed me a thousand times already. I am not afraid of you because I am not afraid to die."

I raised an eyebrow. "Ready to give it all up so soon?"

He regarded me with obvious displeasure. "I have lost those closest to me, and I will spend what life I have left atoning for that loss."

At that moment Kaeleb came back into the room, wrapped in one of the Tahitian fisherman's cloths and looking so ridiculous that I had to force myself to hide my smile. The boy had made a great effort with the garment, but instead of it flowing around the body in loose, easy folds, it looked like he had tried to mummify himself in the colorful cloth. His short sword was strapped to his waist and he was looking at us expectantly, ready to proceed.

Damian coughed into his hand, a false gesture that I assumed was to hide his own amusement at the boy's attempts at Tahitian fashion. He glanced at me and I gave a small shrug. If Kaeleb was happy looking like a strangled salamander, then that was his choice and I would not fault him for it.

Damian led us out, but instead of retracing our steps through the village, we went behind the hut and followed a narrow path through the dense island jungle. The heat was oppressive amongst the trees, the air heavy with moisture. Rivulets of sweat ran down my face, my linen shirt clinging to my back and chest as we walked. Eventually, the path opened onto the beach and the soft breeze was a welcome reprieve for my sweat-soaked skin. The girl was there, sitting in the golden sand, wearing a white dress. The amorphous green-blue forms of the Sirens were lounging nearby, making soft noises as they turned their strange, watery glances towards me. They quieted their gentle cooing, as if waiting to see what I would do next. Beyond them, the sea stretched in a dazzling blue shimmer that rolled out to the horizon.

The girl lifted her head and I felt a familiar tightness in my chest and a knot in my throat that were the lingering remnants of my grief. She looked so much like her mother. The shape of her brows, the tilt of her chin. It was all from Orabelle. I forced myself to swallow the lump that lodged in my throat, pushing aside the vivid memories the child had conjured forth and focusing on the present. Eolande's eyes were red rimmed from crying and there was a disarray of short, pale hair that clung to her head in messy clumps. Her gaze drifted to Kaeleb and her blue eyes widened with peaked curiosity.

She tilted her head to one side and said to him, "You have a sword."

His thin chest puffed up with pride and he placed a hand on the hilt of his weapon. "I am a Leharan warrior."

"But you are just a boy," she pointed out.

"And you are just a girl, but you are the Solvrei," he countered.

Her face darkened at his words. She shook her head and glanced at the Sirens, a shiver rippling over her skin despite the golden warmth of the sun that bathed her. Damian made a motion with his hand at me, indicating the girl.

"What does that mean?" I asked him, waving at his vague gesture.

"It means do something," he snapped. "I did not bring you here just to stand there."

"What would you have me do?"

Damian was growing increasingly annoyed with me, and I was starting to feel a similar irritation with him. He glowered at me and I sighed, taking a step towards the girl.

"Do you remember me?" I asked her, hoping that she did not. I had played a significant role in Gideon's death and I did not want to force her to relive that loss.

"Yes."

Well, so much for that. "Do you know who I am? And why I am here?"

"You are the Fire Keeper. They want you to make me take the Pearl," she answered with another shiver of fear.

"That is not why I am here, Eolande." I came forward slowly and sat beside her on the warm sand. "I can show you how to control the Element and how to use the power, but I will not force you to take it."

She looked down at the ground, tracing whirling designs in the sand with her small fingers. She whispered, so only I could hear her. "I don't like it."

"Why not?"

She hesitated, glancing at the Sirens, who seemed agitated, wringing their hands while their limbs faded back and forth between liquid and human form. "I can hear them."

I narrowed my eyes intently. "The Sirens?"

"No. The other Keepers. The ones who came before."

I stared at her, trying to digest her words, glancing back to make sure that Damian had not heard what she had said. He was standing several yards away, his focus on the sea. I turned back to the child. "How do you know it is the other Keepers?"

"I just know."

"What do they say?"

She wrinkled her nose. "It is hard to listen because there are so many of them speaking."

I leaned back on my elbows, thinking about what she had just said. Either the girl was quite mad, or it was possible she really did have divine blood. But how to know which? The voices in her head could just be delusions, but if it was true that she could hear the Keepers of the past, then it was possible she truly was the Solvrei. I had to admit to myself that this possibility unnerved me. I had never really believed in the old legends. Prophecies were just another tool to control the weak-minded masses.

"Have you told anyone else about this?" I asked her.

"Just the dog."

I grinned. "That is fine. For now, let us keep this a secret between us Keepers and the dog."

"Do you hear them too?"

I hesitated, wondering if I should lie to her. Thinking we were similar would make her trust me. I settled for something between a lie and truth. "I do not hear them, but I can feel them."

She nodded and seemed to accept this. "What was it like for you? When you first became a Keeper."

I felt another shadow pass over my features, wondering if the question had been whispered to her by one of her voices. Something in me was compelling me to help her. Whether it was guilt or sympathy, or something else entirely, I could not determine, but I began to tell her what she wanted to know.

The former king of Veruca had been a hard, unkind man. He was old, much older than Keepers typically were, for controlling the amulet required quite a bit of strength and was usually something reserved for those whose bodies were still hearty and hale. I remembered the fragile bones of his hands and the thin, papery skin that sagged from them as he held out the amulet to me.

"Now you can live up to that foolish name your mother gave you," he had managed to say after a fit of coughing and hacking. "Go ahead! What are you waiting for? Take it already. I know you have been salivating for it, and I wish to die in peace."

I hesitated, seeing my fingers tremble in the air as I reached out my hand. This was what I had been born to do, the destiny that my mother had set forth for me. The reason for everything she had done. Part of me felt that taking it was a betrayal of my brother, Bastion. It would be vindicating my mother and her decision to end his life, giving her the gift she had always longed for, even though she was not alive to relish it. The other part of me felt that not taking it would make Bastion's death meaningless. Being the Keeper of Fire was the only way to make what had happened all those years ago worth something in the end, an act of defiance against my mother, who had only wished it to elevate her own status in life. I was achieving her dreams without her, in spite of her.

The old king noticed my hesitation and laughed, the coarse sound dissolving into a fit of labored breathing. "Don't tell me you are too scared. A weak man will never hold this realm."

"I am not weak," I said, clenching my teeth and snatching the amulet from his grasp.

His skeletal fingers opened and closed convulsively over the empty space where the gleaming jewel had been and for a moment he looked panic-stricken. Then he relaxed, lowering the hand to his chest, a look of peace settling over his creased features. "It is your burden to bear now."

I had gripped the jewel, calling the power to me as he had taught me to do, telling it I was its master now. I felt it burn through me, searing along my skin like a cascade of smoldering embers. I gasped and for a moment I thought it would burn right through me, that he was right and I was too weak and the power would destroy me, that it would use me up and leave no trace of me behind. Then, as quickly as it had overwhelmed me, it faded, curling within me like a sleepy dragon, waiting just on the edge of consciousness for me to summon it again.

"Every day since then it was easier to control," I told the girl.

"Are you still afraid of it?" she asked. I glanced over at Kaeleb who had crept closer and was watching us both carefully.

"Some days I am," I admitted. "Do you think you could try it while I am here with you? Just for a moment."

She bit her lip and shook her head. "No!"

"What if I hold the chain and you hold the Pearl? Then if you get upset I can just yank it away from you. I will be right here with you the whole time and you do not have to do anything but hold it."

Eolande continued to chew on her lip, looking like she was about to cry. Finally, she gave a small nod and I sat up straighter as she lifted her hand to the Sirens. One of the creatures glided over to the edge of the sea, sliding its slender limb into the water that lapped against the shore and returning with the amulet.

I reached out, looping my finger around the length of silver chain that hung from the grey orb. Eolande held up her trembling hand and the Siren set the Pearl gently in her palm. The girl grimaced instantly and I saw her eyes grow wild. Behind me, I could feel the water rising in the sea, a giant wave being pulled towards the shore.

"Blaise," Damian's voice was a warning behind us.

"Eolande, look at me," I told her, ignoring him, my own voice stern. "Look at me, focus on me."

She made a pitiful sound and shook her head. "I can hear them."

"Try to focus on me. Tell them to be quiet." The wave was growing larger, blocking out the sun and casting us in shadow.

"I can't. They are so angry! She says this is your fault, that I am alone because of you, because you are selfish and you could not let her go-"

I yanked the chain, ripping the amulet from her hands, staring at her in shock. The Pearl fell to the ground and the

Sirens were there, snatching it up and cradling it as the creatures melted into the sea. The waters calmed, the giant wave settling back into peaceful swells as if it had never existed.

"What just happened?" Damian demanded, stomping over to loom above us.

I was still staring at the girl, my heart pounding in my chest, hearing the words. Her words. Orabelle's words. The same words she had uttered to me in Veruca. I pushed myself to my feet, shoving past Damian and striding back along the jungle path. I heard Kaeleb's quick footfalls rushing after me, but I did not stop to wait. I wanted to get away from the beach, away from the girl, away from the words that I could not stop hearing.

3

I expected Damian to come barreling after me demanding answers, but he did not follow me back from the beach. I stormed into the hut, slamming the door behind me with such force that there was a sharp crack and the splintering of wood. I prowled back and forth across the threshold, my hands clenched in fists and feeling the rage clawing at my insides. It was good Damian had not followed me, for there was no way that I could tolerate seeing his face in my current mood.

I heard Kaeleb's steps outside and I took a deep breath, trying to calm myself. Of all the things I had thought I would have to face on these islands, the ghost of my dead intended bride was not one of them. I shoved my hands through my hair, trying to be rational. She was not a ghost. It was something about the amulet, something either Eolande or Orabelle had done, and whatever it was, it was likely the same reason that the Sirens were still roaming the seas like masterless waifs.

There was a creak of broken wood and the door swung open, but it was not Kaeleb who stood there. Instead, I found myself facing the nondescript brother with the pale scar through his brow. Seff.

"What do you want?" I demanded, in no frame of mind to deal with him either. "The last time I saw you, you were throwing knives at me."

He shrugged and folded his arms over his chest. His belt of knives gleamed at his waist but he made no move to reach for them. "I threw a knife at the Earth Queen, not you."

"If you want something, spit it out. I am not in the mood for games," I snapped.

"We need you to keep trying with Eolande."

I scoffed. "That girl is either mad or something far worse, and I want nothing to do with her. What does it matter to you, anyway? Are you fighting for the good of Imbria now instead of for silver? A mercenary turned noble warrior?"

"Can I tell you a story?" he asked, ignoring my needling.

"I'd rather you didn't."

He crossed the room and lowered himself into a chair, looking thoughtful and indicating that I should sit as well. I stood stubbornly where I was.

"Do you know why the Gods made the Keepers?"

"Boredom?"

"No," he replied flatly. "They were trying to atone for their failures. The world that was intended to be their beautiful playground had been ravaged by their mortal creations. Instead of peace and harmony, there was starvation, war, greed, and corruption. The mortals required constant vigilance and supervision to suppress their violent natures, and without it they turned on each other. The Gods grew weary of the infinite task of keeping their children in line, and so they created the amulets. They chose the first Keepers, and they did not even bother to stay and see if those Keepers were worthy of their gifts. They were eager to move on from this flawed world and forget their failures."

I narrowed my amber eyes, watching his expressionless face closely. He was not telling a story, not passing down a clever parable like the Samains. There was something in his telling that held a shadow of guilt, of responsibility.

He explained how after the Gods had moved on, Rilian, the first Water Keeper, had become obsessed with pleasing them. Rilian mistook their silence for anger, not realizing they were absent. He constantly worried they were going to come back and take his power away. This was why he had turned on Chaote. They had been in love, but when he found out she was part Fomori, he had become enraged, fearing that this would be the final blow and the Gods would return and strip him of his power. So he had taken her, beaten her and bound her in chains, locking her away underground with the rest of the feared tribe. Then he had come to Tahitia and murdered her family and anyone else who knew what she was. He wanted to erase the stain she had put on him, to make himself perfect in the eyes of the creators. He did not know that those creators were not even watching.

Chaote pleaded and there was one God who came back, one who felt the heavy weight of guilt for abandoning the people that needed their help and guidance. This God was the one who created the Warding Stones. He wanted to balance the unfair power that had been given to the Keepers. The other Gods noticed he was missing and they returned to look for him, learning what he had done, that he had defied their Council and changed the world without the agreement of the others. They banished him to the world forever, to dwell amongst the people he had chosen over his own kind.

"It was you?" I interrupted him. I did not truly believe it, but I could not help remembering what had happened near Gideon's place, when Seff had appeared in the forest not knowing how he had come to be there, somehow having miraculously escaped unscathed from a roomful of savage Fomori women who were determined to rip him to shreds.

He shook his head. "Not me. The Fenris is the banished God."

"The Fenris?" I repeated. I had heard the name before. The halfbreed, Chaote, had screamed it when Maialen and I had released her from her prison.

"The dog."

I stared at him as if he had sprouted another head. "The dog?"

"Yes."

"The dog is a God?" I felt a laugh start to shake my shoulders. "Oh, that is perfect."

"To be precise, he is a wolf, not a dog. Though he does not look much like it now, but that is what centuries of immortality on a mortal plane will do to a creature."

I howled with laughter. "The dog?!"

"Why are you laughing?" he asked, seeming genuinely confused.

I tried to swallow my hilarity. "If that thing is a God, then what are you?"

"My brother and I are his creations, like the Sirens were to Orabelle, only better formed because, obviously, the Fenris was more powerful than a Keeper."

"Obviously," I murmured, my lips still twitching with mirth but my mind racing. "Why are you telling me this? You want something from me."

"I want you to keep trying with the girl. She must learn control; she is our only hope."

"Your only hope of what?" I pressed.

"Of dying."

I sat finally, sinking into one of the cushioned chairs across from him. I needed time to think, to clear my head. Part of me found his tale both hilarious and preposterous, but another part of me felt his sincerity. It would certainly explain the mongrel dog's hideous condition. Only a creature that had lived a thousand years could be that ugly.

"How can Eolande help you die?" I wanted to know.

Seff shook his head. "We are not a fool. We cannot divulge all our secrets. That part you do not need to know. Will you help us or not?"

"If I do this, then you owe me before you embark on your glorious death journey." It seemed I was gathering quite an array of favors for this task. Too bad it was not going to be as easy as I had first thought.

Seff regarded me with his bland expression. "What is it that you want from us?"

"I will let you know, and when I do, you will not hesitate to do as I ask."

"Very well." He stood, walking to the broken doorway.

"She says she hears the Keepers of the past," I said quietly, my intense gaze fixed on the empty space where he had been sitting. I heard him pause, hesitate.

"Is that a problem for you?"

I felt a wash of unease. "It could be."

He left, the door banging closed behind him. I sat, continuing to stare at the empty space, my mind in turmoil, wondering how to decipher what was true and what was madness or lies. I waited for Kaeleb to come in, but there was no movement and the thatched hut remained silent. Finally, I pushed myself out of the chair and went outside, looking around for him. He could not be that hard to find, swaddled in that ridiculous yellow and purple fabric.

"Kaeleb?" I called, but there was no answer. A few of the villagers stopped to look at me with wary glances and I glared back at them. "Kaeleb!"

I skirted around the house and retraced the jungle path that led to the beach, once again breaking into a sweat in the dense foliage. The beach was empty and serene, only a curved indention in the sand as proof we had been there recently. I jogged back up the path to the village, storming into the center of the circular clearing and shouting for the boy.

"What are you doing? You are upsetting people," Damian said impatiently, stomping up to me and waving at the wary villagers who were gathering to stare.

"Where is he?" I demanded, feeling panic start to creep up. Kaeleb had stayed close to me since that day in Kymir, and it was not like him to go running off without telling me where he had gone.

Damian lifted his hands in a gesture of ignorance. "He is a boy. He has wandered off, likely exploring the island."

I took a step closer to him, my eyes narrowed menacingly. "Then you had better find him, because if something happens to that boy, I will burn this pathetic island to the ground."

"Do not think I will let that happen. Keeper or no, you are still a man who can be killed as easily as the rest of us," Damian snarled back.

"Are you threatening me, Tahitian? Because I do not need my power to fight you, I will do it right now with my bare hands!" I shouted back at him.

"Enough, you two!" the weathered voice of Cossiana fell between us and the old woman pushed her son away from me with a gentle shove. "Stop antagonizing him, Damian."

"Me?" The big Tahitian was incredulous. "He is the one who-"

"I said that is enough! You are making a spectacle of yourself and the Fire Keeper's company is already not well received. If people see you two fighting, then it will only make it worse. What are you getting on about, anyway?" she asked me, a false smile plastered to her face for the benefit of those who had been drawn by the commotion.

I matched her smile with a forced grin of my own. "Kaeleb is missing."

"He is not missing," Damian argued. "You just cannot find him."

"That is the definition of missing, you idiot!" I snapped back at him.

Cossiana sighed and pinched the bridge of her nose. "Damian, go down to the docks and look for the boy. Blaise, come with me. Perhaps he has gone to see Eolande. It must be nice for him to have someone his own age to speak to."

Damian threw a last dark glare at me before he stormed off in the opposite direction. Cossiana took my arm and steered me towards one of the huts. Her comment chafed at me, and I could not help but see it as a subtle rebuke, like she was blaming me for the boy's lack of childhood companions.

"I did not ask for him, you know. I took him with me because he had nowhere else to go," I told her.

She patted my arm with her gnarled fingers. "I am aware of what happened."

"Then you know Maialen tried to kill him, like you told her she should," I pointed out, wanting to reciprocate the placing of blame. She and Damian were not as innocent as they liked to portray themselves.

"Yes, I know what the Earth Queen did. I also know that the Maialen I have known all these years would never hurt a child. Something happened to that poor girl, and whatever it was, it happened when she was running around the wilderness with you. I assume that killing her Guardian likely had something to do with it."

I stopped, jerking my arm from her grasp. I was sick and tired of being constantly blamed for deaths that I had not facilitated. "I did not kill Gideon. Even though he attacked me without provocation, I was trying not to hurt him and getting myself beaten to a bloody pulp for my efforts! Then Maialen intervened and Gideon ended up dead, but she was only trying to stop him. She never intended to kill him."

"I assumed the death was her fault. You can see it on her face," Cossiana said sadly as we approached the doorway of the hut she had been leading me to. "We are here."

She rapped lightly on the door and there was a bark from inside. I surprised myself by perking up at the sound, eager to see the wolf-dog-God, or whatever it was, in light of Seff's recent revelations. I wondered again if any of it could be true, or if there was something in the water here on Tahitia making everyone mad.

Cossiana went in and I followed her, stopping just inside the doorway, frozen in place with shock. All around us were flutters of parchment, some heavy and dark with tightly packed words, others with lines of ink standing out stark and bold against the pale paper, one word scrawled across the page like a shouted warning. There were so many that they covered the entire interior like feathered skin, rustling in the breeze from the open window, and I instantly recognized the ancient tongue, the heavy-handed words that a child raised in the woods would not know.

"What is this?" I asked the old woman.

"I do not know. She started writing them after we tried to give her the Pearl."

I walked to the wall and touched one with my finger. The bold characters shaping the word that meant betrayal. Cossiana did not know about the voices, about the child's claim that the Keepers of the past spoke to her. But I did, and I was staring at the sounds of their cries. No wonder the girl did not want to touch the damned thing.

Eolande stepped into the room, her deep blue eyes flickering over the parchment beneath my fingers. She seemed apprehensive, and I wondered if she was afraid I would tell the others her secret. I let my hand fall away from the inked warning and stepped back, giving her a wink. The dog was behind her, its hideous scarred head tilted to one side as it regarded me with one eye.

"Have you seen the boy that he brought with him? Kaeleb?" Cossiana asked her, kneeling in front of the girl and smoothing her short pale hair back from her face. Eolande kept her eyes on me, not breaking away to acknowledge the Elder.

"Eolande, have you seen him?" I repeated when she did not answer.

She shook her head.

"When was the last time you saw him?"

"On the beach, when he went after you," she said.

I felt another burst of anger, this time at myself. I should have controlled my temper, waited for Kaeleb. I turned on Cossiana and said through clenched teeth. "You had better find him, old woman, and you had better do it now."

4

Logaire pulled a comb through her long mane of coppery hair, wishing she could enjoy the visage of herself in the mirrored glass. Instead, her mind was preoccupied with her spiteful cousin and the perverse, supposed son of his that she had been saddled with. Akrin was not even their own flesh and blood. It was completely unfair that she had to share the rule of the kingdom with him. Although she had to admit, he was useful in his own sick way. Fear of him kept many of her would-be enemies in line, and right now she needed to crush the rebellion that Blaise was stirring up.

There was a light tap on the door and for a moment she froze, her eyes rounding in fear as she remembered the day Akrin had murdered Magnus, tapping on her door with the Guardian's severed finger. She swallowed hard and forced the memory away. One day, Akrin would come for her, but it was not today. She had sent him away, to root out the loyalists who were secretly supporting her cousin's return to power. She had been hesitant to unleash him on the countryside, knowing that for every traitor he killed at least a dozen innocents would also die, but it was better than having him there with her and she could tell herself that Blaise was to blame, not her.

"The hawk has returned with a message from Samirra, my Queen," Vishram said, bowing low as she opened the door. He was a practical man, good with numbers, and she had found his services to be invaluable since she had taken control of the kingdom. He was rather boring to look at, stoutly built with the customary auburn hair of the Verucans, his ears a little too big and his nose a heavy block that dominated his long face.

"What does it say?" Logaire demanded impatiently, ushering him into the room and shutting the door behind them.

"She will consider your proposal."

Logaire felt a surge of annoyance, jerking her shimmering golden gown to one side so that she could pace the floor. "That is all?"

"Unfortunately." Vishram handed her the small slip of parchment.

She crumpled it up and tossed it into the fire that blazed in the hearth. "Why would she not leap at the chance for an alliance? It does nothing but strengthen her position."

"Perhaps she deems it unnecessary," he suggested.

"Unnecessary? How can it be unnecessary? She has no other allies. Her war on Maialen must be draining her resources. She will need help and she will need it sooner than she thinks."

"The Fomori are not like us, they do not think like us."

Logaire laughed bitterly. "She is not Fomori, Vishram. She is Tahitian, or at least part of her is. She wants something from me, that is what this is about. I just need to find out what that is and give it to her."

"If I may," Vishram began. "Is it not obvious what she wants? The amulets."

Once again irritation rose in her and she wanted to scream. "Well, I do not have an amulet to give her! All I have is this stupid stone that is practically worthless!"

Logaire lifted her hand, the shimmering milky moonstone glowing on her finger where she had set it in a ring. The Warding Stone was the only thing on Imbria that could dampen the power of the Keeper's amulets, but it was only of use if there was an actual Keeper whose power needed suppressing. It did nothing to impress the people of the kingdom. She could provide no brilliant displays of power like the Keepers could. All she had was the absence of power, a great emptiness to pit against her cousin's fiery wrath.

"There is something else she wants," he began tentatively. She knew the tone. He had an idea, but he was hesitant to share it with her, for it was not something she was going to like. She waited for him to go on.

"The Fomori are also looking for anyone with divine blood. They are seeking the child of Orabelle."

Logaire felt her frown deepen. He had been correct to be hesitant. "I am not in the habit of murdering children, Vishram."

He waved his hands quickly in denial. "I am not suggesting murder, my Queen. Imagine that the child is here in Veruca, with us, where we can provide the halfbreed with just enough blood to keep the child alive and to keep Chaote tethered to us. We would be protecting the child, really, for if the Fomori gets to him first, then they will surely kill him."

Logaire stopped, considering his proposition with a thoughtful tilt of her head. "If the child is real, if he is what they say he is, then you are right and he would be invaluable to us. The problem with your little plan, Vishram, is that the boy is running around Imbria with my cousin, and we both know Blaise will not just hand him over. As of yet, we have been quite unsuccessful at preventing Blaise from doing anything. He is making fools of us! The only good thing about this is that I can send Akrin chasing after him, so at least we do not have to suffer through that bastard's sick whims here at the castle."

"The General is quite useful, my Queen. You need him," Vishram reminded her. "We could send him to seek the child."

"Yes, yes, so you keep telling me. But if Akrin finds the boy first, he will kill him, and then we will have nothing."

Vishram was contemplative. "I do not believe he will. The General would not want a quick death for his adversary. His vendetta with the boy is personal. He believes the child has replaced him, usurped the affections of the former king. He will want to take his time in killing him, which means bringing him back to Veruca, here, where we can control the situation."

Logaire shuddered. Thinking they could control Akrin was a mistake. She had heard the rumors whispered throughout the castle about the things he did down in the tunnels. If it was not for the truth of Vishram's statement, that Akrin was quite useful, she would have poisoned the little runt by now. Some days she was still tempted to, but she knew the fear he inspired kept her on the throne.

"Have you heard anything more from Kymir?" she asked, changing the subject. She was surprised to find herself missing her old home from time to time, and even missing the Earth Queen's company. She had been Maialen's confidant for years, and she supposed some bonds must have inadvertently formed.

"No. Our spies tell me the Kymirran Queen is quite preoccupied with keeping the Fomori out of her kingdom, and with trying to replant her forests that were burned to cinders by the Fire Keeper. The Kymirrans have lost valuable hunting grounds and their food supply will dwindle if she does not repair the damage soon."

Logaire remembered the days after it had happened. The wind had carried the black smoke of the fires towards Veruca and she had looked out the window at the red-orange glow of the horizon, the entire sky stained an eerie shade of yellow. She had never discerned exactly what had happened at the divide that day, only that whatever it was, it had driven a wedge between the Keepers. Logaire had seen the opportunity and pounced on it, doing everything she could to make sure that Maialen did not forgive Blaise. She had sent the Earth Queen messages that hinted as to the purposefulness of the fire, how it was unfathomable that it had been a mere accident. She would have preferred to sow the seeds of doubt in person, but she remained uncertain as to Maialen's loyalties and so, for now, she would do it from afar.

"What are we going to do about our own food shortages?" Logaire asked, feeling annoyed. She was the Queen of Veruca now, and it was ridiculous that she had to suffer for the messes the other realms had made.

"Your cousin has stores of grain saved, more than I expected, but it will be a hard winter. It could be made easier if we were to establish trade with the Leharans," Vishram suggested gently. "The problem there is that the Leharans cannot decide who is in control of their island. How can we strike a deal when we do not know who to bargain with?"

Logaire laughed bitterly. "Thyrr will never trade with Veruca, not after what I did. And if he is willing to, then I am certain he will demand the Warding Stone be returned and I am not ready to give it to him. If we want to deal with the Leharans, then perhaps we need to make sure that Thyrr is not the one who wins their little leadership quarrel."

Vishram nodded appreciatively. "I agree Colwyn would be much more amenable to trade. It would be worthwhile to assist him in securing his regency on the island."

Logaire laughed again, this time her musical voice lilting with mirth. "Bacatha let me take the Stone to stop the assassins she knew would come for it. Perhaps it is time to invite those assassins to return. Put the word out that I am offering a price for the young prince and do it quietly. He had his chance to reconcile with me and he has refused. Whatever happens to him now, it is his own fault."

She leaned over to look in the mirror at the image of herself, pursing her full red lips. She was trying to ignore the twist of her stomach that she had felt at the thought of killing Thyrr. She pictured him lying in bed, his golden hair swept back above his strangely beautiful eyes. She could not afford to be weak now. The young man had been a delightful distraction to her once, and she would miss his clever wit and his virile body, but it had to be done.

She noticed there were fine lines framing her mouth and between her brows and she softened her expression, rubbing her finger over them in annoyance. Then she straightened herself and smoothed the shimmering fabric of her gown over her hips, enjoying the feel of her body beneath the rich fabric. Tonight, she would have a feast for her loyal regents and she wanted to look her best.

"You are perfection," Vishram assured her.

I felt it rising within me, like a beast trying to claw its way out. The power seared through me, heat rolling over my skin as I raged at the stony-faced Tahitian. Damian stood unblinking, his arms clasped behind his back, his eyes on the ground.

"You had better have more answers than just an apology," I snarled.

"The only ship that left the island today went to Lehar. If he is not here, then he must have gone there," Damian said.

"You mean someone took him there," I corrected, clenching my fists at my sides.

"He could have gone to find his family."

"You told him he had no family!" I shouted, tired of his excuses. "Instead of trying to justify what might have happened, I suggest you find a way to get us to Lehar as quickly as possible."

I turned to march back to the hut and collect my things, but Cossiana was behind me and I nearly collided with the old woman. She had a cloth sack in her arms and the man beside her was carrying my sword. I snatched it from him, buckling the sheath around my waist.

"There is a boat ready at the docks. It will take you to Lehar," she informed me, passing me the sack which she had filled with my and Kaeleb's things. I took it from her and started for the beach, shouting at Damian to hurry up. There was no way I was going without him. He had brought us to this cursed island, and whatever happened to Kaeleb was his fault.

"I am sorry, mother," I heard him say in his rumbling baritone.

"Now, Damian!" I hollered back.

"I will take care of the girl. Go, and be safe. Lehar is a dangerous place right now, my son," the old woman said, embracing the giant man before stepping back and allowing him to run after me.

"You have no manners," he muttered, catching up to me easily with his long stride.

"If you want to sit around and have tea parties and hug your mother, then you should have chosen a different life, my friend," I snapped with a bitter laugh.

"I don't even know what that means." Damian was exasperated. "I am doing this to help you. The least you could do is be polite to my mother."

I could not help but take the offered chance to needle him. "Your mother seems to like me just fine. She called me handsome earlier today."

"There is something very wrong with you," Damian said with a shake of his head, his long hair moving over his shoulders.

I grinned at him in response. We were approaching the docks, and as promised, there was a boat waiting. I stopped, turning on Damian with indignation. "You cannot expect me to get into that."

It was his turn to grin. "You wanted to leave right away; this is what you get."

The vessel was an old rowboat that looked like it had been built a hundred years ago. I was not even sure how it was still afloat in its decrepit condition.

"How are you supposed to even get into that without sinking it?" I demanded, waving at his massive bulk.

"It will hold, Fire Keeper. Tahitian boats are made to stay afloat." He dropped his spear into it, then grabbed the bag from me and tossed it into the vessel, causing it to wobble obscenely. He climbed in and picked up two of the long oars, setting them into the worn grooves. "Untie the line and get in."

"What do you mean, untie the line and get in?" I repeated, waiting for the rickety boat to start sinking under his considerable weight. "You want me to jump? Into that thing?"

"Now who is wasting time? Are you scared of the water, Fire Keeper?"

I glowered at him and pulled loose the knot that tethered the vessel to the pier, tossing it into the boat and stepping in behind him as it began to drift away. I nearly stumbled, waving my arms to try to keep myself from tumbling into the sea and sitting down as quickly as I could, water lapping over the shallow sides.

"Row," the Tahitian ordered curtly, and I was tempted to hit him over the head with one of the weathered oars, but there was no way I was going to row his huge bulk by myself. I cursed him soundly, fitting the oars into the second set of grooves as his powerful shoulders began to move, the boat gliding over the gentle swells. It was easier than I had expected and I only had to watch him for a moment before I was able to match his movements.

"If someone took him, then I am sorry for that," Damian said after a long while.

I ignored him, glaring at the back of his head. I did not care for his apologies. All I cared about was finding Kaeleb and shoving a fistful of fire down the throat of whoever had taken him. Though I had to admit, there was a small part of me that wondered if Damian was right, and if Kaeleb had run off on his own for some reason. He had done it to Maialen plenty of times when he had been under her care, but he had never left me.

I thought back to my days as a soldier, before I had been a Keeper and a King. There had been one night when a man had gone missing out on a scouting patrol. He was not in his tent, but all of his things were as he had left them, as if he had just vanished. We searched for days, my commander convinced that someone had taken him, for it did not occur to him that anyone would desert the Verucan army. There were no signs of struggle, no signs that anyone had come to the area, no sign that he had left. He was simply gone. It had nagged at me then, the utter preposterousness of the idea that someone could disappear without a trace. Of course, he had gone somewhere. I remembered trudging through the steep mountains, up and down into valleys and canyons, thinking maybe he had slipped and fallen, hurt himself, been unable to call for help. We were all exhausted by the time the search had been called off and the man had never been found. Though my commander would never accept it, the rest of us were convinced he had run away. I had always expected to run into him somewhere, in a tavern maybe, or as he strolled through the city, carefree and jolly, unburdened by the life he had no longer wanted. My stomach knotted, wondering if perhaps Kaeleb felt that way as well, if he had been waiting for an opportunity to be rid of me, if I would never find him and I would always be left wondering. I shook off the dark thoughts stubbornly. That would not happen this time. I would not let Kaeleb simply be gone.

The day was waning as we neared Lehar, and I was grateful that the islands of the Southern Sea were in such close proximity to each other. Though I would never let on, the muscles of my shoulders and back were aching from rowing and I could feel blisters forming at the base of my thumbs. Damian seemed perfectly at ease, as if he could row us around the entire world without breaking a sweat, which I found quite irritating.

The first thing I noticed about the island was the huge Citadel rising up through the mist, dominating the skyline above the trees. I did not remember the imposing coralstone fortress being quite so tall. Lush, tropical forest blanketed the land beneath the towering cerulean spire, and all of it was surrounded by white sand beaches that stretched out like glittering arcs of moon that melted into the turquoise sea. It looked surreal to me, as if a thing so beautiful should not actually exist.

We landed on the southern side of the island, on an uninhabited beach, and I helped Damian drag the shoddy mess of a boat up the sand past the tide line. I looked around, seeing nothing but an empty beach and jungle. "What now?"

"We find Thyrr."

I lifted a brow. "Going straight to the top, are we?"

"Not quite," he hesitated, rolling his huge shoulders. Perhaps the trip had not been as easy on him as he pretended. He picked up his spear. "Colwyn has taken control of the Citadel. Thyrr is in Orabelle's quarters."

I was startled to hear her name spoken aloud, though I tried not to let it show. It seemed I would be unable to escape the memory of her as long as I was on the islands. She was everywhere here, even after all these years.

Damian trudged down the beach, following the shore as it curved north. I walked at a slower pace behind him, wary that we had not yet seen any Leharans. I was not exactly the most beloved of Imbrians to the islanders, and I began to wonder if I had made a mistake and Damian was leading me into an ambush, or worse. I was about to stop him to ask him just what his intentions were when we turned off from the beach, following a path that led up to a massive beached ship rooted in coralstone. A tall Leharan woman in a crisp blue uniform stood on the bow, watching our approach, and I recognized the severe posture of Bacatha, Thyrr's stringent companion and would-be Guardian.

"Damian." She inclined her head to him before her icy gaze settled on me. She did not seem surprised, but neither did she seem very pleased.

"A pleasure, as always, Bacatha," I called to her.

She spun on her heel and stomped to the staircase that led to the ground, her long-legged stride quickly reaching us as she demanded to know, "What on Imbria are you doing here?"

"We need to see Thyrr. The boy is missing. We believe he may have come to Lehar," Damian began.

I cut in impatiently, "Or someone took him from Tahitia to Lehar. You once tried to convince me to give him to you. Maybe you had something to do with this."

"The boy? You mean the Solvrei?" she asked. Most of Imbria still had no idea that Kaeleb was not the fabled son of Orabelle and her Guardian lover. "I know nothing of this. If I wanted him, I would have taken him then. I do not need to kidnap children, Fire Keeper. Come, you can speak with Thyrr."

She led us onto the ship and I saw Damian's hand linger on the warm teak railing, a nostalgic look in his dark eyes. I felt a stab of jealousy for the look, for the memories he had shared with Orabelle that I never would. Then I remembered that this was probably where she had also shared her memories with Tal, the man who was Eolande's father. I tried to block out the image of them together that rose in my mind, and I gripped my sword hilt with clenched fingers. Bacatha glanced at me and misinterpreted the gesture.

"If you attack him, you will not leave here alive," she warned, her tone as frosty as her pale blue eyes.

"Get away from me before I burn your hair off your scalp," I threatened with a scowl.

"Ignore him," Damian told her. "He has been trying to instigate a fight since the day he was born."

"If you want to fight me, Damian, I am always ready," I countered. He took his own advice and ignored me.

We were standing on the lower deck of the ship and Bacatha tapped her sword on the planks beneath us as the sun dripped its fading golden glow into the placid sea. A few moments later, Thyrr emerged from below. He was just as I remembered, arrogant and golden, like a statue that shone in the rays of the dying sun. He was wearing dark blue pants and a long tunic, and his wild hair was shoved back from his face in haphazard disarray. The strange blue-gold eyes were wide with surprise at the sight of us. A smile tilted crookedly over his lips and he walked up to me, reaching out his hand to grasp my arm in a gesture of friendship I was not prepared for. I supposed he was still grateful to me for letting him escape the trumped-up murder charges that Damek had leveled at him in Kymir not so long ago, though I had not realized that made us friends.

"Blaise. What brings you to Lehar?" he asked.

"I am looking for Kaeleb," I answered, watching him closely to judge his reaction. He seemed genuinely surprised.

"Kaeleb? Why would he be here? I have not seen the boy since that day in Kymir," he said, a shadow falling over his features at the memory of Maialen's betrayal. I had forgotten how young he was, barely more than a boy himself. It was no wonder he had fallen prey to the rest of them so easily. Especially my cousin, who was masterful with her manipulations. Logaire had pretended to care for the young king-to-be so she could steal his Warding Stone right out from under him, just as she had stolen my throne soon after.

"He went missing from Tahitia and the only boat seen leaving was coming here, to Lehar. I need to find him," I said, impatience coloring my tone.

"I know nothing of it, but I will go with you to speak to Colwyn," Thyrr offered.

"I do not need your help with Colwyn," I said derisively. "What I need is for you to get whatever group of islanders are loyal to you these days and go search for him!"

He lifted his hands, placating. "I will help you. After all, he is my nephew. Give me a few moments to gather some of the Guard. We will escort you to the Citadel, then we will search the harbor."

"Is that wise?" Bacatha hissed at him.

"What choice do I have? He is my only family," Thyrr said in response. "And we still owe a debt to the Fire Keeper."

Bacatha was unconvinced, but she did not argue further. "I will gather the Guard. You stay here with them."

She spun on her heel and stomped away like a furious titan.

"She is as delightful as ever," I muttered.

"What is really going on?" Thyrr asked once the Leharan woman had gone. "What are you here for?"

I frowned and leaned on the railing of the ship, staring out over the ocean. Had Orabelle stood in this same spot, staring out at the same darkening sea? Had she laughed here, cried here? Had she stood here cursing my name?

"I am here to find the child," I answered after a long moment.

"Why do you care so much about my nephew?" Thyrr was suspicious and rightfully so, but I knew Damian would not want me to tell him the truth, for the fewer people who knew about Eolande, the better, and I had no desire to endanger the fragile little girl who sang songs and heard the voices of dead Keepers in her head.

"I had a brother once," I began, deciding I might as well tell him a truth, if not the one Thyrr was actually searching for. "He was about Kaeleb's age when he was killed."

"So, you wish to protect Kaeleb because you could not protect your brother?" Damian asked in his gentle baritone, having overheard my admission.

I stiffened at his words, anger creeping up my spine. "You, of all people, should not speak about protecting others, Guardian. You have not championed that endeavor."

Damian sighed and looked out at the sea with me. "Is it not possible for you to put aside your hatred, even for a moment?"

"No."

"Have it your way," the big Tahitian said with a shrug. We waited in stubborn silence, Thyrr looking uncomfortable behind us. Finally, Bacatha returned with a group of lithe, blonde men trailing after her. She led us to the Citadel, and though I would not admit it to any of them, I was grateful for the escort. I had felt out of sorts ever since we had set foot on the islands, and the harsh, bold stares of the Leharans were not helping. I kept darting glances at people who passed, drawn by a flash of pale hair or a movement of gossamer fabric, glimpses that stirred memories of the woman I had once loved. I had been wrong about her ghost being on Tahitia, for it was so much worse here. Orabelle's ghost was everywhere on Lehar.

Bacatha spoke to the men who stood at the entrance to the Citadel and they looked at me with blatant displeasure before reluctantly disappearing into the interior of the fortress.

"Blaise!" Colwyn said with forced enthusiasm, hurrying out to meet us a short while later. "I did not believe it until I saw with my own eyes. What are you doing on Lehar?"

The Captain had widened around the waist a bit since I had seen him last, and his hair was thinner, but he was still as neat and fastidious as ever, his uniform immaculate, and not a single fold out of place. I could see the apprehension in the tense corners of his smile, and I knew he must be panicking inside, wondering why I was here. I was one of the few people who knew that he was the one who had betrayed Orabelle to Chronus all those years ago. One word from me and Lehar would belong to Thyrr, but luckily for the Captain I had not yet decided on which of them I would place my bet.

"Where is the boy?" I did not even bother with greetings. I was tired of their delays and their escorts and their excuses.

"The boy?" Colwyn looked around in nervous agitation.

"Do not play games with me!" I warned him, grabbing the front of his perfectly creased shirt in my fist. Several of his men started forward but Bacatha waved them back with a warning, her hand on her sword hilt. The Leharans were watching me warily, fearfully, and I realized in that moment that they probably all thought I had destroyed half of Kymir on purpose. That was the reason for the escort and for the pretenses. They were afraid of what I would do. I leveled my amber gaze at Colwyn. Good, I hoped they were afraid of me. "Tell me where he is."

"I swear I do not know! There were some men here from Kymir, and they were looking for someone, but I don't know who. They sailed out a few hours ago," Colwyn said quickly. Sweat was starting to bead on his upper lip.

"What men?" I growled.

"Just merchant traders. One of my men overheard them and mentioned it to me because he was worried about the rumors from..." Colwyn's voice trailed off and he darted a panicked glance at Thyrr as if asking for help.

"From Samirra," Thyrr finished for him.

I felt my power stirring, fueled by the rage that was threatening to overwhelm me. I let go of Colwyn so that I would not be tempted to strangle him, and he backed away quickly, smoothing down his shirt and placing several of his men between us.

"Explain," I said to Thyrr.

"There are rumors that some of the merchant vessels are kidnapping people to trade to Samirra. I told Colwyn we needed to be searching every vessel that leaves the harbor, but he refused. I was trying not to divide us further over petty quarrels, but I see now that I should have been more insistent."

My hands were clenched into fists.

"If that boy is on his way to Samirra..." I stopped, unable to finish the thought. Chaote would recognize him and she would either kill him, or she would use him to get to me. Even worse, she would never see him and he would just be a faceless, nameless meal to some random, bloodthirsty Fomori.

"Do you have any eagles?" Bacatha asked Colwyn, thinking logically, which I was grateful for. Colwyn shook his head and she gave him a disgusted look of reproach. It was clear that she had little regard for the fastidious Captain. "Are they all in Kymir doing the Earth Queen's bidding?"

"It does not matter," Thyrr interrupted, not wanting Bacatha's animosity riled further. "We will need a ship ready at first light just in case we do not find him. Tonight, we will search the harbor and the town. I assume you will not oppose me on this?"

Colwyn shook his head. "Of course not. I will supply men to help with the search and I can send a hawk with a message to Kymir if you would like."

"No. Damek would see it first and I don't trust that spidery little wretch as far as I can throw him," I said with a shake of my head. I turned on Damian. "This means that Tahitians were part of this. How could they know Kaeleb and I would be there? Who did you tell? They would have had to plan this."

"No one. I swear it," Damian avowed.

"If we go to the mainland in the morning, then you are coming with me," I told him. He inclined his head in acquiescence.

"I will go too. He is my nephew," Thyrr offered. Bacatha looked perturbed and he gave her a placating smile. "I am of no use here, other than dividing the Leharans. The throne will be here when we return."

"In my experience, that is not always true," I warned him.

"Did you just make a joke about losing your throne?" The young man laughed, clapping me on the back. "Perhaps during all of this we can find time to discuss Logaire and my Warding Stone. It benefits neither of us to let the Stone, or Veruca, remain in her conniving hands. Now, come, let us look for this boy and hope we find him stealing pastries from an angry cook."

6

We searched throughout the night, but there was no sign of Kaeleb and we could find no one who would admit to seeing a boy who matched his description. Thyrr questioned the sailors at the docks, trying to find out more about the men Colwyn had mentioned, and in the morning he told me what he had learned. The rumors of ships going to and from Samirra trading goods were true. Chaote cared nothing for the palace riches and she was all too willing to barter them for what she wanted. Elaborate works of art, gold and silver pieces, precious stones and jewelry, anything that had been the tokens of the royals and regents of Samirra was on the table for trade. What she wanted in return was children.

"She is looking for the Solvrei," Thyrr said, pushing a hand through his wild disarray of hair and grimacing. "And times are hard, people are willing to give her what she wants. One of the men I spoke to claimed he knew a shipmate who refused to be part of any kind of deal with the Fomori, and he was thrown off his vessel by the rest of the crew. I also learned that yesterday, two Tahitians were seen helping to load large barrels onto the Kymirran ship before it sailed. It is possible that they were carrying more than the islanders' famous liquor."

"We must send someone back to Tahitia and tell my mother so she can put an end to this," Damian said with a shake of his head. "It is disgraceful. Believe me when I promise you that if this is true, then whoever was a part of it will be caught and punished."

I glared at the giant man, shrouded in mist. Late in the night, a fog had drifted in and we were enveloped in the haze. The tall masts of the ships in the harbor were barely visible in the dull, grey light that was almost dawn. "That does me little good if they have already taken Kaeleb."

"We have a ship ready," Thyrr cut in. "Let us go to Kymir and hope that we can stop them before this goes further."

I nodded and he grasped my shoulder in sympathy. It was a strange gesture to me, and I felt uncomfortable with his kind look. I still was not sure exactly why he believed we were friends. I had no desire to help him, and I cared little whether he rotted in a cell or was banished to the Wastelands forever. I had only let him go that day in Kymir because the Sirens were there, and because it was what Orabelle would have wanted. It had been a moment of weakness, nothing more.

"Gather the things you will need and we will leave as soon as everyone is on the ship," Thyrr said, turning and waving for Bacatha to follow him.

"He will be a good man if this world does not break him," Damian murmured, watching the young man go.

I snorted derisively. "This world breaks everyone."

He turned his black eyes on me. "Sometimes breaking is good, for then you have the chance to put yourself back together in a better way. Look at you."

"You know I am going to kill everyone who was part of this. Do not try to paint me into something I am not, Tahitian. I am still the monster I have always been, and you would be wise to remember that." I stalked off down the beach after Thyrr. I needed to collect my things I had left on Orabelle's ship and the young man was close to my size. He could provide me with whatever else I would need. I glanced back at the big Tahitian who was standing stoically where I had left him. "Good luck finding winter clothes to fit you!"

I heard his heavy sigh carry through the cool morning and I felt a grin pull at my lips. It did not take long before I had what I needed and we were back on the ship, ready to set sail. The only one we were waiting for was Damian. He finally appeared out of the misty ether, and I chuckled as I watched him walk, straining against the tight fabric of the tunic he had found. His pants were several inches shorter than they should have been, making his booted feet look ridiculous in proportion to the rest of him. He carried a leather overcoat, his huge spear strapped across his back and a bright silver sword curved against his leg.

"Not a word," he warned when I started to remark on his ill-fitting attire. I swallowed my comment but kept grinning and he stomped on board, brushing past me and moving to stand near the ship's captain at the helm.

"We can find you more suitable clothing in Kymir, I am sure," Bacatha said to him, an amused glint in her icy gaze. "Perhaps adding a ruffle to the bottom of the pants would help."

Thyrr snickered and I could not help but laugh, the big Tahitian fuming as he tried to fold his arms over his chest. The fabric made a tearing sound at the seams and we all laughed harder, Damian glowering at us.

It was a somber journey once the humor had faded, everyone finding their own quiet spot to stare out over the sea. I watched the island as it was swallowed in the mist behind us, feeling a wash of relief to be away from it and its ghosts.

"She is everywhere there, isn't she?" Thyrr asked, joining me at the stern. I knew he was speaking of Orabelle, just as he knew I was thinking of her.

"Lehar was everything to her. I just wish I would have realized it sooner," I admitted. I was not sure why I felt like talking to the young man. Perhaps it was the overt gestures of friendship, or the realization that I really did not have any other friends to talk to. I had briefly thought of Maialen as a friend, then as something more, but in the end she could be neither of those things.

"I am sorry for what happened between you and Orabelle," Thyrr offered.

"So am I." It was the first time I had said the words aloud that had been in my heart for so long. It was easier to be angry, to blame everyone else for what happened. It was much harder to admit the role I had played in her death. I had never intended for her to die, but my actions had nonetheless brought it about, and I could not hide from that fact any longer.

"When I was a boy, there was no place for people like me," Thyrr began. He looked uncomfortable, his strange eyes vacillating between me and the broken sea that trailed behind the ship.

"You are still a boy," I told him with a grin.

He shrugged and his crooked smile touched his face. "When I was a much younger boy, we were never welcome anywhere."

"Because you were part Fomori?" I asked him, my amber eyes narrowed.

"Yes. There were others like me and we lived in groups, traveling around the countryside, never staying in one place for very long. I did not know why at the time. I was too young. I thought it was just the way people lived. Later I learned it was because we were afraid," he began.

His father had been one of the leaders of the caravan. They were artists and entertainers, traveling throughout the realms on their wagons, playing music and peddling their crafts. Thyrr had delighted in his childhood, loving the freedom it had brought and the myriad of people he encountered. For a while, a warrior had joined the group, and Thyrr had followed him around doggedly, mimicking everything he did until the man finally relented and agreed to train him to use a sword.

He had not known they were different from other Imbrians until the day the Fomori came. They were in the north, traveling between Samirran villages to reap the benefits of the end of summer harvest. The Fomori had come out of nowhere, but they had not attacked. Instead, they had circled the small band of travelers, looking perplexed and finally calling out for the leader of the caravan to come forward. It was Thyrr's father who had stepped out of the line, his hands trembling with fear but his face brave and determined. The creature had gone up to him, sniffing him and growling low in its throat. Then it had turned and howled, and the Fomori had loped away, leaving the caravan unharmed.

"They knew what we were, that we carried their blood," Thyrr explained. "That was why they did not attack us. My father told me the truth that day, that it was not the Fomori we needed to fear. There was another who hunted us."

"Chronus," I surmised. Thyrr inclined his head slightly to acknowledge that I was correct. Orabelle's father.

Chronus was the constant threat that drove them from town to town, realm to realm. They knew it was only a matter of time before he found them, but there was nothing they could do. No one would help a group of bastard Fomori offspring. So, they kept running, kept moving, until the inevitable happened.

"I tried to fight them, the Earth Keeper's mercenaries. I had been taking lessons, and I was getting quite adept at using a sword, but in the end I was too small and they were too big. They killed everyone they could catch. I watched them slaughter my father in front of me and when I attacked them, they shoved me aside like I was nothing. My father told me to stop, not to fight them, and I stood there crying and helpless while they ran him through."

He paused, turning his tortured gaze back to the sea. "Some of them were reluctant to kill the children. They argued about it, and a few of the men came to blows. This was when we ran. One of them started to chase us, but we were fast and he was tired. He let us go. I kept running and running. It felt like I ran forever and I wondered how I had not reached the edge of the world, I had run so far."

"Why are you telling me this?" I wanted to know.

"Because there is something else I need to tell you," he began. A sudden, loud crack, like a tree breaking in half, boomed through the greyness around us and the sky opened up, rain sheeting down upon us like icy spikes.

"Just a squall!" the old captain yelled. "It will pass in a moment!"

I was grateful for the interruption to Thyrr's sad story. I was not sure if he thought swapping tortured tales of our childhoods would make us bond, but I had no desire to know anymore. I moved away from him, towards the galley where there was a covered doorway I could stand under. Thyrr seemed to understand that I was done with our conversation and he stood silently in the cold rain, his strange eyes bright against the dullness of the storm.

The captain was right and the squall soon passed, the sky thinning out so that streaks of blue peeked out from behind the mottled grey clouds that lingered on. I avoided the others for the rest of the trip, trying to work through the possibilities that awaited us in Kymir and hoping that the boy was unharmed. Kaeleb was not likely to be a compliant prisoner, and this could mean trouble for him. It would be easy for them to just throw him over the side of the ship if they could not control him. But no, Kaeleb was too keen for that. He would know that he had to choose his opportunity to escape wisely.

I had to trust that the boy would take care of himself until I could find him.

It seemed an eternity before we finally reached the shores of Kymir. The winter snow had not yet reached this part of the forested realm, though a cold frost clung to the air. The docks were bustling with ships and people, and I realized as I watched that many of the vessels were unloading weapons. Verucan made weapons. I felt a stab of fury at the sight and as soon as the ramp had been lowered, I had thundered down it. I wanted to toss the crates into the sea, or burn them to ashes, but the boy needed to come first. I was here to find Kaeleb. The rest would have to wait.

"Blaise."

I stopped short, jerking around to find myself face to face with the one person I had been hoping to avoid. Maialen.

"Let me guess, Colwyn sent a hawk and told you we were coming," I surmised. She was clearly not surprised to see me.

Maialen inclined her head to indicate I had guessed correctly and I stared at her, waiting for her to say something more. She looked as beautiful as ever, though there was a hard edge to her clenched jaw that was at odds with the delicateness of her features and the innocent spread of freckles that dotted her nose. Her large, green eyes were filled with sorrow, and I steeled myself against it, knowing that it was better for her to hate me.

"What do you want?" I finally asked after the silence became unbearable.

A shadow passed over her doll-like features and her fingers pleated the dark green folds of her gown beneath the fur cape that draped her shoulders. "You are the one that has come to Kymir. This is my realm, Blaise. Perhaps you should tell me what it is that you want."

"Colwyn did not tell you why?" I practically sneered, hating that I sounded jealous, for that was not my intention.

"He sent a hawk telling me you were coming here from Lehar. That is all."

I glanced back at the ship and was thankful that Bacatha and Thyrr were out of sight. The last thing we needed was Maialen and her spindly little advisor trying once again to drag Thyrr away for Alita's murder. Maialen followed my gaze and I saw her stiffen, her mouth pulling down into a hard frown.

"What is he doing here?" she asked, fixed on Damian.

I would have preferred that he also remained out of her sight, but apparently I had not properly conveyed that request to the stubborn Tahitian, though I distinctly remembered telling him to stay on the ship. I waved at the Guardian in a dismissive gesture, as if his presence were more of an annoyance than anything else. "Damian found me on the road in Veruca."

"That is not an answer! You know I have been searching for him, for the Pearl! Does he have it? Is that what this is about?"

"No, this has nothing to do with that. He is helping me, Maialen. Someone has taken Kaeleb and we believe he was on a ship that would have arrived late in the night or early this morning."

She laughed, a hollow and mirthless sound. "So, after all that happened, you have lost him anyway?"

I felt my temper rising. "I did not lose him, Earth Queen. Someone took him."

"Or he ran away from you. People tend to do that," she spat back at me.

I felt like she had punched me in the stomach and my first instinct was to lash out at her, but I forced myself to remain calm, smiling. "This has been a delightful meeting, my dear, and as much as I would love to continue to enjoy your company, it is imperative that you allow me to search the ships that have arrived."

Damek was hurrying up behind her, his black robes fluttering around his skeletal limbs and his limp hair clinging to his pale forehead. "No, no. That will not do. This is Kymir and you have no authority here, Fire Keeper! The Council says-"

"I do not give a damn about the Council!" I shouted at him, causing Maialen to flinch and step back from me.

"Damek is right. This is my realm. What is left of it anyway," Maialen said and her subtle rebuke was not lost on me. She touched her fingers to the Emerald that was looped around her neck and I felt the peaceful energy of her Element flowing around us. "I will search the ships that have recently docked, but there has been nothing from Lehar for days."

"Nothing from Lehar," I remarked caustically, "but I see you have gotten plenty from Veruca."

She had the decency to let a look of shame wash over her features, but she hid it quickly. "I am doing what I need to do for Kymir. It is not my fault you lost your kingdom."

"I was fighting a war that you asked me to go fight! And saving your life in the process!" I was incredulous.

"I would not have been there if it had not been for your desperate plea for help! I was the one who was saving you!" she retorted, her cheeks flushing crimson.

Damian was beside me, laying his large hand on my shoulder. "Queen of Kymir, we are not here to argue about the past."

She spun on him, furious. "Then why don't you tell me where the Pearl is? What happened in Samirra is your fault! If you had just given it to us, then none of this would be happening! My son would be alive!"

He seemed startled by this and I wondered if no one had told him about Aracellis's death, or if he was merely surprised that the Earth Queen blamed him for it.

Damek was flapping his long fingers, trying to distract us from each other. "This is not the place for this! If you wish to fight amongst yourselves then do it out of sight. Go to the Council chamber. I will look into the ships for you."

I snorted. "Why would I trust you when all you do is lie?"

"You have no place accusing anyone else of being a liar," Maialen interjected before returning her anger to Damian. "Where is the Pearl?"

"He does not have it. He gave it to the Sirens," I answered for him, hoping that would be enough to silence her about the damned amulet. "This is wasting my time and—"

"Enough, Blaise!" Maialen interrupted sternly. "I do not wish to hear anything else you have to say. We will search any ships that have recently arrived, but I am telling you the truth and none have come here from Lehar."

Damian leaned toward me and said in a low voice. "It is possible they have gone directly to Samirra."

My power stirred in me and I wondered what Maialen would do if I turned her entire dock into blackened toothpicks. She sensed the hot edge of my Element and she once again grasped at the Emerald, trying to calm my rising temper.

"Maialen, please," I said through clenched teeth. "I need to find him."

She softened slightly. "I promise if he is here, I will find him. Go back on your ship and wait for me there."

I hesitated, tired of waiting, tired of searching, trying to silence the hateful, insistent voice in my head that was telling me we had gone to the wrong place. Maialen reached out her hand, her delicate fingers touching the knotted muscles of my arm. I pulled away from her, turning and storming back up the ramp onto the ship.

7

The darkness was utter and complete. There was nothing except the gentle sway back and forth, his shoulders rubbing the sides of his confined space with each subtle movement. He knew he was on a ship, that much he could tell, but beyond that he had no clue what was happening. It was good that he was Leharan and the sea was in his blood, otherwise the gentle movement in the dark would likely have made him sick and the last thing he wanted to do was retch all over himself.

Kaeleb lifted his hands, feeling around him. The sides were smooth, rounded. A barrel, most likely. He reached over his head, his elbows bent as he pushed on the lid. It was nailed shut. He sighed and settled back into his crouched position, scowling into the blackness. His legs were aching from being cramped beneath him and he wished he could stand and stretch them, even for a moment. There was a pounding on the side of his head where they had hit him. He had not even seen them coming. Pathetic. Brother Kaden would not be pleased.

He who exercises no forethought and underestimates his opponents is sure to be captured by them.

Kaeleb had underestimated his enemies. He had let the warm embrace of the island lull him into complacency, think-ing he was safe there. He had forgotten briefly, after being in the presence of the girl, that the rest of the world still thought he was the Solvrei. As long as he was protecting her with the lie, he could not afford to be so careless.

He wriggled around in his prison, trying to find a more comfortable position for his knees but there was no relief. He reached for his belt and, as expected, the sword was gone. So was the knife he had taken from one of the fishermen on the beach and stuck in his boot. His stomach rumbled and he wished he had something to eat.

What had Brother Kaden told him to do if he was captured? He tried to remember. There had been so many lessons in such a short time. They were in the black mountains of Veruca, training him to avoid enemy patrols. The tall peaks encircled them, and they were tired, for they had been traversing the rough landscape for days. Kaden was walking ahead of him, his shining blonde hair covered with a dark scarf and wearing a patchwork of leather armor that he had pieced together himself to blend in with the harsh landscape. He was smiling, something he rarely did when they were home and in the presence of Sister Alita, for she had no tolerance for what she considered their foolishness. She insisted their only purpose was to prepare Kaeleb, not to coddle him and make him weak.

Kaeleb walked behind Brother Kaden, stepping where he stepped, noting the path the older man chose to take and trying to determine the reason for his choices so he could pass the test that Kaden would give him later about what he had learned that day. They picked their way over the broken ground, the sky overhead flat and lifeless and tinged with yellow. The Verucan castle rose in the distance like a looming beast.

"Look there," Brother Kaden pointed to a narrow cut between two huge boulders that led higher up into the black mountains.

"Hemmed in ground," Kaeleb answered obediently, knowing that he was being asked a question. "If seen by an enemy patrol, lure them to a position where I have the advantage and can use strategy to defeat them one by one."

"Well done."

Kaeleb beamed with delight at the praise.

"And in the event you are captured, what do you do then?" Kaden wanted to know. He stopped, turning to face the boy.

Kaeleb scrunched up his face in displeasure at the thought. "Getting captured is dishonorable."

Brother Kaden nodded his head. "But it can happen, Kaeleb, and it likely will. There are too many people who would benefit from taking you, so you must be prepared."

"I will fight them off!" the boy had countered with defiance.

"They have taken your weapons and their numbers are greater."

"I will run and outmaneuver them."

"They have boxed you in. There is no escape."

"I hate this game!" Kaeleb had been petulant, rubbing the toe of his boot in the black dirt.

"This is not a game." Brother Kaden came toward him, squatting down so they were eye to eye. "This is your life. If you are captured, there are two things you must do. The first is to be patient and look for weakness. Let your enemy think he has broken you, pretend your fight has left you. Watch him carefully and learn. There will be a weakness and an opportunity, but you must wait for it and be careful."

Kaeleb took a deep breath and digested this information. "What is the second thing?"

"This one you will like. If your enemies are united, you must create disorder among them," Kaden advised, reaching out and ruffling the boy's shock of white hair beneath the dark hood of his cloak. He saw the flash of pleasure in the child's face and it was like a spike being driven through him. He hated what they were doing, hated the way things had become, hated that the boy had so little time to be a child.

"What does that mean?" Kaeleb had asked.

"It means do what you do best and insult them. Degrade them to each other, make them doubt one another, cause animosity between them."

Kaeleb grinned.

Inside the barrel, he was not grinning. So far, he had not seen or heard from his captors, so there was no way for him to divide them. He started to shout, wondering if they would hear him and come, but eventually his dry throat began to ache and he quieted. He would have to be patient. He closed his eyes. There was no point in keeping them open since he could not see anyway. He tried to take himself somewhere else in his mind, thinking back over his memories for one that he would like to experience again.

He was back in Kymir, his belly full of berry fritters and eggs. Blaise was motioning for him to follow, a mischievous glint in his amber eyes. The Keeper was not wearing his armor that day and was dressed in simple clothing, and Kaeleb wondered if they were going to spy on someone. It was good to blend in when you were trying to collect information.

He had trailed after Blaise, licking the last of his breakfast from his fingers. As they stepped outside the older man dipped down, grabbing a handful of mud and flinging it at the boy. Kaeleb's mouth had formed a circle of surprise as the damp earth pelted him in the chest. It did not hurt; the Keeper had tossed it gently and now he stood laughing heartily. Kaeleb felt a smile creeping over his face and he darted forward, grabbing his own glob of mud and hitting Blaise in the leg. They laughed, whooping and hollering and tearing across the gardens, covered in mud, their hair damp with moisture. Kaeleb smiled at the memory. It was one of the only times he had ever played, when there had been no lesson to learn, no task to overcome, only the sheer joy of a moment and the cool dirt in his hands.

He was not sure how much time had passed when he began to hear voices. The ship shuddered and shimmied, a sign that they had bumped up against a dock somewhere. There was scraping and banging, sounds of cargo being unloaded. Then his world tilted precariously and he slammed painfully into the side of the barrel as it was rolled over. He tried to brace against the curved sides, but there was no way to adjust himself in the cramped space and he was tossed about haphazardly. The best he could hope was that he did not sustain a serious injury like a broken bone. Finally, the awful spinning and hurtling stopped and the barrel was once again upright. There was a loud groan and a crunching sound, and light flooded his senses. He cursed, covering his eyes with his hands and shrinking away from the glaring sun that poured into the open barrel.

A meaty hand reached in and grasped the colorful Tahitian fabric he was still wrapped in, hauling him up unceremoniously. He dangled in the air, his legs still bent crookedly beneath him, his knees screaming as he tried to straighten them out.

"Stand up," came the gruff command.

"I'm trying!" he snapped. "Maybe if you had not shoved me into a barrel for so long, then I would be having an easier time of it, you maggoty, dung-eating goat!"

He was dropped to the ground, landing painfully. He blinked, his hand still shading his eyes as he tried to adjust to the overwhelming light. Two men were watching him, their hands fisted on their hips. They were Kymirran from the look of them.

"Get over there with the others," one of the men ordered. Kaeleb followed the line of his arm where he was pointing and saw a group of children huddled nearby, many of them crying. Most of them were also Kymirran, and there was only one other Leharan besides himself.

"What kind of man steals children?" Kaeleb sneered contemptuously. "Are you really so weak that this is the best work you can find?"

The meaty hand that had pulled him from the barrel slapped him hard across the face. He tasted blood in his mouth and he glared at the assailant, his hand going to his hip where his sword should have been. The man laughed at him and grabbed his arm, hauling him over and shoving him towards the other children.

They backed away from Kaeleb quickly, making a space around him as if he were cursed. They did not want to draw the wrath of the men to them and he could understand their fear, even if it was disgustingly weak. He folded his arms over his chest and waited, staring defiantly at his captors. That was when he smelled it, the distinctive rotten odor of the Fomori. He whipped his head around, trying to ascertain where the beast was approaching from, then he saw her. She was an imposing figure, almost regal in her savage demeanor, her grey skin thick and the points of her teeth showing between her slightly parted lips. She had long, dark hair and her body was wrapped in the thick pelt of a bear, the arms of the animal draped across her chest and the head of the creature resting on her shoulder, its eyes staring hatefully forward and teeth bared in a permanent snarl. Kaeleb had never seen a female Fomori and he studied her with intense fascination while the other children fell into terrified fits of wailing.

She paused, her eerie yellow eyes wandering to him. She sniffed curiously as their gazes met, drawing a breath into her mouth as if she were tasting the air around him. Then she turned to the two Kymirran men.

"This is all?" she asked them in her strange and sibilant voice.

They were trying to breathe shallowly through their mouths, not wanting to offend the terrifying beast that regarded them with disdain. The meaty one said, "It is the best we could do without drawing attention. You should be grateful we have even brought you these."

The yellow eyes flashed and she opened her taloned hand, the long nails curving and sharp. She flexed her fingers beneath his chin, regarding him like a cat would a mouse. A tremor went through his thickset body and she laughed. "Next time, do better."

The men took this as their dismissal and hurried off, each grasping opposite sides of a large crate and carrying it towards their ship. They were no longer of consequence, and Kaeleb focused his attention on the female Fomori.

"Are you not afraid, little one?" she asked him. Her features were exaggerated, the cheekbones standing out starkly over the hollows of her face and her brows heavy and dark above her glowing eyes.

"I have never seen one like you," he confessed.

"Give me your hand."

"Why?"

Once again, she was surprised by the child's audacity. This one showed promise. "Because I am the Va'Kul and I have commanded it."

"Is that your name or your title?" he questioned.

"Your hand," she repeated the order.

He stuck out his hand and she took it in hers, her hide surprisingly smooth and warm. She turned it over so the palm was facing up and flexed one taloned finger, clawing it across his skin so that it split. He winced but did not pull away, stubbornly refusing to appear weak beneath her scrutiny.

"It is both what I am and who I am," she told him, as if in reward for his obedience. "There has always been a Va'Kul among us, and there always will be."

She swiped her finger over the red line of blood that welled up in his hand, lifting it to her lips. Her pink tongue darted out and she tasted the crimson liquid, her eyes glittering hopefully. They quickly clouded over in disappointment.

"An ordinary boy, then. I am even more impressed by your courage, little one," she said. "Come with me, you will serve a better purpose than a needless death."

The Va'Kul placed her clawed hand around the back of his neck to steer him forward. Kaeleb wanted to ask what would happen to the other children, but there was nothing he could do to help them and perhaps he was better off not knowing. The Va'Kul led him away from the cargo pier to an eagle that was tethered nearby. A Samirran man stood waiting, thin and wiry, with pale skin and a long braid of dark hair that draped over one shoulder. He wore a sword at his belt and Kaeleb was surprised to see a Samirran with a weapon in the presence of the Fomori.

"Take this one for the games," the Va'Kul said, pushing Kaeleb toward the man. "I believe he will be quite entertaining."

"He is just a child," the man protested. Kaeleb noted that his eyes were haunted, rimmed in dark circles as if he rarely slept, but he had a proud posture and his hand rested lightly on his sword hilt, comfortable with the weapon. Whoever he was, he was a warrior.

The Va'Kul looked displeased with his challenge. "Do not argue with me, Favian. Do as you are told and take him. He is one of yours now."

8

The disagreement over how we would get to Samirra nearly brought us to blows. Maialen had turned up nothing in her search and I listened to her say so with a dull ache weighing on my chest. The more time that passed, the less chance I had of finding Kaeleb alive, and so far I had done nothing but waste time looking for him in all the places that he was not.

"What will you do?" Maialen asked me, her big green eyes looking worried.

"I am going to get him. Give me the eagles. They are the fastest way to reach Samirra."

She shook her head. "I cannot give them to you. There are only a few left and we need them. The eagles are the only reason we are able to keep the Fomori at bay along the divide. Without them, we have no way of scouting such huge stretches of land."

"They are going to kill him!" I cried, slamming my fists down on the table we sat on opposite sides of in the ship's galley.

"I am sorry, Blaise, but I need to protect Kymir."

"You keep saying that, but what is Kymir worth if it survives on the blood of murdered children?" I seethed at her.

She flinched at the words. "You can take the ship. Or I can provide you with horses."

Damian moved from the shadows he had settled into as he watched the exchange. "The ship will be seen. We can take the horses. It will be easier to remain unobserved."

"Are you out of your mind? There is a massive hole in the ground that runs the entire length of the border, thanks to her!" I told him. "Are the horses supposed to just sprout wings and fly over it? Did your mother give you some magical potion to make that happen?"

"Do not bring my mother into this," Damian warned, his black eyes narrowed.

"Your mother is the island Elder. She is in this up to her eyeballs, and it is her fault that-" I stopped abruptly, cut off by Damian's shout of rage. I jumped up, rounding the table so that I was inches away from him, staring directly at his chin as he towered above me. I had been about to say something about the girl and that would have been a mistake. Maialen had no idea that Eolande was on Tahitia and it was better for everyone if the Earth Queen remained ignorant of that fact, for she had already proven that her decision making regarding her sister's child was questionable at best.

"Give me an excuse," Damian threatened, his deep voice rumbling throughout the small galley.

"I have given you plenty, coward," I snarled back.

"I will take you across the border! Just stop fighting, please!" Maialen interrupted us, looking stricken.

I whirled on her. "What does that mean?"

"I will have the eagles take you across the divide, but that is as far as they will carry you. After that, you are on your own. This is the best that I can offer, Blaise. Let me know when you decide." She stood, moving around us and hurrying up the short flight of stairs that led out onto the deck of the ship. She glanced back once before leaving and I turned away from the look in her eyes, not wanting to see it. I could not worry about Maialen's feelings right now, not with everything else that was happening.

"What did you do to her?" Damian asked me once she had gone. He stepped away, relaxing his huge muscles, and I flung myself back down at the table, throwing my booted feet on top of it.

"I did nothing to her."

He raised his dark eyebrows. "She acts as if you definitely did something to her."

Thyrr and Bacatha emerged from the crew's quarters where they had been hiding, Thyrr grinning at us as he said, "Well, it seems that we have found a way into Samirra! Damian is right, though. Something is between you two. Did you and the Earth Queen..."

He trailed off, making a suggestive gesture. I glared at him and Damian started to laugh. Bacatha looked intrigued, her icy blue eyes bright with curiosity.

"No wonder she hates you," the big Tahitian said, his bulk shaking with mirth. "I take it she did not care for your talents?"

"She liked them just fine," I snapped at him. "Enough of that. What are we going to do once we are in Samirra? Walk to the palace?"

Thyrr was still laughing, his hands on his knees as the three of them continued to enjoy the moment at my expense. I waited until they had exhausted themselves over it, glaring at their amused faces.

"There are patrols along the border. We can ambush one of them, take their eagles or their horses," Thyrr suggested.

"The Fomori don't use horses," I pointed out. "The animals will not tolerate them."

"No," Bacatha agreed, "but the Samirrans do."

I was surprised. "The Samirrans are helping the Fomori?"

Thyrr nodded. "That is what our spies have reported. There are patrols made up entirely of Samirran men on horseback."

"I see you learned something from Logaire when she was with you," I said with a grin.

"I learned more than that," he replied suggestively. "I can tell you, if you think it will help things with the Earth Queen."

The three of them once again dissolved into fits of laughter and I got up, stomping out of the cramped room and calling over my shoulder, "Let me know when you are done acting like children!"

"Blaise, come back. We are only teasing," Thyrr called. I felt my own smile tugging at the corners of my lips and I wondered if this was what it was like to have friends. Not that I could consider either of those three as friends, for that was a dangerous way of thinking and a weakness I could not afford. Bacatha would gut me in a second if she felt she needed to. As for the other two, we all knew that ours was a tentative truce and that one day soon it would have to end. Neither the past nor the balance of power on Imbria would allow men like us to be friends.

I stood on the deck alone, watching the gentle sway of the trees in the distance. I would accept Maialen's offer, but I would owe her for it, and I was worried about what she would demand in return. She still wanted something I could never give her, but there was no changing that now. We had both seen too much of each other's souls.

I was grateful that I did not have to see the Earth Queen again that day. I went to her manor to tell her I would accept her offer of help, but Damek was there instead, guarding the entrance like a skeletal knight that had risen from the grave. He had promised the eagles would be ready to take us at first light, throwing me a distrustful glimmer of his beady eyes when I told him there would be two others accompanying me and Damian. He did not ask who, and I wondered what other information Colwyn had sent with his little message. It would not surprise me at all if the two of them had continued on with their duplicitous alliance after Chronus's death.

Luckily for us, Damek was true to his word, and the eagles were waiting for us in the morning as promised, their riders ready to ferry us over into the Fomori's territory. I felt a moment of trepidation as we climbed on behind the riders, wondering if Colwyn and Damek had a plan to murder us all somewhere along the border. It was not the worst idea, and it would benefit the two of them in more ways than one. I hoped that the spidery old man was not as devious as I believed him to be, or that he had some unforeseen use for us that would compel him to keep us alive.

As we soared above the trees, the cold wind tearing at my ruddy face, I could not help but remember the last time I had been on one of the great winged creatures. It was a bittersweet recollection, for Kaeleb had been with me, his blood dripping down and soaking the white feathers of the eagle beneath him. In the distance Kymir had burned, a faint orange glow against the horizon that I should have recognized. We had taken the eagle back to Kymir's Royal City where I had left it, having no use for the majestic creature. There was nowhere for us to go, and the use of an eagle required a destination. Horses were safer, they were slower and allowed time to think. I had stopped long enough to dress Kaeleb's wound and grab the boy some food, then we had ridden off into the woods. I wanted to get as far away from Maialen as I could. The vision of her holding Kaeleb, her knife at his throat, had haunted me for days. Though time had softened the shock of memory, I knew it was one I could never forget.

Beneath the eagles, the trees thinned out and gave way to the vast meadowland that separated the two realms. The blackened scar of the wound we had inflicted on the world could easily be seen. It was a massive, jagged tear, and it reminded me of the scar that tore across my ribs.

The rider in front of me pointed, and in the distance I saw a group of people camped along the Samirran side of the divide. Thyrr had been right, it was men with horses, not the Fomori. I reached over the rider's shoulder and signaled to him where to land, wanting to leave some distance between us and the scouting party. We needed to reach them after night had fallen. Anything sooner invited a skirmish that I wanted to avoid. Fighting would be an unnecessary delay, and there had been too many delays already.

The riders alit just along the western edge of the abyss, true to the promise of only taking us across the divide and no further. One of them wished us luck and then they rose, staying low to the ground until they were far enough to not give away our location if spotted. I looked at my companions, thinking how strange a thing fate was. I had never thought to be standing amongst these three, allied with them for a shared cause.

I felt a flash of guilt for not telling Thyrr the truth about Kaeleb, that the boy was not his nephew and the young man owed him no loyalty, but I swallowed the emotion quickly. I needed his help and so I would let him go on believing that we were saving his sister's child, the revered Solvrei. It was not up to me to educate Thyrr on the members of his own family.

"I would prefer to have the cover of trees," Bacatha muttered, looking around at the vast open field.

"At least we can see them coming as well as they can see us," Thyrr pointed out.

She did not look appeased. Her gleaming silver armor sparkled in the sun and she grimaced at it, then bent, digging into the ground and ripping out a handful of grass and dirt. She rubbed it across her breastplate to dull the shine and Thyrr grabbed another handful, doing the same for her back. The rest of us wore thick leather, which blended in better with the surroundings, but was not nearly as useful in combat. I would make sure that I stayed close to the woman. I could always use her for cover if I needed to.

Suitably dulled, we moved north in the direction of the camp we had spotted. It was cold and the air was brittle and icy. We were spared from the early snows, but it was only a matter of time before the storms brought their fury south and I hoped we would be far away from this place before we had to contend with trudging through the winter sludge. I hated the snow.

Damian fell into step beside me, Bacatha and Thyrr walking ahead. "What is your plan once we reach Iriellestra?"

"I do not have one," I admitted. "So, if you have any ideas, by all means, share them."

"I feel we are walking into the unknown and I do not like it. I have no knowledge of what has happened here since Samirra fell to Chaote."

"Where have you been hiding all these years?" I asked him, changing the subject. There was no point in discussing everything we did not know. Besides, I was curious and since I had lately found myself in need of a place to hide, it was knowledge that could prove useful to me.

"The Wastelands," he said.

I had suspected as much. He was too conspicuous to have been anywhere else. Someone would have seen him, especially with the price Maialen had placed on his head.

"And Kaden is there?"

He whipped his head to look at me in surprise and I knew I had guessed correctly. Damian gave a heavy sigh, realizing he had given away the answer. "I forget that you are clever."

I laughed. "Is that a compliment, Tahitian?"

"Hardly. It is an observation."

"How did you survive there for so long?"

It had been easy in the beginning. Damian had taken supplies with him, food and clothing, a flint to start fires. For shelter, he had chosen the cave Carushka had once inhabited. He knew there was water there, and that was the most important resource in the harsh desert. The blooddrinkers had abandoned the cave, having gone north to join their brethren once Carushka had perished. Damian took advantage of what they had left behind, but soon his supplies dwindled and the harsh reality of the desert existence had set in. There were a few edible plants, the flowers of one cactus were actually quite delicious, and sometimes there were lizards or snakes, but scavenging was exhausting. He made trips to the coast to fish, enduring the grueling journey back and forth beneath the unrelenting sun, but he began to realize he needed to find a more efficient way to get food.

He filled a pack with water and what little stores of food remained and moved further into the caves. The darkness was absolute and he marked his way with carvings on the walls that he could feel with his hands, only using the precious flint and torch when he had to. He walked for what seemed like days, but in the darkness and without sunlight, it was impossible to judge how much time had passed. Eventually, the long tunnels began to slope upward again, and there was a glow of light in the distance. He ran towards it and he found himself in the abundant forest of Kymir.

He was able to hunt, and he carried as much meat back with him as he could, smoking and drying it so that it was easy to transport. He gathered berries and herbs, other edible plants, and he groped his way back through the darkness, feeling the deep grooves he had gouged into the rock that guided his way.

"I made the journey every few weeks. It kept me strong and fit and gave me something to look forward to on the long nights of darkness. It was my brief respite from the bleakness of my existence."

"Sounds as if you were punishing yourself," I said with a sideways glance at his stoic features.

"I was. I blamed myself for my Queen's death, and for Tal." He looked down at the ground, his shoulders sagging beneath the weight of his guilt.

"I did not kill Tal," I confessed to him, relieved to finally be able to say it. "It was Chronus. I knew nothing about it until after it was done."

He seemed to consider this as we continued on in silence. I wanted him to say something more, to absolve the residual guilt that I still carried for that deed, though I had not had a hand in it and could not understand why I felt remorse for it. Perhaps because I had let them believe it was me for so long, or because I knew it was my anger that had prompted Chronus to do what he did.

Night began to fall and the wind grew wilder, threading its way beneath our clothes and chilling us with icy fingers. The sky was clear and the stars glittered overhead, a cosmic array of dazzling lights that was spectacular to behold. We took turns gazing up in wonder, unable to help ourselves from taking in the spectacular sight. I found myself wishing that I could show it to Kaeleb. He loved to find strange shapes and animals amongst the stars, and we often laughed at some of his more ridiculous compositions. The nostalgia brought up a fresh well of fury within me. I did not try to shove it down and instead I let the rage simmer there, ready to boil over. I felt it spread through me with the awakening of my power, a dragon unfurling from its slumber. I flexed my fingers in the leather gloves, no longer aware of the cold, only feeling the searing heat of my anger.

It was then that we came upon the camp. Bacatha stopped, signaling us to be silent, sliding her sword from its sheath. The others did the same, Damian pulling his huge spear from the strap that held it to his back. I did not bother with my sword. There were six men and they had built a small fire in the center of their camp. It was more than I needed. We spread around the perimeter of their circle, silent, deadly, waiting to strike. I glanced to my right and saw the Leharan woman lift her hand, her palm spread. She would close it to a fist when she was ready to attack.

I was tired of waiting. I let the rage burn through me and I lifted my hands, the fire swelling as the men cried out in fright. There were screams and then there was nothing but a curl of black smoke rising up from the charred corpses.

"What have you done?" Damian cried, thundering across the embers of the camp towards me.

"The horses are fine. We have what we came for," I told him with a glare.

He looked horrified. "They were Samirran! They were people, Blaise!"

"Are you suggesting that killing them with your spear was more humane?" I asked in annoyance.

"I was not going to kill them!"

"Then perhaps you should have mentioned that earlier. Before they were all dead." I waved a hand at the circle of bodies.

"What is wrong with you?" he demanded. "We do not even know if they were with the Fomori. They could have escaped! They could have been looking for a way across into Kymir!"

"They could have been a lot of things, Tahitian, but now all they are is dead," I said coldly. "I warned you, this is what I am. It is not my fault you chose not to listen."

"At least it was quick," Bacatha cut in, frowning at the charred remains and sheathing her sword.

"Am I the only one here who does not condone these senseless murders?" Damian asked in disbelief, looking at the other two.

Thyrr looked uncomfortable with the exchange, pushing a hand through his golden hair. "They have weapons, Damian. Odds are they were aligned with Chaote and the Fomori. Either way, there is nothing we can do about it now. Let us get the horses and get out of here, otherwise all of this was for nothing."

I gave Thyrr a small lift of my chin in gratitude, and he returned my look with the ghost of a smile that did not reach his eyes. Let them believe what they wanted about me. Nothing mattered but getting to Kaeleb, and I did not care who or what stood in my way.

9

Kaeleb scowled at the meager dish of slop that had been left for him while he slept. He picked it up, sniffing it, then grimaced, shoving it aside. He knew he would have to eat it, for even slop was better than no food at all and he needed his strength if he was going to escape. He reluctantly pulled the bowl back and stuck his dirty fingers into the gruel, scooping it to his mouth. It tasted worse than it looked.

He was in a cell, in a holding area near the inner courtyard of the palace. The Samirran man, Favian, had brought him there the night before, staunchly ignoring the tirade of insults the boy had heaped upon him. He had given Kaeleb a new set of clothes to replace the soiled Tahitian robes, and they were plain, homespun garments in dull brown that were a little too loose on his thin frame. Favian's eyes had narrowed slightly at the sight of the three long scars that crossed the boy's chest, a gift from the Fomori that had been Kaeleb's first kill.

"Where did you get that scar?" the man had asked as Kaeleb pulled down the tunic to cover the mark.

"Why are you staring at me? Are you some kind of debaucher?" Kaeleb had accused him. "Keep your pox-ridden hands to yourself!"

Favian sighed and averted his gaze. "I was only curious about the scar."

"A Fomori did it, just before I cut off its head."

Favian had left him then, closing the heavy barred door with an ominous thud, the click of the lock sliding into place as he turned the key. He turned and found himself face to face with the Va'Kul. She smiled at him, her wicked fangs gleaming in the torchlight. She had moved quickly, the smell just now catching up to him.

"How is our newest contender?" she asked the Samirran. Kaeleb scooted forward in the cell, listening to their exchange with piqued interest.

"What am I supposed to do with a child? You cannot make him fight," Favian argued.

The Fomori woman laughed, a vicious sound. "He fights or he dies. The celebration is nearly upon us and Mother expects to be entertained. You had better earn your keep, Guardian, or you will find yourself in that arena with them."

She turned her eerie yellow gaze to Kaeleb. "Do not disappoint me, young one. I am betting quite a bit on you."

She disappeared down the torchlit corridor, and Kaeleb heard movement in some of the other cells as the prisoners shrank away from her foul presence. He turned his attention back to the wiry Samirran man with the haunted eyes.

"She called you Guardian," the boy said to him, suspicious. "Who are you? Are you the Samirran Guardian?"

Favian looked as if the weight of the last few months was too heavy for him to bear much longer. "That was a long time ago."

He began to move away and Kaeleb darted forward in the cell, pressing his face against the bars and calling after him, "If you are a Guardian, then why are you helping them?"

"Because I have no choice," was the tired reply, then the man faded into the darkness, following the Va'Kul.

Kaeleb sat eating his gruel, thinking over what he had learned. It was clear the Samirran was unhappy with the arrangement, and that whatever he was doing, he was not doing it willingly. Even if it was done willingly, he still had a distaste for it. Either way, Kaeleb could use that to his advantage. Guilt could be a powerful motivator. Sister Alita had taught him that.

Kaeleb finished his disgusting food and kicked the bowl out through the bars of his cell. Then he began a meticulous examination of his surroundings. He crawled around the perimeter of the small square of stone that housed him, checking for flaws or weaknesses, seeing if there was anything he could use as a weapon. The floor was a layer of dirt over hard stone bricks and the walls were the same blocks of stone, mortared in place and immovable. He tested the bars of his prison and fiddled with the lock on the door. As he did so, he glanced across the corridor and found another man watching him with interest.

"What are you looking at?" Kaeleb asked, glaring at the other prisoner. The man was Samirran, with clear blue eyes and a genial face capped by a dark fold of hair over a high forehead. He had grown a beard that nearly hid his mouth completely so that his voice seemed to float about from nowhere when he spoke.

The man grinned good-naturedly, showing even white teeth. "Did you uncover any hidden treasures in your search?"

Kaeleb frowned at him. "I am not looking for treasure, you foot-licking imbecile. I am looking for a weakness."

The man lifted his eyebrows. "Quite the mouth on you. You will not find a weakness. Favian has made sure that the cells are secure."

"You sound as if you admire him," Kaeleb noted with a tinge of repugnance. How could one admire a traitor who would lock up his own kind? It was disgraceful.

"We were friends once. Maybe we still are, I no longer know," the man said, his tone wistful. "What is your name, boy?"

"Boy," Kaeleb answered flatly. The last thing he needed was for anyone here to think he was the Solvrei.

"Very well, Boy. I am Hovard."

"What are we doing here? What celebration is the Va'Kul speaking of?" Kaeleb wanted to know. If the man wanted to talk, he might as well make himself useful.

The face darkened behind the beard. "Who knows what or why they celebrate? Sometimes I think there is no reason at all. They just pretend for the sake of their cruelty."

"What do they want with us?"

"We are the entertainment," the man said with a resentful laugh.

"Your answers are not very helpful," Kaeleb admonished. "If you want me to get us out of here, then be more forthcoming. We do not have time for you to be coy."

Hovard chuckled. "You've got spirit, Boy. I can see why the Va'Kul likes you. Though be careful, her favor comes with its own set of horrors. The Fomori have made an arena of the inner courtyard and their celebrations are spectacles. They call them games. They make us fight each other, and the loser becomes a sacrifice to the blooddrinkers."

Kaeleb felt his stomach turn. This was not what he had expected to hear, although the idea of an outdoor arena did present possibilities for escape. The man went on to explain how the games were a way for the Fomori to control the population. The farmers and workers had been put to the tasks they were suited for, but the others, the palace guards and the artisans and anyone else that Chaote felt unnecessary, they were expendable and they were mouths to feed. This was a way to cull the herd, and also to give the people just enough hope so that they would stay trapped in their fear. She had promised that at the end of each season, the warrior who had won the most battles would be set free. Hovard himself was the current champion, and if he could survive the winter, then he would be released before spring.

"Why does the Guardian help her?" Kaeleb asked. He had settled himself cross-legged on the floor, scratching at the dirt with his fingernail.

"He is trying to help all of us. After he killed King Astraeus to save this realm, he went to the other rulers and told them what had happened. The Earth Queen offered to let him return here, saying that if he stayed in Kymir he would be executed for killing her husband. So, Favian returned to Samirra to help the people that the Earth Keeper turned away. Chaote forced him into this role, telling him he could train us and arrange the fights, or she would just kill us all at once. He chose the former option," Hovard explained.

Kaeleb was not surprised to hear what the Earth Queen had done to the Guardian. After Maialen had tried to kill him, he knew there was nothing she would not do to get what she wanted and to protect her power and her realm. He was glad Blaise had burned half of it to the ground. "Do you use weapons in the fights?"

"Yes. Favian decides which."

"You do not look like an outstanding fighter. How have you won any of these games?" Kaeleb gave him a long look.

Hovard feigned indignation. "How dare you? I am a champion!"

Kaeleb snorted. "If you are a champion, then I am the next King of Samirra."

"I'm hurt by your doubt."

"It is because you are friends, isn't it? You and the Guardian. He helps you in some way. Is it the weapons?"

Hovard looked panicked for a moment and waved his hand to hush the boy. "Shh. Do not say that where people can hear you."

Kaeleb gave him a smug grin. "Then it is true."

Hovard shrugged. "How do I know? We have never spoken of it."

Kaeleb scooted back into the darkness of his cell, pressing against the wall and disappearing into the shadows to ponder what he had just learned. He could not believe his luck. An arena, outside, with weapons. He had not expected the Fomori to be so stupid. He only had to bide his time until it was his turn to fight, then he would show them just how foolish they were. And he would find some decent food as well.

10

Once again, an argument ensued over what our next course of action would be. Damian was still bemoaning my tactics, and I refused to capitulate to his whining demands of a more subtle approach. As far as I was concerned, we needed to get inside the walled city, and I did not care how it happened or how many worthless Samirrans were hurt in the process.

"We cannot just go barging in the front gates!" Damian was saying irritably. We were in the darkened recesses of a shed, part of an abandoned farm that lay on the outskirts of a small village a few hours' ride from the city. It was a good place to camp and it kept out the cold, but it was close quarters and we were all grating on each other's nerves.

The Tahitian was sitting on the ground, leaning against the wall. Above him hung an array of tools that looked as equally suited for torture as they were for farming. I thought about grabbing one of the clawed hammers and smashing his skull with it. Perhaps it would knock some sense into him. He glanced up to see what I was looking at.

"Try it and I will put a scythe through your chest," he threatened.

I grinned at him. "I was just admiring the collection."

Bacatha strode over and lifted the scythe from the hook it was hanging from. She tested the weight in her hands. "I like it. I will keep it."

"Nothing like an enraged farming Leharan to terrify the Fomori," I sneered.

She shrugged. "A weapon is a weapon and I like this one."

"I think it suits you," Thyrr offered gallantly. "I would be terrified if you were running at me with that thing."

"Thank you, Thyrr, I appreciate that. At least someone around here has an astute perception of clever weaponry," Bacatha replied.

Damian was shaking his head, I'm sure ruing the day that he had gotten tangled up with the rest of us. "Can we please discuss the plan to enter the city?"

"There are other farms in this village that are still being worked. The farmers have to go in and out of the city for supplies and to sell their crops," I mused. I had been surprised that Chaote let the farmers return to their work, but I suppose I should have expected it. She was not a fool, and controlling the grain that fed most of Imbria was quite a powerful position to be in. It also kept people quite busy and busy people were less of a threat.

"So we need to get one of the farmers to help us," Thyrr said.

I shrugged. "Or we kill them and pretend we are them."

Damian pushed himself up from the ground. "No! We are not killing any more innocent people."

"You were perfectly happy killing people when you came to Veruca ten years ago and attacked my kingdom!" I snapped, annoyed by his constant righteousness.

"Ssh!" Bacatha silenced us with a wave of her hand. "Someone is near."

We all froze, straining to hear whatever sound had alerted her to a nearby presence. There was the distinctive clank of metal and the soft snort of a disturbed animal. Someone was stealing our horses.

I shoved past them and threw open the door to the shed, rounding the squat little building to where we had tethered the horses out of sight. A man was there and he looked up at me with wide eyes, clearly not expecting a Verucan to come barreling down on him.

"Get your hands off my horse, you filthy thief!" I snarled, shoving him and sending him sprawling into the dirt.

"No, no!" he cried. "I was not trying to steal them! I thought they were abandoned."

I stepped forward and grabbed the collar of his coat, hauling him to his feet. "What are you doing here?"

"Blaise," Damian warned. "Do not do anything foolish."

"Something foolish like saying my name so this peasant knows who I am?" I snarled back angrily at the Tahitian.

"You did say his name. That was not wise," Bacatha admonished her fellow islander. The terrified Samirran looked at Bacatha's severe visage as she towered over him holding her scythe, and he shrank back in fear, much to her delight. She smiled at us with smug satisfaction. "There, you see? He is afraid of me!"

"Are you..." the man's voice trailed off as he looked up at me. "Are you the Verucan King?"

"Not anymore," Thyrr commented flippantly.

I threw up my hands in exasperation, saying to Damian, "Well, Tahitian, if I was not going to kill him before, I have to now since thanks to you he knows who I am."

"No, no, no!" the man protested, his wild eyes roaming between us, looking for the most reasonable of our group. He could not seem to decide on who that would be and gave up, settling his attention on me once again. "I can help you! I can take you to the Harbonah! He will want to know you are here."

I leveled my amber gaze at him, eyes narrowed. This was quite interesting. "Can this Harbonah help us get into the city?"

The man swallowed hard and nodded. "Yes, yes. He knows the way underground. In the tunnels. We have been waiting for someone to come and liberate us!"

Thyrr snorted in amusement and I shot him a glare before saying, "Of course, we are here to help. Take us to the Harbonah."

"I-I cannot take you to him, but I can send a message and he will come to you," the man said, starting to rise to his feet, his hands still spread in front of him to show his peaceful intent.

I frowned. "How do I know you won't run to the Fomori and tell them I am here?"

A shadow fell over the man's face. "I would never help those beasts. Never."

Bacatha stepped forward, her severe features set in hard lines. "If you are lying, I will use my farming tool to cut you up into tiny pieces and feed you to the crows."

"Thank you, Bacatha, that is quite helpful," I said to her with a shake of my head. I turned back to the man. "Go now, bring us the Harbonah. But I am warning you, do not betray us or-"

"You will meet the sharp end of my farming tool!" Bacatha cut in.

"Stop saying farming tool, it is a scythe!" I cried, exasperated. "You, Samirran, go before I change my mind!"

The man backed away quickly, then turned and fled down the overgrown dirt path that led back to the village. I sighed heavily, watching him go. This Harbonah was either going to be our savior or our downfall, and I did not like leaving such things to chance.

11

Kaeleb trailed behind the line of the men as they walked through the corridor, the stench of the Fomori overwhelming. The beasts were escorting them, but the Samirran Guardian was in the lead giving the orders, and Kaeleb wondered again how Favian could live with himself and the dishonor of his present circumstances.

They shuffled out into the sunlight, the air cold and stark in the empty arena. It was a large, open half-circle in front of the palace where the courtyard had been, and a makeshift wall had been built to separate it from the magnificent marble structure that glistened like a block of ice in the winter sun. Behind the new section of wall was a raised seating area bracketed by poles which held an awning to shade the spectators who sat there. That was where the important ones would be.

Favian was walking down the line of men, handing out training weapons. There were wooden swords and axes, some sticks that Kaeleb assumed were intended to be spear substitutes, and a few other items the boy did not recognize. When the Guardian reached him, he passed over a short wooden sword and a small, round shield.

"None of the others have a shield," Kaeleb said, folding his arms stubbornly over his chest, refusing to take it.

The wiry Samirran stared at him, his clear blue eyes looking decades older than he was. "The others are grown men."

"I will not take it. It will make me seem weak. Give me the sword," Kaeleb ordered, sticking out his hand.

"Take the shield," Favian said, trying to shove it into the boy's arms.

"No!" was the obstinate reply and the shield fell to the ground with a thud. The boy kicked it, sending it skidding across the ground. A few of the men laughed.

Favian gave up. "Have it your way, but if you die before the games even begin, the Va'Kul will be very displeased."

"If I am dead, I will not care what the Va'Kul or anyone else thinks," Kaeleb retorted.

One of the men chuckled again and said, "Are all Leharans like this one?"

Favian motioned for them to be silent, then he divided them into pairs to practice sparring. Kaeleb was placed with the man whose cell was across from him, Hovard. He immediately cried out in protest, refusing to partner with the man. Favian came stomping over, his patience already worn thin.

"I am not fighting him in the arena. You will make me lose!" the boy hissed at the Guardian.

Favian's eyes widened slightly. There was no way the boy could know what he had done. "We are only sparring. It is training, not an actual fight."

Kaeleb still refused. "I know that, you foppish dolt! And I also know that you are helping him and that whoever fights him will lose. Look at him, he is no champion. Look how he holds a sword! The Tahitian Elder is more ferocious than him and she is a hundred-year-old woman!"

Favian grabbed the boy's ear and twisted it, causing him to cry out and writhe in pain. "Be silent! Or I will cut your ear off! You will not be fighting anyone in the games. You think I would put a small boy like you in hand-to-hand combat with fighting men?"

"Let go of me!" Kaeleb cried, jerking away. He felt a moment of panic. Not fighting meant no chance of escape. He had to fight. He had to show this traitor Samirran that he was not just a boy. Kaeleb lunged forward, swinging his sword at the Guardian. It was an easy blow to deflect and the Guardian stepped out of the way, ducking the path of the wooden blade, but Kaeleb had predicted his movement and he spun the other way at the last minute, a blur of white hair and drab brown, and whipped the sword around with his left hand, striking Favian in the back where his kidney was. The man cried out and nearly toppled to the ground. Hovard reached to help him and Kaeleb leapt on the bearded man, grabbing the collar of his shirt and swinging himself onto the man's back, pressing his weapon against his opponent's windpipe. Hovard stumbled, his mouth gaping open and closed beneath the beard like a fish, and the other men started to laugh and cheer. Kaeleb grinned at them and when Hovard dropped to his knees the boy released him, stepping back triumphantly.

Favian was rubbing his lower back. He glanced at Hovard and saw that he would be fine, the bearded man drawing huge gulps of air into his lungs. "Who are you, boy?"

A dark look passed through the steely grey eyes that were out of place on his childlike face. "I am nobody and I come from nowhere."

"Have it your way," Favian muttered. He paired them off again, watching with growing suspicion as the boy continually herded his opponents towards the inner wall. Each time Favian called them back to the center of the arena the boy took his time, dropping his sword or pretending to be out of breath so he could lean against the wall, his thin muscles flexing ever so slightly beneath his clothing as he pressed for weaknesses. Favian could not help but respect the child's determination.

It was obvious he was going to attempt to escape, but Favian knew this was a wasted endeavor, and one that would only get him killed.

The Guardian had returned to Samirra after the Earth Queen had given him no other choice. He had killed a Keeper, her husband. It did not matter what Astraeus had done, she could not be seen to forgive his murderer. Out of respect for what the Guardian had sacrificed, she had allowed him the choice of a quick death, or to go back to his realm and pretend he had never left. He had been tempted to take her up on the offer of death. He was so tired. In the end, though, he could not. That was the coward's way out, and there were still people that needed his help.

Favian had considered going north, finding a quiet farm or somewhere to hide, but if he truly wanted to help his people, then Iriellestra was where he needed to be. The Fomori found him as soon as his eagle had landed outside the walls.

"The Keepers did not want you or your flock, did they?" Chaote asked when he was brought before her. She had managed to gather a full set of golden armor by now and she shone like the sun in the night sky, a strange juxtaposition of beauty, her perfect ebony features as noble and impeccable as ever. She sat on a simple wooden chair with no cushion. She had ensconced herself in the palace, but it was not the same opulent place it had been. It was stripped of its adornments, laid bare, naked and stark. The only room that had not been gutted was the Great Library, for she wanted to know everything she could about her enemies and the library was a wealth of knowledge.

"I killed one of them," Favian reminded her. "There are punishments for such an act."

"You killed a pathetic weakling who only cared for himself. You did this world a favor."

He shrugged, sorrow shadowing his countenance. "Did I?"

She stood and walked to him, a graceful movement with an enticing sway of hips. He still found her beauty painful to look at, and were he another sort of man with different tastes, he might have been drawn to her in a terrifying way.

"You did," she answered with finality. "For that, I will not kill you. I am more reasonable than your Keepers, you see. I know your value."

"I did not think my kind held any value to you."

"Nonsense." She circled around him, a hum of dangerous energy flowing with her. "You will see just how useful to me your kind can be."

She had not told him about the games until later. Perhaps she had not thought of it until then. When she did, she made it sound altruistic, as if she were granting him and the Samirrans a splendid gift. He had seen it for what it was; a tool to control the masses. He had refused, wanting no part of such a barbaric proposal. She took him to the dungeons beneath the city, to the long rows of cells crammed with men.

"These are the men who will be my warriors in the arena. If you do not accept my offer to train and control them, then I will have them all executed." Her voice echoed down the corridor, loud and unwavering, so that all the prisoners could hear what she said.

Favian looked down the row and there, holding the bars of his cell, his gentle face pressed upon the cold iron, was Hovard. The Guardian knew he could never condemn his former lover to death. He would rather die himself. So he relented. Since then, he had done everything he could to keep Hovard alive, even going so far as to damage the weapons before they were given to his opponents, dulling the swords so they could not pierce Hovard's wonderful, beautiful skin. All Favian had to do was get Hovard to win the most games and the man would earn his freedom. Chaote had promised as much, and whatever kind of monster she might be, she kept her word. Or at least a close variation of it.

Now this boy had come, and he was threatening everything. If he tried to escape before the games were finished or before Hovard had his turn to fight, then Chaote could retaliate by reneging on her promise to free a man. Worse, she could just kill them all as punishment. He had to convince the headstrong child to alter his course of action, though as of yet, the boy did not seem amenable to coercion. That left him with the alternative of pleading and appealing to the boy's emotions. Favian was not sure this would be any more effective than using threats. The boy was not like any child he had ever come across. Whoever raised that little monster, they had to be a cold-hearted demon themselves.

Training ended for the day and Favian led the captives back to their cells, pausing as he slid the lock into place, willing the boy to look up at him. Kaeleb noticed he was hesitating and glared up at him in distrust.

"After you are fed, I need you to feign a stomachache. As bad as you can make it seem," Favian whispered.

"No! If you are some kind of diddling pervert then-"

"By the Gods, I am not a pervert, I am trying to help you! Just do it," the Guardian hissed. He moved away, seeing the Fomori guard start forward to find out what the problem was.

"Lock was stuck," Favian mumbled to the beast, jangling the ring of keys.

They moved off down the corridor and Favian could not help but think how strange his world had become, that he was now a jailer to his people, and the fate of a Guardian was now in the hands of one petulant little boy.

12

I stood outside the shed, leaning against it and watching the doddering figure of an old man shuffle up the path. It had been nearly a full day since we had let the man go to summon the infamous Harbonah. With each passing hour I had grown more agitated, believing we had been deceived and that death in the form of a vengeful halfbreed was coming for us. I hardly slept, annoying the others by rising at all hours and pacing incessantly in front of the shed. The night was cold and silent, eerily so, and on one of my pacing rounds the Tahitian had joined me, the darkness of him barely visible in the sliver of moon that waned overhead.

He glanced at the shuttered homestead, the one we had avoided in favor of the cramped shed. The doors and windows were covered with boards and branded with a splash of red paint. Plague had been in that house.

"Have you ever seen what it does? The plague, I mean?" I asked him. A chill wind blew and I pulled my leather coat more tightly around my neck.

"I have not, but I have heard it is not a pleasant way to go."

I shifted on my feet, shivered, told myself it was from the cold. "When I went north to fight the Fomori, Astraeus sent plague victims after us. He wanted to infect my army, to weaken us so we would lose."

Damian watched me with black eyes, his face stoic and unreadable.

"We thought they were soldiers at first," I told him. "Then I realized they were not. There were so many of them. Women and children. A mother holding her dead baby. I do not even know if she was aware it was dead. She kept begging us to help it. We killed them. I killed them. All of them. It was the only thing I could do."

I waited for him to share some of his Tahitian wisdom, for a philosophical quip that would alleviate the guilt that I still carried with me. He remained silent, as inscrutable as the night and just as distant.

I went on, not even sure why I wanted to say the words anymore. "Those men on the border, you want me to feel remorse for their deaths, but I have seen deaths a thousand times worse, killed in ways that were a thousand times worse. We are all monsters here, Tahitian, and now it is children who must reap what we have sown. If something happens to Kaeleb... it will be the last shattering of whatever is unbroken in me."

"Then let us pray to the Gods that he is still alive," Damian said, coming towards me to grasp my shoulder in a gesture of camaraderie. "For I cannot imagine a worse version of you."

I chuckled, and his white teeth gleamed in the faint moonlight as he smiled. We had gone back into the shed, eliciting a string of curses from Bacatha when I jostled her lithe frame while trying to squeeze back into the narrow opening where I was sleeping. The rest of the night continued to creep by slowly, and eventually I must have drifted off to sleep, but when morning came I felt as though I had barely closed my eyes.

I brought my focus back to the decrepit old man as he made his way, achingly slow in his progression. He leaned heavily on a sturdy walking stick, and his booted feet shuffled, dragging through the dirt and grass. His head was bent over and thin wisps of hair danced out from beneath the edge of his hooded cloak.

Thyrr came out to join me, leaning beside me and watching the old man with a crooked grin. "We should have had Damian carry him."

Damian and Bacatha were concealed nearby, in case the appearance of the mystical Harbonah was indeed some kind of ruse. Bacatha had been adamant about taking the scythe with her, even though I had pointed out that the size of the reaping tool would make hiding more difficult. She, in turn, had pointed out that Damian's enormous size was more difficult to hide than the scythe, and he was allowed to carry a spear, and so I had relented.

"So, you are the Harbonah who has caused me so many problems over the years," I called out once the old man was in shouting distance.

"Not as many as you have caused me!" the old man countered, stopping to lean on his stick so he could raise his withered head.

I nearly choked on my own spit. "Astus?!"

The former King of Samirra, father to Astraeus, was the last person I had expected to see. I shook my head. Perhaps I was mistaken, and it was another old man who I had confused with him.

"Yes, it is me."

I was in shock. "You are alive! What on Imbria are you doing here?"

"This is Samirra. I live here," he said, as if I were daft. "Did you think I would just abandon my kingdom?"

"Aren't you mad?" Thyrr interrupted, looking at him quizzically.

Astus lifted his stooped shoulders as if to say it could not be helped. "Being mad was a necessary ruse."

"So, you are not mad?" Thyrr wanted to clarify.

"No, he just pretended to be so he could run around behind everyone's back being the Harbonah," I said flatly. There were a thousand questions I wanted to ask him, and a thousand things I wanted to know.

"You are not as dumb as you look," the old man said with a grin. "I hear you wish to go into the city."

"We believe the Fomori have taken Kaeleb."

A look of panic marched across the old man's face, and he gripped the walking stick with both hands so that he did not topple over. "Kaeleb? The Solvrei? How could you let this happen?"

I felt a flush of indignation. "Well, you and those two lunatics you let raise him did not exactly protect him either, or he would not have ended up with me after nearly being murdered by his aunt, who was trying to drink his blood!"

"His aunt? Maialen? No, she could not have. Maialen would not do that. Tell me she did not!" he wailed, the stick quivering in his arthritic hands.

"No, but only because I stopped her."

"Praise the Gods," he murmured, repeating a string of words in the ancient language and making a whirling gesture in the air with his finger.

My irritation was growing quickly. "Whatever God you think you are conjuring, old man, I can assure you they are not listening. Stop your mumbling and tell me how we can get into the city!"

"There are tunnels. I can take you in tonight, once night has fallen."

More waiting. I was not inclined to be patient any longer. I grabbed his cloak and he teetered unsteadily on his shuffling feet, the stick falling to the ground. He clutched at my arms to hold himself upright.

"I am sick of waiting! Take us to these tunnels now, or I will break your legs and even that stick won't help you then!" I roared.

"Blaise, please," Thyrr laid a restraining hand on my arm, then bent and picked up the old man's walking stick, pressing it back into his hands.

"Thank you, young man, thank you. You are very kind," Astus muttered. I released him once he had regained his balance and he glared at me. "I need time to arrange things, and to find out where the Solvrei is being held. Give me the rest of the day and I promise you I will find him. You do not want to search the entire city. It is crawling with Fomori. Meet me in the village tavern at nightfall. There is only one, you will know it."

"Fine," I ground out through clenched teeth, agreeing because I had no other choice.

"Young man, will you help me back down the road? I am not as spry as I used to be and winter is hard on these old joints," the old man asked, holding out his elbow to Thyrr who took it obediently, guiding him back down the road. There was a wagon waiting for him in the distance, and I was grateful to see it. At least the old man would not be moving at his snail's pace the whole way back to wherever he was going.

"I was certainly not expecting that," Bacatha said, swinging the scythe back and forth as she strode out of her hiding place. "The mad old King of Samirra, who it turns out is not mad at all. I have to say, I am very pleased that I agreed to join in this adventure."

"That makes one of us. As soon as Kaeleb is safe, that old man is going to give me some answers. He is more knowledgeable about everything that is transpiring than anyone else," I said, staring after the slowly retreating figure. His head was bent towards Thyrr and I wondered what secrets or lies the old man might be telling him. The Harbonah was not someone to be trusted, and I was reluctant to leave Astus alive now that I had learned the truth. I hoped he enjoyed the rest of his day, for it was likely to be his last.

We waited until the day began to fade before making our way to the village as the old man had instructed. We had all put on hooded cloaks, but there was no pretending that we would pass as a group of Samirran farmers, despite Bacatha's now ever-present farming tool. I had discovered that she could not correctly pronounce the word scythe, even after I made an effort to visually demonstrate it by writing it in the dirt with my finger. Thyrr howled with laughter at her attempts and she had finally given up, refusing to try again and steadfastly resolute in her determination that it be referred to as a farming tool from then on.

The village was practically deserted, quiet except for a single horse that clopped down the street, its rider not even giving us a sideways glance. The tavern was easy to find, as Astus had promised, the windows glowing with warmth from a hearth fire that burned cozily within. I took a deep breath and opened the door, expecting a roomful of bawdy patrons to turn and stare at us. There was no one there. We filed inside, Thyrr resting his hand on his sword hilt, looking around in wary distrust.

"The Harbonah will be here soon," a woman said, appearing in a doorway that I assumed led to the kitchens. She was Samirran, pale-skinned, thick around the waist and bosom and with a pile of greying hair that towered haphazardly on her head. "Make yourselves comfortable. The fire is warm."

She disappeared into whatever recess she had emerged from. We sat at one of the long tables, Bacatha beside me, straddling the benched seat so that she faced the doorway, with Thyrr and Damian on the opposite side. My fingers tapped a subtle rhythm on the worn surface of the table, a nervous gesture of impatience.

"Do you think she will give us ale if we ask for it?" Thyrr asked, looking around wistfully.

"We are not here for that," I said with reproach.

"How are you planning to pay for it?" Bacatha asked. Damian started to laugh at Thyrr's perplexed expression.

"Around here, no one will care that you are the heir to Lehar," the big Tahitian told him. "They only care that you have silver to spend."

Thyrr frowned and folded his arms over his chest, clearly displeased. It was then that the tavern door swung open, and a stream of Samirran men filed in. All of us were instantly on our feet, our weapons gripped in our hands. My first thought was that Astus had betrayed us. My second was that he should have sent more men and warned them not to light a fire. The hearth flames swelled behind me as I called my power, sweat beading on the foreheads of everyone in the room as we faced off with one another.

"Enough of that! Put that away!" Astus said irritably, ambling into the tavern behind the men and gesturing at the fire. I relaxed, the flames retreating and the oppressive heat dissipating.

"I thought you betrayed us, old man," I muttered. The Samirran men began to spread around the room, sitting at various tables and otherwise ignoring us. I raised an eyebrow at Astus. "That is quite the troop of bodyguards."

"Jealous?" he asked with a phlegmy laugh that broke into a cough. He made his way to our table and lowered himself onto the bench, sighing happily as the weight was relieved from his knees.

"Did you find him?" I asked immediately.

"I know where he is, yes. But he will not be easy to get to," the old man confessed.

"Tell me."

Astus told us that Kaeleb was to be part of a celebration that would take place in front of the palace, in a walled arena where he would have to fight to the death for the entertainment of the Fomori. The tournaments, as Chaote liked to call them, would begin in the morning and they would last the entire day.

Astus spread his hands on the table, stretching his bent fingers. "Your best opportunity to reach him will be at the tournament, when they bring him out of his cell. I have sent someone to deliver a message to him, to tell him to be ready to escape and that you are here for him. I suggest you create a diversion or two, draw the Fomori's attention away from the warriors in the arena. That will be the only chance you have. Once you have him, you must return to the tunnel entrance unseen. My men will be watching and if you try to come there with the enemy at your heels, then we will be forced to stop you. They cannot be allowed to find the tunnels."

"You would sacrifice the Solvrei to keep your little tunnels a secret?" I asked, raising an eyebrow.

"No, we will save the boy. The rest of you, though, you are expendable. The great battle that is coming requires only the savior. He is the most important," Astus preached.

"Glad to know where we stand," I said, with more than a hint of sarcasm. "So be it."

"There is one other thing," the old man began.

"There is always one other thing," Thyrr muttered contemptuously.

Astus was disappointed with him. "I thought you were the polite one."

Thyrr's face tilted into his crooked smile. "You do not know me at all, Harbonah, and I dislike it when strings are attached to bargains. It is your savior we are saving, and that should be enough."

"Hmph." The old man regarded Thyrr with a deep frown creasing his weathered face. "Then prepare yourself, young man, because you will not like this. What I ask is not a request. You must do this for me or we part ways here and now."

I was once again impatient, tired of talking. "What is that you want, Astus?"

"I need you to save another boy. Aracellis."

I stared at him, wondering if we could find the tunnels on our own or if one of the other men in the room would lead us to them after I ripped the old man's head off. My fingers trembled with rage and I clenched them into fists, taking a deep breath.

"Maialen's son is alive?" I demanded. He nodded and my voice was harsher, threatening as I went on, "And you did not think to tell her?"

Astus sighed, wriggling his bony frame on the bench in discomfort. "How was I supposed to do that? I would risk being discovered and Aracellis would have been put in grave danger. The Fomori do not know who he is, and most of the Samirrans have never even seen him since he spent most of his childhood shut away in the palace, avoiding the plague. Nevertheless, I worry that it is only a matter of time until someone recognizes him. I need you to find him and bring him to me before that happens."

Aracellis had been taken by the Fomori when the beasts had searched the countryside for children with divine blood. The children were rounded up and taken to Iriellestra, and some had returned, but many had not. Astus was informed that a few of the children had been taken in by Chaote to serve her. Children were less of a threat, and she did not want to surround herself with servants who might try to kill her. Since the boy could read and write, he would prove very useful to the halfbreed and it was no surprise that she had kept him. He was likely somewhere within the palace, and Astus hoped he would be with Chaote at the tournament, since she liked for all of her subjects to attend the celebratory games.

"You do not know for sure that he will be there?" I asked, doubtful of his story. If he had found Kaeleb so easily, it should not be that difficult to find his grandson.

"I know it does not seem like a difficult task," Astus said, as if he were reading my thoughts. "But Kaeleb is Leharan. It is easy to ask if there is a Leharan boy being held prisoner. It is much more difficult for me to ask the whereabouts of a Samirran boy, especially without revealing his true identity."

"What if we cannot find him?" Damian asked, stirring beneath the heavy hood that was still draped over him. Astus seemed to notice him for the first time, his rheumy eyes growing round as he realized who sat at the table with him.

"Do you have the Pearl?" the old man asked hungrily, suddenly eager.

Damian shook his head and I caught the flash of distrust that crossed his dark features. "I do not have it."

"That is unfortunate," Astus said, the ravenous look fading from his countenance and his shoulders rounding into a stoop once again. "If you do not bring Aracellis, then do not bother returning. You will not leave the city alive unless you have him."

"You make a lot of threats for a helpless old man," I said.

Astus lifted his eroded chin. "They are not threats, Fire Keeper. It is the way things will be. You sneer at me and make jokes, but I am the Harbonah. These people are my acolytes, and you are nothing here. Remember that."

I leveled my amber gaze at him and regarded him thoughtfully for a long moment. "I liked you better when you were mad."

13

The heavy odor of the Fomori hung over the arena like a transparent fog. The day was bright and clear and cold, and looking up at the sky one would have expected to smell the pleasant crispness of the granite cliffs whose tops were tinged with ice, or the faint, billowy aroma of spices and woodsmoke rising from the city. Instead, everything smelled of death.

Kaeleb strained his neck, squinting to see how many Fomori were crowded onto the upper battlements of the inner wall. He realized it was not just Fomori that had come to watch the tournament. Many of the spectators were Samirran. People had brought picnics and snacks with them, colorful ribbons and streamers, which they waved eagerly in the chilled air. Kaeleb was disgusted, shaking his head. How could they be so subservient that they would celebrate their own captivity? He thought back to something Sister Alita had once told him. *The world is made up of vulgar people, and when they can, they will crowd together and this is when they can be swayed by appearances. A ruler must understand this and appear to give them what they want, for the reality does not matter nearly so much.*

Alita's lessons had been complicated, hard for his young mind to grasp the subtle contexts and meanings behind her words, but he listened and memorized them obediently, and he was beginning to understand some of what she meant. Chaote was entertaining the Samirrans, giving them the illusion of freedom, of celebration, and even though they were, in reality, still enslaved and imprisoned, the Samirrans were swallowing it up eagerly.

"Keep moving," the man behind Kaeleb said gruffly, giving him a nudge. The boy nearly stumbled but he righted himself, throwing a glare over his shoulder at the other prisoner.

"Be ready. The Verucan is here," the man said so quietly that at first Kaeleb doubted he had heard the words. He felt his pulse quicken. The man gave him another shove and they continued on, a line of warriors circling the arena, paraded in front of the crowds so the spectators could see who the day's combatants were to be.

It was clear these were not the first games Chaote had hosted, and the crowds had their favorites. A man named Tiberus elicited wild shrieks of delight and hollers of support from the Samirrans. He was tall, handsome, virile. The sort of man the crowd would like. The Fomori were more discerning, not caring for appearances and heaping their support on the most capable fighters, and the most vicious.

As they neared the newer section of wall, Kaeleb glanced up at the rows of seats beneath the awning, his eyes meeting those of the Va'Kul. Her lips parted in a feral smile, the points of her teeth stained pink from a recent meal. There were other Fomori women crowded into the box, all draped in furs and lounging like waiting predators. A few young children wove between them, carrying trays of food and goblets of what might have been wine, but was probably blood. In the center of it all was their halfbreed leader, Chaote.

Kaeleb recognized her instantly from the day at the border when he had stood beside Maialen and faced her across the abyss. She was everything that a warrior should be, and he could not help but feel a shine of admiration for her. She exuded both competence and confidence. Her hair was pulled back from her face in a long ponytail and her skin was like the sky on a summer night, warm and dark and faultless. Chaote caught him staring, and he saw her star-strewn eyes widen slightly in surprise. She recognized him as well. He smiled at her and lifted his chin and her eyes grew slightly more rounded, further surprised by his audacity. She leaned towards the Va'Kul and spoke to her, her fingers waving in Kaeleb's direction. The Va'Kul looked pleased, nodding, and they continued to speak furtively, heads bent close together. If she had not already deduced it from the events that had transpired with Maialen at the divide, there was no doubt now that Chaote was aware of Kaeleb's ordinary blood. He was not the Solvrei he had claimed to be.

The line of warriors finished its march around the arena and the men filed back into the long, dark corridor that led to their cells. They did not return to their individual prisons, though, for one of the rewards on tournament day was to watch their fellow warriors fight. They spread around the darkened opening of the tunnel, just out of sight of the crowds but still able to observe the arena. Kaeleb glanced at the man who had nudged him, but he was pretending as if the boy did not even exist. He had delivered his message and that was the end of it.

Favian joined them and behind him was a cart loaded with weapons pushed by a Fomori. Kaeleb refused to look the Guardian in the eye. He had ignored the man's urgent plea that he feign an illness, believing it was likely to be some ruse to prevent the boy from participating in the tournament that day.

As the cart trundled by, it would have been easy for Kaeleb to grab one of the weapons and kill the beast, but he felt it was too soon in the day to attempt an escape. He would let them settle in first, let their guard down. He wondered if Blaise was there in the crowds, watching. Blaise had to be the Verucan the man had mentioned. No one else would come for him.

The Samirran Guardian took two leaf-shaped swords and handed them to the warriors who were to be the first two combatants. The men stepped close together so that they were toe to toe, bending their heads so their foreheads touched. They held this posture while each of the other warriors touched their shoulders, a ritual they had adopted before combat. When it was done, Favian signaled for them to enter the arena. Everyone pressed forward to watch and Kaeleb let himself slip back towards the cart of weapons. He stood near it, trying to look meek and scared. As he was hoping, the Fomori guard barely noticed him. Kaeleb wanted the beast to think that he was just a terrified child, trying to avoid whatever carnage was happening in the arena.

The crowd broke into wild cries and the Fomori leaned forward, trying to see what was happening. Kaeleb slid his hand into the cart, withdrawing a curved dagger that he had spied lying in easy reach. He dropped the weapon down the length of his trousers, which he had tucked into his boots just for that purpose.

"You do not wish to see?" Hovard asked him. Kaeleb wondered if the bearded man had seen him take the weapon, but the Samirran gave no indication that he had noticed anything amiss.

"I have seen people die," Kaeleb told him with a shrug. Kaeleb turned so that his hip was pressed against the cart, drawing out another knife and pushing it up his sleeve. The Fomori had not even glanced his way, intent on the battle taking place in the arena. Kaeleb moved away from the weapons, sliding forward along the wall. Despite what he had said to Hovard, he was curious as to how the battles in the arena would go. It was obvious the men were holding back during training, for why would you want to show all your best moves to the opponent you would be facing in actual combat?

One combatant in the arena was already wounded, and he was limping away, leaving a bloody trail in the dirt. The other man circled closer, the crowd cheering. Kaeleb knew the injured man would die from the wound in his leg. The blood was gushing out of it with each beat of his heart, but it would take some time. His opponent also knew this and he toyed with him a bit before ending it, turning to the crowd and motioning for them to shout their encouragement. When it was over, the triumphant warrior walked the arena in a long circle, bowing and holding out his hands to the spectators. He returned to the dark tunnel and the prisoners parted to let him through. His work was done for the day. Kaeleb had been told that they held a feast for the winners, the one time they were not forced to eat slop or gruel. He felt a small pain in his chest knowing that his escape would mean missing the promised meal.

Across the arena a heavy door swung open and a Fomori came out to retrieve the body, then disappeared back through the door. That would be Kaeleb's way out. Given that the door was solely being used for the collection of dead bodies, extra guards were unnecessary, and it would provide the most convenient path for escape.

Kaeleb waited patiently for his turn as the men paired off one by one. Some fought with swords, others with spears or maces. Hovard won his match and he returned with a pinched look on his face, his eyes haunted. He did not like killing, that was evident, but the will to survive was often greater than the will to spare another. He would choose himself, he had to. Kaeleb saw Favian grip Hovard's shoulder as he passed by, an intimate look of hope passing between them.

A shout from the arena drew his attention. Was this what he had been waiting for? A signal that it was time to escape? He peered out into the stark, cool air and saw the Va'Kul standing at the railing of the boxed seats, leaning over and shouting down at the field. Favian sighed heavily and jogged out, going to see what had disturbed the imposing creature.

"Where is the boy? I want to see him fight," she said to the Guardian.

The wiry man looked uncomfortable, tugging at the end of his long braid. "There is no other boy for him to fight. I will not put him in the arena with a grown man."

Kaeleb felt a surge of annoyance. He had already proven to the traitor Guardian that he could fight as well as any of them, and he resented the man for treating him like he was a weak child. The Va'Kul also seemed annoyed. She did not like her authority being challenged. She turned to Chaote and spoke a few quiet words, then she stalked over and grabbed one of the child servants around the neck, shoving him towards the rail.

"Very well, here is a boy for him to fight," the Va'Kul announced.

The color drained from Favian's face and for a moment he looked as though he would faint. He finally regained his composure and tried pleading with the beast. "The crowd will not want to watch a child die. It is not a wise decision."

"You are the one who wanted two children to fight," the Va'Kul pointed out. "So if a child dies then it is your fault, Guardian."

Kaeleb was rubbing his toe in the dirt in agitation. It was one thing to fight a man who was a warrior, another to have to fight a scared little boy who stood no chance against him. He snatched a sword from the cart before the Fomori guard could stop him, and he darted out onto the field to stand beside Favian.

"That boy is not worth my skill," Kaeleb sneered contemptuously. "I can take on any of the men in that tunnel. I can even fight the Guardian if you desire!"

"Are you out of your mind?" Favian hissed down at him.

"It is done," the Va'Kul said, her voice final and harsh. "The boys will fight. Do not challenge my authority again, Guardian, or your champion who is to go free will suffer a very different fate."

Favian looked stricken and he shook his head, spinning on his heel and storming back to the dark tunnel of prisoners. One of the Fomori women was hauling the servant boy down the steps behind their seats and a short while later he emerged from the tunnel, a sword being dragged along in the sand behind him. He was small, younger than Kaeleb, and soft in the way that a regent or noble child was. His pale skin was unblemished, smooth and cherubic around his cheeks, and his round, frightened eyes were a clear sky blue. He had a sweep of dark hair that lifted off his high forehead and even from a distance Kaeleb could see he was trembling in fright.

Kaeleb turned back to the halfbreed, hoping that he could reason with her since the Va'Kul would not be budged. "Mother," he called, using the honorary Fomori title for her, "Do not make me fight this sniveling wretch. Give me a worthy opponent."

Chaote leaned forward, the flecks of yellow in her eyes glittering against the endless black. "I remember you. You are the Earth Queen's little demon. I have seen you kill and I do not doubt your skill, young warrior. What I wish to test now is your resolve."

She settled back and motioned with a flick of her wrist for the fight to continue. Kaeleb scowled, turning back to face the frightened child and moving just outside of striking distance to him. He began circling the terrified little boy.

"Pick up your sword!" Kaeleb ordered harshly.

"I...I do not even know how to use it," the boy admitted, looking forlornly down at the heavy weapon.

"Pick it up with both hands, hold it like I am. Set your feet apart, like this."

The boy did as he instructed, the blade of the sword throwing gashes of light around the arena as it shook visibly in his hands.

"That is good. Now swing it at me," Kaeleb told him.

"But what if I hurt you?" the child asked softly.

Kaeleb grinned at him. "You won't hurt me, but I have an idea and I need you to trust me. Swing your sword!"

The child did as Kaeleb wished, swinging the sword in a clumsy motion that caused him to spin around in a circle. Kaeleb kicked him in the back as he tried to right himself, sending him sprawling in the dirt. The crowd cheered and Kaeleb lifted his arms to them as he had seen the other men do.

"Get up!"

The younger boy was on his knees, crying softly, tears welling out of the corners of his eyes. Kaeleb steeled himself against it.

"You are not hurt, get up! Get on your feet! I am going to swing at you, and I need you to hold the blade across your chest to block me. After that, I want you to back up several steps. Do you understand?"

The younger boy wiped his nose with the back of his hand and got to his feet, lifting his sword. Kaeleb swung, pulling the blow at the last second, using every ounce of his control to make it look like a powerful swing while barely tapping the boy's sword as it appeared to block the move. Kaeleb glanced around at the crowd and he saw a flash of golden skin and an edge of pale hair beneath a heavy cloak. It was a woman, a Leharan, and she was hastening towards the area above where the door was. He knew she was there for him and his heart soared. This was his chance.

"Good, now back up! Keep your sword up! I am sorry, this might hurt a bit," Kaeleb apologized with a sheepish grin, then he turned his own sword away and ran at the boy, barreling into him with his shoulder and sending him flailing through the air. The child hit the dirt with a hard thud and a cry, his sword skidding across the dirt away from him.

"Now I need you to die!" Kaeleb said, hoping the boy was intelligent enough to know what was happening. He was gasping for breath, his eyes wild, stricken with panic. Kaeleb straddled him and lifted his sword, plunging it down as hard as he could.

14

I watched the scene unfolding in the arena below me with a sick sense of dread. I had been waiting for hours for Kaeleb to appear, and I was starting to fear that something had already happened to him, or that Astus had been wrong, but finally he was there. He marched out of the dark hollow beneath the wall and stormed up to yell at the Fomori elite, and I could not help but smile. He was still Kaeleb; they had not broken him.

The commotion ended and Kaeleb stood in the arena, waiting. The sunlight glinted off his pale shock of hair and even from a distance I could see the firm set of his jaw. His eyes flickered through the crowd and I wondered if he was searching for me, if he had received Astus's message that I had come for him.

A solitary figure crept from the dimly lit tunnel which the warriors had been using as an entrance. There was something familiar about the boy and I squinted harder, trying to see, hoping that my luck was not as terrible as I was beginning to think it was.

Aracellis.

Maialen's son was in the arena, his sword trembling in his hands. Kaeleb was saying something to him and I turned to the far battlement, trying to find Damian in the crowd. He would not recognize Aracellis, he had never seen him, and I needed to find some way to signal the Tahitian, to let him know, but I could not pinpoint him among the throngs of spectators.

The boys were fighting and I could tell Kaeleb was holding back, trying not to hurt the other child. To everyone else it was a believable sparring, but not to me. I knew what he could do. Aracellis went flying across the ground and then Kaeleb was on top of him, lifting his sword and plunging it down. I wanted to scream at him to stop, but I knew I could not, and it was too late anyway. Kaeleb stood, wiping blood on his pants, his sword still sticking up out of the body of the other boy. He backed away, gesturing for the crowd to congratulate him on his victory. Some Samirrans were sickened, and they looked away as a Fomori came out to collect the boy's body, but most of them were cheering wildly. The beast bent over the child, tilting its head curiously and lifting the sword from the corpse.

The beast spun to face Kaeleb and I knew something was wrong. I closed my eyes, calling my power to me. For the first time since that day at the border, I did not hesitate or shrink back from it. I called it all to me, reaching out across the city, searching for what I wanted. I found it. I could feel them all, the thousands of flames that flickered within the walls. Hearths burning, food being cooked, torches lit, candles lighting the dark. I found them all and then I released it.

The city exploded. Bursts of fire thundered into the air from all over Iriellestra and people began to flee the area in shock. I opened my eyes, the sky around us filling with columns of smoke. In the arena, Kaeleb leapt onto the startled Fomori, a knife suddenly in his hand, slicing the beast's throat. The Fomori females shrieked in anger as Bacatha vaulted down into the arena, running at Kaeleb, her long legs carrying her swiftly. Her hood fell back and her blonde hair streamed out behind her like a beacon. She grabbed Kaeleb's wrist but he pointed at the prostrate child and Bacatha jerked Aracellis to his feet, blood smeared on his chest but somehow still alive. They ran for the doorway the Fomori had left open and Chaote was shouting, pointing at them, looking around desperately for a weapon. Suddenly a spear pierced through the awning, nearly impaling her and she screamed in rage, turning to see who had flung the weapon. The female Fomori were leaping down onto the field, running after the fleeing Leharan and the children. Chaote jerked the spear from where it had stuck and turned, flinging the weapon at Bacatha. It hit just as the Leharan shoved the door closed behind them, falling uselessly to the ground. The other Fomori were trying to open the door, and I was about to call my power again when there was a loud chorus of roaring indignation. The tournament competitors came tearing out of their dark tunnel, weapons in hand, going straight for the Fomori. They fell on the beasts with savage ferocity and I spun around, pushing my way through the panicked crowd, satisfied that the warriors would fend off the Fomori long enough for Kaeleb to escape.

Smoke was drifting over the palace and my eyes stung as I pressed against the wall, edging around the clamoring throngs. I needed to get to the place we had designated as our rendezvous, and I needed to do it quickly, before the Fomori were crawling all over the city looking for us.

I managed to escape the chaotic inner sanctum with the rest of the fleeing Samirrans, narrowly avoiding being trampled. As I turned onto one of the roads leading south, the sounds of panicked footsteps faded away. Ahead of me, long tongues of flame were pouring out from the windows of a cramped little row of houses. A few people were clustered together, watching helplessly as their homes burned. I skirted by, keeping my hood pulled up over my face. I could have stopped to help, but I had seen enough of the cheering Samirrans at the tournament that I was not feeling inclined to be so benevolent. I wound through the burning streets of the city and finally turned the corner to the small tea shop where we were to meet. I pushed open the door, a knot in my chest, praying to the Gods I knew were not listening that the boy was safe.

I nearly fell over, such was the force with which Kaeleb threw himself on me. His thin arms wrapped around me, his face buried in the folds of my cloak. I had never felt a comparable sense of relief in all my life, and in that moment I admitted to myself the doubt that I had always held within me, the fear that I would never find him again, that he would be gone forever like the others. I hugged him back, just as fiercely. Then I kicked the door shut and Bacatha was there, grinning, her frosty gaze dancing with excitement. Behind her Aracellis cowered, his face stained with dried tears.

"Did you see them?" Bacatha asked me breathlessly, closing her eyes to savor the memory in her mind. "All of those Fomori running at us, and that spear! I slammed the door shut just in time, a second later and it would have gone right through me! It was glorious."

"You were quite impressive," I told her magnanimously. I peeled myself out of Kaeleb's grasp so I could look him over. "Are you hurt?"

He shook his head, beaming up at me.

My gaze traveled back to Aracellis. "And you?"

"He has a few scrapes and bruises but he is unharmed," Bacatha answered for him. "The boys were quite clever. Kaeleb, tell him how you did it. Tell him how you fooled them in the arena."

Kaeleb's dirty face practically shone with joy at the attention being heaped upon him. "I pretended to stab him, but the sword went here, between his arm and his chest. Then I cut my own hand on the blade and rubbed the blood on him."

"You must be very proud of him," Bacatha said to me. I had to wonder for a moment just what her family life had been like if this was the measure of pride in a child, then I remembered she came from generations of Leharan Guards.

"I am quite proud," I assured both her and Kaeleb.

Bacatha's expression darkened, the light fading from her crystalline eyes as she went on, "The old man will not be pleased that we did not rescue his nephew. We may have a problem getting out of the city."

I grinned at her. "Oh, but we did find him. Bacatha, Kaeleb, meet Aracellis."

The Samirran child waved his hand in an awkward greeting and Bacatha laughed heartily, slapping me on the back. "You are one lucky Verucan, you know that?"

"Sometimes it does not feel that way. Where is Damian?" I asked, striding to the broken window and peering out. Dark breaths of smoke were wafting down the street, making visibility difficult. Upon our arrival in the city, Thyrr had pretended to go with us. Then he had split off and circled back to wait near the entrance to the tunnels, hiding and watching in case we could not fulfill our end of the bargain. He would be ready if we needed to overpower Astus's band of zealots and ensure they did not betray us or lead us back into a trap.

"The Tahitian will be here soon. I am sure of it." Bacatha was confident.

Kaeleb joined me at the window, staring out impatiently. I could not blame him. I was sure he was ready to get out of this cursed city of death as soon as possible.

Time seemed to drag on forever and there was no sign of Damian. I began to pace back and forth, prowling the room like a caged animal. My trepidation grew with each passing moment, and finally I could stand waiting no longer.

"I am going to look for him," I said, starting for the door. Kaeleb darted in front of me, blocking it with his body.

"No!" Bacatha protested. "We need to get the children out of here. We have given him enough time, Blaise."

"You want to just leave him here?" I demanded, incredulous. I was incredulous with myself as well, for caring about what happened to the Tahitian.

"He knew the plan. He will understand. It is possible that he realized he would not make it here in time and went straight to the tunnels to meet us," she said reasonably.

Perhaps she was right. Either way, we needed to leave. I nodded my head and Bacatha grabbed Aracellis by the hand, dragging him behind her in a dazed stupor as we headed out into the street. We had barely turned the corner when we came face to face with a group of Fomori, the charred scent of the fires that ravaged the city masking their telltale smell.

"If you had let me bring the farming tool, this would be much easier," Bacatha complained, throwing back her heavy cloak and whipping her sword from its sheath.

"You needed to be fast. It was cumbersome and would have slowed you down," I pointed out yet again. She drew back to strike, but before either of us could attack there was a blur of white and brown.

Kaeleb shot out like lightning, sliding in the dirt at the last minute and skidding between the legs of the closest beast, slicing their ankles with a curved dagger, the perfect weapon for the task to which he employed it.

There was fire all around us and it was easy to summon it to the snarling Fomori as they bent to try to catch the quick boy who was slashing maniacally at the tender spots behind their knees and ankles. In moments, they were engulfed in flames and Kaeleb crawled back to us as the creatures howled in rage, trying in vain to outrun the fire that burned them. He was wiping at the sprays of black blood with disgust.

"How many knives do you have?" I asked him, raising an eyebrow. This was the second weapon he had produced from the folds of his clothing.

"They left a whole cart of weapons just sitting there with one Fomori guarding it," he explained, as if it was their fault for leaving so tempting an offer out for him. He tucked the knife into his waistband.

I recognized the weapon. It was an ornamental item from the palace, made by the finest craftsmen for deadly precision but never intended to actually be used in combat. "Keep that one. It is quite the prize."

Aracellis was watching all of this with wide, watery eyes, and I feared he would start crying at any moment. Bacatha snatched him up again and this time she tossed him over her shoulder as we ran.

Thyrr was waiting where we had left him, stepping out from his hiding spot as we raced past him. I assumed this meant that nothing had gone awry with the Samirrans and our escape was still guaranteed.

"Where is Damian?" he called, stopping to look in the direction from which we had come.

I shook my head. "We were hoping he was here already."

Thyrr pushed a hand through his hair and hesitated, indecision pulling at his arrogant features. It was at that moment the group of Harbonah acolytes streamed out of hiding and surrounded us, ushering us towards the ramshackle little hovel that leaned haphazardly against the outer wall of the city. One of the Samirrans held up the trapdoor and I grabbed the bar that had been placed across the opening and swung myself down, dropping into the ten-foot shaft that led to the tunnels. Kaeleb followed me, then Bacatha, still awkwardly carrying Aracellis, and I gave her a slight nod in acknowledgement of her agility. I could hear Thyrr arguing with the men, wanting to wait for Damian, but they were adamant that we leave now.

"Thyrr! He knows where to go. There is no point in waiting," I called up from the shaft.

The young man relented and dropped down behind us. We ran through the tunnels, out of the burning city, and I found myself once more praying to the absent Gods that the Tahitian would come thundering after us.

15

Logaire frowned at the man who stood before her. He was a dour-looking peasant with a pinched face named Carsican, and he had come to the castle to protest the foul and unjust murder of his two brothers. Akrin, the accused murderer, sat beside Logaire, a smile toying at his thin lips. She hated that he had brought another throne into the room, and that it was slightly taller than the one she occupied. The little weasel had done it on purpose, just to get under her skin, and it had worked.

"Your brethren were accused of treason," Akrin said, as if this whole charade was too preposterous to be bothered with. "The penalty for treason is death."

"They were not traitors!" Carsican insisted, addressing Logaire and refusing to look at the dour young man. Logaire could not blame him. She wished she did not have to look at Akrin either.

"They confessed," Akrin countered.

"Because you tortured them," the peasant exclaimed. "Please, Your Highness, my brothers were not traitors! Ask the oracle if you do not believe me! They did not deserve to die."

Akrin made a noise of disgust and flopped back on his throne. "Logaire, why are you listening to this nonsense?"

She clenched her teeth. She detested the sound of her name on his lips. "It is my duty to hear the grievances of my subjects."

"You mean OUR subjects," Akrin reminded her.

She ignored him, focusing her attention back on the middle-aged man who stood before her. "I am sorry for the loss you have suffered, but it is all too common for a family to defend its members staunchly, no matter how much proof there is to the contrary."

"What proof?" Carsican demanded. "He has no proof because it is not true!"

Logaire smiled pityingly. "You have admitted yourself that they confessed. What can I do? They are confessed traitors, and besides, I cannot bring them back to life. What I can do is return half of your tithe for the upcoming season. This should help mitigate the cost of losing your kin."

Carsican sighed and nodded, bowing slightly before backing away. He must have known he would never get justice for his murdered family, and he was wise to accept her offer and move on before Akrin decided he was also a danger to the kingdom. Once the man was gone, Logaire glanced at Vishram who stood nearby with the scroll of grievances for that day. She was relieved when he shook his head, showing that she was finally done hearing everyone's incessant, trivial complaints.

"I cannot believe you are letting him have half a tithe," Akrin muttered, the smile gone now that he had no prey to toy with. He was once again sullen and pouting, his heavy brows drawn together.

"And I cannot believe that you are unable to do one simple task without going on a murderous rampage," she snapped at him. "One of these days someone is going to come seeking revenge for the things you have done."

"Is that someone you?" he asked, his slightly nasal voice trying to be low and threatening. She wanted to laugh at him, but she knew that would not go well for her.

"Of course not. I am just concerned for your welfare. You know I find you invaluable, and I would hate it should something unfortunate befall you," Logaire assured him, wishing with all her heart that something unfortunate would befall him. She was not discerning; she would be pleased with any sort of unfortunate event. A falling rock crushing his head, some bad mushrooms in the stew, a slip off the deck of a ship. She did not care how it happened, she only wanted him gone.

Logaire rose, her golden folds of gown cascading down her long legs and puddling on the obsidian rock beneath her feet. She could not even enjoy wearing her new gown when Akrin was around. He ruined everything with his sullen, sick presence.

She paused, thinking back over the encounter with Carsican. "What did he mean when he said to ask the oracle?"

Akrin's brows drew even further together. "Ridiculous notions some of the villagers are claiming. It is completely preposterous."

"Tell me these claims," Logaire said silkily.

"There is a woman they claim can foretell the future. It is a peasant with mad ramblings, nothing more, and as soon as I find her I will put an end to it," Akrin promised.

Vishram stepped out of the shadows where he had been waiting, indicating that it was time to proceed to the feast. Another feast, another charade to pacify the regents and nobles where she would be forced to smile and laugh at their ill attempts to humor and flatter her. The gatherings had been exciting at first, but now the mundane tedium of the evenings bored her to tears and she understood why her cousin had avoided such encounters.

Vishram walked beside her as they made their way to the dining hall, leaving Akrin to sulk on his throne. Logaire hoped he would remain there and not join the lavish dinner, for he tended to make her guests quite uncomfortable. It was one thing to keep a dog in the house to chase the vermin, quite another to have the dog dine at the table with you.

"I believe Akrin is trying to conceal knowledge from you, my Queen," Vishram said in hushed tones.

"What sort of knowledge?" Logaire asked, impatient and wanting to think of anything besides the horrible young man.

"The Oracle."

Logaire stopped, her interest peaked. She turned to face Vishram with eager golden eyes. "Tell me what you know."

"There is a woman who claims to see the future, that much is true. But this is not some simple peasant. She has grown immensely popular with the people. I hear whispers of her spoken throughout the castle and Verucans are traveling from all over the realm to see her and hear her prophecies. They speak of her reverently, as the teller of truths and the seer of the unseen," Vishram explained.

"So, she is clever," Logaire deduced.

"Quite," Vishram agreed. "And I believe she presents you with a unique opportunity, my Queen. You must go and see this woman."

Logaire laughed in disbelief. "I do not believe in such nonsense, Vishram, and I am surprised that you would be taken in by it."

"Of course, I do not believe it myself, but what does it matter if we believe? Your people believe. This is a way for you to become beloved by them. Go to the Oracle, win her to your side, then you will publicly show your support of her. Build her a temple, a place where you can cultivate worshippers who will blindly follow whatever the Oracle says. The Oracle that you will guide and provide patronage to."

Logaire was warming to his words, her tongue darting across her lips as her mind skipped ahead of Vishram. "We can end the rebellion by giving the peasants what they want. They will not care about Blaise or his silly fire tricks any longer. We can also counter the influence of the Solvrei and the Tahitian prophecies."

"Precisely. You are a wise woman, my Queen," Vishram said, bowing low in deference. "Give the people someone else to worship. Take away the power of the former king and this supposed savior and return that power and influence to Veruca and you will be beloved for it!"

"Vishram, plan this little excursion into the countryside. I am eager to meet the new beneficiary of our patronage as soon as possible," Logaire told him, her full red lips smiling with pleasure.

16

Damian gritted his teeth as he was pushed to his knees in the dirt, the clawed hands of the Fomori heavy on his shoulders. The fight was still raging around them, a fight that he had instigated, and he let himself smile with satisfaction.

"Do not be too pleased with yourself. They will all be dead soon," Chaote snapped, wiping blood from her lip where he had struck her.

After the city had gone up in flames, Damian had stood amongst the fleeing Samirrans, throwing back his hood and bellowing the blood-curdling Tahitian war cry.

His voice carried over the panicked throngs as he shouted, "How can you let your invaders sit comfortably on the Samirran throne? How can you let them entertain themselves with games at the expense of your own people? Look, Samirrans! Look at the bravest among you, and he is not even one of you! Look at the one who has challenged your enslavers, your captors! A boy! Am I to believe that one Leharan boy is braver than all the men of Samirra? Rise up, show them you will not be tamed by their evil deeds, that you will not be meek in the face of their threats. Rise up and fight with me, fight for Samirra!"

The big islander had turned, hurtling his spear through the air at Chaote. She hollered with rage and Damian bellowed once again. Samirrans began to turn on the Fomori, grabbing whatever they could to use as weapons. In the arena he saw the other warriors were fighting the Fomori women, but Bacatha and the boys were gone. They had escaped.

"My brother!" a voice pierced through the cacophony that surrounded Damian and there, in the center of the arena, was Chaote, shining in the sun like a dazzling jewel, her gaze fixed on him.

"I am not your brother," he shouted back at her.

"Have it your way," she said with a shrug, her armor glinting with every movement. A man rushed at her and she sidestepped him, twisting his arm back so that his sword sliced open his own abdomen. She had never even taken her eyes off Damian. "Come down here and fight me!"

This was what he had wanted for the last ten years, what he had been waiting for. The chance for redemption or to die a warrior's death. He did not care which happened, he only knew that he had to fight her. He shoved through the angry mob and dropped down from the wall, landing lightly on his feet in the arena. One of the Fomori women saw him and started forward with a snarl but Chaote let out a warning shout, motioning for the creature to back away.

"No, Va'Kul. This one will be mine." Chaote spread her arms wide in invitation. She had no weapon, nothing other than her own body ensconced in gleaming golden armor. Damian circled her warily, watching her, looking for weaknesses, but she gave nothing away. She turned slowly with him, her arms still spread wide, a knowing smile adorning her perfect face. He had never seen anything so beautiful.

"You do not have to do this," he began.

She laughed, a warm, throaty sound. "If you knew how many times I have heard that speech, Tahitian, you would not bother. The other mouths that uttered those same words are now silenced forever."

"My name is Damian and you are one of us, you are Tahitian. Come home, be with your people," he urged, his deep baritone resonating with gentleness.

"Words of invitation as you attack me, and you expect me to listen?" she challenged. "The promises of a liar, descended from liars. I tried to come home once, Damian. It did not end well for me."

He stopped circling, stood facing her. She ran at him and he was not prepared for such a direct attack. She swung her left foot up into the air, kicking him under the chin and tossing him back in the dirt. He was on his feet in a heartbeat, shaking his head to clear it. He had underestimated her. She lunged for him again and he was prepared for her now, ducking the blow, his elbow connecting with her face. Blood pooled over her lip and she spat it onto the ground. She ran at him once again but this time she parried at the last minute, twisting to the side and delivering him a solid blow to the gut before dancing away.

"Getting tired?" she asked with a bloody grin.

He looked around and realized they were surrounded by the Fomori. No matter what happened next, he accepted that he would not be leaving the arena alive.

He struck out with his fist and she grabbed the arm, using his own momentum against him, pulling him towards her and kicking his feet out from under him while tossing him to the ground. She was on his back, one arm around his throat and one hand splayed on the back of his head, pressing his face into the dirt.

"You are lucky you drew blood," she whispered in his ear. "Otherwise, I would rip your head off."

"I am prepared to die," Damian managed to spit out through the dirt. "But I deserve to die on my feet."

"I am not killing you, my brother. Not just yet," she promised, her voice a melody against his ear. She motioned to the nearby Fomori. "Come, take him."

The one they called the Va'Kul intervened. "We should kill him."

"Did I not just give an order?" Chaote's voice hardened, was now the promise of death if she was not obeyed.

The Va'Kul stepped back, inclining her head in acquiescence, though Damian could see the flare of resentment in the eerie yellow eyes. "Yes, Mother."

He was now on his knees in the dirt, waiting to hear what punishment the leader of the Fomori had in store for him.

"I want him clean and properly attired, then bring him to me," Chaote said curtly before stalking off. "I want the others found. As for the rebellious Samirrans, anyone who has raised a hand against us today will be put to death!"

The Va'Kul was scowling at Damian hatefully, her inhuman gaze never wavering as the Fomori who held him dragged him to his feet and led him away, several other beasts crowding around them to ensure that he would have no further opportunity to escape. They took him through the dark tunnel the warriors had used, now awash in blood. Bodies littered the floor and the Fomori shoved them out of the way callously with their feet. They passed one man who was still alive, a bent man whose head hung low, his face obscured as he wept. A body was draped across his feet and he held it against him, resting the lifeless head gently on his chest and stroking the dead man's bearded face. His long braid of hair was stained with blood, both human and Fomori, and Damian felt a jolt of recognition.

"Favian!" he exclaimed, trying to turn toward his fellow Guardian. The Fomori forced him to keep moving down the corridor and he twisted his head around, shouting back over the throng of beasts that encircled him. The man lifted his tear-stained face and his expression was so tortured, so haunted, that Damian flinched involuntarily at the sight of him. His cries died in his throat. The man that stared back at him was not the man he had known. Favian was broken.

17

"You must take him with you," Astus was insisting, trying to press my hands between his own in a gesture of pleading. Feeling the damp, papery skin of his aging palms was an unsettling sensation, one that caused me to jerk away in disgust. Less than a day had passed since the old man had threatened to kill me, and I was not inclined to be granting him favors. Especially not when Damian was still missing, trapped somewhere inside Iriellestra.

"I do not have the time or the means to take care of a child," I said. "If you want to take him to his mother, which you should have done a long time ago, that is your choice. Do not try to saddle me with your burdens."

"But you already have one child with you," Astus protested.

I scoffed, reminding the old man of the lie they still believed. "Kaeleb is no child, he is the Solvrei."

"Yes, you are right, he is no ordinary boy, but look at me, Fire Keeper. I am an old man. I cannot protect Aracellis," Astus confessed. He motioned at the child, Maialen's child, who slept peacefully in the corner of the room, Bacatha's cloak wrapped around him. Astus stepped closer to me as if he could sense a crack in my resolve. The stray hairs quivered on his age-spotted scalp and he looked so desperate that I worried my continued refusal would cause him to prostrate himself on the ground and beg.

"You have an entire flock of addle-brained worshippers at your disposal who can watch over him for you," I pointed out, waving at the Samirrans who were grouped together across the tavern.

The old man's rheumy eyes flashed with irritation. "I cannot trust anyone but you. Please, you must take him!"

"When did I become Imbria's babysitter and the man to be entrusted with all of its children? This is ridiculous and I will not be swayed," I insisted stubbornly. I could not help but wonder what it was about me that was making everyone believe I was the savior of lost children. I had come for Kaeleb twice now, but aside from that, my history of deeds would not lend one to believe that I should be given the care of helpless waifs. If Damian was there, he could have attested to that.

Thyrr cleared his throat, stirring from his silence as sat at the table beside us, leaning on his elbows. "Even if we agreed to take the child, we are not leaving without Damian."

"You are fools!" Astus cried in exasperation. He spun on Kaeleb, who was now seated beside Thyrr. "Solvrei, I beg of you. Take my grandson with you, protect him with your divine power!"

Kaeleb stared at the old man, his steely gaze flat and unmoved. There was a line of tension in his body and I wondered what the extent of Astus's influence over Kaeleb's upbringing had truly been. The boy was not pleased to see him. When we entered the tavern Kaeleb had not spoken a word. He simply stared at the old man, just as he was staring now. Astus had attempted to fuss over him and Aracellis, mumbling prayers of gratitude in the ancient language that I grasped pieces of but did not fully comprehend. Kaeleb had scowled, recoiling from the old man's grasping, fluttering hands and moving away to sit, keeping the safety of a table between him and the former king.

"Do not put your burdens on him," I warned Astus, my tone growing harsh.

Kaeleb began swinging his feet under the bench, his face scrunched up in thought. "We should take Aracellis. He should not be left with the Harbonah."

I glared at Astus, my amber eyes burning with hostility, wondering once again what he had done to the boy to make him say such things. Perhaps it was better if I did not know. I had the nagging suspicion that whatever it was, my learning of it would lead to me killing the old man. "Very well. We will take the child to Maialen, but we are not leaving until we have found Damian."

Astus gestured to a man who rose obediently and left the tavern. I assumed he was assigned the task of discovering what had happened to Damian, and we would be forced to sit here and wait in the Harbonah's unsettling company.

"The least you could do is give us some food," Thyrr muttered. Kaeleb perked up beside him, looking around in eager anticipation. Astus made another motion and another man stood, disappearing into the kitchens. Soon we were all eating, all but Aracellis, who was still sleeping soundly in the corner of the room, snoring softly. The meal was not a lavish affair, and the cracked plates held meager amounts of bland food, a few turnips and some slices of potato. Kaeleb dug in heartily, though without joy, grimacing with disappointment after every bite.

I looked at Astus thoughtfully as I chewed, saying between mouthfuls, "Tell me, old man, how you have reconciled being the Harbonah who calls for the destruction of the amulets when you and your son were both Keepers."

Astus sighed and his shoulders rounded forward, as if pressed down by the weight of the world. "I always hated the power, the awful pull of it, like something cruel and vicious calling to you from the shadows. You must know what I mean, for now it flows even more strongly within you than ever before."

As soon as he said the words his face paled and he looked down, shoving a large spoonful of soupy turnips into his mouth. Suspicion curled within my gut.

"What do you know about my power?" I demanded.

"Nothing, nothing," he insisted, waving his hands. "I am only rambling."

"Astus," I warned. "You can no longer claim mad ramblings. If there is something you know about the Elements, you had better tell me now or I will take your grandson back to the Fomori and this time I will make sure that Chaote knows exactly who he is."

Astus glared at me, defiant. "You would not."

"Try me."

He shook his head. "It is not of consequence, Fire Keeper. What I have done has made no difference. None of you knew anything was different."

My temper was rising with each cryptic admission. "What did you do?"

Astus looked as uncomfortable as I had ever seen him. His voice lowered and Thyrr and Bacatha both leaned forward, straining to hear as he admitted, "I made a bargain to save my son."

"Your son is dead," I pointed out cruelly.

"I am quite aware of that! I was there when he died."

"I am growing weary of having to coerce the truth from you, old man. Spit it out."

"You will not believe me," Astus said, shaking his head, the white hairs fluttering. He began to tell us about a God who walked among us, one who had been banished to Imbria as punishment for defying the others. Astus had found this God and begged them for help. Astus hated the amulet, hated the power, and he wanted to be rid of it. He did not want to feel it any longer, but he was too afraid to admit to the other Keepers how he felt, and too weak to tell his wife that he did not want to pass the amulet to their son. He knew, even then, that Astraeus was the sort of man who would be corrupted by the Element. His son would not be able to resist the dark whispers of the power. He asked the God to have mercy on him and his son, and the God granted his request, as long as he did something for them in return. They wanted him to gather followers for the coming war, followers that would be loyal to the Solvrei. He agreed.

"What form did the mercy of the Fenris take?" I asked him, wanting to see how he would react to my knowledge of his mysterious divine being. The old man's eyes widened and his lips parted slightly as he inhaled a sharp breath.

"You know of them? How? Where are they? I have been waiting for so long and they have not returned." Astus seemed despondent for a moment, then he recovered his wits. "I will have patience. Wherever they are, I am sure they are doing what is needed."

"Or they have no further use for an old man who let his kingdom fall to the enemy while he was too busy pretending to be mad," I suggested unkindly. "And gathering followers for the Solvrei is not the same as plotting against Keepers and trying to murder them."

"I did not sanction your murder, if that is what you speak of. That attempt was made by Alita and her father," Astus protested.

"Because of your teachings."

"Alita never followed the teachings properly, that was her mistake in the end," Astus said, shaking his head. He glanced at Kaeleb, a look full of guilt and fear.

I raised my eyebrows. "You had Alita murdered."

His eyes roamed around the room as if searching for someone to save him. I waved a hand in front of his face, causing him to flinch and focus his attention back on me. The old man stammered, "Alita never would listen. She always believed that her way was better. She was not supposed to take the boy to the Council at Kymir. It was too soon. Then she was taken captive.... she knew too much. I could not risk what she would say to save herself."

"So even your own devoted followers are not immune to your treachery." I was repulsed but I hid my revulsion, grinning in condescension, knowing he would hate it.

A shadow passed over his face. "You are trying to goad me, Fire Keeper. I will not let you."

I shrugged. "Tell me about the bargain with the Fenris."

It was revealed to Astus that the amulets and the power of the Elements had not been created by the Fenris, and so they could not be destroyed by them either. The Fenris had also grown weaker over the years. Centuries of living in a mortal world had eroded the essence of their being. The only thing the God could do for Astus was to manipulate the power between the amulets. They took away as much of the Sapphire's power as they could and forced it into the other amulets.

I sat watching him, my fingers tapping a subtle rhythm on the table. I kept the smile on my face, an easy grin that belied the tumultuous thoughts that were racing through my mind. What Astus had done changed all of us. This was why Astraeus had been so weak and why the rest of us were stronger than the Keepers who had existed before, why I felt the overwhelming presence of the Fire Opal constantly burning in me, why Orabelle had been able to do things like create the Sirens, why she could still speak to her child through the amulet. I thought it was the Water Queen who had done something to bring about the strange happenings, but it had been Astus. He had tried to ease his own burden by cursing the rest of us, and Orabelle must have taken on more than anyone.

I thought it over for a moment, knowing what I wanted to do, wondering briefly if it was the best decision, realizing there would be consequences I had not yet foreseen. I remembered Kaeleb's face as he looked at the old man, his warning that we could not leave Aracellis with him. I glanced at the boy now and he was staring back at me intently, his grey eyes alert, his spoon paused halfway to his mouth. He gave me a slight nod, the barest movement of his head. That was all the justification I needed.

I lunged across the table and grabbed the former king's head in my hands, seeing the dull blue eyes, the whites tinged yellow with aged and tangled with blood-red veins. I twisted my hands and his neck snapped with a crack that seemed to echo throughout the room. I released him and he collapsed on the table, splattering food.

My companions were on their feet, weapons drawn, facing the shocked group of Samirrans who were staring, mouths agape, at the corpse of their former leader.

"There is no reason for all of you to die," Bacatha warned them. "We will wait for word of Damian and then we will leave here peacefully."

One man began wailing with grief and he ran at the Leharan, throwing himself on her. He was weaponless, and she shoved him off, striking him across the back with the scythe. I saw the indecision warring on the faces of the others, wondering if they would survive, if it was their duty to try to avenge their dead leader. Before they could react, I lifted my palm and fire poured out of the hearth, weaving through the room and circling all of them in its hot embrace. I let it recede after a moment and the Samirrans retreated to the back of the room once more, heeding my not-so-subtle warning.

"Grandfather?" Aracellis had awoken and was staring wide eyed at the fire, his cherubic face puffy with sleep.

"Your grandfather has exhausted himself. He is sleeping," I said gruffly.

Kaeleb stood up and lifted the old man's head off the plate of food, resting it back on the table and taking the plate to Aracellis. Kaeleb sat in front of the child, blocking the view of the body while the boy took small bites, his hands still trembling. I felt a wave of pity for him. He had been through so much recently, and the least we could do for him now that I had killed his grandfather was to take him to his mother. I also could not help but consider the benefit of Maialen's gratitude when I returned her son to her. The Earth Queen would owe me, and I needed as many favors now as I could gather.

The Samirrans began to whisper to one another and Thyrr chastised them with a click of his tongue. "None of that. There will be no plotting. You will remain silent or my friend here will make sure that you never speak with that tongue again."

Bacatha smiled, clearly pleased to have been named the harbinger of torture and doom. She stood watching over the men, her favored farming tool grasped in her hands.

"That was not the wisest course of action, my friend," Thyrr hissed at me, indicating the lifeless form of the former Samirran king.

I lifted my hand as if to say it could not be helped. "That old man was of no use to anyone alive."

"That may be true, but now the Samirrans will not help us."

"If Damian is dead, then we do not need their help," I pointed out.

Thyrr said nothing more, folding his arms over his chest and returning to his seat. We all waited, the tension in the room building with each passing moment.

18

Damian was escorted out into the high upper courtyard of the Samirran palace, the balconied expanse between the domed minarets. An eagle was perched in the center of the clearing, preening its immaculate white feathers with quick dips of its massive head. The Fomori guard pushed him forward, and he saw Chaote standing on the other side of the winged creature, leaning on the elaborately carved lattice that encircled the open space. She was still adorned in her golden armor, the setting sun glaring off the metal and reflecting around the palace like a thousand sparks. She turned her head to look at Damian, the movement so graceful and powerful that it was hard to watch.

"Come, my brother," she said, motioning him to join her. "Look out at the city you have set fire to."

He did as she commanded, his head held high despite the chains that shackled his wrists. He stared off at the horizon, over the tall pillars of smoke that billowed around them.

"You do not wish to see?" she remarked, and there was a hint of humor in her tone, as if she was amused that he preferred not to look.

"Samirra is burning because of you," he said darkly.

She laughed. "This entire realm was a festering sore when I took it. It was only a matter of time before it collapsed in on itself. Could you not see that? Or were you hiding from it all, locked away from the rest of the world in the Keeper's Wasteland? They created it for me, you know. The Wasteland. It was their first attempt at a prison for me and my brethren. A failure in the end, but nevertheless a painful one to endure for so many years."

"You do not want this realm. You want revenge. Let the Samirrans go," Damian said.

She squinted up at him curiously. It had been a long time since she had seen another Tahitian. He was not as dark as her, though he was still one of the beautiful shades of night. Tall, broad, muscular. A warrior. His face was strong planes and distinct lines, a noble face. Long dreadlocks hung down his back, still the preferred style of the men, that had not changed. Or perhaps it had, but she had been gone so long that the favored look had circled back and been born anew. There were silver hooks through his ears and she wondered when the islanders had stopped using bone in favor of the shiny metal.

She said, "I let the Samirrans go. They came running back to me, like pathetic lost sheep, turned away by the wolves that roam your land in the guise of Keepers. They are the ones who stopped the Samirrans from reaching Kymir. It was the Keepers who tore open the land and filled it with fire, not me."

"Then leave the city to the Samirrans. You do not want it."

Anger flashed across the perfection of her face. Vicious, deep, unending wrath. "They do not deserve it! Let me tell you a story, my brother, a story that the Samains of Tahitia and your precious Keepers have forgotten."

Damian stood impassive, still fixed on the horizon. He had no choice but to listen as she began to tell him of the world in her time, before she had been trapped underground for centuries. The four realms did not yet exist and the world was smaller then. The land was divided by tribes, each existing almost entirely on their own, independent and autonomous. The Fomori were the cruelest of them all, this much was true, but they were part of the world and their land was the fertile land that was now called Samirra.

"The Keepers did not care about the Fomori or their atrocities," Chaote sneered. "The first of them to wield the amulets were clan leaders, tribal chiefs, men and women who led others but had never lifted a finger to save anyone from the savage Fomori. Then they were given their powers, bestowed with the great gifts of the amulets, and all of that changed. They began to bring the tribes together, to consolidate power and land and claim it for their own, all under the guise of protecting people. They realized they would have to feed these people they were gathering together, and they turned their ravenous gazes to the northwest. The land was fertile, the rivers flowed, and the valleys were wide and perfect for farming. It was then that the Keepers decided they could no longer tolerate the hateful deeds of the dreaded Fomori. They inflamed the other tribes, embellished the accounts of cruelty, sowed fear across the world. Then they came for us, and I was caught up in it all, an unwilling pawn, a piece of refuse to be discarded. The Keepers stole this land from the Fomori, and they did it savagely and without remorse, driving those of us they could find to that hateful wasteland in the south, slaughtering others, and forcing the rest to flee into the inhospitable mountains of the north. I have taken nothing from the Samirrans. I have simply taken back what was ours all along."

Damian was silent for a long while, the columns of smoke dancing with the wind, the smell of char and death floating on the air with fragile bits of ash that clung to their hair and marred the shining splendor of her armor. Finally, he said to her, "Come home. End all this and come home to Tahitia."

Chaote's endless gaze was suddenly filled with so much pain that it seemed unendurable. It was a bottomless chasm, a plea, a cry, a desperate grasping for something, someone, anyone, to pull her out of the nightmarish abyss where she was trapped. Then her features softened and smoothed and she was cold, unreachable once again.

She said, "I can never go home. They took my home from me."

Damian was surprised to feel pity, even after all she had done. "You can still come home. Let the Fomori have Samirra and release the Samirrans. We will find a place for them. The Keepers were afraid before, unprepared. There was plague."

"A plague that I ended," she practically snarled. "And yet they still pretend I am a monster! I am trying to keep this cursed kingdom and its ungrateful populace alive and look at what I get for my troubles! Rebellion and bloodshed. I have held back the Fomori, kept them from slaughtering this wretched race of weaklings."

"You cannot keep living between two worlds. You claim to be a Fomori, but you are a Tahitian. I can see it. It is in your blood and it is in your every movement, your every word."

She was unmoved. "The Tahitians will never accept what I am or what I have to do. I will not stop until I have destroyed the amulets and rid this world of their corrupted power. Tell me, Damian, would your fellow islanders join me in this fight? Would they offer restitution for the crimes committed against me and my family in the past? No, they will not. The Tahitians cower behind the Keepers, weak-willed servants to their vile whims, and you are the worst of them, a Guardian. You, my brother, you are their champion."

"Why am I here, Chaote?" Damian asked, his deep baritone barely audible.

She smiled at him, a dazzling sight, the kind of sight that one wishes to see before the world ends. "I know the Tahitians have the Solvrei, and I am hoping they will be foolish enough to bring her here to save you."

19

The awkward standoff in the tavern ended when the messenger returned to tell us that Damian was a captive of the Fomori and he was being held in the palace by Chaote herself. There was no way that we could reach him on our own, not even with my power, for the Fomori still held the Warding Stones and I would be useless in proximity to them. We needed help. If we could bring the armies of Kymir, Lehar and Tahitia together against the Fomori, we could save Damian, liberate Samirra and crush Chaote and her advance before they even looked towards Veruca. I had to admit, Damian's capture could prove quite useful to me in the end. The return of Maialen's child was all that we needed to bring her to our side, and with her came Lehar.

"Do not do anything rash," Bacatha was cautioning the Samirrans as we backed out of the tavern. She had picked up Aracellis and I could hear him asking her why his grandfather had not awoken. She ignored him. I was the last one out the door, and I touched my fingers to the edge of my amulet as the tavern burst into flames.

I turned to find Kaeleb scowling at me.

"It had to be done. They knew too much about us. They would have ratted us out in half a second or hunted us down themselves," I told him, not caring to be reproached for my methods.

"You could have waited till he was out of sight of it," Kaeleb admonished, pointing at Aracellis. Bacatha had thrown her hooded cape over his head to keep him from seeing the raging flames that were devouring the building his grandfather was supposedly sleeping in.

"Well, I did not think about that," I retorted irritably. "I was thinking about keeping us alive."

Kaeleb nodded, his face clearing. He walked along beside me as we untethered the horses the Samirran acolytes had left outside. "When we are in Kymir, do you think I can have some of the berry fritters from the manor?"

"Kaeleb, did you offer to take Aracellis just so we could go to Kymir and get pastries?" I questioned him with a sidelong glance as I settled into the saddle of my horse.

The boy was grinning. "They have the best pastries on Imbria. And I have eaten nothing but slop for days now. It is a miracle I have not starved to death."

We rode northeast, away from the smoldering city of Iriellestra, taking the longest and most indirect path to Kymir and hoping that Chaote would waste most of her resources looking for us in the south. It was a cold, bitter trek, and we were soon knee deep in snow, which I detested above all other things. The horses did not seem to mind, and we raided yet another abandoned farm for warmer clothes for the boys, so we were all at least somewhat properly attired. Kaeleb complained constantly about his lack of a sword, and at the farm Bacatha scoured the property for tools that could be used as weapons, but anything useful had been taken. She had grudgingly given him her own sword to hold, but the weapon was much too long for his compact frame and it dragged on the ground as he walked. He returned the sword to her and resigned himself to the decorative knife he had stolen in Samirra that he kept stuck in his waistband.

"I had not expected you to be so mothering," Thyrr commented to Bacatha with a laugh one evening. We had decided to camp for the night at the deserted farm. It was risky, for the solid structure could attract other wayward vagabonds with the promise of a warm shelter, but we were tired of the cold and decided it was worth the risk. We were in the main house, horses and all, our sleeping mats spread in a circle in the large kitchen. A fire burned in the fireplace and it must have been a charming cottage once, before it had been ransacked and left to rot.

Bacatha glowered at Thyrr. "I only tolerate it because none of you have offered to help. The child smells horrible, like all children do."

Aracellis was sleeping in front of the fire, curled in her cloak. He was a quiet, contemplative child. Once the shock of what had happened in the arena had worn off, he had been no trouble, obeying commands without question and staying mostly silent, speaking in soft, hushed tones when spoken to. He did not ask questions about his mother and accepted that we were taking him to her with emotionless acquiescence. I wondered if he blamed her for not coming for him after his father died. Children did those sorts of things, blamed their parents for not knowing the truth. It was only later, when the world had pressed its boot upon their own necks and they knew the insistent bitterness of regret, that they could begin to understand the choices their parents had made.

"I want to come back with you when you return for the Tahitian," Kaeleb said to me that same evening.

"I would prefer you to be safely away from that fight," I countered, smiling at him to ease the sting I knew those words would bring.

He shook his head. "Damian was captured saving me. It is the right thing to do. I will go back with you or I will follow you there on my own."

"You are a stubborn lad," I told him, giving him a gentle nudge on the shoulder. "Very well, you may return and fight for the glory of Samirra."

"Ugh, no!" he countered. "I would never fight for Samirrans. They are soft and weak, with pale limbs like swan necks and just as easy to break. It is no wonder their entire kingdom was captured."

"Tell me, my boy, how would you get into the city with your army? What should our strategy be?" I asked, and he grinned up at me. We stayed up late into the night debating plans, Bacatha and Thyrr joining in with bold exclamations, mocking each other's ridiculous ideas and leaving all of us in fits of laughter.

The next day we left the warm comradery of the farm behind us and trudged back into the snow. The icy chill of winter bit through my clothing and caused me to shiver constantly, a state of being that infuriated me immensely. I was tempted to use my power to carry a small flame with me for warmth, but I did not want to risk being seen or drawing unwanted attention, and so I suffered in silence. Mountains rose in the distance, shadowed monoliths that promised pain. Eventually, a few sparse trees began to appear on our path and we saw the first blackened remains of an ancient pine. We were nearing the divide.

Besides the incessant shivering that it caused, there was a desolation to the snow that I had always hated. The pale whiteness of it was too fragile, too harsh. To me, it was the silent component that death was made of, a cold and empty thing that ended life where it lay. Here, surrounded by the skeletal trees of the forest I had inadvertently burned, the cessation of life was even more poignant.

"There," Thyrr interrupted the bleak quiet. He was pointing to the long, black scar that ripped across the land. The divide between Samirra and Kymir. I had hoped it would be narrow enough to cross over since we had come so far north, but it was still as wide and gaping as the southern end of it.

"Should we ride further north and see if it narrows?" Bacatha asked.

"It does not." It was Aracellis's quiet voice that spoke. We all turned to look at him where he was perched on the saddle in front of the Leharan woman. "In Samirra, when the Fomori captured me, I heard them speaking of it. They said it was unpassable as far as the eagles had gone. They were trying to find a place to build a bridge, somewhere my mother would not see, but she always sees. She lets them build, lets them waste their time and resources, then she destroys them before they can be used."

I chuckled appreciatively. "Your mother is quite clever."

"So, how do we get across?" Thyrr asked, leaning forward in his saddle and squinting into the distance, as if the answer would magically appear somewhere in the snowy shadows.

"We build a bridge," I answered. "If Maialen sees it she will come. If not, we will have our bridge and we will cross it. Either way, we will be in Kymir."

"With berry fritters," Kaeleb added, as if that was all the motivation any of us would need.

We slid from our horses and tethered them to the burnt stump of a tree. I walked forward to the edge, gauging the distance. The burnt trees would be a problem, as they were too weak and could not be used for our little endeavor. We would have to go back quite a distance and drag the living trees back here, find a way to split the wood, lash them together, and somehow get them across the opening without dropping them into the gaping abyss.

"Aracellis, get back from the edge," Bacatha warned as the boy peered over into the dark recesses of the world.

"My mother did this?" he asked, turning back to blink at us solemnly.

"She did. I was there when it happened," I told him. He nodded, seeming to consider this. His father hated Maialen for a long time and Astraeus had probably portrayed her as weak and sniveling to their son. I was glad for her sake that her child would now be able to see her in a different light.

"We will have to go back for living trees. We need the wood to be strong," I said to Thyrr. "I can use my Element to fell them, then we can have the horses drag them back here. Bacatha, you and Kaeleb look for something we can use to lash them together."

"I have a rope," Kaeleb offered.

"Where did you get a rope?" I wanted to know.

"The farm. I rose early and found a few things I thought might be useful," he said, going to his horse and pulling down the large sack that was tied to his saddle. He pulled out items, spreading them on the sooty branch of a nearby tree. There was a length of rope, a fraying wicker cup, a ball of twine and a wooden spoon. I shook my head, laughing to myself, taking the rope and pulling it taut to test the strength.

"It will help, but we may need more. See what you can find."

"Blaise." Bacatha said my name, quiet and insistent.

I sighed. "Bacatha, it is not woman's work. We need the supplies and I do not wish to hear you argue about this."

"Blaise!" she repeated, louder this time, with a note of panic. I whipped around, my heart pounding, thinking that Chaote and the Fomori had found us.

There was nothing. Just the still, snowy world and the great black scar that cut across it. Then I saw where she was looking and my eyes rounded in disbelief.

"No!"

"I was not watching," she said, shaking her head.

I stepped close to the yawning chasm, beside the line of footprints that ended in two sloping chutes that led to the edge of the abyss. There was nothing but darkness that seemed to go on forever. I turned back to Bacatha, incredulous. "He fell in?!"

"I-I was not watching. He was there, and then he was gone," she stammered. I had never seen her lose her composure before and she was pale beneath her golden tan.

"How could he fall? Aracellis!" I shouted down into the ravine. "ARACELLIS!"

There was no answer. Thyrr and Kaeleb joined me at the edge of the divide, their voices echoing through the unforgiving darkness below as they shouted for the boy.

I shoved my hands through my hair, stomping away from the scene, wanting to burn the rest of the forest to the ground. I had just lost the one thing that would have won me the loyalty of the other realms and given me my kingdom back. I let out a bellow of rage that echoed through the dead land. I looked over at the rope, wondering if I could lower myself into the abyss and look for him, but in my heart I knew it was futile. The fire that had come up out of the crack had come from the center of the world. It was deeper than any of us could imagine. Aracellis was gone.

20

Logaire winced, bracing herself against the harsh sting of the winter air. She was forced to abandon the luxury of the warm wagon she was traveling in once they reached the shoddy village called Halig, the birthplace of the supposed oracle. The squalid assortment of shacks had one road that passed through it, and it was a pitted, snowed-in, tarry mess. Logaire lifted the skirts of her heavy velvet gown, cringing as she saw the mottled stains that now adorned the lace-trimmed hem. A troop of soldiers flanked their little party, positioned both at the front and back. Vishram stood beside her, visibly uncomfortable in the biting cold, his large block of a nose red and chapped.

"Tell me again, Vishram, why we could not summon this oracle to the castle?" Logaire asked through gritted teeth. She pulled her fur-trimmed cloak more tightly around her, cursing the advisor and the oracle under her breath.

"She would not have come, and that would put you in an unfavorable position. If you allow your summons to be ignored, you are weak. If you punish the oracle for ignoring you, then you are a tyrant trying to subdue the hope of the common people," Vishram explained. "By coming here to Halig, you are magnanimous, a benevolent ruler who walks amongst her people."

"If I have to walk amongst them, the least they could do is clear the snow," she muttered. She glanced around at the wretched village. The buildings were squat and simple in design, made of the black mud bricks that were common in Veruca. Layered shingles on the roofs were patched and torn, creating a motley of textures and colors, as if the houses were wearing shabby old hats. Bits of cracked barrels and discarded tools dotted the snowy ground, and a few wooly sheep wandered aimlessly, muddied and looking as miserable as she felt. On the surrounding hilltops she saw a broken-down waterwheel, a forgotten wheelbarrow, troughs that no longer had a destination. The remnants of what had once been working mines.

"This is where you want me to build a temple?" she hissed to Vishram in disbelief.

· "The temple will bring greatness and prosperity, my Queen. People will come from all over Imbria to pay homage," Vishram assured her.

She considered his words. She knew she needed to be careful with Vishram. He was quite intelligent, and she had been the puppeteer herself once, so she knew when strings were being pulled. She also knew that he was immensely helpful to her, and as of yet she saw no need to dispatch him. She would keep her eye on him, though. The last thing she wanted was another man controlling her, even if he twisted their fates with velvet gloves.

"We are here," Vishram announced, indicating the residence where the oracle resided. Logaire had expected it to be better maintained than the others, but its shoddiness was concurrent with the rest of Halig. The soldiers circled around her as Vishram rapped on the door, a loud, jarring sound that was discordant in the quiet winter air. Off in the distance a sheep bleated an agitated response.

The door swung open and a middle-aged woman stood, hands on hips, looking over the group with a sardonic smirk.

"The Queen of Veruca seeks an audience with the Oracle," Vishram said, bowing to the woman.

"Well, well. I must be more gossiped about than I expected! Come in, fair lady, and I will tell you all you wish to know!" the woman offered expansively.

"You are the Oracle?" Logaire asked, disbelief coloring her words.

The woman looked slightly miffed but she let it pass, smiling once more. "I am."

"We beg your pardon, Oracle," Vishram intervened. "But the Queen's safety is our greatest priority. If you would allow the men to search your home before we enter, we would be most grateful."

"Sly tongue on this one," she said to Logaire with a bawdy wink. "Go ahead then! Nothing in there but my washing that needs to be done."

Logaire regarded the woman thoughtfully as the soldiers moved about, their heavy footfalls a chorus of thuds. The Oracle was Verucan, rather homely looking except for the bright orange-red of her hair. She was thin, with a small chin which she compensated for by jutting her face out over her neck like a turkey when she smiled. Crow's feet framed her eyes, which were a light shade of brown, almost tan, ringed with short, sparse lashes. When their eyes met, Logaire could see that the woman was assessing her in much the same way.

"Not what you were expecting?" the woman asked with a knowing look.

"Not at all," Logaire murmured. "But I have learned not to judge a woman's abilities before I have seen the extent of her determination to overcome her situation."

The Oracle widened her smile and nodded her head in appreciation. The soldiers came trickling back out through the doorway and Logaire motioned for them to wait outside as she stepped across the threshold into the dilapidated house.

"Not afraid I will take a stab at you?" the woman teased.

"I can see you are too clever for such sordid things as murder by your own hands," Logaire purred. "Besides, you will like what I have come to offer you."

The woman led her into a small, cramped sitting area. A meager fire burned in the hearth and Logaire pushed back the fur-lined hood, her coppery hair spilling over her shoulders. Two chairs were placed on opposite sides of a little round table that was littered with small bottles, candles, and bundles of dried herbs.

"Thorn apple," Logaire said, eyeing the herbs. "A dangerous plant."

"Not if one knows how to use it properly. It allows you to have the most spectacular visions." The Oracle slid into one chair, motioning for Logaire to take the other. Vishram had entered with them and he stood to one side, head slightly bent, his large ears absorbing everything.

"I see you also have betel nut. So, this is how you do it? You give them concoctions to make them delirious?" Logaire asked eagerly, picking up one of the small red berries with her long fingernails.

"Not entirely. I give them the betel nut. It puts people at ease. The others are for me," the Oracle explained.

"What is your name?"

"Sybylla. But you can call me The Oracle."

Logaire laughed, the musical sound bright and sharp. "I believe I will call you Sybylla."

Sybylla gave her a knowing smirk. "Very well, Queen of Veruca. What is it you wish to learn from me?"

Logaire leaned forward, licking her red lips. "I do not wish to learn anything from you. I know you are a charlatan, so let us not deal in false pretenses and instead be honest with one another. I need you and you need me."

Sybylla's tawny eyes narrowed slightly and she stuck out her soft chin. "What is it you believe I need from you?"

"My patronage, darling Sybylla. You see, as of now, you are merely an entertaining pastime trapped in this horrid little village. Something for the life-worn commoners to seek as a respite from their miserable existence. But I can make you so much more. I can make you the great Oracle of Halig. Once I am your patron, the wealthiest and most influential of regents and nobles from all of Imbria will come to seek your advice and your sage counsel. You will be showered with gifts, residing in splendor in your glorious temple that I will build for you."

Sybylla's eyes shone with avarice and she gripped the arms of her shoddy chair. "I have learned that nothing in this life comes without a price, dear Queen. What is it that you will want in return?"

"I only ask that you continue to do as you are doing. I assume that the Gods, or fate, or whatever you claim has granted you this divine power, will have interests that are conveniently aligned with mine. After all, it must be destiny that has brought us together."

"Yes, it must be," Sybylla mused. "And I suppose you will need a test of my abilities to secure our contract?"

"Perhaps you are a genuine prophet, after all!" Logaire laughed. "To prove your loyalty to me, I want you to support my claim to the throne and help end this uprising the Fire Keeper has been stirring up."

Sybylla nodded. "Of course, I have already foreseen this omen. The Fire Keeper will not return to rule this land, for you are the one true Queen."

"Perfect!" Logaire chimed, clapping her hands enthusiastically. "There is one other thing I will need you to do. Denounce the Solvrei."

Sybylla raised her eyebrows, relaxing her grip on the arms of her chair and settling back into the threadbare cushion to regard the Verucan Queen thoughtfully.

"Why would you want me to do that?" she asked suspiciously.

Logaire wondered if she had made a mistake, if this charlatan oracle was another one of the mindless devotees who were obsessed with the legend of the Solvrei. Vishram shifted on his feet, a subtle movement to draw her attention to him, but she ignored it. She did not need his advice or his help. She knew women better than he did, and she would find out just what this supposed oracle was hiding.

Logaire eyed the thin woman, weighing her words carefully before speaking. "Are you involved with the Harbonah?"

"The who?" Sybylla repeated, appearing to be genuinely confused before recognition dawned on her. "You speak of the zealots who want to take down the Keepers. I cannot say they are wrong for their beliefs, but I have no time for all of that nonsense. You see what it is like here in Halig. I am merely trying to survive, my dear Queen, not save the world."

Logaire was satisfied with the woman's answer for the time being. "We are all trying to survive this world, darling Sybylla. But together we can do more than survive. We can build an empire where no one can touch us."

21

I sat across from Maialen, staring out the window and trying to avoid the searching look in her big green eyes. I wanted more than anything to get up and leave the room, to escape from her oppressive, prying gaze, but I needed to get back to the islands and there was no one else I could ask for help. She sipped her tea and I pushed mine away with disinterest as it swirled untouched in my cup.

"What was it like in Samirra?" she asked in her gentle voice.

"What do you think it was like in a realm completely enslaved by the Fomori?" I retorted, taking my impatience with the situation out on her. "If you prefer, I can tell you it was lovely, that they were all frolicking together happily and showering each other with flower petals. Would that assuage some of your guilt?"

She looked hurt and I tried to ignore it, despite the quick twinge of regret that her injured countenance brought me. She tucked a wayward strand of chestnut hair behind her ear. "You saved the boy. You are both here and appear unharmed. Why are you angry?"

Because I let your son fall off into a giant hole and lost the man who promised to help me take back my kingdom.

"I am tired. It has been a long journey and I need to get to Tahitia," I told her instead.

We had all decided as we built our bridge to cross the divide that it was best not to mention Aracellis, or his untimely slip into the abyss, to the Earth Queen. Bacatha had shaken her head as she went about weaving the rope through the long planks of wood Thyrr and I had brought to her.

"If she discovers the truth from someone else it will be far worse than if you tell her yourself," the Leharan warned.

"The four of us are the only ones who know," I pointed out. "Astus and the Samirrans who were witnesses are dead. There is no one who can tell her."

"What if Astus told another? And what if they send a message to Kymir, asking if the boy arrived safely with us?" Bacatha questioned further.

I shook my head. "They could not even be bothered to send a message to his mother telling her he was alive. I doubt that any of the Harbonah's followers will care enough about a Keeper's son to ask after him."

"If keeping it from her is what you wish to do, then I will be forever silent on the matter," Bacatha relented.

I looked at the golden-haired young man. "Thyrr?"

"The Earth Queen is no friend of mine, we all know that, but I feel that telling her will only hurt her further. It would be cruel and I fear she will blame us for what happened. I will also remain silent," Thyrr agreed.

I glanced at Kaeleb. He was sitting on one of the boards, watching us quietly. His eyes drifted over the long expanse of the black divide. "He is gone. It cannot be helped."

"Then we are agreed," I said with finality.

We finished lashing the long planks together as best we could, then we used Kaeleb's pilfered wicker cup and spoon to dig a trench into the snow where we could raise and pivot the planks end over end, praying that we had calculated the distance correctly and the bridge would fall safely to the other side instead of tumbling into the deep ravine. It crashed down as intended, spanning the gap, but I noticed that the movement had jostled the planks within the loops of rope on one end. It might hold, but with each crossing there was a chance the boards would work themselves loose from the binding.

"Kaeleb goes first," I said, my tone making it clear there was to be no debate. Not that Thyrr or Bacatha would have argued against it. They were both too heroically arrogant to put themselves before a child.

The boy stood and went to get his horse but I stopped him, indicating that he should walk across on his own. I would bring his horse behind me when I went. Kaeleb was annoyed by this, but he also knew my mood was sour and I was in no state to be argued with. He stepped onto the boards, wobbling slightly as he found his footing. He stomped on the ends of the bridge to dislodge the snow from his boots, then he stepped forward, over the yawning abyss. He paused, taking a breath and letting it out slowly, then he moved his other foot. The bridge was four planks wide, large enough for a horse to cross it, but we had not had any tools to cut the wood properly and I had resorted to using my power to burn the long sections so they could be split apart. It was a painstaking and tedious process, requiring such precision and skill that it had made my head pound. But it appeared as though they were holding.

Another step and Kaeleb was over the center of the ravine. He turned his head to look down and he wobbled slightly, his arms windmilling around him as he tried to regain his balance.

"Do not look down!" I shouted at him.

"I was looking for Aracellis," he called back. He seemed to find his footing and he started forward once more, this time taking quicker steps, eager to be on the approaching land of Kymir. He stepped off into the snow and turned, lifting his arms in triumph.

I motioned for Bacatha to go next and she bristled, just as Kaeleb had done.

"It is not because you are a woman," I assured her. "It is because I want to watch how you do it before I try it myself."

This seemed to satisfy her abundant sense of pride, and she swung herself onto her horse and guided the creature to the edge of the bridge. At first, the horse refused to be coerced onto the planks, backing away from the deep ravine and snorting with displeasure. Thyrr grabbed the bridle and pulled it forward, and Kaeleb made encouraging noises from the other side. As soon as the beast had stepped onto the planks, Bacatha spurred it forward and it darted across the bridge in a terrifying clatter of hooves. I watched the ties loosen a little more.

"After you," I offered to Thyrr. He shook his head. "You have the boy to look after. I will be last."

Though I never would have admitted it, I felt relieved by his offer and climbed up on my horse, taking the long reins of Kaeleb's animal and guiding it behind me. I did not tear across the weakening bridge as Bacatha had done, but walked steadily across it at an even pace. I tried not to glance down at the infinite darkness that gaped below, but I could not help wondering just how far poor Aracellis had fallen. He had not even screamed.

Kaeleb let out a whoop of joy as I safely alit on the other side. Thyrr was next, his face fixed with a stern expression as he walked ahead of his mount, guiding it along behind him. He was almost a third of the way across when the horse whinnied in agitation, the loose plank shifting under its hoofs. Thyrr desperately tried to calm the horse, but the unstable plank beneath them only made it more anxious. The tie loosened further and we began shouting at Thyrr to hurry. He looked up at us for just a moment, his strange blue-gold eyes panic-stricken. Then he dropped the reins and ran across the span of the bridge, leaping onto the other side and rolling in the snow. His horse, not wanting to be left behind, had followed his lead and nearly trampled Kaeleb as it landed, the bridge teetering horribly, then splitting apart, one plank tumbling down into the abyss and the others perching precariously on the edge.

Thyrr was laying in the snow and howling with gleeful laughter, thrilled to be amongst the living. I stuck out my hand and pulled him up while Kaeleb darted around him in circles, exclaiming his bravery and luck.

The rest of the way through Kymir was uneventful, something we were not accustomed to and which caused all of us to be quite unsettled by the time we reached the Royal City. I was half expecting to find it had been razed to the ground, a desolate graveyard where the vibrant center of the forested kingdom had once been, and I was overwhelmed with relief to see that it was as bustling as ever. Maialen quickly heard of our arrival, summoning me to the manor where I now sat across from her, sipping tea and wishing I was anywhere else.

"What is in Tahitia that you are so eager to get back to?" she was asking. I thought I heard a bitter thread of jealousy in her tone.

"The only person I wish to see in Tahitia is Cossiana. I need to tell her what has happened to Damian," I told her.

A shadow passed over her doll-like features. "He deserves to rot there for what he has done. If it was not for him, everything would be different! Aracellis would still be alive!"

I felt my ruddy skin flush at the mention of the child and had to remind myself that Maialen was referring to the boy's death that she believed occurred months ago. "It was not Damian's fault," I began.

"Why do you defend him?" her voice rose shrilly. "I thought you hated him."

"I did. Maybe I still do. Either way, I need him and he is no good to me if he is being tortured to death in some grimy Samirran dungeon. Maialen, this is an opportunity. We can all work together to destroy the Fomori, drive them out of Iriellestra and take back the city."

She stood abruptly, her chair scraping across the ground. "What do you care about Samirra? Last time we spoke you claimed to care nothing about whether Samirrans lived or died. You want something else, Blaise, something Damian has promised you."

I leaned back, resting my booted feet on the table, more to annoy her than because I found it comfortable. "You will not help me reclaim my kingdom, even though you were instrumental in its loss, so I have gone elsewhere to find allies. The Tahitian has promised me his support, but that has no bearing on your decision now. Maialen, what I am proposing will benefit all of us. We can defeat the Fomori once and for all. There is no downside here for you."

"It is Damian's fault, Blaise. He took Pearl. If he had not done that... I am sorry, I cannot help him," she insisted, her eyes taking on the haunted look they shone with when she was lost in her memories of the past.

I dropped my feet to the ground, standing up to circle the table and stand in front of her. I did not want to do it, but I could think of no other way to persuade her. I knew she still had feelings for me. I stood close, my amber eyes burning into hers, and I could see her breath quicken. "Maialen, we need your help. I told you before, Damian did not have the Pearl. The Sirens were the ones who held the amulet and they are still part of Orabelle, it was she who-"

Maialen shoved me away from her suddenly, crying out, "Do not say her name to me!"

I backed away, caught off guard by the vehemence of her response. Her cheeks were flushed a deep scarlet and her eyes were round and wild as she spat, "I hate her! I hate my sister for what she has done and I will never forgive her! Never mention her name in my presence again!"

"Maialen," I began again.

She shrieked once more, gripping her teacup and flinging it at me. I ducked, and it shattered against the wall behind me, the arc of brown liquid dripping down the wooden panels. "Leave at once!"

I strode from the room, slamming the door behind me just in time to hear the other teacup crash against it. Kaeleb was waiting, leaning against the wall, his face smeared with the dark purple juice that oozed from the inside of the fritters he loved so much.

"Does she know?" he asked, worried, and I knew he was referring to Aracellis.

"No. She hates me enough, even without that knowledge," I muttered with bitterness. "You have fritter on your face. You had better clean it up before the cooks see you."

He wiped frantically at his face with his sleeve, falling into step beside me as we left the manor. Bacatha and Thyrr had gone down to the docks to try to bribe us passage to Tahitia, a precaution they had prudently taken in case the Earth Queen was unwilling to help.

I tried not to look around as we stormed down the wintery paths, ignoring the smell of jasmine and the bright red blooms of the ice flowers. I was angry at her, and I had no desire to be surrounded by Maialen's infernal plants. If I never returned to Kymir, it would be too soon.

We found Bacatha and Thyrr standing on the pier near a large, two-masted Kymirran vessel. It looked like a new ship, and I wondered how many more Maialen was planning to acquire through her alliance with Colwyn and the Leharans, and exactly what she was planning to do with them since it did not appear that reclaiming Samirra was on her list of priorities.

Bacatha was leaning on the scythe, talking to a handful of the ship's crew. "It is a farming tool," she was saying proudly. "Useful for crops but deadly in combat."

The men nodded appreciatively and she preened, pleased with the attention her new weapon was garnering. She saw us approach and left off her conversation, turning to me and remarking on my murderous appearance.

"I take it from the look on your face that your meeting with the Earth Queen did not go well."

"No, it did not," I snarled.

"Does she know?" Bacatha queried.

I felt my power uncurling as my rage grew. "No, I am not an imbecile! Do you think I cannot last a few moments in the room with her without spilling all my secrets?"

"We all knew that without the gift we were going to bring her, it was not likely that she would be inclined to help us," Thyrr pointed out, referring to Aracellis. "Lucky for us, I have secured us passage on the ship you see before you! We leave for Tahitia at midday."

"Let us hope that Cossiana has a better gift for diplomacy," I said darkly. "There will be no avoiding the truth about her son."

22

Our return to Tahitia was just as acrimonious as our reception in Kymir. I was beginning to wonder if I would ever feel the nostalgic pleasure of a homecoming again, for it seemed no matter where on Imbria I went, I was not welcome there. I thought of Veruca, expecting to feel some sense of longing or fondness for the place that had been my home, but I only felt a cold antipathy. I had to admit, it had never felt much like a home. Veruca was somewhere to rule, the place where I was in control. It was the black mountains littered with memories as unpleasant as the hot, pungent gases that escaped the mines. The truth was that Veruca had ceased to be my home the day my brother died. Bastion and Logaire were where I had belonged, back when we were wild, carefree children, before the world gripped us in its unremitting vice. Veruca had just been the setting for our story.

The thought of Logaire cast a shadow over my heart. I was still stung by her treachery, though I had known that eventually the day would come when she would betray me. Logaire the woman was an entirely different person than Logaire the child had been, and it was the relentless dismay of her young life that had melded her into this new creature.

As a child she was bright, sunny, carefree. Even in the days when her father still slunk around, bringing misery everywhere he went, she could still laugh and smile, hoping for a better and brighter future. It was later, once her father was gone, that the thorns of bitterness had become lodged beneath her skin. Her mother, my aunt, was a weak woman, and too foolish to see that the men she expected to save her from herself were not the chivalrous sort and would only drag her down further. She invited the demons into her house, and it was Logaire who paid the price. My cousin had come to me once, her dress torn, smeared with blood, her face stained with tears. I had taken one look at her and stormed off in the direction of their miserable hovel, determined to avenge the wrongs that had been done to her. I was in a strange space at the time, the space that lies somewhere between a man and a boy. I was thin with muscles that were just beginning to form and my hair was worn long, tied back from my face in a knot. I had no home, my family was dead, and I should have been sent to an orphanage, but I stayed out of the way, not drawing attention to myself, hiding in the shadows. My mother, Maritka, had a box of silver coins she had been miserly hiding away for years for some obscure purpose that I would never know, and after her death it was this silver that sustained me.

Logaire had rushed after me on my charge to redeem her honor, begging me not to do anything, to let it lie. I ignored her, throwing open the front door with a loud bang and glaring at the man who lounged insolently in their kitchen, picking his teeth with the bones of whatever rodent had been his supper.

"What is this?" he cried in irritation. "Do not come barging in here, disturbing my meal, you little runt."

I walked up to him and slapped the bone out of his hand. He was shocked and for a moment he just sat there, uncomprehending. Then he rose to his feet, towering over me, a hulking mass of sweaty rage. He swung with a roar and I ducked, dancing out of the way, grinning at him. I should not have been so pleased with myself, for it was the last of his fists I was able to dodge and he had beaten me bloody and senseless. I could still feel the echoes of the blows, shocking and severe against my youthful face. I could hear the crunch of cartilage and feel the way the blood ran down my cheeks. I tried to shove him off of me but his bulk was like a fallen tree that had pinned me to the ground and was crushing me. Logaire screamed at him to stop, but as soon as he turned his attention to her, she paled and fled through the doorway. I was spared merely because he had tired out, climbing off me with heaving breaths, his face red and sweating. Later, when I went to find my cousin, my face a mess of bruises and blood, she had glared at me and cursed me soundly.

"I do not need you to die for me," she snapped. Her golden eyes narrowed and her jaw was clenched and I knew her well enough to know she was steeling herself against the wretched sight of me. It was obvious she had been crying.

"I was trying to protect you," I mumbled bitterly, spitting blood.

"You have only made it worse. Men make everything worse and I do not want to be saved by you, any of you! I will save myself!" She had spun in a flurry of coppery hair and left me standing there, angry that she was so ungrateful for my efforts. We had never been children again, for the last of what we were so desperately clinging to was ripped away from us that day. Logaire became a woman after that, distant and aloof, a dark streak of fierce self-preservation running through her. I could not understand how she felt until much later, and by then it was too late for understanding, for the wedge that was driven between us had grown as wide as the divide between Kymir and Samirra.

I shook myself out of the memory as Kaeleb stood beside me on the beach, frowning and rubbing the toe of his boot in the sand, a deep trench forming with his growing agitation as Cossiana showered me with an angry tirade of words. She had barely waited for me to disembark the ship before she assaulted me with questions that rapidly turned to accusations once she learned that her son had been left behind.

"Everywhere you go there is death!" Cossiana railed. "And now it is Damian who pays the price for your follies, because taking one son from me was not enough for you!"

Anger bristled along my body, like coarse fabric chafing my skin. The memory of Logaire was still fresh in my mind, her anger at me even though I was the one who was trying to save her. All my life I had been blamed for the actions of others, for the pain others had caused. The misery of the wretched was constantly thrown at my feet and then I was berated for it as if I were the cause. I glared at the old woman, my amber eyes bright with my indignation. "You brought me here in the first place because you needed me. I did not seek you out. Do not come to me and pretend you are faultless in this, Cossiana, for it was Tahitians who kidnapped the boy. I am well aware that everyone on Imbria would like to lay their burdens of blame on my shoulders, but this is because of you and your people."

She stopped in mid-sentence, her mouth slowly closing as the wrath poured out of her, ebbing like the tide and leaving her tired face slack and wretched. "I only want my son back."

"Bring me the child," I commanded, my voice ringing with determination. "Assemble your warriors, and together we will retrieve him."

"I cannot."

Her answer startled me in its unexpectedness. One thing I had never doubted was that Cossiana would move mountains to save her son. I narrowed my eyes. Sweat tricked beneath my heavy shirt as the bright sun crested overhead.

"What do you mean, you cannot?" I asked.

"The child is more important than Damian. I will not send Eolande there to be sacrificed for him. She is the one thing the halfbreed wants most in this world. She cannot go to that place," Cossiana said with a shake of her head.

"And the Tahitian warriors? Do they not wish to save their brother?" I challenged.

"They are needed here, to protect the Solvrei."

"For all we know that child is completely mad! She is no savior. She cannot even hold the Pearl without fits of incoherent babbling!" I exploded.

"She is the Solvrei," Cossiana was insistent, resolute in her determination to abandon her son.

"Who do you need protecting from? Who is going to attack you here on Tahitia?" I demanded. "The Fomori cannot sail, and the Samirrans are not adept at that craft either. The Leharans would destroy them if they came by sea. Your warriors can sit here growing idle, babysitting a deranged child and thinking of ways to steal more children, or you can send them to Samirra with me so they can fight, the thing they are meant to do."

"Why are you so determined to save my son, a man you hate?" she demanded.

I stared at her, not knowing how to answer. I could not even explain to myself why I felt so determined to save Damian. I did not particularly enjoy his condescending and self-righteous presence, so it was not some new sentiment of friendship that pushed me. Maybe it was my longing to escape the island and the memories that came with it, to find any reason to avoid confronting the little girl whose dead mother spoke to me. A mother I had once loved, still loved, but who hated me. Regret was a powerful emotion, and not one I cared to wallow in. It could have been that, or maybe there was a part of me silently longing for a chance at redemption. I wanted to save her Guardian, to show Orabelle that I was not the monster she always believed I was. But I dared not say any of this to Cossiana and so I stood there staring at her.

"I can stay to protect the Solvrei," Kaeleb said with quiet and steady determination in his young voice.

I faced him, appreciative of the interruption that ended the awkward silence. "I thought you wanted to help save Damian."

"The old woman is right. The Solvrei is more important. I will stay and I will guard her," he informed me as if the decision was made and that was all that needed to be said.

"You may call me Elder, not old woman," Cossiana admonished him with a hint of annoyance.

"Last time we were here, someone took you and shipped you to the Fomori in a barrel," I pointed out unnecessarily to Kaeleb, ignoring her.

He scowled at me, grey eyes steely. "I was not prepared then. I did not know the Tahitians were as treacherous as the Verucans. I will be prepared now. But I must have a sword."

Of course. I could not help but grin at him. He had been trying to get someone to give him a sword since we left Samirra.

Cossiana put her hand on my shoulder, the weathered appendage warm and insistent. "The men who took the boy have been found. An example was made of them and I promise you it will not happen again. He will be safe here."

"So you will send warriors to Samirra?"

She let her hand drop from my shoulder as I turned back to her. She said, "No. I will come with you."

I felt the overwhelming urge to smash something, but I managed to refrain since the only thing around us on the docks were piles of slippery silver fish and I did not care to be covered in fish guts. "I have never heard a plan so utterly doomed to fail in my entire life. You cannot fight!"

"Not everything can be solved with fighting," she flung back at me. "We will use diplomacy. Damian has no value to the Fomori, his only value is to me."

"And you are the island Elder. You want to trade your life for his," I surmised.

"I will suggest an exchange of prisoners. You will be nearby in case they are not honorable in their dealings. The halfbreed must know your power by now, and although she will never say it aloud, she must fear you."

"I cannot use my power in her presence. She has Warding Stones," I countered.

"Yes," Cossiana agreed, "but she needs Samirrans to survive in Samirra. You will threaten what is left of the kingdom and we must hope the threat will be enough. You are the only person she will believe is capable of sacrificing an entire realm to get what they want."

"Somehow, that does not seem like a compliment," I retorted. "I came all the way back here for warriors, old woman, not for you."

She smiled, and I was unsettled by the knowing look in her wise eyes. "I will summon you once we are ready to depart, Fire Keeper."

Cossiana left us standing on the beach, squinting in the bright light as she walked away, her movements slow and measured.

"She is going to get me killed," I grumbled irritably.

Kaeleb shrugged. "Perhaps she is right. Brother Kaden said that one should strive to win a war without ever going into battle."

"You wish to remain here? You are certain?" I asked him, searching the determined lines of his youthful face.

He nodded and blinked at me solemnly. "I do not wish to leave you unprotected, but I feel this is what I must do."

I chuckled in amusement. "I will ask Bacatha to stay and watch over the two of you, if you are amenable to that?"

"I do not need anyone to watch over me, but she is a fine warrior and I would be glad of her presence. There are moves I wish her to teach me with her farming tool."

"Scythe," I corrected.

He looked confused.

"Never mind," I said. "Come, let us return to the ship and see if Bacatha is willing."

Bacatha was not as agreeable as I expected her to be, insisting that her place was with Thyrr when he returned to Lehar. We stood on the ship which was preparing to sail to their island, and the tall Leharan woman was methodically wiping the blade of the scythe with an oiled rag.

"We have been gone from Lehar for too long already. It weakens Thyrr's position. Every moment we are not there is an opportunity for Colwyn to garner more favor amongst our people. Thyrr must remind them that he is the rightful heir," she explained.

Thyrr stood beside her, the salty wind playing in his golden hair. There was a strange look on his face, as if he were uncomfortable with her words. I could not shake the feeling that there was something he was not telling us, a hidden truth he was guarding.

"Colwyn has no position," I scoffed, annoyed with everyone around me and tired of feeling like I was constantly begging for support. I was a Keeper, I was the rightful King of Veruca. I should not have to beg someone to watch over a child. Colwyn was just another usurper, and not even a worthy one at that. He had long outlived his usefulness and was now nothing more than a hindrance. "You want to end Colwyn's bid for regency of Lehar? Then tell the Leharans that he is the traitor."

Bacatha's icy gaze was suddenly sharp. "What do you mean, Keeper?"

"I mean, Colwyn was the one who was informing Chronus of Orabelle's every move. How do you think the Captain became the puppet of Kymir? He has no affinity for the Earth Queen. It is because Damek holds sway over him. That sniveling weasel was the liaison between Colwyn and Chronus," I finished, folding my arms over my chest as Thyrr and Bacatha gaped at me.

"Is it really true?" she demanded to know, her knuckles whitening on the grip of her scythe.

"Yes, and he knows I know. That is why he helped us search for Kaeleb."

"You said nothing all this time," Thyrr said quietly, his blue-gold gaze fixed on me but seeing something far away.

I shrugged. "I can keep secrets if I need to. It was useful to me to have Colwyn under Maialen's thumb when she and I were allied."

"We must tell the others, the Guard. My father." Bacatha shook her head in disbelief. "A traitor cannot be allowed to control our island for one moment longer. I will go with Thyrr and see that this filth is removed from the Citadel, and then I will return to look after your boy."

"I do not need looking after!" Kaeleb scowled. "I am merely grateful for the company of another warrior while Blaise is away."

Bacatha barely heard him, still absorbed with this new morsel of information I had fed her. "Yes, fine. As soon as Thyrr has reclaimed the throne I will return. It should not take long. Once word of his treachery spreads, Colwyn will no longer have any support amongst the Leharans. Thyrr will be the rightful and unchallenged ruler of Lehar!"

Thyrr was still looking uncomfortable, and I wondered again what the young man was hiding. I remembered his words as we had sailed to Kymir, that there was something he wanted me to know. I was tempted to ask him, but I refrained, knowing the others were present and that whatever it was would be more useful to me if I was the only one who knew it.

23

Logaire waved her arm irritably at the maid who was trying to comb her wild mane of hair, saying harshly, "Get out!"

The woman bowed and fled from the room, nearly colliding with the Verucan royal falconer who stood in the doorway. He was still wearing his thick, padded leather glove on one hand and in the other he clutched a tiny scroll.

"Word from Kymir," he told her, passing over the scroll. She snatched it from his grasp and forced herself to be patient, thanking and dismissing him before she allowed herself to look at it.

Logaire smiled, tucking the small slip of paper under the bosom of her gown. Such a tiny thing, the message. Only a few hastily scrawled words and yet in it the power to change the world. She lifted her skirts and hurried from her chambers, eager to find Vishram and tell him their plan had worked. The Oracle was making her way along the corridor, watching the retreating figure of the falconer with undisguised curiosity.

"Logaire, I was just coming to see you," Sybylla said, bowing deeply. She was clothed in long, white robes that draped her thin frame, accentuating the brightness of her blood-orange hair. Logaire had brought Sybylla back to the castle with her, promising to return her to Halig once the construction of her temple had begun. After all, she could not have her prized possession wallowing in squalor in the countryside, waiting to be attacked or kidnapped, or worse. Sybylla was too important to what was coming. Vishram was already having plans drawn up for the magnificent monument they were to build, and it would be a glorious testament to Logaire's reign as Queen of Veruca, but it would take time.

"Sybylla," Logaire inclined her head in greeting. "Are you in need of something?"

"Just your company," Sybylla said with a grin. Logaire felt a little thrill in her stomach. The woman had turned out to be much more than she expected, and she enjoyed their private meetings as much as she enjoyed their public displays of power. On the way back from Halig, Logaire had questioned her incessantly, not surprised to learn Sybylla's story and the echoes of familiarity it had with her own.

Sybylla was born into a poor family, miners who could find no work after the mines near their village had been depleted. Her brothers were the first to leave, forced to go elsewhere in search of a livelihood. Her mother died soon after, leaving Sybylla to care for her father, a bitter and angry man who turned to drink. He was cruel, though he never laid a hand on her. When he too passed away, she was compelled to marry as she had no other means to sustain herself and there were no opportunities in the village, especially not for a woman. It was an unhappy union, and one that was fraught with strife. She had two sons who were miserable louts, bullies that grew up to be bigger bullies, and she was grateful for the day they left home for good. Attending to her sons had diverted her attention from her unhappy marriage, and once they were grown and departed, she found herself solely with her husband, with whom she engaged in dreadful arguments. One day, he struck her with the back of his hand. She had clutched her stinging cheek as he had stomped from the room without apology. The next day, he fell quite ill, vomiting and retching so violently that his bile turned bloody. He almost died, though somehow he clung to life and made a slow recovery. Sybylla had tended to him sweetly, both of them well aware that it was she who had brought about his incapacitating condition, and both knowing that she had meant to kill him. One day, she went to fetch water from the well, but when she came back, he had vanished. He never returned. It was then that Sybylla started performing her tricks as the Oracle. She had a knack for reading people, for knowing what they wanted to hear and what would make them open their miserly purses. She would weave grand tales brought about by her prophetic visions, and her patrons, plied with betel nut, would absorb it all in slack-jawed wonder. Logaire had seen the gift for herself since they had arrived back at the castle. The Oracle had performed her little tricks on several of the nobles and regents Logaire was closest to, and Sybylla was true to her word, interpreting her visions in ways that would benefit the Queen, and displaying quite a knack for manipulation and strategy.

"I am afraid you will have to make a request for my company at a later time," Logaire told her with a sensual pout of her lips. "I have pressing matters to attend to."

"What matters?" Sybylla asked, seemingly an innocent question.

Logaire hesitated for a moment, but she knew there was no point in keeping the truth from the other woman, for she would need her help with what came next. "The hawk has brought us a message from the Earth Queen. She wishes to accept my proposal that we be allies."

Sybylla's smile widened. "As it was foreseen, so it has come to pass. What will you tell Vishram?"

Logaire shrugged her shoulders, bare and finely sculpted above the low neck of her glittering gown. "Only as much as he needs to know. Once it is done, you must return to Halig to oversee the building of the temple, and to make sure that no one discovers the truth."

"My fate is your fate," Sybylla whispered. She stepped aside and Logaire swept past her, a cloud of sweet floral amongst the torpid scents of Veruca.

Logaire was pleased. Sybylla was everything she had hoped for and more. Clever and quick, the woman knew that for now her survival depended on Logaire remaining as Queen. Logaire would just have to make sure that it remained that way. The Oracle had the potential to grow too powerful on her own.

Logaire made her way through the castle to the small chambers Vishram kept, rapping impatiently on the door. She had made several efforts to convince him to occupy one of the castle's more extravagant chambers, situated conveniently near her own, but Vishram declined, asserting his preference for humble surroundings.

He opened the door, torchlight flickering off the blocky features of his face, making him look as if he had been broken into pieces and put back together again, slightly askew. She stepped inside the austere space, frowning.

"I wish you would accept my offer for better quarters," she muttered, settling herself into the only chair, a hard wooden object with no cushion that was quite uncomfortable. The only other furnishings in the room were a thin bed that looked as if it barely held one man, and a long wooden table piled with neat stacks of books and scrolls, and a tidy arrangement of ink bottles and quills. A single torch burned on the wall.

"I am quite comfortable here, my Queen," he replied.

She reached into her gown, noting how he glanced away at the attention she drew to her bosom. Logaire did not know where his proclivities lay regarding women. If he had any, he was much too discreet to be discovered. She only knew that he had never looked upon her or anyone else in the castle in a lustful way, something she had always liked about him. She flourished the tiny scroll. "We have received word from the Kymirran Queen. She will accept the alliance."

Vishram nodded slowly and Logaire was disappointed in his lackluster response. She expected him to exhibit at least some level of enthusiasm now that all their plans were bearing fruition.

"What is the reason for the Earth Keeper's change of heart?" he asked, ever the logician.

"You are no fun at all," Logaire pouted with a heavy sigh. "She does not say, but our spies on Lehar have sent word that Colwyn is dead. Executed by the Guard for being a traitor. Which he was, so I do not feel any pity for him, though I imagine Maialen is quite distraught. Thyrr's ascension to the Leharan throne poses a threat to both of us. Maialen knows this, and it must be why she has finally agreed."

"I did not hear of Colwyn's removal," Vishram remarked, seeming perturbed.

Logaire's red lips pulled into a smile. "I am the Queen, Vishram, and therefore I am the one who decides what you know. Did you think you were the only man in my employ? There are a dozen others just like you."

She enjoyed the shadow that crossed his cumbersome features. It was good to remind him of his place, to make him remember that he was useful but not necessary.

"What preparations would you like me to make, Queen Logaire?" he asked, deciding to let her needling pass with no further comment.

"It will be just as we discussed but with one caveat. I will need to send Akrin," she replied, deliberately vague.

"Akrin?" Vishram raised a heavy brow. "I thought you wanted him kept out of things."

"He will only know his small part, nothing of the grand design. Besides, I will be glad to have somewhere to send him where I will not have to look upon his horrid face or his atrocities," Logaire muttered with a slight tremble of revulsion running down her spine.

It was Vishram's turn to sigh. "Yes, he has been causing quite a stir lately. I am afraid that keeping him cooped up here is drawing too much attention to his inclinations. There are whispers of an accusation from one of the noble houses. A favored servant has gone missing and Akrin was seen speaking to her before she disappeared."

"Make sure that nothing can be traced back to him, and that she is not in the castle somewhere. Put an end to the accusation before it is made." Logaire felt a twist in her stomach. She wished she could remove the sullen young man's head from his neck right then. If Sybylla continued to rise in the esteem of the Verucans and other Imbrians, then soon she would have no need for him. She could kill him, or she could banish him as she had done to her cousin. He and Blaise could wander Imbria together, bemoaning their lost kingdom. The thought made her laugh, the musical sound filling the solemn chamber.

"It will be done, my Queen," Vishram promised, wondering what caused her laughter and knowing it was better not to ask. The Queen liked to have her secrets, and as long as she was busy hoarding hers, she would not think to look for his.

After she was gone, Vishram pulled out a clean piece of parchment, picking up a tiny bottle of blue-black ink and a quill. It would be dangerous to send a message now, but he had to warn the others of what was coming. The Harbonah had tasked him with steering the course of events in the kingdom, to make sure that those loyal to them grew in the Verucan ruler's estimation, garnering favor. None of them could have imagined that what Logaire was scheming would actually come to pass. Vishram had to do something, and if he could not reach the Harbonah, then he was on his own, a thought that chilled him to his very bones. He would have to be more careful than ever.

He dipped his quill into the ink and began to carefully craft the cryptic message. It had been so long since he had heard from the Harbonah, and he worried for the old man's safety. The network of acolytes that was spread across the land had become fractured, split apart by the siege in Samirra and the great divide the Earth Queen had torn through the world. The information that had once flowed freely, whispered from place to place by devoted followers, was now a feeble trickle of insensible words.

Vishram took a breath, squaring his shoulders. He had accepted the task he had been given, knowing the risk. He could not afford to succumb to his fear now. He remembered when he had first received the orders. He had been sitting in this very room, a lowly scribe in the hierarchy of the castle, overlooked and underappreciated. Blaise was still the ruler then, had yet to venture out for the war that would claim his kingdom, even though it was fought on the other side of the world. There had been a soft knock at the door and Vishram had opened it, peering out into the empty hallway. There was no one there, but a scrap of parchment lay on the ground at his feet. He bent, picking it up, his thick brows drawing together thoughtfully.

The time is at hand to arise in glory to the Gods. Come and see the sunset over the harbor.

He felt a thrill inside of him. It was finally time. After all these years of devotion, he was finally being called upon to serve the Gods and the Harbonah. He took the scrap of paper to the single torch that burned in his sparse chamber and touched the edge of it to the flame, dropping it to the floor as it crumbled and blackened. Then he tossed on his robe and hurried out the door, eager to meet whoever it was that awaited him, wondering if it would be the great man himself, though he dared not hope too much for such an honor.

He had gone to the wall that overlooked the blackened sea, for everyone knew it was the best place to watch the sun set behind the mountains. He was surprised to see a woman there. She was thin, with long auburn hair and big, soulful eyes.

"Vishram," she said in greeting. He noticed her eyes were not as innocent as they first seemed, and they gleamed with a flash of cunning. "I am glad you have come."

"I am the humble servant of the Gods," he murmured. "Tell me, why have you summoned me here?"

"You are needed, called upon by the Harbonah himself," she said, pausing so he could relish in the honor. "He wishes you to elevate your status in the castle."

"How... how can I do that?"

"Come now, Vishram," the woman prodded. "You are no fool. You can do better than you have done. The Solvrei will soon be revealed and everything will change. We will need someone we can trust, someone who can bend the ear of the Verucan ruler."

"The Solvrei?" he repeated, nearly breathless. It was finally happening.

She had nodded and grasped his hands, pressing them tightly, telling him that he was the chosen of the Harbonah, of the Gods. Vishram had listened with wide eyes, his heart singing. All the years of devotion, of prayers, they were finally being rewarded. She had laid out a plan for him and he had listened intently, hanging on every word. When she was done, she simply turned and walked away from him.

"Who are you?" he called after her.

"Who I am is not important," she had answered. "I am the servant of the Harbonah and the one who was chosen by the Gods to mold the Solvrei."

His eyes had rounded and he rubbed a hand over his protruding features, as if she were an apparition that would fade when he looked again. He learned some time later that it was Alita. She had smiled one last time, then she disappeared around the bend of the wall, the last time he had ever seen her before she met her violent end in Kymir.

Vishram said a quiet prayer for the woman he had met so many years ago and then blew gently on the parchment to dry the ink. He had not heard a word from any of the other followers since that day, and he could only presume that this was because they were pleased with his progress and saw no need to interfere. But now he needed them, needed to warn them about what was coming, what Logaire would do. He prayed again and slipped the paper into a small scroll case, setting it aside with the other messages to be sent out with the hawks the next morning.

24

Time seemed to stand still as I waited on Tahitia. With each day that passed, I grew more and more uneasy, cringing at the smallness of the island and my inability to escape it and its inhabitants. This included the Sirens, who seemed to rise from the ocean every time I ventured near the beach, their beseeching hands beckoning to me as they moaned. I thought perhaps they were trying to lure me into the sea to drown me, revenge for the wrongs that Orabelle believed I had perpetrated, but I soon realized they were not trying to draw me out into the turquoise ocean and instead wanted me to follow them along the coastline.

"Should we go with them?" Kaeleb asked, squinting up at me in the harsh glare of the sun. He was wrapped in a bright yellow cloth and was no better at mastering the draping of the fabric than he had been the first time he tried. He sat in the sand, his feet bare and his toes wriggling down into the coarse grains. Water lapped at his ankles, filling in the spaces that he had dug out with his toes.

I stood over him, wearing linen but with my heavy leather vest over the light fabric of the tunic and my sword belt strapped around my waist. I did not fully trust the Tahitians any longer, and I did not go anywhere on the island unarmed.

I shook my head. If the Sirens were not trying to kill me, then they must be trying to lead me to the girl, and I was in no hurry to see her again. Seff, Vayk and the dog had left the island while we were gone, and I wondered what could have drawn the banished God away from his precious prophet. Perhaps they also doubted her validity and her sanity.

"Do you wish to follow them?" I asked Kaeleb, surprising myself. I was feeling guilty about the departure I would soon make, leaving him alone just when I had promised that I would not do so again.

"Yes," he said eagerly, with a grin at the ephemeral creatures. He stood, brushing sand off while one siren cooed happily, waving her barbed hands in welcome. He started after them and I followed, somewhat reluctantly. They danced along the curve of the island, twirling and shimmering like amorphous jewels as the sun glistened off their damp bodies. It was not difficult to see Orabelle in their graceful movements, to imagine her dancing along the pale sand, her smile radiant and her pale hair billowing around her like a cloud.

The Sirens stopped suddenly and turned to look up the beach where the girl stood, arms crossed over her chest, scowling with irritation.

"Finally!" she cried, stomping one of her golden feet. She wore a simple white dress, and her hair, though still shorn off, had been tidied up to look somewhat presentable and slightly less wretched.

"Is no one looking after you?" I wanted to know, glancing around at the empty beach.

"You are supposed to be," she accused. She looked at Kaeleb, her face softening. "I like your robe. Yellow is my favorite color."

He preened, unable to stop the grin that spread over his face. I rolled my eyes.

"Did Cossiana tell you I would look after you?" I asked her.

She shook her head, blue eyes solemn, then lifted her hand to the Sirens. "She did."

I stared at the creatures, thinking of what Seff had told me. The Sirens were like he and his brother, and he and his brother were part of the God, Fenris, the same being as the dog, yet different, separate. One of the Sirens reached into the waves and took out the Pearl. I sighed heavily, not wanting to have a repetition of what had happened the last time.

"Keep it," I said to the Siren, motioning for her to stay away from the child. "I want to try something different. Eolande, can you hear the voices when the Pearl is near?"

She nodded, frowning. "They are just whispers though."

"Ignore them. They are only yelling because they are angry for being dead," I told her with a grin. She giggled and I went on, "We are going to try to make them go away. Can you feel the water around you?"

She shook her head.

"Close your eyes. Do not be afraid. Kaeleb is beside you. He will protect you," I said. I gave the boy a nod and he moved next to the girl and she grabbed his hand, gripping it tightly, her eyes squeezed shut obediently. "Very good. Now I want you to reach out with your mind, to find the water. You don't need the Pearl or the other Keepers. You are the Solvrei. Make them be silent. Show them you do not need them."

One of the Sirens made an agitated noise and I ignored it. Orabelle would not be pleased that I was telling her daughter not to listen to her, but I needed to know if the girl was what they claimed she was. It was one thing for a child to manipulate an Element using an amulet, quite another to not need the amulet at all.

Eolande's lip curled up in concentration, her eyes still tightly shut. I felt something wet beneath my feet and looked down to see a trickle of water snaking up through the sand from the ocean. It wound around me, then moved to where Kaeleb and Eolande stood, circling them.

"You are doing well," I murmured, not wanting to break her concentration. "Now, I want you to try harder."

The flow of water expanded to a small stream as I watched in disbelief. It rose up from the ground, weaving through the air in a shower of crystalline droplets. Then Kaeleb gasped in pain and jerked his hand away as if she had burned him. The water fell to the ground, sliding back into the ocean it came from.

I grabbed Kaeleb's arm, turning it over to examine his hand. "Are you hurt? Did she hurt you?"

"No... not in a way that I know how to say," he said quietly. "It was like she was taking something out of me. It hurt, but I did not feel injured."

"What were you doing to him? What did you do to Kaeleb?" I demanded of the girl. She was watching us with wide eyes, her small hands trembling.

"I needed him," she whispered. "To do what you wanted me to do."

I pushed a hand through my red hair, feeling that it had gotten longer and was curling over my shoulders. I had a thousand questions, but I was not sure who could answer them. The dog perhaps, but he was conspicuously absent. The Sirens possibly, but the girl would have to interpret their answers, and I could not even be sure it was them speaking. It could be any of the former Water Keepers using the Pearl to be heard, and I was certain that not all of them had motives that could be trusted. I wanted to shout in frustration. I was sick and tired of this cursed island, of prophecies and gods and the Solvrei and amulets and fighting. I was sick of all of it.

I took the girl's hand in mine. "Do it again. I want to know what you did."

She shook her head.

"Eolande, do it again!" I yelled at her. One of the Sirens keened in warning, her face distorting to reveal sharp rows of teeth, like the mouth of a shark. Eolande bit down on her lip and closed her eyes and instantly I felt it, a horrible sensation, not painful in a way that could be described, but worse than anything I had ever felt before. It was as if she was pouring icy fire into my veins, as if she were crushing my hand and ripping it apart at the same time. I felt the damp caress of water against my cheek and we were surrounded by a swirling mass of droplets. I waited, trying to endure as long as I could, to understand what it was that she was doing, but I could take no more and I tore my hand from her grasp, knocking her to the sand. The Sirens shrieked at me, rushing to her and covering her with gentle caresses, cooing at her tenderly. I backed away, staring down at my hand, expecting to see a gnarled stump or to find my skin sliced to ribbons. Instead, it looked perfectly normal. Scarred, tanned, strong. I opened and closed my fist. It was as it had always been.

Kaeleb was thoughtful, his pale brows drawn together. "She takes something from us. Instead of using the amulet. That is how she draws power."

"How did you know how to do that?" I asked her.

"The dog told me. It said when the time came, that was how it would die," she said in a soft voice, tears welling up in her eyes. "I do not want the dog to die."

The dog. The wolf. The creature that Seff claimed was the God, Fenris. My mind was still spinning, still trying to understand what was happening. I needed time to think, but I also needed more answers. I began to muse aloud, watching the girl's face intently to see if any of my thoughts struck a chord within her. "The dog wants you to end its life, and it told you this is how you will do it. So, you are killing whoever you draw power from?"

"No! The dog said it was not killing, that it was drawing out the life that is left in you," she was vehement in her protest.

I wanted to tell her that sounded a lot like killing, but it was clear that her fragile child's mind could not grasp the nuances of the situation. The dog told her it was not killing, and she believed it because she needed to believe it. I tried to think of another way to ask what I wanted to know. "How much life did you draw from me just now?"

Her bottom lip trembled. "Only a few moments! The dog said no one would notice a few moments."

I glanced at Kaeleb and he spread his hand, fingers splayed, as if looking to see if the flesh there had aged faster than the rest of him.

"You cannot see it," she said to him. "It is inside you."

"Does the same thing happen when you use an amulet?" I wanted to know.

She shook her head. "No, but I hate the amulets. There are too many voices, they scream at me. Even yours. I can hear them whispering even from here. I will not touch one ever again!"

I sat beside her and the three of us sat watching the sea, the Sirens singing out a tender lullaby. The girl joined in, her voice clear and bright. The gloom that had settled over the child lifted and she looked so much like her mother that it caused my throat to tighten. I did not even know if Orabelle liked to sing. I claimed to have loved her, but in all honesty I had barely known her. I coveted the idea of her, the woman I wanted her to be, more than the woman she actually was. I sighed, a heavy exhale, as if part of the past was being released into the balmy island air and one of the Sirens turned her head to me, a smile playing at the edges of her lips. I stared back at the creature, trying to tell her without words that I was sorry, and hoping that some small part of Orabelle understood.

25

Damian rolled the muscles of his shoulders, shaking off the reverberations of the blow the Mother of the Fomori had dealt him. She laughed, the warm, throaty sound filling the cold air between them.

"Tired already, Guardian?" Chaote taunted. She danced around him, the sparring staff she gripped in her hands spinning in front of her. She was wearing leather armor striped with iron bands, the shining golden suit set aside for more auspicious occasions than training in the arena. Her hair was pulled back from her face in an elaborate weaving of braids and knots, and the darkness of her skin was smooth and unbroken.

"I do not tire out so easily," Damian reminded her. He held his own staff ready, angled across his chest, his feet braced far apart. He was also clad in leather armor, though his was simple and well-worn, and did not have the protection of the iron bands that adorned Chaote's.

She moved like liquid, running at him and dropping the end of her staff to the ground so she could lean over on it, kicking out with her foot. He blocked the maneuver and she spun, lifting the staff and using a turning kick to deliver a sharp blow to his forearm. Before he could recover she lurched her body back into a reverse hook kick. Landing on both feet, she swung the staff upward, nearly colliding with his chin had he not thrown himself back out of her reach at the last moment. She was incredible in her agility, the most skillful fighter he had encountered since his brother, Tal.

"Well done," he said graciously. He could see sweat beading along her forehead and he could feel rivulets of it running down his back despite the chill air. Snow was already blanketing the cliffs to the west and soon all of Samirra would be in the grip of winter.

She smiled, her black eyes sparkling. "That is enough for this day. You may be the champion of the arena come spring. If you are still with us in the spring."

"Are you planning to let me leave?" he asked, knowing that she was not.

"Your mother has requested a parlay," she told him, watching closely to gauge his reaction. He did not seem surprised, but he often kept his face carefully blank, stoic and unreadable. "What do you suppose she wishes to trade for you?"

He shrugged, throwing his long dreadlocks over his shoulder. "She will not give you what you want."

"You would be surprised what mothers will do for their children," she said, and he heard the shadow in her words.

"You speak of your own mother?"

Chaote looked away at the icy cliffs that glistened in the distance. "She would not deny me. Even at the end, when she faced Rilian and knew she would die for it, she did not deny me as her child. She was the only one who stood up to him, and he slaughtered my entire family because of it."

Damian was silent, watching her, studying her. He did not have to say the words again, the words he had said to her countless times by now. That it had been long ago, that she needed to let go of the past, of the pain, of the hate.

She looked at him and the yellow flecks in her eyes were stars in the darkness. "I know what you are thinking, but you seem to forget that for me, time has not passed. This is not an ancient story that happened hundreds of years ago. When I was trapped underground by the Keepers, it was as if I were asleep. I dreamt, and sometimes I could hear the Fomori calling to me, but it was a timeless sense of existing. When I awoke, for me, it had been mere moments, not centuries. Their deaths are too recent and I have not been allowed the luxury of passing time to soften my need for vengeance."

"I felt the same way you did after my brother died, but I learned later that the man I blamed for killing him was not the man who had done it. If I had given in to my anger, if I had killed him for revenge, it would have been for nothing."

She laughed, a bitter sound this time. "I am not mistaken and I will not regret what I do, just as I do not regret ridding the world of the pathetic Samirran king. The Keepers are to blame and their atrocities continue to this day. You truly do not know what they are capable of, do you?"

"They are not all the same," Damian countered.

"They are and some day you will come to see it. I cannot tolerate their corrupt power any longer. Go now and wash yourself. I will see you for the evening meal," she dismissed him with a callous wave of her hand. He walked past her, taking the tunnel that led from the arena to the prisoner's quarters. She insisted he share a meal with her each night, and it had quickly become a strange habit of theirs. He would be bathed, dressed, brought to dine with her in the palace, and afterwards he was returned to the dungeon, locked in the filthy, squalid cell until the next time she decided she wanted his company. He recognized that part of her was clinging to the human side of herself, to the Tahitian ways in which she had lived most of her life. The Fomori were not her people. She had been forced among them, trapped among them, but they were not her people. Whether she wanted to admit it or not, she was Tahitian and she craved the bond of their origin that Damian shared with her.

Damian also saw the way the Va'Kul watched them together. The female was the most powerful Fomori after Chaote herself, intelligent and brutal in her cruelty, and he had seen the flashes of jealousy from her, even if Chaote had not. The Va'Kul resented the Mother's affinity for the Tahitian, and it was sowing the seeds of distrust between them. He considered telling Chaote what he observed, that he believed the Va'Kul would attempt to overthrow her soon, but perhaps that was the most fortuitous outcome. If the Fomori turned to fighting amongst themselves, then the rest of the realms could band together and defeat them.

A Fomori guard was waiting for him inside the tunnel and the beast escorted him back to his cell, slamming shut the iron bars and stalking away. Damian had grown used to the horrible scent of the creatures, but he was still grateful when they were out of sight, and he did not have to look upon their unsettling countenances.

Damian waited until he was sure the beast was gone, then he pressed himself against the stone wall, listening for any sounds of life from the cell beside his. There was only silence. There was always silence.

"Favian!" he called furtively, not wanting his voice to carry too far. There was no response. There never was. "A message has arrived from Tahitia. They have requested a parlay with the Mother of the Fomori."

Unending silence.

"I will do what I can to see that you are freed from this place. Have hope, Guardian," Damian urged, his gentle baritone rumbling over the stone. He sighed. Favian had not spoken a word since the day Damian arrived in Samirra, when they had rescued Kaeleb from the arena in a bloody battle that left most of the Samirran warriors dead. This included Hovard, the man Favian had loved, the one he had sacrificed everything to save. Hovard was the last stitch that held the Guardian together and when that thread had been cut, Favian had fallen apart. He was a shell, a shadow of the man he once was, and try as he might, Damian could not seem to draw him back from the darkness.

Damian sat, waiting for the Fomori guard to return for him. There was nothing else to do but wait. Endless hours of waiting, and always waiting for her. Chaote was the center of his world now, the thing that his existence revolved around, and it was her whims that decided his every moment. He clung to the foolish hope that one of these days he would get through to her, that he would find the right words, the perfect words that would finally reach her and convince her to stop this war. There was no one else who could, and so he would not give up.

Sometimes when he was waiting he would close his eyes and think of home. He would picture the shimmering sand of the beaches and the azure water teeming with life. The boats that slid in and out of the harbors and coves, and the colorful nets laden with fish. He would hear the laughter of his people, smell the scent of herbs and spices and tropical flowers. For a few moments, in the isolation of his own mind, he could make himself believe he was home. Sometimes he would imagine his brother, Tal, was there with him, and Orabelle was beside him, their daughter playing on the beach. His mother was there too, not as old as she had become, but younger, more vibrant, the way she was before Tal's death. He smiled. It was a dream that would never come to pass, but it was one he longed for more than any other.

The smell of death chased away the daydream and Damian opened his eyes just as the Fomori approached his cell. He rose to his feet, stepping back as the beast swung the door open and motioned for him to follow. He stepped out, glancing quickly into Favian's cell as they moved past it, but the Guardian was nothing more than a heap of misery piled into the dark corner, his long hair obscuring his face. Damian prayed silently for him to look up, for any sign that he was still the man he had once known, but Favian was as still and silent as ever.

The Fomori led him to the bathing area where he undressed while the beast unceremoniously tossed buckets of cold water onto him. Once that unpleasantness was done he was given clean clothing and led further down the corridor, up the stairs that ascended to the outer courtyard, behind the area that had become the arena. They walked up the palace steps, and Damian could see that the structure was already falling into disrepair. The white marble was dull and sooty and the domes that topped it were drab and muted, an effect of the fires that had now ravaged the city twice. The inner palace was not faring much better, for the Fomori cared nothing for arts and culture, and the entire structure looked as if it had been scraped bare. There were still dark sprays of dried blood on some of the walls, and dust and dirt collected in the corners.

Chaote was waiting in the dining hall, seated at the end of the long table. Her hair was long and loose, like a glossy black curtain of satin, and she was draped in the fur robes that were the traditional garments of the Fomori women. He could see the edge of the scar on her chest where she had embedded a Warding Stone beneath her skin, but the single blemish did not mar her appearance, instead it seemed to enhance it, as the rest of her beauty radiated out in stark comparison.

She motioned for him to sit and he did so, at the opposite end of the table, where he was at what she deemed to be a safe distance. He could not catch her unawares with the shard of a smashed plate slicing her throat, or a heavy goblet crushed against her temple. From a distance she could see him coming, and she could stop any attack that he made.

The Va'Kul stood beside her, off to one side, and Damian tried not to look at the formidable creature, not wishing to let her know that he was aware of her animosity towards her ruler. The Va'Kul made a motion with her hand and Samirran servants brought in plates of food. It was a simple meal, as it always was, for Chaote did not believe in extravagance, and Damian had always appreciated this about her. They ate in silence for a while, the Va'Kul standing back, watching them both with her shrewd yellow eyes.

"Your mother wishes to meet on the Isle of Clouds. Do you know the place?" Chaote asked, finally breaking the strained silence.

"I know of it, though I have not been there myself. It is rumored to be a beautiful and rugged place," Damian answered.

"Do you enjoy beautiful and rugged things, Damian?" Chaote asked, a teasing glint in her black eyes. He saw the Va'Kul frown.

"I will decide when we get there and I have seen it for myself," he answered, trying to find words that would pacify both of the women. Chaote was no fool, and he wondered if she knew the dangerous game they were playing. It seemed impossible to him that she did not, and that would mean she was deliberately trying to provoke the Va'Kul, but to what end he could not fathom.

"In my time, it was said the Isle was the playground of the Gods and that was why no one settled there."

Damian shrugged, taking a sip of wine from his cup. "I would think it has more to do with the harsh winters. It is said the sea air often blows with the force of a storm and carries shards of ice on it."

"A strange place to parlay," Chaote mused. "I wonder why she chose it."

"If your aim is to ascertain my mother's thoughts through me, it is a wasted endeavor. I have given up trying to understand women, even my mother, a long time ago."

Chaote laughed and the Va'Kul's frown deepened. She was staring at Damian and he was finding it difficult not to meet her intense gaze, though he somehow kept his eyes fixed on Chaote. The meal was finished and the Va'Kul once more motioned the servants forward to collect the empty dishes. Chaote tipped back her goblet of wine, draining the liquid and setting it on the table with a loud thud.

"Come with me, Guardian. I wish to show you something," she said, rising from the table.

The Va'Kul seemed startled, her heavy brows knitting together as she hissed to Chaote, "What are you doing?"

"Whatever I wish to do," Chaote responded without so much as glancing at her. She started to stride from the room and Damian rose quickly to follow. The Va'Kul's malevolent gaze followed him through the doorway and he could feel it burning into his back as he followed Chaote down the hallway. They went up the staircase to the upper levels, and he was pleasantly surprised when she turned and pushed open the doors to the Great Library.

The library was unchanged, as if the war and the passing of time had somehow skipped over the place. The statues remained, the works of art still hanging on the walls, and the gilded shelves still crammed with the knowledge of centuries. Damian looked around in awe and Chaote seemed pleased with his response.

"Did you think I would destroy it?" she asked.

He turned to look at her, the wonder fading and replaced with the stoic detachment she was accustomed to from the former Guardian. He simply said, "Yes."

"This place is the greatest treasure on Imbria, greater than the amulets. There is power here, knowledge of the past that is irreplaceable. I am not a fool, Damian." She walked slowly beside one shelf, running her finger over the edges of the tomes, her movements graceful yet predatory. "Do you know that he is here, in these recordings of history?"

"You speak of Rilian."

She nodded, pleased that he understood her. "It is strange to read about such mundane things as the cost of his wedding feast. Even stranger to read the accounts revering his deeds. He is a murderer, a vile, loathsome traitor, and yet here he sits, immortalized in these scrolls and books as a hero. A man instead of a monster. It is difficult for me to learn that he carried on without consequence after I was gone, that he had a family, was perhaps happy."

"History is often distorted by the victors," Damian said in his quiet way.

Her eyes gleamed as she turned to look out the window over the scarred city. "One day I plan to write my own history, Damian."

"You provoke your Va'Kul," he said suddenly, before he could convince himself not to.

She glanced back at him, the curve of her cheek carved out of silver by the fading light of day that filtered through the window. "I am aware of the Va'Kul."

"Then why do it?" he questioned.

"I know she is too proud to let me, a halfbreed, rule her people forever. It is one thing to be a legend, locked away in an unescapable prison, quite another to be a person of flesh and blood, flawed and imperfect. She will challenge me. That is inevitable. Why do you think I have been training with you? Did you believe it was because I enjoyed your company?" She laughed again. "I want to be ready when the day comes. I still need the Fomori and I am not yet ready to relinquish my rule over them."

"But you do intend to relinquish it?" Damian wanted to know. He wondered if she heard the faint hope in his voice, prayed that she did not.

"Once the Keepers are destroyed, I have no desire to rule anyone. I never wanted power, Damian, not the way others covet it. I became the leader of the Fomori for self-preservation, because I had to. I am a halfbreed. It was lead or die, be the strongest or be the weakest. Now that I have obtained that power, willingly or not, it would be foolish of me not to use it to achieve my desires."

He wanted to ask her if there was nothing else she desired besides revenge, but he knew she would not give him the answer he sought and so he remained silent. She came closer to him, close enough so that he could smell her. There was something warm and inviting in her scent, but underneath, the cloying fragrance of death lingered.

"There is a chance your mother will bring me something I seek," she said, tilting her head to one side. "And then I will have to release you."

He watched the impeccable perfection of her features, the tilt of her full lips as they played at the edges of a smile. She lifted her hand, laying it on his chest, just over his heart.

"Perhaps I will even miss you when you are gone," she said softly, leaning in closer to him. "Give me a reason to miss you, Damian."

He kissed her then, before he even realized what was happening. The rest of the world fell silent. There was no war, no destiny, no prophecy. His mind shoved out everything else and there was only her, the exquisite beauty of her face, the sharpness of her mind, the savageness of her fighting. He knew that whatever they felt for each other would never leave this room, that when they walked out they would still be enemies, but for this one moment he did not care. He had given his entire life to serve others, and he would take this one moment for himself.

26

"I cannot think of a worse place to be," I muttered disconsolately at the bleak surroundings. I had heard tales of the island's fabled beauty, and I wondered just what sort of deviant individual had created that myth, for they were either blind or a flagrant liar.

The island was slightly larger than Tahitia but smaller than Lehar. The rocky coastline where we docked abated in a series of shallow pools before giving way to an extraordinary assemblage of peculiar rock formations that jutted up from the heaving landscape in strange peaks and pinnacles. The towering rocks were dusted with thick white frost and the wind howled between them, whipping along in icy currents.

"One of the old legends claims the Gods made giants here before they made man, and the rocks you see are the remains of those titanic creatures, uncovered by centuries of harsh wind," Cossiana said.

"How inviting," I retorted sarcastically. "I would probably lay down and die as well if I were forced to live on this wretched island."

"We will prepare for the halfbreed's arrival. You will stay on the ship, out of sight unless you are needed," the old woman ordered crisply.

"I do not take orders from you," I reminded her, a hard edge to my voice.

She glared at me. "Fire Keeper, would you be so kind as to remain out of sight so that I can try to save my son from the monsters you let capture him?"

"Fine. Yes," I said with a wave of my hand. She pulled her fur-trimmed cloak more tightly around her and moved off, overseeing the men who were loading the small boats with supplies they would ferry to the island. Cossiana planned to erect a temporary shelter against one of the larger rock pinnacles, a place where she and Chaote could meet comfortably. She glanced back at me and I smiled amicably at her, walking towards the stairway that led down into the quarters where I would presumably be hiding. As soon as she turned her back again I veered to my right, hopping into one of the boats and wedging myself between the crates of cargo. Kaeleb told me he had learned not to trust the Tahitians, and I was heeding his warning. The more Cossiana wanted me to stay behind, the more I began to feel that I must go.

I felt my knees cramping from the awkward position I had tucked myself into and I silently cursed the men for being so abysmally slow. Finally, the boat was lowered into the water and several men who were piled in behind the crates and baskets began to row for the desolate shore. They jumped out as the boat hit the rocky ground, hauling it up and fastening it beyond the reach of the tide. They grouped together, discussing the best way to unload the cargo, and I took advantage of their distraction to roll myself over the side, landing rather painfully on the hard surface of the hellish island. I shook off the pain and scrambled behind the nearest pinnacle of rock, flattening myself against it and waiting. The wind was bitterly cold, tearing into my heavy coat and dragging tears from my eyes, and I was reminded yet again of why I hated the snow.

The men finished stacking the supplies where Cossiana had directed and they set about unpacking them and creating the shelter. It was nothing more than a simple lean-to, erected on the leeward side of the rock face, out of the ferocious wind. I was forced to wait until they were done before I could slide closer, coming about the windward side of the rock, the gusts stinging my face till it felt raw. I pressed myself into the shadowed crevice between the shelter and the rock, out of sight of the ships but where I could still hear what was said in the tent. I reached for my amulet, using my power to cause the tiniest flare of warmth, closing my eyes and relishing the feel of it. I felt a stab of anger at being forced to hide in a cold, dark corner like some pathetic spy, but I had no choice, not if I was unwilling to leave our destinies up to Cossiana.

"She is here. Return to the ship, all of you. Await my signal," Cossiana commanded the other islanders. I tried to get comfortable, grateful for the howling wind, miserable though it was, for at least it masked any sounds that I made.

I did not hear them till they were in the tent. The same wind that masked me also hid their movements, but I felt her coming. Rather, I felt the absence of power Chaote carried with her. The bottomless nothing that was the Warding Stone curled around me just as their booted footfalls crunched on the ground and I heard two sets of feet. I prayed that one of them was Damian.

"Where is my son?" Cossiana asked. I felt a surge of annoyance and cursed the silent gods for ignoring my request.

"He is safe nearby," the warm voice of Chaote flowed through the screeching wind. "This is my Va'Kul. Tell me, old woman, why are we here?"

Cossiana's retort was sharp and harsh. "You are Tahitian and I am your Elder! You will address me with respect!"

I nodded in my hiding place, grinning, impressed with the old woman.

Chaote laughed. "Very well, Elder. Tell me what you have brought me in exchange for your son."

"I have brought myself."

The younger woman laughed again. "You must be teasing me, Elder. Surely, you would not have wasted all our time by bringing me here with only yourself to offer."

"I told you we should not have come," the seething voice of the Va'Kul hissed.

There was a moment of silence, then Cossiana said, "I am the Tahitian Elder. Damian is nothing, he is no one of importance. He is only my son. Accept me in his place."

"But I enjoy having your son," Chaote said, taunting.

"You are no fool, girl. You must see that I am worth more than he is."

Chaote's voice lowered slightly. "Your son is a Guardian, and that is worth something. He is a symbol of the Keepers. You are the one who is worthless, not him. You are lucky that I respect him, Elder, or I would have your head removed from your stooping shoulders for dragging me to this place on a worthless errand."

"You should kill her," the sibilant voice of the Va'Kul once again interjected.

"Wait!" Cossiana interrupted. She took a long pause as she carefully considered something in her mind. "There is something else I can offer you."

Chaote's voice was smug. "I thought as much. Tell me this other offer."

"I can give you the Verucan."

I narrowed my eyes, wishing that I could burn them all to the ground, gripping the Opal that hung from my neck like a useless trinket. I could have charged into their little soiree with just my sword, but I knew that between Chaote and the Va'Kul my chances of victory were slim. The idea of engaging in hand-to-hand combat with one of them seemed feasible, but the thought of taking on both together felt like tempting fate. I tried to swallow the burning rage that was simmering in me, forcing myself to breathe. I knew I could not trust Cossiana. She was lucky that the halfbreed had the Warding Stone, but that would not save her from me later.

"The Fire Keeper?" Chaote was asking curiously. "And how will you manage that?"

Cossiana did not even pretend to hesitate this time. "He is on our ship. He believes he is here to help persuade you to trade me for Damian. I will give him to you."

"He came to save your son and you offer him up as a sacrifice? Have you no honor?" Chaote let anger color her words. At least she saw the deceptive Tahitians for what they were. "Va'Kul, go and bring Damian here. We will let him decide."

"This is a mistake, we should kill them all," the Va'Kul snapped. There was a moment of silence, then I heard the heavy footfalls of her boots as she stormed away. The unmistakable sound of an eagle's repetitive chirping resonated over the howling wind, indicating the nearby presence of one of the massive birds. So, they had not come by ship.

"You are Tahitian, child. You are one of us," Cossiana began once the Va'Kul was out of earshot.

"Your son has tried those words with me. They will not have the effect you wish them to," Chaote responded flatly. "You are a liar and you are weak. I am nothing like you."

"You wish to kill an innocent child. Who are you to look down on me?"

"I do not wish to kill the divine child. I wish to use her blood to accomplish my goals," Chaote snapped. "Ah, I see you are surprised, Elder. Did you not think I knew about the girl, about your lies? I know the Solvrei is not the boy you pretended it was, the boy you were willing to sacrifice, so which of us is willing to kill innocent children? Is it me or is it you? Because from where I sit, it appears to be you."

"We are only trying to protect the Solvrei," Cossiana insisted.

"So you claim. I am not inclined to believe your lies. Be silent now, or I will cut your tongue in half. I have agreed to let your son decide his fate, and unlike you and your Keepers, I am true to my word."

I was tired of hiding in the shadows, shivering like an imbecile while the women bickered. They already knew I had come here on the ship, Cossiana had made sure of that when she offered me up to them like a prized pony. There was no point in hiding any longer, and I had no desire to remain a passive listener while they bartered with my life. I pushed myself out of the crevice, coming around and throwing open the tent flap. A cozy fire burned between them and the women were seated around it on crates padded with cushions. They both turned to stare at me, eyes round, and I glared hatefully at Cossiana.

"If you are going to discuss my fate, I will not freeze to death while you are doing it," I muttered irritably, holding my hands over the fire to warm them.

Chaote leapt up, grabbing her sword from its sheath.

"I do not have it with me," I told her, pulling open my coat so she could see my neck. The Opal was not there. "Do you really think I trusted this old woman with my life? I have given the amulet to someone else to keep safe, and if you kill me, this will just start all over for you with a new Keeper."

I could see Chaote's eyes darting between us, weighing the potential threat I posed. Eventually, she seemed to accept that I was harmless enough for now. She sheathed her sword just as the Va'Kul returned, pushing Damian into the tent before her.

"Blaise!" Damian exclaimed, his mouth falling open in surprise.

"What is the meaning of this?" the Va'Kul demanded. She had a knife pressed to the back of Damian's neck.

"It seems the Keeper would like to be included in our negotiations," Chaote said, a hint of amusement in her tone. "I must say, Fire Keeper, you are my favorite of this new lot. The rest are a little spineless, don't you think?"

"I have been saying that for years," I concurred. Damian made a face at me.

Chaote settled herself back onto her crate, motioning for the rest of us to sit. There were only four crates and so I stood, arms folded over my chest, glaring at each of them in turn. "Now what?"

Cossiana was smiling at her son, her face gentle and mothering. "Are you well? They have not hurt you?"

"I am fine," he assured her, stoic as always.

"Damian, your mother has offered to give us the Fire Keeper in exchange for you," Chaote told him. I couldn't help but notice the subtle, intimate look that passed between them when he glanced at her and I raised an eyebrow. Perhaps Damian had not been suffering too greatly in his captivity.

"An arrangement that I did not agree to," I pointed out. "Besides, I have given the Opal to another for safekeeping. It will do her no good to take me with her. I am just like any other man."

Damian's lingering stare made me wonder if he was aware of the hidden amulet in my boot. Surely he, of all people, would not believe that I had given the jewel to someone else.

"I will not trade my life for his," Damian said with finality.

"Then take me!" Cossiana wailed. "Please, I beg you!"

Chaote was thoughtful, almost playful, like a cat toying with mice. She tilted her head, her perfect features delicate and strong. "It may not matter soon, anyway. Tell me, have any of you bothered to look and see what your Earth Keeper has been up to?"

"Maialen?" I asked. "What has she got to do with this?"

Chaote turned her starry gaze back to me. "She has everything to do with it. You claim to have left the Fire Opal with someone for safekeeping, and you have just come from the islands, so if you are telling the truth, then someone there has it. That is also where the divine child resides, is it not?"

My mind was racing with possibilities, trying to ascertain what she was hinting at, but I could not grasp it. "Spit it out," I snarled at her.

She laughed. "Your Queens have decided they no longer need the rest of you."

Damian started to stand, his dark eyes growing round. "What are you saying?"

"The Earth Keeper and the Verucan wish to put an end to this war, and so we have come to an agreement. While you are here wasting your time with us, they are invading your islands and they have agreed to bring me the child, as long as I let them both continue to rule their lands after the amulets are destroyed."

I lunged at Chaote, wanting to break her perfectly formed neck, kicking the fire in a shower of sparks. The Va'Kul shrieked and her long talons sliced at my arms just as I wrapped them around Chaote's neck. Damian was behind them and he picked up the crate he had been sitting on, smashing it over the Va'Kul's head. She toppled to the ground, releasing me just as Chaote kicked me squarely in the chest, tossing me backwards.

"What have you done?" Damian asked her, his voice pained.

"What I must," Chaote said through gritted teeth. She had her sword in her hand and was backing away, moving toward the opening of the tent.

"Kill her!" I shouted at Damian. I was still flat on the ground, trying to draw my sword, but the Va'Kul had recovered from the Guardian's blow and she grabbed my arm once more, wresting it to her poisonous jaws. I wrapped my legs around her neck and squeezed so she would not be able to bite me while she thrashed about, clawing at me viciously. There was a flurry of movement and Chaote was gone, the flap of the tent flung out by the wind so I could see her running across the barren landscape of rock and ice. I looked at Damian in disbelief, still trying to wrestle the savage Va'Kul. "You let her get away?"

He ignored me and kicked the Va'Kul in the face. She released me, once more unconscious. I scrambled to my feet, running after Chaote. I could see her dark form sprinting towards the eagles, and I knew I would not reach her in time. It did not matter; I was not after her. All I wanted was to take the other eagle and to get to Tahitia as quickly as I could. I had left Kaeleb there. I told him I would protect him and I had left him there and he would die. I prayed that Bacatha was with him, that she would protect him, but I knew in my heart that if what Chaote said was true, if Maialen was the one to attack, then no one could stop her. Only another Keeper could stop her. I was the only one who could have stopped her, and I was not there.

Chaote was frantically trying to loose the other eagle so I could not follow her, but the creature was agitated, flapping its wings and ducking its massive head up and down so that she was forced to dodge the enormous beak. I heard her scream in frustration, then she leapt onto the bird whose tethers she had already untied from the rock, vaulting into the air with a rush of icy wind. I lifted my sword, hacking through the thick leather ties that held the remaining eagle, trying to calm it as it reared back, great wings flapping, showering me in a stinging curtain of ice and snow. It cared nothing for my soothing placations, hopping backwards and screeching maniacally. I wrapped the tethers around my fist and yanked down. The enormous head turned slightly, its eye facing me while it decided whether or not to obey my commands. Then it dipped its shoulder and I climbed onto it just as the creature spread its wings and soared into the air.

I looked down below as we circled higher over the barren island and I saw Damian looking up, waving his arms. For a moment I was tempted to go back for him, but he was too heavy and he would only slow me down. I was not even sure the winged creature would make it all the way to Tahitia with just me atop it, let alone his massive bulk. Damian had his mother and her ship, he could find his own way back. He was no longer my concern. Kaeleb was all that mattered now. I pulled the tethers and turned south, leaving them behind.

27

The gentle spattering of raindrops became a torrent as the islands finally appeared on the dim horizon. The eagle dipped low in the sky, skimming over the waves as I stared in disbelief at the wreckage that was scattered through the sea. Uprooted trees, twisted planks of wood, pieces of ships, all of it tossed about on a churning grey ocean. I lifted my eyes to what I knew was Lehar, but the island was unrecognizable. With night quickly approaching, the towering Citadel should have illuminated the landscape but it was not there, and its absence was so disturbing that I felt my chest tighten. *Where was the Citadel?*

The debris grew thicker, congesting the water as we approached, and I stared in disbelief at the entire eastern edge of the island that was now missing. Orabelle's ship, the coralstone wall, it was all gone and the ocean frothed turbulently against the mountain of shining blue rubble that had once been the great Citadel. I turned my head away, squeezing the flanks of the eagle, urging it to beat its wings faster for Tahitia.

The smaller island was still intact, the shape of its coastline just as I remembered it, and for a moment I felt a surge of relief. Rain pelted my face, stinging my eyes, and I wiped it away, trying to see through the storm. My relief quickly faded.

Tahitia was a wasteland. It looked as if one of the giants from Cossiana's old tales had walked the perimeter of the island, kicking down everything in its path and flattening it to the ground. Further in, beyond the ring of complete destruction, there was more chaos. I could see people moving, hear their cries tossed about by the wind. The village in the center of the island was in shambles and I saw a dead eagle laying brokenly in the clearing, its neck bent at an impossible angle. The black armored bodies of Verucans were still trapped beneath it. I spurred my eagle higher, not wanting to risk the survivors mistaking me for another assault, coming around the southern side of the island, to the beach where Kaeleb and Eolande liked to sit. I guided the eagle down onto the sand and slid off it, looking around, feeling completely helpless for the first time in my life.

"Kaeleb!" I shouted. Rain poured down on me, plastering my hair to my forehead and running down the sharp planes of my face. I shoved my hair back, wiping at my eyes again to clear them. "Kaeleb!"

I ran to the flattened tree line, clamoring over fallen trunks and broken branches. The sky was nearly black, the moonlight obscured by the storm. I reached into my boot, pulling out the Opal and looping it around my neck, calling my power to me. I felt the hot sear of it, the familiar burn that raced along the edges of my skin. I lifted my hands, lighting up the decimated jungle.

"Kaeleb!"

"Fire Keeper!" a Tahitian voice called to me from the darkness. I wove my hand, the flames arcing in their direction so I could see them. It was one of the island's healers and she was on her knees, bent over a prostrate man, her hands pressed against the deep gash that scored the man's leg. "Fire Keeper, help us. Stop the bleeding."

I gave her a curt nod and she moved her hands, blood pouring out. I waved two of my fingers and the man screamed as the heat from the flames cauterized the wound.

"Have you seen the boy? The one I brought here?" I demanded of the woman.

She shook her head. "No, but the healers are gathering the wounded in the houses that remain standing in the village. He may be there."

I started to run. The flattened destruction that ringed the outer edge of the island ended abruptly, and I fought my way through the shredded jungle that followed. Great gouges of earth had been ripped out of the ground and the vines were like cobwebs between the trees, so thick and their spikes so sharp that it was nearly impossible to get through them. That was when I looked up and realized why. The thorny web of vines was woven with bodies. It was Maialen. No one else could have done it, and I stared in horror at the atrocities. I forced myself to look at each of them, searching for Kaeleb's slight frame and pale hair, my heart pounding. He was not among them. I closed my eyes, relieved but unable to reconcile the doll-like gentleness of the Earth Queen that I had known for so long with whatever monster had done this.

I kept going, burning my way through Maialen's tangle of horrors. I needed to find Kaeleb. My mind was reeling with images of him, of my brother, of Logaire, Orabelle, all the ones I had loved but could not protect. I failed again. Nothing had changed. I was still the same boy, weak and ineffectual, unable to save the people who mattered most to me.

I burst into the clearing in a shower of sparks and fire. Villagers gasped and shrieked, some of them calling out for my help. I spread the fire around the open space so we could see, and I wound my way through the maze of bodies. More Verucans, a few Kymirrans. Eagle feathers everywhere. This was why Maialen had been hoarding her eagles, why she would not let us take one. She knew she was going to need them for the attack. My mind went back to the docks of Kymir, to the new ships that sat proudly in the harbor. She had known she would do this. She planned it.

"Have you seen Kaeleb? The boy, the Leharan boy!" I shouted at one man who was hurrying past me.

"No, but the Leharan woman is that way," he said quickly before moving out of the ring of firelight and disappearing into the rain and shadows.

I sprinted in the direction he had pointed, calling out Bacatha's name.

"Here! I am here!" Her lilting Leharan voice was hoarse and strained. I lifted my hand, a flame catching in the air, burning despite the rain. She looked at it and grinned. "I never thought I would be so happy to see you."

She was sitting on a fallen tree, her armor cracked, her face and neck covered in dozens of shallow cuts. The rain had washed most of the blood away, but her hair held a faint pink tint from being soaked with it.

"Where is Kaeleb?" I demanded.

She shook her head and I felt a knot form in my throat, choking me. Then she said, "He was beside me; we were fighting. Then the Earth Queen came. Everything... it was as if the world had turned upside down. I lost him. I tried to hold on to him and the girl, but they slipped away and then there was so much pain."

"Where did this happen? Where were you when you lost him?" I asked, gripping her shoulders and shaking her out of the stupor she was falling into.

"I do not know!" she cried, her eyes wild. "I am still struggling to understand what happened. I thought Kaeleb was the Solvrei, but it wasn't him, was it? It never was. It was that girl, the girl who turned the world over."

I took a breath, trying to stay calm, to speak over the knot that restricted my throat. I forced her to look at me, my amber eyes burning with intensity. I needed her to focus on me. "Bacatha, tell me everything that happened."

They had come in the middle of the day, without warning. Lehar was attacked first. The Kymirrans sailed their ships into the harbor peacefully, as they always did, but this time those ships were filled with soldiers from Kymir and Veruca. They poured out, taking the Leharans by surprise. The mainland armies would have been no match for the battle-trained islanders, but then the Earth Queen came on her eagle, and she brought Akrin with her. Maialen laid waste to Lehar, toppling the Citadel and rending the island in two, shoving part of it out to sea. Bacatha and the Tahitians could see that something was happening on the other island, but they had no way of knowing the extent of the violent destruction the Queen was inflicting.

"We knew something was happening, that something was wrong. The Tahitians were prepared. They were ready for them when they came, but the Earth Queen was too powerful. We could have defeated the soldiers, but what could we do against a Keeper? We tried to take her down. I even hit her eagle with an arrow, but then she did this to me." Bacatha indicated the myriad of cuts that crisscrossed her face. "Thorns. She wrapped me in them, my whole body. It was agonizing. Kaeleb was helping me, pulling them off, but then the girl began to scream."

Akrin had landed on the island, cutting down anyone who got in his way until he found Eolande. He grabbed her and was trying to drag her back to his eagle, but she fought him. Then the Sirens were there, screaming with her, attacking him. As soon as she saw them, Maialen forgot about Bacatha and the writhing thorns, staring at the Sirens and the child with unimaginable enmity. The Sirens turned to look up at Maialen as she circled overhead. They were crying, as if trying to understand why she was there, why she was doing this. Bacatha took advantage of the Earth Queen's distraction and managed to free herself from the tangle of thorns. She charged at Akrin, knocking him to the ground and sending the little girl sprawling in the dirt. Kaeleb dove for Eolande, gripping her hand, and Bacatha reached out for his, ready to run. Before she could, she felt an unimaginable pain radiate up her arm. That was when the world moved.

Maialen and Eolande both called their power at the same time. Bacatha watched helplessly as the ground began to dissolve beneath them, rippling and buckling, and the ocean rose into the air. Not just a few droplets of water, but the entire sea surrounding Tahitia. Maialen stared at the child, open-mouthed, gaping, unable to believe the extent of her niece's power. She brought her eagle down to the island and stood across from the girl, clutching the Emerald and trying to use her own power to stop the child. The Sirens came up to her then, wailing, a horrible, sorrowful sound. The Earth Queen screamed at them, reaching out and snatching the Pearl away from the one who held it. They raised their hands to her, a pleading gesture, but Maialen turned her back, running to the eagle as the sea continued to rise into the air above them. It was then that Akrin grabbed the girl again, hitting her over the head. When he did, the sea plummeted from the sky, crashing into the land with a force that shook everything. Bacatha was thrown down, landing on her head, stars and blackness exploding in front of her eyes.

I felt hope leaching out of me as she spoke, the first faint tendrils of rotting grief curling in my gut. I waited for her to go on, to say something that would take away the pain that was filling me, to tell me anything that would allow me to go on believing he was alive.

"When I awoke Kaeleb was not there," Bacatha said, hanging her head in shame, rain dripping down her golden features, her voice colored with remorse. "I am sorry. I tried to protect him."

"I told you I did not need protecting."

I jerked my head up and spun around. Kaeleb was standing there, leaning on the hilt of his sword, his wet hair stuck to his head and a bandage wrapped around the left side of his face, covering one eye. He grinned at me and took a step forward and I grabbed him up, embracing him tightly until he made a suffocating sound and then I set him back on his feet. I could not have put into words what I felt at that moment. I did not care about the amulets or the throne or anything else. All that mattered to me was that Kaeleb was still alive.

"What happened here?" I asked, my voice rough with emotion, which I tried to hide. I lifted the edge of the bandage. There was a dark, empty socket where his eye had been, the wound crusted with dried blood.

"I lost the eye," he said, his face scrunching up with displeasure and his remaining grey eye casting downward.

"Good thing you have another," I told him, ruffling his wet hair and wishing I could strangle whoever had done this to him. I was beyond grateful that he was alive, but I should have been there. I should have protected him, protected all of them.

"They took the Solvrei. I could not stop them," he said.

"Bacatha said you fought bravely. You did well, my boy," I assured him. Bacatha nodded in agreement and Kaeleb dug his toe into the muddy ground.

"What do we do now?"

I felt my eyes burning with the wrath that was a bottomless well within me. "We need to find a healer to look at that eye of yours, then we help the islanders as much as we can tonight. Tomorrow I am going to see the Earth Queen, and she will not like the welcome I intend to bring her."

28

The morning came too soon. I had not slept, for fear that if I closed my eyes, Kaeleb would not be there when I opened them. Instead, I watched over him and Bacatha as they curled together under two pieces of thatched roof we had leaned against each other, remnants from one of the collapsed houses. It was not the most stable of shelters, but the storm was past and it was not as if we had many choices in accommodations. The few structures that remained standing in the island village were full of the wounded, their cries and gasps filling the air as the surviving healers moved between them, doing what little they could. I had walked amidst the wounded, Kaeleb trailing behind me, in search of someone to provide care for his eye, using my abilities to illuminate the healer's work and cauterize wounds as required. I finally found a woman who could help us and she lifted the makeshift bandage from the boy's face, letting out a low whistle.

"You are certainly brave, little one," she murmured, dipping a strip of cloth into a bowl of pungent herbs and smearing it across his face with gentle, nimble fingers. "How did this happen?"

He gritted his teeth at the pain from her ministrations and I saw tears gathering in the corner of his remaining eye. I looked away so he would not be embarrassed, placing my hand on his shoulder for comfort.

"I do not know. I was with the Solvrei, then the Verucan man hit her and the water fell and I remember feeling like I was being thrown about. Then everything went dark," he told her. "When I woke up again my eye was gone."

There was something in his voice that made me think he was lying, or at the very least holding back some part of the truth, but I did not question him further. He had been through enough for one night. The healer made a small noise of understanding while she padded the eye with some sort of fluffy plant fiber. Then she wrapped a clean bandage around his head, tying it securely and causing him to give a sharp yelp of pain. I looked back at him and he was staring up at me expectantly, as if needing me to reaffirm that the healer had done all that she could.

"You look very dangerous now. I rather like it. Perhaps I should take one of mine out too," I told him, ruffling the pale shock of white hair. The healer gave me a kind smile, then rose and moved on. We made our way back outside to where Bacatha was waiting. She was pale, unsteady on her feet.

"I cannot find my farming tool," she said, the words nearly choking her. I felt sympathy for the woman, knowing that her grief at the lost weapon was her way of coping with what was happening.

"We can find you another or have a better one crafted for you. I still know Verucan blacksmiths who are loyal to me and will forge weapons," I assured her. She nodded and took a deep breath, grateful for the steadiness of my voice.

"I need to get to Lehar," she said, staring at the darkness that harbored the other island. I knew what she was leaving unsaid, that she needed to know if her family and Thyrr were still alive.

"I will take you in the morning before we go to Kymir," I promised her. "Tonight, you must rest. You cannot help anyone in this condition."

She considered arguing, but in the end she was too fatigued and simply nodded in reluctant agreement. I kept my word, and as soon as the sun was cresting the horizon I shook them both awake, telling them it was time to leave.

"You did not sleep," Kaeleb accused. I did not have to see myself to know there were dark smudges under my eyes and I was still covered in dirt and blood. We all were. The healer who had helped us the night before had brought us clean clothing sometime in the night and we changed quickly, glad to at least not be soaked in mud and gore. I saw Bacatha glance over at me as I pulled the shirt over my head and I raised an eyebrow at her.

"I thought you did not care for my kind," I teased her.

"I don't," she tossed back. "I was looking at your amulet. Perhaps the halfbreed is right and it is too much power for one person to hold."

She dropped her broken armor in pieces on the ground and I looked away as she peeled off her tunic and pants and replaced them with clean ones.

I touched my fingers to the golden edge of the amulet, thinking of the destruction around us, the complete desecration of Lehar, and I murmured in assent, "Perhaps she is."

We went to the eagle which I had tethered nearby, unwilling to let the creature out of my sight. Three of us were quite a heavy load for the poor bird, but it was only a short distance to Lehar and we could fly low over the water.

"We will be too heavy," Bacatha said, echoing my thoughts. "I will take a boat. There are some small fishing vessels still intact."

"The eagle will be faster," I pointed out.

She considered this before deciding. "No, I will take a boat and I will bring a healer with me. It will be needed."

Kaeleb walked up and wrapped his arms around her waist, hugging her tightly. Her icy blue eyes widened a bit in surprise and she patted him awkwardly, cringing though he could not see it. Then he released her and swung up behind me on the eagle. We lifted into the air, soaring towards Kymir. I glanced back at the scattered remnants of the island, now littered with death and destruction, and once again anger unfurled inside me, growing stronger as we neared the Kymirran shores.

"Maialen!" I bellowed as we reached the sky over the mainland, slashing the air with my hand and watching one of her ships burst into flame. I felt a smile pulling at my lips as I looked upon the burning wreckage, feeding my power into it until it was nothing but ash floating over the sea. Men were fleeing the docks as I circled overhead on the eagle, Kaeleb perched behind me and ducking his head behind my shoulder so the wind would not tear at the bandage that covered his missing eye.

A troop of archers streamed towards us from the forest and I chuckled. She would need to do better than that. Flames surrounded them and they huddled together in panic, pressing close to each other to avoid the swirling tongues of fire that encircled them. I called her name again. If the Earth Queen did not show herself soon then I was going to burn all of Kymir to the ground. Perhaps I would burn it all anyway. I could feel the power of my Element growing inside of me, filling me until I could barely contain it. I could release it all onto Kymir, burn the Royal City, leave Maialen with nothing but a kingdom of ashes, which was all she deserved.

There was a subtle movement in the balance, and I felt the cool breath of the Pearl. For a moment I was disconcerted by the unexpected sensation, then I remembered what Bacatha had said. Maialen had taken the Pearl from the Sirens.

Droplets rose out of the sea and dampened the flames that surrounded the soldiers. Through the smoke, I saw Maialen walking towards me. She was wearing a long winter gown of deep green etched in gold, her hair falling in loose waves around her shoulders. There was not a mark on her, as if she had just woken from a restful sleep and had not spent the previous day obliterating an entire realm. I saw the golden bracelets on her arms, a tribute to her dead father perhaps, and I wondered if it was Damek's influence and Chronus's warped memory that had brought about this change in her.

"Blaise," she said flatly, clearly not pleased to see me. Her eyes moved past me to the burning cinders of her ship and her frown deepened. "I thought you were off in the north, playing champion to my sister's Guardian."

I settled the eagle on the ground, passing the reins back to Kaeleb and leaving him astride the creature in case he needed to make a hasty escape. His single grey eye narrowed slightly, conveying his worry, and I responded with a nonchalant grin. I refused to be afraid of Maialen.

"Who has the Pearl?" I asked her, looking around at the assembled men, wondering if it was one of them.

"I do," she said defiantly, lifting her chin. It was a gesture too much like her sister, and I felt a chill run down my spine. She went on, not bothering to hide her triumph. "No one has ever held two amulets before. Damek was not even sure it was possible, but I am able to do it. I am the first. It is exhilarating."

I was shaking my head, appalled, unsure who the woman was who faced me as I tried to reason with her. "Maialen, you cannot do this. It is not done and there is a reason it is not done."

She scoffed, big green eyes flashing. "You would have done it yourself, given the chance. And the Council forbade it, but the Council is gone thanks to the rest of you. If no one will follow the rules of the Edicts, then why should I?"

"You do not know what it will do to you," my voice was stern, warning. "There are things happening that you do not understand."

"I know exactly what it will do, Blaise. It will make me the most powerful person on Imbria. I am not the fool you think I am! I am sick of being a pawn in the games the rest of you play. All of you use me when it is convenient and then you toss me aside like I am nothing!" She was angry, resentful, and I knew she was speaking of me, of how I had treated her.

"It was not like that, Maialen," I said softly. "What happened between us-"

"What happened between us was a mistake," she interrupted. "That is what you believe, isn't it? You wish it had never happened because no matter how much I try, no matter what I do, I am not her!"

I shoved a hand through my hair, looking up at the blue sky. Guilt was heavy on my shoulders, pressing me down with the weight of my thoughts. Maialen had done what she did because of me. She destroyed Lehar and Tahitia because of me and because she was jealous of Orabelle. That was why she shattered the island, tossed everything that was a monument to her sister's memory into the ocean. It was my fault. Whatever justifications for destroying Lehar that Logaire's silver tongue had slipped into her ear were just excuses.

"Maialen," I began, letting her see my regret, the pain in my heart. "I wanted to give you what you needed, but I told you I could not. I did not lie to you. I never lied to you. My feelings for you have nothing to do with Orabelle. You think I am the one who cannot let go of her memory, but it is you who clings to it so bitterly."

Tears welled in her eyes. "I hate you."

I sighed. "Then hate me. But you cannot destroy the world because of me. What have you done with the girl? Give her back to me and we can end this. You cannot give her to Chaote, you are a Keeper. You are the thing Chaote wants to kill most, and now you have two amulets. You are the first person she will come for."

Maialen laughed bitterly. She twirled her finger in the air and a flower rose up from the cold, hard ground. Moisture gathered around it and it grew taller, blooming into a beautiful spray of red and yellow petals as the water curled, caressing the stem. Then it began to blacken, withering and crumbling to the land, a dried and dead husk. She lifted her green eyes to me. "I do not have the girl. Your cousin sent Akrin to find Eolande and he was supposed to bring her back to Kymir after the attack but he never returned here. I suppose he took her to Veruca. We were never going to give her to Chaote, that was a lie."

"You were going to keep her for yourself."

She shrugged. "I was, but that was before I had the Pearl. Logaire can have the girl. I do not need her now. You see, Blaise, I am the Solvrei. I can unite the Elements. I can be the one to save Imbria."

I stared at her as if she were mad, apprehension curling in my gut. "You are not the Solvrei, Maialen. How can you say that? How can you claim you want to save Imbria when you just obliterated one of its kingdoms? Look at Kaeleb! Look at his face. You have decimated Lehar and Tahitia, crushed the greatest army on Imbria just when it is needed the most. If you really wanted to stop all of this you would not have made shadowy pacts with my duplicitous cousin. You would have helped me take back Veruca! We could have done this togeth-er, Maialen. We could have saved Imbria without destroying it."

"I saw the way you looked at me. That day at the divide. There is no together for us, there never will be," she practically spat.

I could not argue, for she was right. I would never have trusted her again after that day, and what was happening now only proved that my instincts were correct. We stood there together in the cold winter morning, neither of us knowing what to do next.

"I loved you, you know," she finally whispered. Tears slid down her freckled cheeks. "Go now, I do not wish to fight you. It will only end badly for both of us."

I nodded. "I will go for now, but I cannot let what you have done go unanswered."

"Then build your army and come for me. I will be ready."

29

Thyrr coughed, spitting water from his mouth and gripping the piece of wreckage desperately. He had dozed off, his cramped muscles easing their clutching hold on the debris. He had slipped under the cool, salty waves, mercifully weightless for a moment, silent and still in the darkness beneath the sea. He forced his mind to focus, kicking back up to the bright surface and once again clinging onto the broken piece of hull as he drifted, bobbing on the endless expanse of ocean. He knew that if he had been tossed into the eastern sea surrounding Lehar, eventually he would drift into the current to the south, carrying him towards Tahitia. Thyrr held on, laying his head on the splintered wood that had once been part of Orabelle's magnificent ship.

He wondered if he should have seen the attack coming, if there were signs he ignored. Had Colwyn not been executed, then perhaps Maialen would not have come, wreaking havoc. Thyrr did not want the man to die, that was never his wish. When he and Bacatha returned to Lehar, they had gone to Brogan, Bacatha's father and one of the oldest living members of the Guard. They sat around a table in their kitchen, and Bacatha told him what they had learned, that Colwyn was the traitor. Brogan nodded, did not seem surprised, but rather he was melancholy, as if he knew this day would come but he was not yet prepared for it.

"I thought it might be him," Brogan said in a low voice. "I kept picturing those days in my head. Who had been where, who had the opportunity. It could only have been Colwyn or Damian, and it was hard to believe that it could be the Tahitian, but I still needed proof."

"Now that we are certain, he cannot continue to speak for Lehar," Bacatha insisted vehemently, banging her fist on the table.

Her father smiled at her, slightly indulgent. He was proud of her, proud of her fierce convictions and her resolve to do what was best for her kingdom. "You have never cared for the man's policies, but Colwyn has tried to do what he thought was best for Lehar."

Thyrr leaned forward, his strange gaze intense. "He is the reason my sister is dead."

Brogan seemed to chafe at the reminder. "You did not even know her, boy. I served Orabelle for years. She was my Queen and I loved her, as all Leharans loved her. I am not asking for his crimes to be overlooked. I merely state that his intentions were not so devious as you might want to believe. Chronus was not a man to be trifled with, Colwyn was no match for him. There is no telling what manipulations the old Earth Keeper used to get the Captain under his thumb."

Bacatha was unmoved. "He is a traitor and it does not matter why. I would die before I betrayed Lehar."

"It is easy to accept death when you are not being faced with it, daughter," Brogan cautioned her.

Thyrr interrupted them. "So, what do we do now?"

Brogan regarded the young man carefully. Thyrr was also trying to do what was best for the island, that much Brogan could see. But like Bacatha, he was young and headstrong, and he needed to learn that every action a ruler took had consequences that reverberated through generations. Thyrr did not know how to rule. If he did, then Logaire never would have taken the Warding Stone, and Colwyn would never have been able to challenge him the way he had. Brogan was not convinced that Thyrr was the best choice for Lehar.

"We will assemble the Guard," Brogan suggested, though it was more of a statement than a proposal. "They will vote and decide."

Bacatha sat back, content with this course of action. She knew what the Guard would choose, and so did her father. She also knew that his aim in assembling a vote had nothing to do with Colwyn's fate. He was setting a precedent, giving the Guard the power to rule alongside the monarch. It was an intelligent ploy, and she was pleased at the way he had brought it about.

The Guard had gathered to hear Blaise's words repeated to them by Bacatha. There were shouts of denial, arguments, and a heated debate. They summoned Colwyn to them, to confront him with the accusations and to hear his defense, but the moment he stepped into the room they all knew he was guilty. It was written all over his face, in the way he hung his head in shame.

Thyrr petitioned that the Captain be banished for his crimes, but the Guard was insistent that he would need to die for them. It was their way. Their honor was everything, and Colwyn had besmirched it. To let him live was to let all of them continue to live with his shame, and this they could not abide. He was taken on a ship, far out into the southern sea, bound with rocks, and tossed into the ocean. Thyrr was there, he had to be there, and he tried to stare at the man's forehead as Colwyn was waiting to die, avoiding his eyes. The others knotted the ropes that held the heavy stones around him and stepped back, looking to Thyrr. He would have to give the order, even though he was given no choice in what order he was forced to give. He stared at the forehead, at the hair that was receding back, at the pale strands of blond and grey that clung to the sides of the face above the heavy jowls. Anywhere but at the eyes, the soft blue eyes filled with fear and regret.

Thyrr moved his hand and the men gave Colwyn a gentle shove. A quiet splash and he was gone, swallowed by the ocean. Thyrr would never have to look at those terrified eyes again.

Now, as Thyrr bobbed on that same frothing sea, he wondered if Colwyn was somewhere beneath him. If he let go, slipped between the waves, sunk into the vast depths of the darkness below, would he find the other man? Would Colwyn be there waiting for him, his eyes still open, frightened and alone?

Thyrr shook his head, trying to clear it of the morose thoughts. He needed to stay awake, to not think about the weightless embrace of the sea. He needed to live. After everything he had been through to get here, he would not die now.

He remembered his father, how much he wanted a life that was not filled with fear, how much he wanted to stop running. His father never had a chance to live that life, and so Thyrr had tried to live it for him. He thought that if he was someone special, if he was the brother of the Leharan Queen, then his life would be better.

"You must tell no one what you are," his father warned him. "There are people who would not accept you, people who will want to harm you just because you are part Fomori."

Thyrr remembered how similar he and his father had been, how much he looked like him. They both sported the same golden hair and unique eyes, blue like the summer sky streaked with sunlight, the same crooked smile. His father was a man who laughed often, the lines around his mouth deepening as he did, though the night Thyrr's mind drifted back to was humorless, his father's face stern and serious. They lay in the back of their wagon, Thyrr tucked onto the shelf above his father's bed that he had taken over when he was too large to fit in the wicker basket that had served as his bassinet. His father was stretched out below, hands folded behind his head, staring up at the roof of the wagon that was painted with a wild mural of a stag running through a meadow. The colors in the painting were all wrong, the stag bright red instead of muted brown, the sky lemon yellow, and the meadow grass too vibrant, dotted with flowers in every color imaginable. Thyrr loved it.

"Why do they blame us for what we are?" Thyrr asked, always curious. "We did not have a choice. And it saved our lives today. The Fomori did not attack us."

"They hate us because there is a secret that we know."

"A secret?" Thyrr pushed himself up on his elbow, interested in this new revelation. "I want to know it!"

His father stared overhead, his eyes tracing along the grass of the painted meadow. "I can tell you, but must promise me you will never speak of it to anyone."

"I promise," Thyrr had vowed solemnly. He swung his feet over the shelf and dropped to the floor of the wagon beside his father, settling onto the covers next to him and getting ready for a wonderful tale. His father was the best storyteller in the caravan and he wove tales so vivid that if you closed your eyes while he was speaking you could believe you were there.

"This is not a story, my boy," his father warned. "This is something that can get us all killed, but as I have taught you, knowledge is power. If something happens to me, then I want you to use what I tell you."

"Use it how?" Thyrr questioned. He was still a child, not quite ready to grasp the context his father laid out.

"You will know if the time comes," his father assured him. "There is one like us that is quite powerful, possibly the most powerful person on Imbria."

"Like us... you mean part Fomori? Who?" Thyrr demanded, his eyes growing round.

"The Water Keeper. Orabelle, Queen of Lehar."

Thyrr drew his eyebrows together, thinking over this new revelation. He had not expected someone so prestigious to be a descendent of the Fomori. "How do you know?"

"Her father traveled with us for a time, before he returned to Samirra. We were friends."

"But her father is the Kymirran king," Thyrr protested, trying to recall what he knew of the Keepers and the royal families.

"Chronus is not her true father. You will understand more when you are older, my son. For now, believe me when I tell you that the Leharan Queen is one of us, though I doubt even she knows it."

Thyrr mulled this over. "She has an entire family she does not even know about?"

"Not an entire family, no. Just a father and a brother."

Thyrr had taken the rest of the night to mull over his father's revelation, to imagine what it would be like to have a secret family somewhere that no one ever told you existed. He did not know then that he would one day use what his father had told him, just as his father wanted him to. He would spend years becoming the brother of the Leharan Queen, training himself to believe it, learning everything he could about the flawed and broken family that he would now claim to be a part of. Thyrr had spent so long convincing himself and everyone around him of who he was supposed to be that he had almost forgotten it was not true.

The ocean began to sway insistently and Thyrr opened his eyes, trying to look around. Perhaps he was near the shore, or he had finally found a current. He adjusted his aching arms on the piece of wooden hull that he clung to, wondering how much longer he could hold on. He was not ready to die. He had gone through too much, fought too hard to get where he was, and he would not give up now. Thyrr lifted his head, his neck screaming, pain radiating through his back and shoulders. There was a boat. That was what was making the water move. He tried to call out, but his voice was a hoarse croak. He kicked his feet, the movements taking an enormous amount of effort, though his limbs were barely able to obey.

He closed his eyes, worried that he was imagining the small craft, but when he opened them again the boat was closer. There were two figures in it, silhouetted against the sun so that he could not make out who they were. He did not care. All he wanted was to get out of the water. Thyrr forced his feet to kick harder, then suddenly the piece of debris he had been clinging to slipped out of his grasp, carried away quickly by the wake of the boat. He tried to curse but instead swallowed a mouthful of seawater, choking and sputtering as he thrashed about, trying not to sink between the waves.

He would not die here.

Thyrr tried to swim, tried to keep the boat in his sight, but the waves were rolling over him and he could not catch his breath, could not kick hard enough to stay afloat. Below, it was calm and peaceful. Quiet. Serene. Colwyn was down there, waiting for him. He would not be alone.

30

After leaving Maialen to her tears and her delusions of being the savior of the world, Kaeleb and I took the eagle back to Lehar. I still could not reconcile the woman I had known with who she had become, though a nagging voice in the back of my head told me I should have seen it coming. A thousand moments raced through my mind, the small, telling signs of her bitterness that I should have noticed, and they added up to her insurmountable jealous rage. I should never have encouraged her feelings for me, though at the time I had believed that we could share a night of intimacy and move on from it. I had cared for her, in a way. I wanted to give her something that she desperately needed and that her husband refused to give her. If I had known her husband would be dead so soon afterwards, I would never have laid a hand on her, knowing that his demise would only make her cling to me more. But it was too late to take back what had happened. My only consolation for my guilt was that I had never lied to her. She knew that I would never be able to love her the way she wanted me to. I had admitted as much to her, even if she stubbornly wanted to believe otherwise.

I felt another chill run down my back as I thought of the Earth Queen commanding her sister's Element. It was not just my personal discomfort with the idea, though that was immense, it was something in the way the power itself was moving. There was something wrong. I remembered the flower Maialen had coaxed from the ground, how it withered and died, and I wondered if that was her doing, as I had first presumed, or if the effect was a consequence.

"The Harbonah always insisted that only the Solvrei could wield more than one Element," Kaeleb had whispered to me as I returned to the eagle, Maialen watching us with her tear-stained face. "What she is doing is wrong. She will change things."

"She already has," I muttered back. I swung onto the creature's back and pulled at the tethers, lifting us into the air. I was tempted to burn the rest of her ships, but I let the urge pass. At this point, I had no clue about the extent of her power or her intentions, and I was not about to put Kaeleb in harm's way yet again.

"She could have given us some food for the journey," Kaeleb sighed disconsolately. Then, his voice tinged with worry, he said, "If we are at war with Kymir, then that means no more pastries and fritters."

I chuckled. "Yes, that means you will be deprived of pastries for the time being."

He was silent the rest of the flight, grieving more for the loss of the pastries than he had for his eye. As we neared the island that had once been Lehar, I swooped around the western shore, following it south to where Bacatha would have come from Tahitia. I needed to know if Thyrr was still alive, and I needed to find men who could fight. I could not let Logaire keep the girl. I would take back the Solvrei and Veruca, by any means necessary, and then I would deal with Maialen.

I spotted a small boat on the Leharan beach, just as I had hoped, and the marks in the sand showed that someone had been dragged from the boat into the blighted jungle. I flew low over the tangle of twisted and broken trees and saw three figures, two women hauling a third man between them. The sun shone off his golden hair and I knew it was Thyrr. Bacatha looked up at me, waving her hand for us to land and help.

"Is he alive?" I asked, climbing off the eagle and walking over to inspect the young man.

"Yes," Thyrr croaked, a miserable sound.

"Take him," Bacatha ordered me. "Put all those muscles to good use."

"I knew you were looking," I said to her with a grin, moving to do as she wanted. She scoffed, shaking her head. I took Thyrr's weight on my right side, hoisting him half over my shoulder. Bacatha stepped away, rubbing her lower back with a grimace. The Tahitian woman who flanked his other side was the same healer from the night before, the one who had bandaged Kaeleb and brought us clothing. She looked tired but determined, displaying the infamous Tahitian resolve. I asked her what her name was.

"Gula," she told me.

"Thank you for helping us, Gula," I said, grateful that she endured under Thyrr's weight and did not abandon me to be his sole carrier as Bacatha had. She was a sturdy woman, kind in the eyes, with a gentle smile between rounded cheeks and a halo of curly black hair.

"I never thought the Keeper of Fire would be thanking me," she exclaimed with a laugh.

"These are strange times, indeed," I agreed. "Where are we dragging him to, exactly?"

Bacatha's face was pinched. "We must take him somewhere. He needs food and water, and he could be injured. My father's house..."

She trailed off, staring through the distorted line of broken trees. I knew she was struggling with her emotions.

"Let us go there first, to your father's house. Perhaps he can help," I said. She gave me a grateful look and we moved on, Kaeleb leading the eagle behind him. The creature was bobbing its head, poking its beak at the shredded palms as if it were trying to ask what had happened there.

"I spoke to Maialen," I told them as we walked. Gula looked at me in surprise. I shrugged. She was helping us, and it was her home that had been destroyed. I would say what I needed to say in front of her. "She has the Pearl. She is controlling both amulets and now she believes she is the Solvrei."

Bacatha let out a low whistle and Thyrr grunted to show his displeasure at my words.

"She is tempting the Gods to intervene again," Gula said, her voice tinged with trepidation. "They will not be pleased."

"Your Gods stopped caring about Imbria a long time ago," I retorted.

"That means you are the only one we can look to," Gula went on. "You are the only other Keeper that remains."

A frown creased my face, my lips turning downwards. I could not even protect one small child. "I am not trying to be anyone's savior."

"That is what a savior would say," Gula quipped.

"Enough of that," I said with a shake of my head. "If you want me to burn something to ashes, I will gladly do so, but I will not be held responsible for saving the lot of you."

Bacatha glanced back, a grin teasing at her lips. "Yet look at you, Fire Keeper, out here traipsing through the mud to save Leharans."

"Perhaps the world really has turned upside down." I felt my own rueful grin spreading over my face, replacing the deep frown, and I wondered how, with all that was going on, we were still able to smile. Kaeleb was also beaming, proud of my ridiculous new status the healer had bestowed upon me and swinging the reins of the eagle as if we were just out for a stroll and not walking through the wreckage of a kingdom after being maimed in battle.

"There," Bacatha said, her humor draining quickly from her face and leaving it pale. She pointed and I followed the line of her arm to the crumbled structure that had once been her home. Cracks spread like veins over the ground beneath the rubble, radiating away from the eastern shore where Maialen had torn the island asunder. Part of one wall was still standing and around it were the coralstones and memories that had built Bacatha's life. She walked slowly, stopping to touch the pieces of her home as she passed them. Part of a chair, the pages of a book flapping in the breeze, a broken clay pot. Gula and I lowered Thyrr to the ground and the rest of us stood watching as the proud Leharan wove through the remains of her past.

She reached the edge of the broken wall and hesitated, looking back at us, her icy blue eyes pleading. Kaeleb ran forward, shoving the eagle's tether at Gula as he went. Bacatha stood back as the boy clamored through the wreckage, small and quick and agile.

"There is no one here," he announced.

"Thank you," Bacatha breathed in relief. "I should have been able to look, but I could not bring myself to."

Kaeleb shrugged as if it were an ordinary thing to search for a companion's dead relatives in the rubble that had once been their home. He scampered back over to where I stood and nudged Thyrr with his toe. "He does not look well."

Thyrr was mumbling something and I leaned closer so that I could hear what he was saying. His eyes were bright, feverish, and sweat was beading on his forehead, though his skin was waxy and grey. Kaeleb was right, he did not look well.

"I need to tell you," Thyrr was whispering, clutching at my arm.

"Tell me what?"

"I am not her brother."

I stared at him. He had barely breathed the words, barely given life to them, and yet they echoed through my head as if he had shouted them. The others could not have heard and I pulled his hand from my arm, settling it on his chest as if he had said nothing of consequence.

"Put him on the eagle and take him to Tahitia," I told Gula. "Tend to him there."

The healer again expressed surprise at my decisions regarding her. "You trust me with the only eagle you have?"

"If you like, I can threaten your life, tell you that if you do anything foolish then I will murder you and your firstborn children. Would that be more helpful to you?" I offered.

She snorted with mirth. "You are not what I expected, Fire Keeper. Cossiana should say nicer things about you."

"What does the old woman say?" I demanded, but Gula simply laughed and waved me off, nudging the eagle forward so that it was beside Thyrr. She pressed down on the wing and it dipped its shoulder for us, letting us hoist the prostrate man over it. Gula climbed on behind him.

"Stay low, it will be heavy with both of you," I instructed her, showing her how to control the beast with the tethers. I stepped away and the eagle vaulted into the air, eliciting a startled shriek from Gula, but she held on and kept Thyrr on with her.

"Are you going to tell him I am not his nephew?" Kaeleb wanted to know after they had disappeared into the horizon. It was understandable that he ask, for Bacatha had already seen the truth for herself, that he was not the Solvrei, and it was only a matter of time before she told the other Leharans.

"I believe he already knows," I answered quietly, still letting Thyrr's words sink in. *I am not her brother.* I felt a smile once again tugging at my lips and I grinned, nodding in silent appreciation. It took guts to claim a throne that was not yours, and I did not care in the least who he was or where he came from. After what Maialen and Logaire had done, Thyrr would be an ally for life and someone who could rally the Leharans to follow me. He could not do that if he was not Orabelle's brother. If he lived, I was going to have to convince him to keep that bit of knowledge to himself, for I needed him and I needed him to be the ruler of Lehar.

I turned to Bacatha. "Where would your father have gone in a battle?"

She grimaced. "To the Citadel. He would have taken my mother and sisters there as well, thinking they would be safer. He could not have known it would fall."

"They may not have made it that far. Maialen would have attacked the Citadel first. It might have fallen before they reached it. Come, show us the path they would have taken." I gestured for her to lead the way and we trudged after her.

31

Akrin strode into the throne room, pushing the girl ahead of him. He had covered her head with a cloth sack and her hands were bound together, encased in the thickest leather gloves he could find. She took small, shuffling steps and he prodded her relentlessly between the stark bones of her shoulder blades. She was a skinny little thing, almost frail looking, though he had learned on Tahitia that her looks were quite deceiving.

Logaire was waiting for him, pretending to be serene and indifferent to the prize he had returned with. She could not seem too eager, or the pugnacious young general would be inclined to toy with her. Her full, red lips curved upward as she rose from her place on Blaise's throne, her gown falling around her in a shimmering cascade of golden cloth. She was draped in jewels, even more than the last time he had seen her, and Akrin found himself wondering how she moved about with so much adornment weighing her down.

"Is this her?" Logaire asked, her voice purring, trying to contain her excitement.

Akrin leered at her, the closest he could get to a genuine smile. His brooding brown eyes were shining beneath his heavy brows. There was a deep cut on his chin that went up through his bottom lip, swelling and distorting the lower part of his face. "I have brought the Solvrei."

"We must thank the gods that Maialen told us who she really was," Logaire murmured, stepping down from the elevated stage where the thrones sat. "Take off that covering. I want to see her."

"Do not let her touch you," he warned. "She does something to you when she touches you. I saw it on Tahitia."

Logaire snatched back the hand she was extending towards the child and let Akrin remove the cloth covering from the girl's head. She raised her arched brows at the dreadful sight of the child and murmured. "Oh my."

Eolande was glaring at her, her blue eyes red-rimmed from crying. Her face was scratched and bruised and her hair had been shorn off, cut close to the scalp, much like Akrin's and the other soldiers. Logaire tilted her head to one side, watching the girl with peaked interest. The child looked just like her mother, though Logaire had never seen Orabelle in such an unkempt state. They had the same eyes that angled upwards, the same sharp nose and full lips. Eolande still had a cherubic fullness to her cheeks, so she did not yet have the haughty, imperious look of the former Water Keeper, but you could see that it would come in time.

"How delightful," Logaire said with a laugh, clapping her hands together. "Did Maialen try to stop you from taking her?"

Akrin's look of pleasure soured. "No, the Earth Queen was interested in something else. She took the Pearl."

Logaire's eyes narrowed. "And you let her?"

"It was that or the child. You told me to bring the girl. I have brought you the girl," he said obstinately.

Logaire sighed, walking back up to her throne and folding herself into it. The man had no imagination at all, no ability to strategize or think on his feet. He was a blunt instrument, nothing more. She made a gesture to push her wild mane of hair back from her head, forgetting that it was already en-trapped by the gold circlet she wore. She dropped her hand in irritation, settling her annoyance on Akrin.

"I have brought you a gift besides the girl," Akrin said, his voice oily and persuasive, eager. The voice that meant she would not be pleased with whatever gift he was offering.

"You have done enough, Akrin. You have brought me the only thing I asked for. I need nothing else," she purred, hoping to discourage him from giving her whatever foul token he was about to offer.

"I insist." He reached into his pocket and she felt her stom-ach turn as he pulled out a small, bloody orb, holding it out to her in his palm. She shrank away from it, seeing the spark of pleasure in his eyes as he asked her, "Do you not like it?"

"What is it?" she asked, forcing herself to remain calm. She knew how to deal with Akrin. She just needed to remain calm.

"Blaise's new pet lost his eyeball," Akrin explained with a laugh.

"The... an eye? Whose... whose eye?" Logaire stammered, breathing deeply, trying not to show him that he had upset her. If he knew she was affected by it, then she would have a dozen gouged out eyeballs in her chambers by dinner.

"The boy that my so-called father has replaced me with," Akrin practically snarled, his mood once more turning dark at the thought of Kaeleb. Logaire could barely keep up with the pendulating swings of his mental state. The little girl began to cry and Akrin shoved the eye under her nose, causing her to wail pitifully.

"Take a look at your little friend," he told her, flexing the eye between his fingers. "Right after I hit you over the head that stupid boy tried to stop me from taking you. He cut my face, so in return I took his eye. He screamed so much, I was surprised it did not wake you."

Akrin continued to squeeze the eye between his fingers, taunting the girl. Logaire had a horrible vision of the eye being crushed in his hand, juices splattering the poor child's face. Her stomach turned again and she fanned herself with her hand, not allowing herself to be sick.

"Have the girl taken to the tower and locked away for now. No one will speak to her but me," she commanded, turning to Vishram to carry out the task. He stepped out of the shadows and waved over several men to escort the girl.

"The gloves stay on!" Akrin called after them as they ushered her out of the room. She went with them, still crying pitifully.

"That was unkind," Logaire said to him. "She is a child."

Akrin shrugged, putting the eye back in his pocket. "You did not see what she could do. She is no ordinary child."

"Tell me everything that happened," Logaire reached over and patted the arm of the throne that sat infuriatingly beside her own. The last thing she wanted to do was spend another second in his horrible presence, but she needed to know. He slid into the seat, continuing to leer at her while his hand slipped into his pocket to caress the severed eye. She shuddered to think what he would do with his little trophy when he was alone.

At her prompting, Akrin told her how they had assembled in Kymir, how Maialen's ships had gone ahead, sailing innocently into the Leharan harbor, laden with archers who were hidden below deck. Akrin and the Queen followed later, on the eagles, screeching through the sky above the harbor, the signal to attack. The Leharans were taken completely by surprise. Akrin watched Maialen as she watched the battle below, saw her enmity, the way she seethed as she stared at the island.

"I knew she wanted to destroy it. I could see it in her face. You were right, she hates her sister, hates anything that reminds her of Orabelle. It was easier than you thought it would be," Akrin told Logaire with an appreciative sneer. "All I had to do was give her a little nudge. I told her how the Leharans thought she was weak, how they knew she would never measure up to her older sister, that she would always be found wanting. Then I told her how Blaise used to laugh at her, to call her a doll and a puppet. How he had boasted that he could manipulate her with her weak emotions. She went completely mad."

Maialen had channeled her power in a fury of rage, breaking the island and sending the eastern edge crumbling into the sea. The Citadel collapsed in a thunderous pile of rubble, and the Earth Queen laughed, spreading her hands, opening up crevices all over the island and swallowing anyone she saw moving.

"It was over in moments," Akrin said wistfully. For him, the bloodshed would have ended too soon. "I could see that Lehar was done for and there was no need for me there, so I went to Tahitia. They were better prepared for us. They put up quite a fight in the beginning, though it did not last long. Most of the warriors were gathered in the village, protecting one little hut. Stupid of them. It was obvious that was where I would find the girl. Maialen followed me, and once she arrived there was nothing the Tahitians could do to stop her. I thought she would take the girl, but as soon as she saw the Sirens with the Pearl she forgot about the child. All she wanted was the other amulet."

"The Sirens gave it to her?" Logaire interrupted sharply in disbelief.

"I do not think the sea witches expected her to take it. She just snatched it from them and flew off on her eagle."

"You said the girl did something, used her power somehow?" Logaire prodded.

Akrin looked sullen. "Some beastly Leharan attacked me and the girl began calling the Water Element. The entire sea around Tahitia rose into the air. I thought she was going to kill us all."

"She did it without the Pearl?" Logaire asked, trying to keep her eagerness from her face so that Akrin would not toy with her, withholding information to aggravate her further.

"It was something she did with her hands. She was holding onto the Leharans, doing something to them. Their faces were so pained, as if she was torturing them," he explained, his tone colored with jealous longing for the child's gift of inflicting pain.

Logaire sat back on her throne, thinking over what Akrin had recounted. She wanted to rush out right then, to find Sybylla and tell her what she had learned, but she forced herself to stay, to be patient, to tolerate Akrin's obscene presence a little longer. She glanced at Vishram, his blocky face half hidden in the shadows. He made a slight gesture and she nodded, relieved when he stepped forward and offered to escort Akrin to the dining hall, for surely he must be hungry after his ordeal and a feast had been prepared.

Akrin pushed himself up out of the throne, his dour face glancing back at Logaire. "You will have to kill him. He will not forgive us for this."

Logaire shrugged her bare shoulders, a delicate gesture that caused the rubies around her neck to shimmer in the torchlight. She knew he was speaking of Blaise, but she had a plan to appease her cousin that she did not want to share with Akrin just yet. The young man had mutilated Kaeleb, a mistake on his part, for they both knew Blaise would not be forgiving of that infraction. Of course Akrin would now want Blaise dead. He feared the Keeper's legendary wrath, but Logaire was reconciled to the fact that her cousin seemed impervious to death, refusing to die even in the most hopeless of circumstances. The safest thing for her was to bring him back to her side, and she would use the girl to do it. Everything now depended on the child.

32

Damian was wary of the Va'Kul, watching her carefully as she stood on the bow of the ship. She had her hands spread wide so the Fomori on the docks could see that it was one of their own who approached Samirra on the Tahitian vessel. Her head was held high even though she was supposed to be his captive, and he wondered if it was actually he himself that was the captive and he was only fooling himself with the illusion of control.

His mother was frowning at the Fomori woman, her dark eyes as full of mistrust as his own. Cossiana had been hesitant to follow his proposed plan. She too had seen the look that passed between her son and the halfbreed and she had to consider that whatever feelings he had for Chaote were clouding his judgement. She tried to dissuade him, but he was insistent, saying this was the only way to stop the wars that now seemed inevitable. Her thoughts kept straying to her beloved island, knowing as the Elder she should be there with her people, but she had agreed to let Damian try to end things his way.

The Va'Kul had awoken on the Isle of Clouds with a horrible screeching epithet, spewing curses and profanity at them as she wrestled against the bindings they had wrapped around her wrists and legs. Damian had attempted to calm her, speaking to her in his reasonable, gentle baritone.

"I did not kill you, though I could have," he told her. "I wish to speak with you. I believe we want the same things."

She laughed, a sound that made the hairs raise on his arms like a surge of nearby lightning. "You have no idea what I want, Guardian."

"You want to rule the Fomori," he said, sitting on the crate he had vacated earlier to stop her attack. "I want to return your people to your control. It is the same thing."

The yellow eyes gleamed with interest and she twisted herself into a sitting position on the cold, frosted ground beneath the shelter that covered them. Her features were prominent, unsettling in their blend of savagery and femininity. "You want Mother to come back to your pathetic island, but there is nothing left for any of you there. That was part of the agreement. Chaote wanted her home obliterated, wiped away so she would never be tempted to return."

Damian felt a knot form in his stomach at her words. He prayed that Tahitia would withstand the assault. His first instinct had been to use the ship to race after Blaise, but he knew that the Fire Keeper was the only one who could truly oppose Maialen. Damian's presence would not change the outcome there, no matter how much he wished it could.

"I have seen your face, watched you when she gives orders. You think Chaote is making mistakes, that you can do better," Damian surmised.

"She has been asleep for hundreds of years. We are not the same as we were before," the Va'Kul said through clenched teeth.

"You do not wish to live in Samirra." It was not a question, but a statement laced with understanding, with empathy.

"Our tribe was content in the North! This dream of waking the Mother was nothing more than that. A dream, a story to tell our young. She was a hallowed visage to worship and pray to when we needed it. She never should have left her prison. It was those like Carushka that longed for a different life, but he was wrong and look where it led him. Murdered at the hands of his own granddaughter. He could not accept that we had gone too far beyond what we once were, that we could never be what we were before. We will never be part of the four realms. That dream ended the day the Keepers first turned their sights on us. We are beasts, monsters, demons, the creatures your kind needed us to be. We are not farmers, we are not weavers, nor blacksmiths or scholars. We do not belong here."

Damian glanced at his mother as she silently observed the exchange, seeing the deep lines of concentration between her brows. If there was a large sect of the Fomori who wanted to go back to the north, and they could convince them to go, then Chaote would lose her army and her hold on Samirra.

Damian looked back at the Va'Kul. She was rubbing at the grey hide that covered her neck, her lip curled up in disgust that Blaise had almost been able to choke her. The Keeper was stronger than she expected, and she detested the thought that he remained alive after he had put his hands on her.

Damian went on, "What if I agree to give you leave to return to the north?"

The beast laughed again, the sound even more brittle than before. "You, Guardian? You rule over nothing. No one cares what you give leave to."

"I will tell the others. I can convince Blaise. If you leave Samirra with your blooddrinkers, we will not follow you and we will not attack the north again. You will have your sanctuary there."

Her sinister yellow gaze slid to Cossiana. "And you, Elder? You will agree to abide by this? You know we will not stop killing your kind. We could not stop if we wanted to, for it is who we are."

"This is not my decision, it is my son's," Cossiana said evasively.

The Va'Kul shook her head. "See there, Guardian. Already your people slide into half-truths and lies of omission. She will not give her word because she has no intention of abiding by our agreement. We will never coexist peacefully, that is true, but the Fomori cannot exist without the Imbrians, just as you cannot exist without the Fomori. Have you not realized this? What will your people do if they have no one to fear? What will they do if they have no one to hate? Already they turn on each other. Imagine what it would be like if they did not have us, the nightmares that terrify their children into obedience, who have kept the realms looking upon their kings with pleading eyes to save them. We are the darkness, the warnings of what you will become if you follow the path of evil. We are as necessary to you as you are to us."

Damian could not help but hear the truth in the words she spoke, though he hated to admit it, even to himself. Chronus and Blaise had made a shrewd decision when they had bartered with Carushka, knowing that the fear instilled by the Fomori could be used to manipulate the realms.

"I see the wisdom of your words, Va'Kul," he deferred. He nodded his head slightly, the only acquiescence he was willing to grant her reasonings even though he knew she was right. "Let us end this now and return things to the way they are meant to be."

The Va'Kul was still wary, her eyes fixed on Cossiana, but she inclined her head in agreement. "This war threatens all of us, and for this reason, I will consider your proposal, but only if you return me to Samirra."

Damian had one more request. "You must promise me that you will not challenge Chaote. Let me speak to her first, convince her that this will be the best way."

The Fomori woman smiled, revealing her sharp, fanged teeth. "Are you afraid I will win?"

"No, I am afraid you will lose." He did not add the unsaid words he could not stop himself from thinking. *And then I will lose her forever.*

"You are a foolish man, Guardian. Come, let us leave this godforsaken place. I do not wish to die in a graveyard of giants," she said with another curl of her lip.

They had sailed back to the mainland, the Va'Kul remaining bound until they reached the port of Samirra, where they had been challenged by the Fomori guarding the docks. She now addressed them from the bow of the ship, free of her restraints.

"I am your Va'Kul!" she called out. "I have returned from the Isle of Clouds with great tidings and I wish to speak with the Mother right away."

The Fomori caught the lines the Tahitian sailors tossed down to them, towing the ship in against the pier so they could disembark. The Va'Kul walked back to Damian and smiled at him, rubbing her wrists where the rope had bound her.

"Take them all prisoner!" she commanded with a shout. "Everyone on the ship!"

Damian's eyes darkened and he instinctively reached for his spear, forgetting it was not there. The Va'Kul smiled at him and whispered, "This is how it needs to be. Do not fight them."

She stalked away, her predatory gait carrying her quickly to the ramp the Fomori were using to storm the ship. Damian motioned for the other islanders to remain calm. Fighting would only lead to useless deaths. They were outnumbered here and the only thing he could do was trust the Va'Kul and pray that his words had gotten through to her.

"I hope you know what you are doing, my son," Cossiana said to him, lifting her hands in surrender as the beasts surrounded them.

"I have to try," he told her, dark eyes pleading with her to understand. She smiled at him. No matter what happened, he was her son and she loved him.

The Va'Kul led them off the ship, past the groups of Fomori and Samirrans who were stacking barrels and crates, to a line of wagons that waited efficiently at the port to transport goods. The Tahitians were piled into the carts and Damian wondered if the efficiency of imports and exports was Chaote's doing, a way to prepare her supply lines for battle, or if it had always been that way and he had never bothered to notice. Astraeus, in his previous rule of the western realm, had been an ineffectual and vain man, more obsessed with his own image than with helping his people, and Damian could not imagine he had ever taken time out of his day to think about how his port was functioning. For a fleeting moment he thought perhaps Chaote was not the most terrible ruler the Samirrans could have had, then he saw the savage face of the Va'Kul, the inhuman gaze that stared at him hungrily as she gestured for him to get in the cart. The Fomori could never peacefully exist with the rest of Imbria. They would always be the masters, the lions looking upon the rest of them as lambs. They would crush the world if he did not stop them.

Chaote was waiting on the steps of the palace. The Va'Kul had ordered the other Tahitians to the cells beneath the arena, leaving Damian and his mother to confront the halfbreed. The Va'Kul walked behind them as they approached the palace, her long shadow falling over them like an ominous warning.

Chaote was adorned in her golden armor, her hair tied back in a long ponytail, gleaming like the sun itself in the cold winter air. The proud and delicate bones of her face were noble, regal, and she looked like a goddess herself standing there.

Her black eyes, flecked with bits of starry yellow, regarded the three of them with open hostility.

"How have you come to find yourself our prisoner once again, Guardian?" she asked, not trying to hide the disappointment in her voice. She despised weakness, found it dissatisfying that Damian had allowed himself to be captured by the Va'Kul when he clearly had the upper hand on the Isle of Clouds. Surely he was not so inept.

"It was by choice, so I could speak to you," he told her.

She descended the steps to meet him, her armor clattering, dazzling in the light. "That seems sentimental and unwise. Why would you not go home to protect Tahitia, knowing it is threatened?"

"One warrior will not turn the tide of a battle, but I have a way to end this war for good, before any more people have to die. Let us speak alone. I have given up my freedom and put my mother in danger to come here again. All I request in return is that you hear me out."

Chaote glanced up at the Va'Kul, wondering what the Fomori woman had promised the Tahitians in exchange for her freedom. She felt a line of tension in her shoulders. She knew the challenge would come soon, and she was prepared for it. There was no doubt in her mind that she could best the Va'Kul in combat. It was whatever was happening now that she was wary of. She cared nothing for war or for ruling any of the realms. All that mattered to her was destroying the Keepers and ripping their corrupt power from their hands.

She lifted her fingers, motioning for Damian to follow her into the palace. Cossiana started up the stairs after them and Chaote stopped, turning her exquisite head back to look at the old woman.

"You said you wished to speak alone," Chaote said, her words directed at Damian.

Damian frowned. "She is the Elder. You cannot put her in a cell in a dungeon."

Chaote smiled at the old woman, but the expression held no warmth. "Of course. Va'Kul, escort the Elder to the kitchens and instruct the Samirrans to prepare food for her, then find suitable accommodations for her in the palace."

They entered the palace and Chaote led Damian up to the library. A shadow passed over his face as he stepped into the massive space and Chaote saw it, commenting, "Remembering the last time we were here?"

"I have not forgotten," was the Guardian's stoic reply.

"What is it you want, Damian?" she asked, the pretense gone, weariness creeping into her voice.

"You are tired," he noticed.

"Of course, I am tired," she said irritably. "Too tired for games. Speak plainly or go and join your mother and your new friend."

"The Va'Kul is not my friend and she is not yours either. She wishes to challenge you."

"Why do you think I left her on that cursed island?" Chaote hissed. "Then you come traipsing in here, carrying her right back to me. Do you think I am a fool? I will defeat the Va'Kul. She does not stand a chance against me, but when I do there are many among the Fomori who will be angry and it will cause a divide. She is loved by our people."

"They are not your people," he reminded her once again, trying to be gentle, understanding.

"They are the only family I have left!" she snapped back.

"I know your story, Chaote. You do not have to tell it again. But you are wasting the life you have left with this vendetta. Let the Va'Kul and the Fomori return to the north. She claims this is what she wants, what the Fomori want."

Chaote scoffed. "And then what? Return to Tahitia with you? Be your wife? Make you supper every night in our little hovel, living every day beneath the weight of the stares of others who know what I am? They will look upon me with disgust and I will be unable to bear it, just as I am unable to bear the sight of Tahitia. I will never set foot on that island again. All I will see there are the ghosts of those I loved."

"I will go anywhere with you. Anywhere on Imbria. Just tell me where." Damian's offer was so genuine, his voice so earnest, that she almost believed him.

When she answered it was with fierce self-preservation. "I have taken that path before. It did not end well for me."

"I am not Rilian," he vowed with a shake of his head, his long dreadlocks sweeping the shoulders of his coat. "I would not betray you."

"You barely know me. You cannot say what you will do for me."

"I have spent every day with you since I arrived here. I know how you fight, how you think, what the slightest gesture of your hand means. I know you are not happy, that you want more than this life is giving you. I know you feel something for me, even though you do not wish to," he countered.

She walked to one of the small tables, lifting a piece of parchment. "I could not read before I arrived here. One of the Samirrans taught me. An old woman. She made me laugh, was kind to me even though I was an intruder in her realm. I have not seen her for weeks now. I suppose she is dead, but I have been afraid to ask. Is that not a strange thing to fear? I am not afraid of death for myself, not afraid of the Va'Kul, or the Keepers, but I fear someone telling me that this old woman is dead. Can you imagine what I would have to feel for you if I let myself believe what you say?"

His dark eyes widened slightly, caught off guard by her un-expected vulnerability. "Life is uncertain, Chaote, that is what makes it worth living. It is the uncertainty and the fragility of it that make it meaningful."

"Says the man who came here wishing to die."

Once again, he was taken by surprise, but deep down he knew what she said was true. He had never let go of the deaths of his brother and Orabelle. He held them close to him, nursing the pain of his failures, wishing to be redeemed and knowing that the only redemption that would satisfy him would come with death. "That was before I met you."

She laughed, bitter and cold. "We will never be what you want us to be. I will never stop fighting as long as the Keepers control the Elements, and you will never stand against them. You claim you will do anything for me, but the one thing I needed to end all of this was that child, and you hid her from me."

"She is just a child," he argued. "I swore to protect her. It was her mother's dying wish. I would have no honor if I did not keep my word."

"Then it seems we are at an impasse, for I also made a promise to the dead. You claim we deserve to have a life, but we are both still bound by our obligations to those we have lost. Go back to your mother now. I must have time to think."

He ignored the command and stepped towards her. The ghost of a smile passed over her features, a smile that held no happiness, only the faint glimmers of what might have been. Damian took her hand, pulling her to him. She allowed it, staring up at his strong face with eyes that were the sky at night, and just as unreachable. He tilted his head down to hers and kissed her. She gave in to the moment, surrendering for just that brief flash of time, then she pulled back, pushing him away and motioning for him to go.

33

I watched the land below us pass away like memories as we glided overhead on the eagle. Kaeleb was with me, his eye now covered by a wide leather strip that was tied around his head over the bandage. The wound smelled terrible, pungent with the herbal remedies Gula had crushed and packed into the dark socket, but I pretended not to notice. She had assured him it would heal well, and he had touched the bindings gingerly, sniffing his fingers and wrinkling his nose in disgust at the putrid aroma. To compensate for his missing eye, he now carried two swords instead of one, having plucked the second from the ground on Lehar, where the hilt of it was barely visible sticking up out of the muddy sand. It was then that we realized why we could not find the bodies of the island's fallen warriors. Maialen had buried them in the ground.

We had gone to the Citadel, or rather the pile of rubble that had once been the gleaming coralstone fortress. The Leharans who survived were gathered near it, for the Citadel had stood for centuries as the center of their world. Now that it was gone, they seemed lost, disoriented, not knowing where else to go. Bacatha had run through the sparse crowd, shouting for her father.

Brogan was alive, and though I wanted to feel pleased for Bacatha, I could not help the thought that twisted through my mind, telling me Bacatha would have been more useful to me with her father dead. Her need for vengeance would have assured that she would fight beside me.

She had run to him, thrown her arms around him, and Brogan returned the embrace, his grey head leaning over hers. He whispered to her that her mother and sister were safe, both helping to tend to the wounded. He looked tired, older than when we had last seen him. I was surprised at their open display of affection, for neither of them seemed the sort, but I supposed with the destruction of their home and their realm in ruins, they were allowed a reprieve from the stringent stoicism of the Leharan Guard.

"I am surprised to see you here, Fire Keeper," Brogan said, turning his weathered face to me.

I felt a twinge of annoyance. "People keep saying that to me, and I am beginning to see it as an insult."

Brogan shook his head. "Not an insult. We will take all the help we can get."

I surveyed the war-torn landscape with a frown. "I am afraid I am not here to help patch wounds and hold hands. I need to know who is still able to fight."

"You think another attack is coming?" Brogan asked sharply, suddenly alert.

"No," I assured him. "Maialen has taken the Pearl and she has crushed any opposition that Lehar may have posed. She has no need to return here."

"And Veruca?" the old Guard asked, a hint of accusation creeping into his voice.

I glared at him. "Veruca also has what they want. They have taken the Solvrei."

He looked confused, his eyes going to Kaeleb then back to me. "The Solvrei is here."

"It is not me," Kaeleb interjected helpfully. "I am nobody!"

"You aren't nobody," I corrected him, then returned my attention to the Guard. "Damian lied about who the child was in order to protect them. It is a long story and your daughter can fill you in later. Right now, I need men who will fight to come with me to Veruca and rescue the true Solvrei before they can hand her over to Chaote."

Brogan looked around at the wasteland the island had become. "I am sorry, Keeper, but this is not our fight. Seeing what the Earth Queen has done here, and now you tell me she has more power... if it were up to me, I would give the halfbreed Fomori woman the amulets and be done with the lot of you. She is right. One person is not meant for this kind of power."

"It was the manipulating of the amulets that led to this in the first place," I exclaimed, frustrated, though I knew he would not understand what I was speaking of. Astus and the Fenris had changed the balance of the Elements, and there was no way of knowing what the destruction of another amulet would bring. It was likely to make the remaining amulets even stronger, and a vision of the dead Tahitians, their gnarled bodies threaded through with thorny tangles of vines, ran through my mind. The last thing Maialen needed was more power.

The old Guard continued to shake his head. "I am sorry, Keeper, but your problems are your own."

I turned to Bacatha, incredulous. "Do you agree with this?"

She looked chagrined. "We are in no position to fight, and the few of us who remain cannot leave Lehar undefended."

I turned back to Brogan, my amber eyes glittering with rage. "I will not forget this."

I stalked off, storming past the gathering of Leharans that had been drawn by my presence. They hurried to step out of the way, letting me pass, their fear evident. It was disconcerting to see them in such a state, the proud, fierce islanders that Orabelle had once led to battle now reduced to cowering skittishly.

"If none of you cowards will go, then I will!" Kaeleb yelled at them as he darted after me. I remembered then that I had sent the eagle with Gula and Thyrr and I whirled back, stomping up to Bacatha, my rage now boiling inside of me at the humiliation of having to ask them for anything else.

"Take the boat we left on the southern beach," she said before I could ask. I knew it was her way of apologizing, of sparing me from having to make the request.

"We will!" Kaeleb said defiantly.

I saw the corners of her lips twitch before Bacatha knelt before him and said, "Take care of him, boy."

Kaeleb scowled at her but gave a curt nod of his head. Then he once more hurried to keep up with me as we began to weave through the wreckage, returning the way we had come. I was furious. Furious with myself for being so naïve as to think the Leharans would help us, furious that I had wasted time trying, furious that I would be wasting more time rowing some feeble little boat back to Tahitia to get the eagle that I had been sentimental to let Thyrr take, and furious at Thyrr for being in a fevered stupor instead of rallying his people to support me.

It was an eternity before we reached the southern beach, and another eternity as we rowed through the churning wreckage to the other island. The seas were calm at least, and for that I was grateful. I watched the fathomless blue water as our oars broke through it, wondering if the Sirens were somewhere below, if they were grieving what had happened. If Orabelle was grieving.

When we reached Tahitia I wasted no time, not even bothering to drag the boat above the tide line before hurrying to find Gula and my eagle. She had kept the bird safe, refusing to let anyone else touch it, and after she had fed us and tended to Kaeleb's wounds, she had taken us to it.

"Thyrr will live," she told me quietly as she passed me the tethers of the creature. "But he is feverish and he is saying things."

I looked into her dark eyes. She knew. "Do not let anyone else near him until he can recover his wits and when he does, you need to give him a message from me. Tell him to stop being a fool and to be the man he was born to be, the ruler of Lehar. This world needs him still."

She nodded and stepped away. Kaeleb swung himself up behind me, the foul smell of his eye poultice nearly making me gag. Gula gave me an understanding grimace as I nudged the giant bird with my legs, launching it into the air.

Our journey took us over the plains that stretched between Kymir and the Wastelands, the dark mountains of Veruca towering ominously in the north, capped with fresh snow. I had no plan, no thought as to how we would get into the city, let alone the castle. The tunnels that ran beneath the ground were our best chance, but I had been told that Logaire had sealed them off as soon as she had taken the throne. She did not know the tunnels like I did, though. No one did. I could only hope that she had missed something, overlooked an entry point.

I landed the eagle as soon as we reached the foot of the black monoliths. Kaeleb slid down from the eagle's shoulder, looking around with his one good eye.

"Where do we leave it?" he asked, speaking of the bird. There was a scattering of pine trees nearby, and the rocky outcroppings of the foothills that were the beginning steps to the mountains. The eagle would likely perch atop one of them, and we could only hope that it would wait there, resting, until we returned and whistled for it. Kaeleb seemed to find this a dubious plan, but he shrugged and we both stepped away from the eagle, letting it hobble off before it vaulted into the air.

"This way," I told him. He followed me as we threaded through the sparse winter foliage that clung to the slope of the mountain base. There was a sheer face that towered above us where part of the cliff had torn away, and we climbed over the tumbled rocks and boulders that had broken off from the peak long ago.

The air was starkly cold and frost clung to everything, and as we climbed higher, the white-tipped massif above us was threatening with heavy seracs and cornices. I was glad we would be going underground. It was beginning to feel like this damned winter would never end.

The cave entrance appeared untouched as we approached it, plodding up a steep escarpment that I doubted anyone would willingly ascend out of curiosity. My chest was heaving from the effort and the thin mountain air burned my throat. Kaeleb seemed unphased behind me, stopping to squint up at the dark crevice we were making our way towards as if he wanted to be sure it was really there.

"How did you find this?" he asked me.

I paused, grateful for the chance to catch my breath. I considered myself able-bodied, quite muscular and of good health, but I was being taxed by the lack of sleep and the unrelenting harshness of the cold. "I found it from the other side. It was much warmer that way."

He gave a short laugh then carried on. Soon we reached the entrance to the cave. I stepped inside the darkened cavern first, sniffing the stale air for any signs of the Fomori. I smelled nothing but damp earth and rock. I lifted my hand and firelight flared to life. I no longer needed to use the flint. I could conjure my Element without even a spark, something that both pleased me and caused me trepidation. If my power was growing, then so was Maialen's.

The tunnels were shining obsidian, cut in rough planes by someone or something long ago. The fire reflected off them, dancing around us so that the smallest flame sent light cascading down into the depths.

"What will we do when we get there?" Kaeleb asked suddenly. There was no fear in his voice, no doubt, only curiosity, as if he wanted to know what we might be eating for dinner that night.

I sighed, for I had been wondering the same thing myself and had no answer to give him.

34

Logaire stood beside Sybylla, scrutinizing the little girl who was displayed before them. She frowned, her red lips pulling down into a pout. "She looks too... something."

Sybylla twisted her face in thought. "You are right. She looks too innocent."

They had cleaned and scrubbed the child, dressed her in a new white gown that was slightly too large for her slender frame. Eolande had submitted to their grooming of her, listening with careful consideration and wide eyes as they explained to her what she was expected to do that day. The child rubbed at the bandage around her wrist where the small cut was and Logaire saw a drop of bright red blood seeping out from the shallow wound.

"Stop fussing with that," she chastised the girl, pushing her fingertips away from the injury. "You are wasting what is most precious in you. Go and put your old dress back on."

The child turned and walked back behind the dressing curtain and Logaire waited, hands clasped behind her back, until the waiflike creature emerged once again, this time looking properly shoddy. The white dress she had been wearing when she was brought to them was coated in grime and splattered with dark droplets of blood, torn at the hem and quite ugly. It was perfect. Logaire's lips lifted into a sultry smile.

"Ahh," she breathed. "Now you have the look of a false prophet, my dear! Come along, we do not want to be late for your ceremony."

Logaire grabbed the child's gloved hand and began to tow her from the room in the tower, but as soon as they reached the staircase, she was compelled to release her grip on the girl. The child insisted on clutching the railing with both hands, cautiously descending at a pace that was painfully slow. Sybylla trailed after Eolande, patiently taking small steps herself so as not to rush the girl. The Oracle's robes flowed around her like an aura, dazzling in their whiteness so that she radiated light and purity. Her ginger hair was worn in an elaborate upward sweep Logaire had insisted on, and Sybylla inwardly wondered if it was so that she would not compete with the coppery majesty of Logaire's own locks. She did not mind; she had no desire to threaten the Queen in any way, and if adopting the complicated arrangement of braids and curls was the way to keep her benefactor happy, then she would gladly oblige.

Vishram waited for them at the first landing, a bundle of scrolls tucked neatly under his arm. "Everything is prepared for today," he assured them. Logaire smiled with delight and Sybylla gave him a small nod, making sure to keep her eyes from meeting his.

"Are you certain this is what you wish to do?" the advisor asked after a moment of hesitation. "It is dangerous."

Logaire arched her manicured brow. "You have just promised me that everything is prepared. There is no turning back now, Vishram, it must be done."

He stole a glance at the child, her eyes red-rimmed and puffy from crying. She seemed to have shed all the tears she had in her, and she stared back at him with uncorrupted resolve. He found the look unsettling, and he avoided glancing her way again. He motioned for them to follow him and they moved towards the open balcony that presided over the main courtyard below.

Logaire could hear the sounds of the crowd as they approached, but she made sure she and Sybylla remained out of sight, so the gathered masses would not catch a glimpse of them before she was ready. She nearly collided with Akrin, who was sulking in the shadows, and she quickly pushed herself away from him, disconcerted by the feel of his hands on her arms as he tried to steady her.

"I am fine. I do not require your assistance," Logaire said, shaking out of his grasp.

Akrin leered at her, his small eyes gleaming with something dark, then he focused on Eolande and his sick smile widened. It seemed he had found a new pet to torture. He was dressed in his black soldier's uniform, the collar embroidered with the general's crest, boots polished and gleaming, and a decorative sword hanging from his waist. His closely cropped hair matched Eolande's in length, though hers was a striking pale white compared to his dark auburn.

"Did they tell you what today is?" he asked the child, kneeling in front of her. She did not flinch from his gaze, merely watched him with her deep blue eyes. She gave a small nod of her head.

Akrin laughed and pushed himself back to his feet. "And you say I am the cruel one, Logaire. You and your Oracle may have surpassed me with this one."

Logaire wanted to smash him over the head, imagined what it would be like to see his brains scattered on the obsidian walls of the castle behind her. Sybylla was wary, her eyes darting to Logaire with a questioning glance, as if asking her if Akrin knew what they were doing. Logaire returned the seeking glance with a small shake of her head, a gesture so infinitesimal that only Sybylla noticed it. Logaire had been careful in her plans. Only Sybylla and Vishram knew what she was going to do.

"It would be cruel not to tell her," Logaire said smoothly, interjecting herself between Akrin and the child so he could not question her further.

"I feel there is something else at play here," Akrin mused, tilting his body so he could peer around Logaire's resplendently draped golden gown at the child. He was staring at the bandage on Eolande's arm. "What are you not telling me?"

Logaire felt a moment of panic, her throat knotting. She forced herself to remain calm as she fumbled in her mind for an answer, cursing herself, for she was not this dimwitted. Akrin was getting under her skin. This entire ordeal was getting under her skin and she wanted it over with.

It was Sybylla who spoke, drawing his attention. She jutted out her small chin, smiling, speaking in the purring way that Logaire had taught her. "Today the Queen will announce that the construction of the Temple of the Oracle has begun. We were hoping to keep it a surprise, but it seems you are too clever and you have found us out."

Akrin sneered at her. "This temple is a foolish idea and a waste of resources. We are at war, there are better things we could do to-"

"I will end this war," Logaire interrupted. Her eyes sparkled beneath the heavy fringe of lashes. "I will end it and this temple will be our legacy."

"How will you end it? Blaise still lives, and the Earth Queen is more powerful than you will ever be," Akrin pointed out with a vicious laugh. "And what do you think that halfbreed in Samirra will do when she learns what has happened today and realizes you have broken your word?"

Logaire laughed, the sound grating on Akrin's ears. "Chaote knew I was never going to keep my word. She also knows that I want peace, and I will do whatever I have to in order to secure it. War is a drain on resources, Akrin. Men who crave violence always have a hard time seeing that. It is costly and drawn out and deadly and in the end rarely amounts to anything. An exchange of land, a newly bestowed title. These are the things men crave with their wars, but we women can find ways to take them without those costs."

"It is one of you women who now enslaves Samirra and one of you women who just destroyed Lehar," Akrin reminded her.

Logaire gave a pretty shrug, as if he had made an irrelevant point. "The Keepers are corrupted. If not for them, there would be no need for all of this violence."

Akrin shook his head, beady eyes flashing with distrust. "You don't truly believe that. You are lying and I will not be deceived by your silvery tongue. Perhaps I should remove it from your mouth until you learn to speak the truth."

"I would love to see you try," Logaire hissed back, a momentary lapse in her calculated demeanor and one that she instantly regretted. The young man leaned close to her and his hand played at the hilt of his sword.

"Enough of this," Sybylla interrupted, throwing Vishram a desperate plea for help.

The stocky advisor stepped forward, resting a hand on Akrin's shoulder. "General, perhaps you would like to address the crowd first? Speak to them of your heroic deeds on Tahitia?"

Akrin slunk back away from Logaire, allowing Vishram to guide him to the balcony. Logaire could not help but smirk as he stepped out onto the terrace, greeted not with cheers but with a hushed silence. They would never love him, not the way they would love her. She felt the child's eyes on her and she turned to the girl with a wide smile, trailing her long fingernails over the short wisps of her hair. This child would change everything and no one, especially not Akrin, would ever see it coming.

35

I pulled on the door, my muscles heaving beneath my thick leather armor. Kaeleb was standing to one side, arms folded and leaning against the wall, watching me with a slight frown. I heaved again, but the heavy iron did not budge.

"Not this one either?" the boy asked.

I shook my head. Sweat beaded on my forehead under the fringe of red curls. I rubbed a hand over my face, feeling the coarse stubble on my cheeks and chin. "There is another. One that Akrin knew of and was fond of using. He may have kept it from being sealed."

Kaeleb nodded and fell into step behind me as we once more began to wind our way through the tunnels, asking, "Did all the kings of Veruca know about this place?"

"No," I answered him. "They must have known they existed, but I believe most were afraid of the underground. The Fomori were known to dwell here."

Kaeleb made a noise of disgust. "Disgraceful. It is pathetic that kings would let those beasts run wild under their kingdom because they were afraid of them."

"Fear can be a useful tool, Kaeleb. It keeps us alive."

"But you were not afraid."

I chuckled. "No, my boy, I was never afraid of these tunnels. I knew the blooddrinkers served a purpose for our world. They were useful to us when they stayed underground, lurking in the shadows."

"Useful how?"

"You are full of questions today," I remarked. I wondered how much I should share with him, if he would look at me differently if he knew the things I had done. It was strange to think that one boy's opinion mattered more to me than anyone else's on Imbria. "Did Alita tell you about me? About my pact with the Fomori?"

"She did, but I did not know if I should believe her," Kaeleb confessed. "Brother Kaden said she did not always tell the entire truth. Then when I met you, I knew you were not the sort of man she told me you were."

I lifted the firelight higher as we rounded a corner, sniffing the air. It was cool and musty, with a faint hint of herbs from Gula's poultice. "I did what needed to be done. Kaden was right, the stories that Alita and her Harbonah sympathizers told were embellished, if not downright lies. I was not some monster feeding scared children to the blooddrinkers. I gave them people who were already dead or who very much deserved to be dead. Had I not done what I did, the blooddrinkers would have caused much more harm, just as they did after Carushka was killed. My pact with them kept them controlled and it kept Imbria safe, even if it seemed to others that I was committing an atrocity. In some situations, one must perform an undesirable action in order to prevent a more undesirable outcome."

"You are saying that sometimes you must do something bad to prevent something worse," the boy concluded.

I was grateful that my revelations had not frightened him. "That is what we are doing every day. Everyone, even Chaote and Maialen and Logaire, they all believe they are doing the right thing, that what they are doing is best for Imbria, even though they are truly only doing what is best for themselves."

Kaeleb stopped suddenly, his head tilting to one side. I smelled the air, but the foul stench of the Fomori was still nowhere near us. I gave him a questioning look and he shrugged. "I thought I heard something."

"Someone in the tunnels?" I asked.

"No. It sounded like people shouting from far away."

I furrowed my brow, staring into the darkness at the end of the corridor as I tried to listen for whatever he had heard. "Maybe losing an eye has improved the function of your ears."

He snorted, his fingers touching the edge of the leather band as if he had forgotten about the injury. He once more fell into step behind me. We finally reached the place I was searching for and as we entered the chamber I stopped short, looking around at the macabre collection of horrors that surrounded us.

"Akrin has definitely kept this door unsealed," I said, revolted. The room was littered with remains. Small bones, broken and twisted. Rotting pieces. I saw a string of human ears hanging from a hook. There were several wooden boxes of all sizes stacked on the ground and arranged neatly on stone shelves that had been cut into the tunnel walls. I shuddered to think what was in them.

Kaeleb walked through, looking around and grimacing. "Is that the door?"

He clearly did not want to linger in this place any longer than I did. We went to the door and I placed my hands on it, giving it a push. It moved slightly, then the latch on the lock caught with a metallic clang and I winced as the sound echoed down the passage like rolling thunder. I listened intently, waiting for someone in the castle to come and investigate, but there was only silence.

I spent a moment debating my next course of action. It was obvious the door was only held by the single key lock; it had not been barred or sealed shut like the others. I could try to break the lock by bashing it with my sword, or I could try to use my amulet. My strengthened powers might allow me to burn fire hot enough to melt the metal.

Before I could decide, Kaeleb had slipped around me, crouching in front of the lock and pulling two sharp metal objects from his pocket.

"The Tahitians wear them in their ears," he said, displaying them to me in his palm. "I thought they might be useful."

"You stole them?"

Kaeleb nodded enthusiastically, and I chuckled, stepping back and leaving him to his task. He slid both the earrings into the lock, wiggling them around until there was a faint click. He exclaimed proudly, "Brother Kaden taught me how."

"Well done," I granted, ruffling a hand in his pale hair. He smiled, pleased with the attention, and he was so much like a child in that moment that it caused a pain in my chest. Guilt washed over me for the constant danger I had put him in since the moment I had taken him from Maialen. He should have been playing games and making friends, not fighting off Keepers and Fomori, or being kidnapped or losing his eye, or picking locks in a dungeon of horrors.

"What is wrong?" he asked, seeing the shadow that passed over my features.

"Nothing. I only wish I could give you a better life," I confessed.

He looked at me as if I were mad, scrunching up his face in the way he did when he was pensive. "Honestly, the quality of our meals could be better, but other than that, this is the best my life has ever been."

The pain in my chest moved to lodge in my throat and a wave of emotion washed over me, one that I was not comfortable in feeling, but with everything that had happened I was forced to accept that I loved the boy, as much as if he were my own flesh and blood, and he loved me. It was an unsettling revelation for me. I was no longer sure what it was like to be loved by someone, for it had been so long since anyone had. I shook my head and told him gruffly to move aside, pushing the door open as carefully and quietly as I could. I peered around it into the hallway. Torches flickered in sconces on the walls, but there was no other movement. I pushed the door open all the way and stepped into the castle, the first time I had done so since leaving to fight the Fomori in the north. It seemed a lifetime ago, and as I looked around, I felt only an empty acknowledgment of our present circumstances. There was no sense of coming home, no rush of relief. We were simply there, in a place that felt like any other place. It was disconcerting to feel, and I shook it off, closing the door softly behind us.

"This way," I whispered. "Stay against the walls."

"I know how to not be seen," Kaeleb hissed back, mildly annoyed that I did not trust in his ability to go undetected.

We moved down the hallway to where it intersected with another corridor. I waited, listening, but again there was nothing but silence inside the castle.

"There it is again," Kaeleb spoke softly. "Do you hear it?"

I nodded. The faint din of a crowd cheering.

We turned down the second corridor, taking a short flight of stairs up to the area where my bed chambers had been. I wondered how long it had taken Logaire to toss my things out after she had stolen my kingdom. We reached the door that had once been mine, and I drew my sword, then opened it slowly, ready in case my deceitful cousin was lying in wait for me.

I stopped on the threshold, narrowing my eyes in distrust at the sight that greeted me. There was no one there and my rooms were unchanged, untouched, everything exactly where

I had left it. I went in, Kaeleb behind me, one of his short swords also held ready in his hands. I pushed the door shut behind us and looked around, unsure of what to think.

"She left it how it was," I murmured.

Kaeleb looked around curiously at the glimpse into my somber inner sanctum. "It is rather dull."

"What did you expect, piles of golden treasure strewn about?" I threw back at him.

He grinned. "Now that would be something worth seeing!"

I went straight to the wardrobe, pulling open the door and sighing with relief. Aside from my leather armor, I had been wearing secondhand clothes for months now. I told Kaeleb to watch the door as I quickly shed the garments Gula had given me, pulling on a black tunic and pants, and donning a black padded jacket that buckled up the side. I slid my feet into tall boots, closing my eyes for a moment in bliss at the soft feel of them, for they fitted my feet perfectly. I stole a look at the mirrored glass and paused, unnerved by the sight that greeted me. My hair was longer than I had ever kept it as an adult, brushing over my shoulders in loose red curls, and my face was swarthy and tanned bronze, most of it covered with the dark shadow of a beard. There were smudges under my amber eyes, and lines around them I had not noticed before.

"Are you done admiring yourself?" Kaeleb asked impertinently.

I glowered at him. "If there is anything you would like, take it."

"It won't fit me. I am content."

I nodded and grabbed two heavy winter cloaks, tossing one to him. It would be large, but I needed something that would cover his head. He pulled it on and I chuckled as he paraded around the room, an abundance of fabric dragging along the ground behind him. I took his knife from him and cut the bottom third of the cloak, ripping off the fabric so it fell around his ankles.

We went back out into the hallway, and again I was struck by the eerie silence inside the castle. Whatever Logaire was doing, the entire kingdom must have been called to watch, which meant she would be on the terrace overlooking the courtyard. I needed to know if she had the girl with her, because if she didn't, then this might be our only chance to search the castle for the child. I led Kaeleb through the expansive rooms of the keep, going down and taking the servant's entrance out into the courtyard. I pulled up the hood of my cloak, motioning for Kaeleb to do the same, and we stepped out into the gathered crowd.

Logaire was standing on the upper terrace before a scarlet red curtain, glittering in gold and rubies, her hands held out in supplication. I felt the awful emptiness of the Warding Stone reaching out for me, and even from the distance I could see the milky moonstone shine on her finger where she wore it as a ring. There was a woman next to her, unremarkable except for the brilliant white of her robes and the deep orange of her hair. A few other men stood nearby, and a few paces behind I saw Akrin, his sullen face half in shadow, beady eyes glaring at the back of Logaire. Both sides of the balcony were flanked by black-armored soldiers.

"And now, Verucans, I will let our revered Oracle speak to you," Logaire announced. The crowd cheered and she smiled beatifically, turning to the woman shrouded in the white robes. The woman stepped forward, clasping her hands together in front of her and bowing her head, her lips moving though no sound came from them. She then lifted her head, pushed her chin forward and began to orate.

"The Gods are displeased!" she avowed. "When first I heard them mention the Solvrei, there were whispers of anger, but they have now turned into shouts of rage!"

The crowd gasped and murmured. I looked around, amazed that anyone was believing the farce that was being perpetrated up there. This woman was no more an oracle than I was.

The woman went on. "You have not decried the false prophet! You have not denounced the travesty that is an abomination to the will of the Gods and for this they are furious! We wish to save you, to restore you to the favor of the merciful Gods, but we can only do so by ridding Imbria of this scourge. The Solvrei is the bringer of lies, and the bringer of death! She will poison our waters and blight our lands. Look at what is happening in Samirra as a result of her existence. You must deny the imposter, deny the Solvrei! We have brought her here to you, so that you may be redeemed by the Gods."

Logaire motioned to one man and he pulled back the red curtain of fabric. Eolande was there, standing on a small platform with a rope around her neck. I felt my stomach turn and Kaeleb clutched at my arm, his small hand gripping my wrist in panic.

Logaire was going to kill the child.

The jeers of the crowd intensified, but the girl stood resolute, her face betraying no emotion, her eyes locked forward. There were shouts for her death, chants of encouragement for those who would end her life. One of the men on the balcony slipped a cloth covering over her head, and my stomach churned again at the sight, still thinking that surely they would not publicly hang a child. The woman in white stepped back as Logaire once more commanded the attention.

"Verucans! Do you wish us to deny this false prophet? Do you wish us to save you from her evil treachery, from the path to darkness she has set the world upon?"

The crowd erupted in cheers. Kaeleb released my arm and spun, darting through the spectators and heading straight for the servant's entrance. He was going to try to stop them.

"Kaeleb!" I shouted, but it was lost in the noise of the crowd. I muttered a curse and pushed my way through the throngs of people, chasing after him. There was no way he could fight off all the soldiers on the terrace, not with Akrin there as well. The boy was rushing to his death and I had to stop him.

I tore into the castle and sprinted down the hallways, racing up the staircase that led to the upper level of the terrace. The crowd was cheering wildly and then there was a moment of silence, a hush that I knew in my gut meant that Eolande was swinging from her neck. Then cheers once more filled the air.

"No!"

I heard the tortured shout from Kaeleb before I saw him, the cry full of defiance and denial. I rounded the corner and felt a stab of temporary relief that he was not dead, though it did not appear that he would be long for this world. He held his two swords, one in each hand, one small boy facing off against a wall of Verucan soldiers.

I threw back my hood and drew my blade, falling on the assembled soldiers with a shout of rage. Most of them were too startled by the sight of me to react quickly and they fell back, scattering, unsure of what they should be doing. Kaeleb was darting around them, trying to get to where the girl was.

"I see you have come to offer me your remaining eye," Akrin's voice broke through the melee and I spun to find him holding Kaeleb around the neck, the blade of his sword at the boy's throat. The young man I had once called my son grinned at me, pressing the blade further. Behind him, I could see Eolande's feet kicking in the air. Then her legs went slack.

"Let him go," I said to Akrin, my rage at him incomparable.

"We will not harm him," Logaire sauntered up to stand before me. The soldiers fell back, clearly relieved at not having to decide who they should be fighting. "Not if you do as I ask."

"I will cut your head off for this, you vile, traitorous witch!" I roared at her.

She smiled, unmoved by my threats. "If you do, then your boy dies, and we both know Akrin will not make it a pleasant death. Come, cousin, I wish to speak with you alone."

I stared at her as if she were mad. "You just killed a child! You hung her in front of the entire realm!"

"And another does not have to die. Come and listen to what I offer," she was insistent. I looked at Kaeleb, squirming in Akrin's grasp, at the soldiers that surrounded us. They had been caught off guard by the sight of me and hesitated at first, but the moment they resolved to follow Logaire's orders, I would be dead.

"I won't leave the boy with him," I said to her through gritted teeth.

"A wise decision," she agreed, her musical laugh tinkling through the air, the sound horridly out of place amongst the sickening events that were transpiring around us. She glanced back at the woman in white and the soldiers nearest to her. "Dismiss the crowd and keep the boy safe. You three, guard him. He is not to be harmed."

Akrin's small eyes flashed with defiance and I saw the arm that held the blade to Kaeleb's throat tense.

"Don't," I warned him, my voice low and threatening. "Whatever pain you think you have felt in this life, it will be nothing compared to what I will do to you."

Akrin shoved Kaeleb at the soldiers with a baleful glare, his eyes burning. "You are just delaying the inevitable. I will finish what I started," he said, tapping his own face beneath his left eye and laughing.

"This way," Logaire said briskly, motioning for me to follow her. I did, glancing back to make sure the soldiers were doing as they had been told. I saw the woman in white come to

Kaeleb's side, her hand on his shoulder, then we turned the corner.

Logaire led me to a room with a long table, the corners filled with brass candelabras. She sat in a chair, kicking off her slippers and rubbing at her ankles. "Standing for so long is dreadful."

"You killed the girl," I said, still hardly able to believe what I had just seen.

"It needed to happen. She was a threat to all of Imbria," Logaire said matter-of-factly. "If you were not so caught up in your sentimental attachment to her mother, then you would have seen that."

I threw myself down in a chair on the opposite side of the table. "So, you think that murdering children is a worthy cause? Did your ridiculous Oracle tell you that?"

Logaire laughed again. "Sybylla is her name, and is she not wonderful? The people adore her. They swallow the fodder we feed them without even hesitating because of her. It makes it so much easier to rule. But I did not bring you here to talk about Veruca."

"You did not bring me here at all," I countered.

She shrugged, shaking her coppery hair back off her delicate shoulders. "You are being petulant, and I am here to be magnanimous. I have something to offer you."

"Unless it is your head on a platter, I am not interested," I muttered.

"What if I am offering you a kingdom?" she asked eagerly, leaning forward.

Suspicion colored my thoughts. I did not trust my cousin as far as I could throw her. "Speak plainly, Logaire, I do not wish to play your games."

Her lips turned down in a pout. "You used to be more fun. As you wish, dear cousin, I will speak plainly. I am offering you Samirra."

I scoffed. "Samirra is not yours to give."

"It is when I have this," she said, reaching into the bosom of her gown and proudly displaying a small glass vial. "The blood of the Solvrei. Now that the girl is dead, this can be used to bargain with Chaote. We will burn the body and there will be nothing left, no more blood. This will be the only vial of it in existence."

She paused, shaking the vial and looking at me expectantly. I glared at her.

"Fine," she sighed. "Be stubborn. But I am willing to do this for you, cousin, to make right all that has passed between us. I will offer the blood to Chaote, and in exchange she and her foul Fomori must leave the western realm forever. It is impossible for her to decline. She will go, and I will give you the rule of Samirra."

"You will give it to me?" I asked, raising an eyebrow. "You think quite highly of yourself these days. There is one problem with your clever little scheme. I do not know if you noticed the events that have transpired lately, cousin, but Chaote wishes to kill me and that blood will help her do it. Or is that part of your plan?"

Logaire was annoyed. "I am doing this for us. If I wanted you dead I could have killed you already, and you know it. Chaote does not care about you. She wants the amulets. Let her have the Opal or don't, that is between the two of you. Or convince her that Maialen is the bigger threat so that you will have more time to prepare your defenses. Think on it, cousin, would a world without the amulets be so terrible?"

"The power cannot be destroyed, not in the way she thinks it can."

Logaire raised her arched brows in interest. "Oh?"

"She tried to destroy the Sapphire, but all she did was weaken it and make the other Elements stronger."

"This is good. This knowledge will bolster our bargaining position," Logaire said eagerly. "Maialen already has two amulets. Killing you or taking the Opal from you would give her more power and make her nearly invincible. Chaote cannot risk that. We can easily turn her against the Earth Keeper first."

"Is there no one on Imbria who is safe from your treachery?" I asked in disgust.

"I suppose not," she replied, smiling, not offended in the slightest.

I stared at her, remembering the skinny girl from my childhood, the girl who held my hand and whispered that everything would be fine. The girl who brought me food when I was hungry, who tickled Bastion's feet as we lay in the warm summer grass. The girl who once laughed with untamed joy, running through the mountains beside me to feel free. "Where did you go, Logaire?"

The shadow that passed over her features told me she knew exactly what I was asking. "You know where. Blaise, this is the only way. Please do not make me kill you and the boy. We were family once, but that sentimental attachment to the past cannot deter me from my path. I have proven today that I am willing to do whatever is necessary. Take my offer and go to Samirra."

36

Damian stood across from Chaote in the library, watching the way the light filtered in through the window, playing off the perfect curves and hollows of her face, gilding the muscles of her arms. She was toying with a small scroll, the kind he recognized as a message from the falconer.

"There is troubling news from Veruca," she told him, her expression unreadable.

"What does it say?" he asked, wary, eyeing the slip of paper as if it were something alive, a coiled snake waiting to strike.

She turned to stare out the window. "I do not wish to be the one to tell you."

Damian felt apprehension crawling over him. "Tahitia?"

"No. Though I doubt the island is unscathed," she admitted. There was a long pause that seemed to stretch on forever before she finally took a breath and said, "The Verucans took the child, Damian. They took her and killed her, to put an end to all of this."

He felt the air leave his lungs and he closed his eyes, praying that she was wrong, that she had read the message wrong, misunderstood the meaning. He opened his eyes, holding out his hand, and she dropped the small slip of parchment into it.

The child is dead and her body burned. All that remains is one vial of her blood. Leave Samirra forever and it is yours. -L

Damian's hands trembled as he balled up the parchment and flung it away with an angry roar. He had failed again. Failed his brother, failed Orabelle, failed all of Imbria. Shame crawled across his skin like lice.

"I must tell my mother what has happened," he managed to say, his voice choking on the words. Chaote watched him with pity, the proud and stoic Guardian struggling to comprehend his own futility while drowning in his grief. She knew how he felt. She had felt it herself standing on Tahitia all those years ago, staring at the remnants of her desecrated home.

"Damian," she began, but he shook his head, pushing her gently away from him.

"No. I should have been there with her, not here with you."

Chaote stepped away from him, stung by his words, though she knew what he said was true. "Then go."

He was torn with grief, so full of it that it seemed to press upon him from above, weighing him down beneath the immense burden of it so that he could not move. He could see his brother in his mind's eye, see the look that would have haunted Tal's face if he had known that Damian had let his only child die. "She was my brother's child. Eolande was all that was left of him, all that was left of Tal and Orabelle, and we destroyed her. She was just a child. She was happy, laughing and singing and dancing. Then we did this to her."

Tears slid down his face, shimmering against his ebony skin, and his grief was as real to her as her own. She felt the pain of it deep within her, the pain she knew so well. "Let me help you."

"What will you do?" Damian demanded. "Avenge her death? Take more lives in your crusade for justice? What will you do to help me, Chaote? Tell me, because unlike you, I do not wish for more innocent people to die."

"There are no innocent people," she whispered.

"That child was innocent!" he cried.

Chaote watched him for a long moment, her emotions warring within her. She knew she could not stay in Samirra. The Va'Kul would rise against her, and the other rulers had just made it clear they would continue to oppose her, especially now that the divine child was dead. It was a fight she would not win, and one she cared nothing about. Let them have their pathetic kingdom back, and they could ruin it just as they had before.

"I will go."

Damian lifted his head, his dark round eyes haunted. "Go where?"

"With you," she said simply. "I will take what they offer and we will leave Samirra. I will send the Va'Kul back to the north with the Fomori."

"And the Keepers?" he wanted to know.

"I will not stop fighting them. If I go with you now, you will join me in that fight, but I will do what I can to spare the lives of the ones you claim are innocent. That is the compromise I will make." She was adamant and he knew she would never relent until the amulets were destroyed.

Damian never imagined he would find himself considering her proposal, but the world was not the same as it had been before. His old life was gone. The Solvrei, his niece, his brother's child, was dead. The last tie to Tal was severed, the last tie to Orabelle, to everything that had mattered to him. The Council had been abandoned by the Keepers and the Edicts were worthless without anyone to obey them. There was no one to challenge the unchecked rule of the Keepers, and already the world was descending into chaos. He had done everything he could for Imbria, and still he had failed. Perhaps it was time to try another way.

"Send the message, accept the offer. I will stay by your side." There was a quiet resignation in his voice.

A smile touched the corners of Chaote's lips. She knew he was in pain, that his very soul was hurting, but she also knew in that moment that she loved him, that she felt for him what she had not believed she could ever feel again. It was both terrifying and thrilling. Chaote wanted to tell him how she felt, to love him with the wild abandon that he deserved and that she had once felt for Rilian, but her heart was not ready yet. She might never be ready, never able to put into words and say aloud the things that would make her so vulnerable. The only thing she could do was show him, slowly, over time. She would not have to say it, not to Damian. He would know.

"You have surprised me, Guardian," was her only reply.

"I am not a Guardian any longer," he said. "Never speak that title to me again."

"Very well. Go and tell your mother what has transpired and I will tell the Va'Kul that I have decided to give up this kingdom."

"I should be with you when you speak to her," Damian offered. He still did not trust the forbidding Fomori woman.

Chaote shook her head. "I do not fear the Va'Kul. She is getting what she wants. She will not be foolish."

Damian stared at her for a long moment, wondering if he should make some gesture, some token to cement the pact they had made. Chaote sensed his uncertainty and she gave a small shake of her head. They would have time for that later.

Damian left her then, making his way through the palace to the rooms Chaote had given to Cossiana. He found his mother standing at one of the long windows near her bed, staring out at the glaring white cliffs in the distance, searching for a glimpse of the sea beyond. She turned at the approach of her son, smiling warmly, but her smile faded when she saw his ravaged face.

"What has happened?" she breathed, her voice barely a whisper, afraid to hear the answer.

Damian took a deep breath and his mother rushed to him, wrapping her arms around his huge shoulders as he trembled with emotion. She petted his back, stroking it in a gentle, soothing motion and softly murmuring words of compassion. He stepped away, wiping at his dark eyes.

"There was a message from Logaire and the Verucans. The Solvrei.... Eolande is dead." He was blunt, not knowing how to soften the words that hit his mother like a fist.

"She cannot be dead," Cossiana gasped, shaking her head in denial. "They are lying!"

"Logaire claims that they have killed the child and burned the body. She saved one vial of blood and has offered it to Chaote in exchange for Samirra's freedom. I am sorry, mother, I know that I have failed this family."

"Nonsense!" she said harshly. "You did not fail me, or any of us. Do not allow your mind to be consumed by such thoughts! You have gone far beyond your duty to this world, my son. What does the halfbreed say about this?"

Damian hesitated. "Chaote will leave Samirra and send the Fomori to the north."

"There is something else you are not telling me," Cossiana intuited. She knew her son better than anyone else on Imbria.

"I am going with her."

The old woman's eyes rounded. "Oh, my son, you cannot do this. Not with her."

"I have to. It is the only way that she will agree."

Cossiana walked to the bed and sat on it, the strength gone out of her. He spoke as if he were bound by duty, but she was his mother. She knew better than that. He had feelings for Chaote, had allowed himself to be drawn in by her, and it filled Cossiana with trepidation. "She will be the death of you."

Damian was resolved. "Perhaps if someone had loved her enough before, none of this would have happened."

Cossiana wanted to laugh, not believing that her son could be so naïve, but she knew it would only push him further towards Chaote and so she refrained. She gazed up at him, at the powerful muscle that knotted his massive form, the noble face, the kind and serious eyes. "Damian, my son, you cannot go with her. She will not give up on her determination to destroy the amulets."

Damian gave his mother a small, sad smile. "I know she won't."

"Damian, do not do this! That woman will drag you into a fight that you cannot win! You are not like them," his mother pleaded. She was gripping the bed cover with her gnarled hands, the fabric twisting in her fingers.

"It is already done, mother. I will make sure that you are escorted safely back to Tahitia, and then I will confirm that the Va'Kul and the Fomori have kept their word before I go."

"And who will rule Samirra when she has gone?" Cossiana wanted to know, trying to find some flaw in his plan that she could exploit to make him reconsider. "You must stay here to look after the people."

"I am sure the other rulers have already decided on who the next monarch will be, but in the meantime I know someone far better suited to it than I. Please, mother, accept my decision."

Cossiana heard the plea in his voice, and she sighed heavily, patting the bed beside her. "Come then, sit with me for a while and let me be your mother for what little time we have left."

Damian had gone to her, letting her put her comforting arms around him as she leaned her head on his shoulder. They sat for a long time, watching the light fade through the window, neither of them speaking.

Keeping her word, Chaote sought out the Va'Kul and spoke the words that would change her fate. It did not take long for the Fomori to assemble and be ready to depart, and Damian was sure that the Va'Kul had begun making preparations for the occurrence as soon as she had returned from the Isle of Clouds.

A few days before the Fomori's departure, Damian had returned Cossiana and the other Tahitians to their ship. His mother had pleaded with him once more to return with her, but he was steadfast in his decision, even though it tore at his heart not to know what had happened to his homeland, or if the Tahitians might be suffering after the attack. But he had made his choice and given his word. He would stay with Chaote. He watched as the ship glided away on the rolling sea, not taking his eyes from the vessel till it was a speck on the horizon. As it disappeared, it took with it the life he had known before, and he was left with something new, something wholly his own and not connected to the past. While part of him grieved, there was another, smaller piece of himself that felt the fragile glimmer of hope.

"We have no choice but to depart with the Va'Kul. The Samirrans will not allow me to remain here, not without the protection of the Fomori," Chaote said when he returned from the port. She was standing on the platform above the arena, radiant in her golden armor. Her eyes swept over the city and she was wistful for a moment, then the feeling passed.

"We need to entrust someone with the responsibility of overseeing things here. The kingdom cannot be without a ruler," he told her.

Chaote's black eyes went to the dark archway that led to the prisoners' cells. "You want the Guardian?"

"I do," Damian said, nodding, hoping that the haunted creature he had seen down there still held a vestige of his former self.

"He is not the same as he was. His lover was killed during your riot, and I believe it was the last thread that was tethering his sanity to him," Chaote warned.

"Let me speak with him."

She gave a nod and motioned with her hand for him to go. He descended from the platform, using the same entrance that was used to remove the bodies from the arena and striding across the open space. As his footsteps left the marks of his boots on the arena floor, he remembered the first day he had seen her there. So much had happened since that day. He never imagined that he would be there again, beneath Chaote's watchful gaze, walking freely about Samirra without hesitation. Once again, the glimmer of hope shone on the future, and he prayed he could convince her to forget her plans for vengeance and embrace a life with him, the life that had been denied to her in her own time.

Damian entered the dimly lit tunnel, taking a moment for his eyes to adjust to the faded light. He found the cell where the Guardian was crouched, huddled in the shadowed corner like a warrior's ghost. Favian's clothes were dirty and a beard had grown on his chin, patchy and sparse. Rather than his usual neat braid, his long hair was in a state of disarray, tangled and greasy, hanging lifelessly over his face.

"Favian," Damian said gently, kneeling in the dirt in front of the cell. "Favian, can you hear me?"

The man turned haunted eyes on him. "Go away."

"They are leaving, Favian. The Fomori are leaving," Damian said.

"Does that mean everyone is dead?" Favian muttered the question, expecting the worst answer.

Damian shook his head. "No, they are not dead. The Fomori wish to leave, to follow the Va'Kul back to the north."

There was a faint spark of something living in the Samirran's dead eyes. "Why would they do that?"

"The Verucans have killed the Solvrei. It is over." Damian could not keep the grief from his voice.

"Orabelle's child... I am sorry to hear that, old friend." Favian tucked his greasy hair behind one ear. He scooted forward on the dirt, his face becoming visible in the light as he moved out of the shadows. His cheeks were thin and gaunt, his sharp features stark under his pale skin. "And Chaote?"

"We are leaving this place together."

"Together?" Favian repeated.

"We wish for you to take control of Samirra when we are gone," Damian told him, trying to ignore the contempt in the other man's eyes.

"We? So, you are with her now? Do you know what she is, Damian? Do you know what she has done?"

"It is the only way to free this kingdom."

Favian laughed, a hoarse and brittle bark. "Do not try that with me. You can lie to yourself if you want to, old friend, but do not lie to me. You love her?"

Damian hesitated, staring down at the ground. "I do not know. Perhaps I do."

"I loved someone once. He is dead now. They are all dead, everyone I loved," Favian said, tortured and melancholy.

Damian wondered if this was the curse of being a Guardian. To watch those around you die while you somehow lived on, no matter how much you prayed to the Gods to end your suffering.

"Will you do it, Favian?"

The Samirran gave him a weak smile. "I will do it. I have given everything for Samirra. I should like to see her returned to the people."

Damian reached through the bars and grasped the other man's hands in his own. "I will see that you are released as soon as possible."

"Thank you," Favian murmured, tears shining in his eyes.

Damian rose, leaving him then and returning to Chaote, who still stood watching the arena with a thoughtful gaze.

"Favian is willing," he told her. "Have him released, fed and washed. The people will not need to see a captive, they will need to see a leader they can trust."

She nodded and slipped her hand into his, a gesture that surprised him with its unexpectedness and its intimacy. The feel of her was always a revelation to him, as if he could not bring himself to believe that she was real and not some ephemeral goddess, too beautiful to remain in their cruel world. He held onto her, the wind cold and crisp as it blew around them.

By the time they were prepared to leave, Favian was ready, and the Fomori assembled in a mass behind the Va'Kul at the outer gate. The Samirran Guardian squinted around at the crowds of people who lined the battlements of the wall on either side of him, all of them waiting in breathless anticipation, wondering the same thing that he was. *Would they really go? Would they just leave so easily after everything that had happened?*

He had his doubts, and he tugged on his long braid of hair, now clean and plaited so that it draped over one shoulder. He had shaved his face smooth, but instead of feeling more like himself, it was a stranger that had confronted him in the mirrored glass. Whoever this man was that he had become, he was not the same man he had been before.

The Va'Kul shouted an order and the Fomori began to move, an endless river of death snaking its way out of the city. Favian wondered again how it could all end so easily, so painlessly. After everything that had happened, they were just walking away. He had to steel his mind against the images of bloody bodies, against the memory of his forearm pressing into Astraeus's throat, of Hovard's lifeless corpse laying defenseless at his feet.

A flash of gold caught his eye and Favian turned to where Chaote and Damian stood beside two eagles, still inside the city walls. They were waiting until all the Fomori were gone before they would follow them out. The halfbreed was resplendent as always, a creature so glorious that he had trouble keeping his eyes fixed on her, though he forced himself to try. She held the tethers to her eagle in her gloved hand and Favian stared down at her intently, his eyes burning into her. She was the reason all of this had happened. She was the one who brought the Fomori, who forced him to kill Astraeus, who he had thought killed Aracellis and Astus. Favian felt a brief flush of relief at the thought of the child who had escaped from the arena that day. He hoped the boy was back with his mother. The shock of seeing him alive had left Favian feeling as though he had seen a ghost. He would have to send a message to Maialen when this was all over, to ask after the boy and assure the Earth Queen that her son's line of succession in Samirra was still secure.

The Guardian watched as Chaote leaned over to say something to Damian, and the Tahitian nodded. The last of the Fomori were through the gate and the two dark figures followed, leading their eagles behind them. Once they were clear of the city they would climb onto the winged creatures and fly to wherever it was they were going. Favian did not care where they went, as long as it was far away from Samirra. He had been surprised by the public demonstration of their departure. The procession had been Damian's idea, a sort of gift for the people of Samirra, so they would know that their captors were truly gone and they were once again safe.

Favian followed the golden gleams of Chaote's armor as she moved, thinking of Hovard, of the things he had done to keep the other man safe, the lives he had sacrificed, the honor he had sacrificed. It had all been for naught. Chaote had dangled Hovard's freedom in front of him like a carrot and then she had snatched it back, sending her Fomori to slaughter the arena warriors without hesitation. Hovard had not even fought back. He was not one of the rebellious fighters who had gone charging into the arena. He had stayed in the dark tunnel, waiting till it was over, afraid to risk his upcoming release. The Fomori had walked in and struck him down with a single blow, then they had fallen on him, ripping pieces of him out with their sharp teeth. Favian had found him there later, his body torn and mutilated, and he had stood over him helplessly, worthlessly, unable to do anything, unable to put the life back into him they had ripped away.

Favian gripped the bow he held in his hand as the Samirrans began to cheer along the wall, hope blossoming within them that the Fomori really were leaving, that it was over. Before he could stop himself, he swung his arm out, pushing back those nearest to him and lifting the bow, notching an arrow in it. He tilted it down, aimed at the base of her neck, above the collar of her golden armor. She had done too much and he could not let her simply walk away from it all. He pulled back on the string, the cheers growing louder, and Damian turned, looking back at the walled city before he was to climb astride the eagle.

Damian saw the arrow just as Favian released it and he dove for Chaote with a cry of warning. She threw herself to the ground, rolling behind the bird for cover. Favian quickly notched another arrow, piercing her eagle in the side. The second bird flew off with a cry of alarm. Favian lowered the bow, his haunted eyes wide as he stared at the body of the

Guardian sprawled on the ground, an arrow piercing his chest and blood pooling around him.

The shriek that erupted from Chaote was a sound Favian never wanted to hear again. It was the sound of a rage and pain so immense that it could not be contained within a single body, and it echoed the silent torment of his own heart. She crawled around the eagle, pressing her hands around the arrow, trying to staunch the flow of blood, but Favian knew it would not help. There was too much blood. Damian was gone.

Favian whistled and the enormous gate swung shut with a heavy thud that echoed over the land. Chaote screamed again, a piercing, agonizing sound. She dropped Damian's body, sprinting for the gate, her hands covered in his blood.

"Open it!" Chaote shrieked wildly, reaching the gate and pounding on it. "Let me in so I can kill you!"

Favian leaned over the upper wall, watching her with dead eyes. She looked up at him, wild and ferocious, her beautiful lips pulled back in a vicious snarl, her face wet with tears he had not thought her capable of shedding.

The Fomori army had already advanced beyond the reach of the Samirran's arrows and they stopped, their ranks parting for the Va'Kul. The savage creature's icterine eyes flickered over the scene, and Favian wondered for a moment if the Fomori would return to avenge the one they had called Mother.

"Open the gate!" Chaote demanded. Beyond her the Va'Kul turned away, the Fomori resuming their march to the north.

Favian shook his head with a gesture of refusal, then he too withdrew, walking away. Chaote deserved to suffer the same fate that she had inflicted upon him. She deserved to know what it felt like to lose the last person you were able to bravely bring yourself to care for. He had not meant to kill Damian, but perhaps the Gods had intervened, granting him a justice that was far more poetic than her death would have ever been. As he neared the inner wall, where the deserted arena stood in silence like a mausoleum, he could still hear her screams. She was cursing his name, her fists pounding on the gate, unrelenting. She stayed there for hours, beating at the gate, shouting and screaming. Throughout the cold, bleak night the Samirrans could hear her and they shuddered at the sounds, but she refused to relent, even when her voice grew hoarse and she had fallen to her knees, her fists bloody and bruised. In the morning, her cries finally faded, her screams spent. She pushed herself to her feet as dawn rose over the city, then she turned, walking away, stepping over Damian's body without looking down.

37

I emerged from the tunnels into the biting wind that swept through the black mountains. I took a few steps then let out the bellow of rage I had been holding in, my fists clenched at my sides. I could feel my power growing in me, pulling at me, begging me to use it. I was a knotted mess of hurt, betrayal, frustration, and futility. I wanted to burn everything, to melt all of Veruca down to a molten stream, to look out where the castle had once stood and see nothing but clouds of smoke and ash.

I knelt on the ground, pounding my fists against the hard dirt, trying to release the insistent anger that was overwhelming me. I finally stopped, sitting back, accepting that it was futile because I was not angry at anything or anyone I could beat or destroy. I was angry with myself. I should have killed Logaire, but I was weak, sentimental. I could not do it. At first, I tried to tell myself it was because I did not know what would happen to the Warding Stone after her death. Would it have ceased to work without someone to wield it, or would I still be without my powers, outnumbered and sure to get both Kaeleb and I killed? I had not known and so I had hesitated. Then I heard her speak, heard the voice of the girl I had grown up with, and knew I could not do it. Not to Logaire, despite all she had done.

I gazed at the darkening sky, streaked with muted colors as if the world was bleeding into it. I had never been so lost. I always had a plan, a course of action, something I was striving to achieve. Now I had nothing, nowhere to go, no one to turn to, and the heaviness of that thought fell upon me like a boulder tumbling down from the mountainside. I was not a soldier, not a king, not a Verucan. I was nothing anymore but who I was, my sole existence limited to what I held within my own mind and body, and to the amulet that hung around my neck. I was still a Keeper, for whatever that was worth.

"She did not kill you either," Kaeleb said behind me in his quiet voice, with an uncanny awareness of the inner turmoil that was consuming me.

I turned my head to look at him. He was rubbing the toe of one boot in the dirt, watching the marks it made on the ground.

"She could have," he went on. "She could have killed both of us, but she didn't."

"No," I agreed, my voice rough, "She did not. But she killed Eolande."

Kaeleb frowned, sniffing, and I looked away so that he could shed his tears without embarrassment. "I should have tried harder to stop them from taking her."

I stood and came to him, folding him into my arms, holding his slight frame while he cried, the pain in his voice tearing at my guts as I tried to assure him, "You could not have done more."

He clutched at me for a moment, an anchor in a world that seemed untethered from reality, a child seeking the comforting embrace of a father. I waited until he pushed away, wiping at his nose with the back of his hand. "Will you be angry with me if I kill Akrin?"

I sighed, shoving a hand through my hair. "Why didn't you tell me he took your eye? Why did you lie?"

Kaeleb shrugged. "I did not want you to blame yourself for it."

"But it is because of me. I made him what he is," I said bitterly, thinking of the sullen young man I had tried to raise as my own. He was a mistake, a monster that should have been blotted out of existence, but instead I had sheltered him, given him a place of power where he could perpetrate his morbid inclinations. Now he sat upon a pretender's throne, with only my willful cousin to keep his darkness contained. It was Akrin who had guided us back to the tunnels after I agreed to Logaire's proposal, flanked by my cousin and a group of soldiers. He had watched Kaeleb the entire time, staring at him with such fixed determination that it was disconcerting. He pulled open the door, exposing his chamber of horrifying trophies, and moved aside.

"I will not forget that you betrayed me," I told him, a warning and a promise.

Akrin smiled, a leering grin, still looking at Kaeleb instead of me. "You were never going to make me your heir, and he is all the proof I needed of that. You never thought I was good enough, no matter how much I did for you. You chose this boy over me, but now neither of you will ever be able to forget about me, because I still have a piece of you, don't I, boy?"

"Your face is just as ugly as mine," Kaeleb threw back at him. "That torn lip will never heal properly, leaving you scarred forever and burdened with the shame of everyone knowing a mere boy caused it!"

As soon as I heard their exchange of words, I knew what had happened to Kaeleb's eye. Anger rolled across my skin and the torches in the hall flared brightly for a moment then dimmed, the bottomless emptiness of the Warding Stone swallowing it up. I looked at Logaire and she was fidgeting with the ring on her finger, her face thoughtful. For a moment, I believed she would remove the ring and let me kill Akrin. Our eyes met and she smiled, motioning for me to go through the opened doorway.

Akrin laughed, a malevolent sound filled with scorn, mistaking her gesture for a declaration of loyalty towards him. "Harm me and your deal with Logaire is done. You did not see my worth, but she does. She has made me her equal, not her servant."

"You are a fool," I said to her. Her face remained impassive as Kaeleb and I stepped through the doorway, hearing it slam behind us with a resounding boom that echoed through the dark. I waited until the siphoning power of the Warding Stone faded, then I lifted my hand and fire flared to life, illuminating the long chamber of macabre souvenirs.

"Burn it all," Kaeleb said, storming through the center of the room and turning down the hallway at the end, out of sight. I followed, the flames swelling behind me, swallowing up everything in the chamber, brilliant and hot and blazing. It was over too quickly, the room filled with thick smoke that forced us to hastily retreat further into the underground labyrinth.

Kaeleb now stood at the base of the mountain with me, waiting for me to come to grips with what Akrin had become. His young face was full of trust that, no matter what else happened, I would be there for him. I reached out and ruffled his pale hair. "I will not be angry with you," I promised.

He squinted his one eye up at the rocky crags that towered over us. "Do you think the eagle is still near?"

I whistled and we heard the whooshing sound of wings beating the air. The eagle glided down towards us, and I whistled again, bringing it to land in front of us. It bobbed its head up and down, and Kaeleb made gentle sounds of praise, petting the feathered head.

"At least the bird is loyal," I muttered, swinging up onto its back and leaning over to help Kaeleb up.

"Where will we go?" the boy wanted to know. Once again, there was no hint of frustration or impatience, no blame. Wherever I would lead, he would follow. I realized in that moment how many people had come and gone from us. Only the boy remained, loyal and steadfast. Maialen, Thyrr, Damian, Bacatha, Akrin, Logaire. Even Orabelle and Bastion. Each one of them had been part of my journey, but they all eventually disappeared from my life. Kaeleb was the only one who stayed.

"We are going to make a choice," I answered him, nudging the eagle so it lifted into the air.

Night was approaching and the wise thing to do was to find somewhere we could seek shelter until the morning. There were still Verucans loyal to me, but I did not wish to risk their lives or their loyalty by going to them now, especially since arriving on an eagle would draw quite a bit of unwanted attention. I searched my mind, but I could think of nowhere that seemed safe, no place that made sense for us. Everywhere was a risk.

I pulled at the eagle's tethers and maneuvered the creature in a wide, sweeping arc to the north. We could avoid Maialen's notice by crossing the burnt wreckage of her northern lands, now uninhabited. It would be the first time I would see the charred remains of the once abundant forest without feeling guilt and regret for marring her realm. Instead, I wished I had burnt more of it. Kaeleb leaned on my shoulder, his hood pulled over his head and soon I could hear the quiet rhythm of his breaths as he slept. Rest was good. Perhaps someday I would have it as well.

The sky grew dark, heavy with night, hiding the pain of the day from my sight. Ice and snow sparkled faintly on the ground below, coating the limbs of the few blackened trees that still remained standing. I noticed the orange glow of a fire in the distance, standing out like a beacon amidst the nothingness of the dead forest. I brought the eagle around to circle over the small clearing, dipping lower and seeing a rough shelter made of stretched hide and broken tree limbs standing beside the crackling fire. I wondered why on Imbria anyone would make camp in this desolate area. A dog barked, shattering the stillness of the night, and Kaeleb jerked awake just as I saw two figures stand up, their movements in unison. The Fenris.

"You knew they were here?" Kaeleb asked me, surprised.

"No," was my curt reply. It seemed impossible to me that finding the Fenris here was merely a random occurrence and questions raced through my mind at the sight of them. Had the dog-God known we would be there? Had they lit the fire as a signal? Why had they not stopped the attack on the islands? At the very least, they could have taken Eolande with them and spared her life.

I guided the eagle down lower and the brothers shielded their faces as the creature's wings threw a stark blast of icy wind over them. It settled onto the snowy ground and lifted its feet in turn, hopping back and forth as if expressing distaste for the frigid landscape. The twins were as unassuming and ordinary as they were when we first met, clad in thick furs to protect against the harsh winter. Beside their makeshift tent was a sled loaded with provisions, as if they were planning to be out in the frozen wilderness for quite some time. The unsightly dog paced back and forth before the fire, its gnarled head low to the ground, scar tissue glistening and undulating in the orange glow of the flames.

"What on Imbria are you doing out here in the middle of nowhere? Do you have any idea what has been happening?" I demanded of them, furious and grateful to finally have some-where to direct the rage that had been gnawing away at me for too long. I swung off the eagle, tossing Kaeleb the tethers and striding up to Seff till we were nearly nose to nose. "You and your dog had better explain yourselves."

Seff backed away and the brothers exchanged looks of surprise, the dog letting out a low whine.

"You don't know?" I asked them, my amber eyes narrowed. "I thought your dog could see into the future."

Vayk let a slight frown mar his bland face. "We have never made this claim. We do not see the future; we only predict possibilities."

"Did you predict that Maialen and Logaire were going to attack the islands?"

"We thought it was possible," Seff admitted.

"They killed the girl." I was deliberately blunt, my gaze oscillating between the twins and the dog, judging their reactions.

Vayk's frown deepened. "That was unforeseen."

"Why did you leave her there, unprotected?" I wanted to know.

Seff glanced at Kaeleb. "She was not unprotected."

I saw the look of guilt and hurt that passed over the boy's features at Seff's insinuation and fury rose in me once more. I grabbed a handful of the fur pelt that was draped over Seff and shoved him to the ground. "Do not dare try to blame him!"

The dog let out a soft growl, circling around the fallen man as he got to his feet, brushing ice and snow from his clothes. I glared at the beast, as if daring it to do something. I was not averse to trying to kill a God, and he had already confessed to me once that he wished to die.

"We meant nothing by it," Vayk intervened. "If she is dead, where is her body?"

"Burned. In Veruca. There is nothing left, nothing but one vial of blood that Logaire has promised to give Chaote," I told them.

The men once again exchanged looks between them. "Do you have it? The blood?"

"No," I lied. It was the one thing I would not concede in Veruca. Logaire had tried to argue, but I stubbornly insisted that the only way I would accept her bargain was if I was the one to take Chaote the blood. She relented, too easily in my opinion, but that was something to ponder at a later date. Right now, I needed to focus on the mysterious trio who stood before me. There was something they were hiding. Probably many things they were hiding. I decided to tell them about Maialen, to gauge their reactions to her recent claims of grandeur. "The Earth Keeper has taken the Pearl. She believes she is the Solvrei and will wield both Elements."

"This is an unfortunate turn of events," Seff murmured. "It is not done. She cannot be the Solvrei."

"I am well aware of that, and I tried to tell her so, but the Earth Queen is not exactly displaying the most reasonable behavior these days. She obliterated the entire Leharan kingdom," I sharply retorted.

Vayk focused on Kaeleb. "You saw the girl die? Eolande. You are sure that she is dead?"

Kaeleb squirmed, swiping the toe of his boot on the snowy ground. "I saw her face as they took the body away. I made them take off the hood, to be sure it was her."

"We must have time to think on this," Seff said. The dog came and rubbed its flanks against Kaeleb's legs, a comforting gesture. The boy reached down, absently petting the mangled beast, and I could not help but notice the irony of the two empty eye sockets, one on each of them.

"Is that what you are doing out here? Pondering your poor life choices while the rest of Imbria is being torn apart? Perhaps it is time for you to actually do something," I suggested, my frustration with the Fenris growing with each passing moment.

Seff regarded us for a long moment with his placid stare, then he glanced at the dog and nodded, as if the beast had given him a command. Kaeleb continued to stroke the mottled brown fur, and I almost laughed at the absurdity of it all.

"We are not as strong as we once were," Seff said to me. "There was a time when we could have done what you wished, but those days are long past. Now we are merely an observer, a guide."

"A guide," I repeated sardonically. "It seems to me you are only guiding things to your own end."

Seff motioned for us to sit on the blackened log they had pulled up next to the fire. I hesitated, but in the back of my mind I knew we had nowhere else to be, so it would not matter if we stayed and listened to what they had to say. I sat down, Kaeleb coming to join me, pulling off his gloves and sticking his hands over the warmth of the fire. I fed the flames surreptitiously, helping him to stay warm.

Seff walked to the opposite side of the fire, the light dancing over his dull features so they seemed sharper, more sinister. The scar across his eyebrow was stark white, like the snow beneath his boots. He began, "It was only a matter of time before the Keepers abused the power they were given. Men had shown they could not be trusted. We knew this from the beginning, though the rest of our kind refused to believe it. This is why we created the Warding Stones."

"And creating the stones got you banished to the world. I know all of this already," I interrupted.

Seff ignored me and went on. "You do not understand what it is like for us to be here, on this world. Every day is torture, painful and harsh. We have learned that it is because of this that you are the way you are. You cannot help it. Your brief lives are spent in agony on a cruel world, always striving for something, reaching for something that you can never attain. You are flawed in this way, and perhaps that is the fault of those who created you. They gave you the ability to feel things much greater than we ourselves can feel. Joy, love, friendship, bliss. But to allow you to feel those things, they have opened you up to the darkness, to sorrow, hate and greed. Tell me, if you were one of us, what would you want for your children? Would you want them to feel love so deeply that it is like a miracle inside of them, or would you want to spare them from ever having to feel the loss of that love?"

I looked at Kaeleb, his innocent child's face and the steely grey eye, already so much older and wiser than it should have been. I felt my chest tighten as I considered the question. Would I spare him pain and deprive him of love? Or would allowing him to feel happiness and joy be worth the hurt that accompanied it? I shook my head at Seff. I did not have an answer.

"So you understand our predicament. The other Gods believed that making the amulets was the cure, that if the world were not as harsh then your kind would do better, be less cruel, feel less pain, but that was a mistaken sentiment. Despite our attempts to make them understand, the others refused to acknowledge the inevitable corruption the power of the amulets would bring. The Warding Stones were meant to be a balance, not a weapon. We were trying to help. Now, we fear that the only way to prevent the end of this world is to destroy all of what was given. The stones and the amulets. We wish to leave you with a world free from our influence, to let you decide the lives you wish to lead. But to do this we need the halfbreed and we need the blood of the child."

"Why do you need Chaote?" I asked, though I had a feeling I already knew what he would say.

"Chaote believes she is the bastard offspring of a Fomori and a Tahitian, and she is, but there is much more to her story than that. Her father, the Fomori side of her, was a direct descendent from the first of his line."

I pressed my hand to my forehead, pushing back the hair that was falling over my eyes, wondering if anyone on Imbria was who they claimed to be. "You created the Fomori. She is your descendant."

Seff gave a small smile. "Her blood is still strong, pure and preserved, not weakened from centuries of banishment."

Kaeleb took a deep breath beside me, his face scrunched up in thought as he tried to understand what this meant. "That is why you came to her all those years ago. You put her in the wall in the north, to keep her safe from the Keepers until you needed her."

"The boy is clever," Seff commented. "Yes, it was us who influenced those events."

"You have been influencing everything ever since. All of this, everything that is happening, it is because you wanted it to," I accused.

"The war needs to come."

I chuckled. "Because you are tired of living. So you expect the rest of us to die for you."

Seff was bland, unmoved. "You die anyway. You kill each other anyway. Your lives are brief mortal flickers in the unending stretch of time. It has always been the way of it, and it always will be. We are not just asking you to help us die, but to destroy all the remnants of the Gods' powers on this world, to leave you to your own fates and your own free will. Is this not what you want?"

"How do you expect us to help you?" I questioned. My mind was reeling, but I tried to keep my face as blank as his was. I forced myself not to reach for the vial of blood in my jacket, not to reassure myself it was still there even though I wanted to.

"Find the blood and find the halfbreed and prepare for what comes. What you have seen will not be the end of it, the fight will be much worse. Your Edicts demand that you relinquish the Fire Opal after twenty years. We ask that you refuse this tradition. The Opal is stronger than ever, another may not be able to control it as you do, and we will need you. Imbria will need you."

"It is years before I would be called upon to pass on the amulet," I said, my eyes narrowing. "How long is this war to last?"

Seff looked at the dog who was staring into the fire, his one eye gleaming and his tongue hanging out of his gnarled mouth. "The war has not even begun."

38

Logaire looked down along the line of wagons being loaded with supplies, all of them heading to Halig for the Oracle. The construction of the temple would be underway as soon as the first breaths of spring began to thaw the frozen ground. Vishram had done his part well, ensuring that the structure would have the smaller, inner chambers built first to provide Sybylla with a place for her worshippers to flock to while the rest of the grand design was completed. Logaire was not pleased to see the woman go, for she had come to enjoy her companionship as well as her counsel.

"You have Vishram here. You do not need me," Sybylla assured her. "And now that your cousin is pacified, you are in no danger."

Logaire frowned, the faint lines between her eyes deepening. "I do not believe that Blaise has been pacified in the least. He agreed to my proposal because we threatened the boy and it was prudent for him to do so at the time, but I must be careful of him still."

"Perhaps he and the halfbreed will kill each other and save the rest of us the trouble. At least that wretched boy is gone," Sybylla said with a shudder. She had never met a more foul-mouthed brat. The entire time that Logaire and Blaise were conversing, the child was hurling insults at her and everyone else.

"You hedge-born doxy wench! Get off of me!" Kaeleb shouted at her when she tried to lay a restraining hand on his shoulder. "You and your pig-faced, tallow ketch, buckets of spew."

Sybylla snatched her hand back as if he had bitten her as he continued to rant.

"You have fewer brains than a maggot! It is a wonder you have lived this long, being as utterly dullwitted as a clotpole. Your mother must have cried after giving birth to a canker blossom like you!"

"By the Gods, you are a foul little wretch," Sybylla had murmured. She moved away, keeping an eye on him as he continued to berate the soldiers who stood guarding him. She cast her eyes to Akrin, who was still lurking across the room and watching the boy with a fixation that made her shiver. It occurred to her once again that she should ignore Logaire's promises that the disturbed young man was necessary to them and slip something into his food so they could be rid of him once and for all.

"Knock-kneed, horse-faced buffoon!" Kaeleb continued to rail at the soldiers, only falling silent when Vishram ushered past him with the men who were carrying Eolande's body. Kaeleb stared at the unmoving figure of the girl child, the cloth still covering her head. Then he darted forward, the soldiers managing to restrain him just before he reached her.

"Take that thing off her face!" the boy yelled at them. "Take it off her, please, she can't see!"

Sybylla felt a pang of sympathy for the boy and she walked forward and lifted the cloth from the little girl's head, making sure that Kaeleb could see her for a moment. "She is gone, boy. She cannot see anything anymore."

Sybylla replaced the cloth, pulling it quickly over Eolande's face. The men continued on, taking the body away so it could be burned. A single tear formed in the corner of the boy's eye as he shot Sybylla a venomous glare, spitting on her immaculate white robes. She reacted instinctively, slapping him across the face. He gaped at her, startled by the blow, then he closed his mouth, thankfully silent. Sybylla felt another wave of sympathy for him, a twinge of regret for striking a child, but she needed him to stop calling attention to the girl's body and her nerves were already on edge.

Akrin was watching everything that transpired with undiminished zeal. Sybylla had given Vishram a pleading look and Vishram had leaned towards her and whispered for her not to worry. Then he followed the procession of the body down the corridor and out of sight.

Sybylla shook her head at the memory of the ill-tempered boy as she walked with Logaire along the line of wagons to the plush and ornate carriage that she would be riding in, a gift from one of her wealthy benefactors. Logaire was pleased that Sybylla was already securing the patronage of the nobles and regents. She was far better at being the Oracle than they had expected her to be.

"Will you be safe here? Are you sure this is what you wish to do?" Sybylla asked, stopping to look into the Queen's golden eyes. She reached up and touched the other woman's cheek, the skin smooth and soft, the lines around the mouth beginning to deepen. It was difficult to be the sole ruler of an entire realm, and she felt a moment of compassion for Logaire, for the toll that the role was already taking on her.

"We have everything now," Logaire said, her eyes sparkling. She pulled Sybylla's hand from her face, squeezing it between her own. "We have won."

Sybylla was unconvinced. Akrin was still looming over them, his dark presence always a threat, the nightmare she could not awaken from. "Be careful. I will let you know as soon as the first structure is completed."

"Your temple will be glorious, my darling," Logaire assured her, full red lips pulled into a satisfied smile. "Now go, before I change my mind and go with you."

The women embraced each other tightly for a moment, Sybylla closing her eyes and breathing in the faint floral scent that clung to the Queen, praying to the Gods that it was not the last time she would hold her in her arms. It was a dangerous game they were playing, and one wrong move would end in death.

Logaire walked back to the castle, her hips swaying, head held high. She could not help the rush of elation that washed over her as she thought about everything that had happened. The outcome could not have been better. She glanced around at the bustling kingdom, the people moving about industriously, full of purpose. The hammer of the forges echoed across the mountains and it was the sound of prosperity. It was a new era, an era where the Verucans would hold the power instead of being held down. They would no longer be pressed beneath the thumb of the Council and the other realms. And Logaire had been the one to bring this new era about.

Vishram was waiting for her near the castle entrance, nodding in greeting as she approached. The soldiers who had guarded her dispersed as they entered the fortress, and she could not help but laugh delightedly once they were alone.

"Vishram, you are a genius of a man," she praised. "Has everything been destroyed? I want nothing left of it, not even one scrap of wood or fray of rope."

"It has been taken care of," he assured her. He smiled, but it was not suffused with joy and she wondered if he ever allowed himself to feel that emotion. He was always so controlled, so mediocre in his expression of pleasure.

"I need you to make sure there is no one left who can speak to any of it. The craftsman, anyone who worked with him, they must all be dealt with," she ordered. She did not want any loose ends.

Vishram inclined his head. "It is done."

Logaire fidgeted with the ring on her finger. "Bring some supplies and meet me in the tower. A sharp knife, some clean cloths, a needle and thread."

She thought she caught the flash of something in his eyes, but he simply nodded and moved away to do as she wished. She went to the long stairway that led up to the tower room, thinking as she walked that perhaps it was a mistake to keep Vishram alive. He knew more than anyone, aside from Sybylla, but unlike the Oracle, she had no way to control him. He had no family, he was immune to seduction, celibate and seemingly unmoved by either of the sexes, and he did not care about material objects. Vishram professed that his sole desire was to serve Veruca, and she trusted that his altruism was genuine. So long as he continued to believe that she was the best ruler for Veruca, his loyalty and usefulness would be unwavering. She only hoped that she would be able to see the difference in him should he ever change his mind.

Logaire reached the upper landing, trying not to gasp for breath. She hated the damned tower, but it was the only place that Akrin would not creep around and she could keep it locked, hiding what was in there from his prying, sullen gaze.

Logaire slipped the key into the lock and it glided smoothly, the locking mechanism recently replaced so that she held the only copy. She felt a pang of sympathy for the lockmaker, a rather pleasant old man who, unfortunately, was now very dead if Vishram was telling the truth.

"Hello, darling," she purred, entering the room and smiling widely at the morose little girl who was huddled in the corner with her arms wrapped around her knees. "Are you feeling better?"

Eolande lifted her head, staring at Logaire with bottomless blue eyes, deep like the far-off sea. Logaire saw that the tray of food was empty, so the girl had eaten, which was a good sign.

"I was afraid the herbs might have a lingering effect that was unpleasant," Logaire said. "But we had to make it look like you had died. Did it hurt? Vishram's clever little device?"

The child nodded and rubbed beneath her arm. Vishram had created a leather harness of sorts that Logaire had put beneath the child's dress, which he had attached a rope to. The noose that had circled the child's neck was never pulled taut, it merely tied onto the rope that would hang from the harness and when she dropped, it would appear that she had hanged. Logaire and Sybylla had slipped Eolande a mixture of herbs just before the execution that would render her unconscious, putting her in such a deep slumber that she would seem dead at a glance. It had been an ambitious ploy, and a thousand things could have gone wrong, but it had all worked perfectly, and Logaire was still thrilled by the excitement of it all.

"We have everything we want now, darling," she told the girl. "But there is one more thing we must do."

Logaire heard Vishram's sturdy footfalls on the stairs below. She opened the door to let him in and closed it behind them, locking it once more in case the girl tried to run. Eolande would not like what came next.

Vishram set his little collection of supplies on the small table beside the bed and then grabbed the child by the arm, hauling her up and forcing her to the bed. Eolande writhed in his grasp, eyes wide as she stared at the knife and rags he had set down. Then she grabbed his arm and his face changed, the blocky, unmoving features distorting into a mask of pain as he cried out. The air around the room shifted, sending the contents of the table scattering on the floor and the skirts of

Logaire's gown flapped around her legs. Vishram jerked his arm away and then shoved the child, sending her sprawling face first onto the floor. He quickly knelt on her back, calling for Logaire to help him and pointing at the leather gloves that lay discarded in the corner.

"Remarkable," Logaire murmured, delighted. She picked up the gloves and passed them to Vishram, not willing to risk touching the child herself. He forced the girl's hands into the leather mitts, and then he once again hauled her up and shoved her onto the bed.

"You will have to hold her," he told Logaire.

The Queen shook her head and took a few of the rags he had brought, tossing them at him. "I will not risk touching her. Tie her down."

Eolande was squirming, fighting with all of her tiny strength, but Vishram was as solid as a stone. He bound her, then he held out his hand to Logaire and she pulled off the ring that held the Warding Stone, dropping it into his outstretched palm. He took the knife and pried the stone out of the setting, then cut away the dress from Eolande's back. Vishram stopped for a moment, closing his eyes briefly and murmuring an apology to the screaming child, then he lowered the knife, making a long cut along the center of her back. He winced every time she shrieked beneath him, but he did as Logaire wanted, shoving the stone into the open wound and sewing it closed with the needle and thread.

Logaire could have given her something to render her unconscious, to spare her the awful pain, but she feared the child and she hoped that the memory of this moment would remind the girl of her place, keep her docile and afraid.

When it was done they walked out, leaving Eolande there on the bed, crying, her face pressed into the blankets. Just before Logaire shut the door, the child turned to look at her, and the face was so much like her mother's that it shook

Logaire to the core. It was no longer the face of a child and Logaire wondered with a shudder if they had made a mistake keeping her alive.

39

Kaeleb and I stood on the edge of the great divide, the precipice that now split the world in two. It was just after dawn and the air was silent and still, the rising red sun cascading over the snow-drenched fields that flanked the jagged rift. We had spent the night at the camp with the Fenris, and I had been grateful to finally sleep, though it was a fitful slumber, filled with dreams of death and destruction. We had risen before first light, leaving the Fenris to do whatever it was they did out in the wilderness alone. I had guided the eagle here, to the divide, the only place I could think of going.

Kaeleb peered over the edge of the ravine, the hood of his cloak thrown back and his shock of pale hair falling over his forehead, obscuring the bandage that still covered his missing eye. I noticed he was careful not to get too close, for we had learned from Aracellis the dangers of that on the icy terrain.

"Why are we here?" he asked me, tilting his head back to look up at me curiously.

"We have a choice to make," I told him. Kaeleb stepped away from the edge and walked back over to where I stood, waiting for me to explain. I was struck once again by his un-marred trust in me, his constant assurance that whatever I did, I would protect him. Not since my beloved brother Bastion had anyone looked at me that way. It had been a long time since I had felt such a willingness to give up everything for another person.

I thought about the twists of fate that had brought Kaeleb and I together. I remembered him on the road back from the north when he had run up to us, hurling insults and telling me how I should have won the battle. I remembered him in Kymir with his mouth stuffed full of pastries and his legs swinging beneath a chair as he ate happily. I remembered the first time I had seen him carefree, like a child should be, when I had thrown a handful of mud at him and his look of utter shock had split into a boyish grin. I remembered him hiding under the table, kicking Maialen to avoid the wrath of the cooks, and him standing at the divide, a knife in his hands, ready to defend the Earth Queen with his last breath. I remembered him in the arena in Samirra, saving Aracellis, and in Tahitia, walking out of the rain, his face bloody and his eye gone, sacrificed for Eolande. He deserved so much more than he had been given, and so much more than I could ever give him. He deserved a life that was his own, not the one that had been forced upon him by others since his birth. He deserved a choice.

I lifted the Opal from around my neck, holding it in one hand while I reached into my jacket for the vial of blood. I held them both out to him and he scrunched up his face, staring at the objects with one steely grey eye.

"I can throw them into the divide if that is what you wish," I offered him. "I can throw them in and we can walk away from all of this forever and never look back. You have given up enough and you deserve to have the life that you choose to have. We can find a place where we can live, without Gods and Keepers and Kings and Queens and wars that have nothing to do with us. We can walk away from all of it, just say the word."

The frosty wind tugged at the edges of his cloak and pulled at his hair. He stared at the small objects, the causes of so much pain and misery, his brow furrowed in thought. Then he lifted his grey eye and a smile spread over his face. I grinned back at him, knowing what he had decided and knowing that neither of us would ever look back.

NEXT IN SERIES

EOLANDE: THE KEEPERS OF IMBRIA BOOK 4

The exciting final installment in the Keepers of Imbria series

About the Author

Jenna Barrett is an award winning author who writes fantasy novels and is currently at work on the Keepers of Imbria series following the release of her debut novel, Orabelle. She weaves complex emotional dichotomies and breathes life into strong female heroines and villains that you love to hate. Jenna is a recent breast cancer survivor and currently resides in Texas with her three-legged dog, Artemis. When she is not writing, she spends her time doing freelance photography and is an avid adventurer who enjoys anything outdoors, especially rock climbing and mountaineering.

Visit her on the web at www.jbarrettauthor.com
on Twitter and Instagram @jbarrettauthor
or on Facebook J Barrett Author

www.ingramcontent.com/pod-product-compliance
Lightning Source LLC
Chambersburg PA
CBHW021216310726
48971CB00006B/1586